WHERE THE WIND BLOWS
The Sound

by Dorothy Gable

The wind blows where it wishes, and you hear its sound,
but you do not know where it comes from or where it goes.
So it is with everyone who is born of the Spirit.

– John 3:8
English Standard Version

Where the Wind Blows — The Sound
Copyright © 2020 by Dorothy Gable

ISBN: 978-0-9996874-2-0 (sc)
ISBN: 978-0-9996874-3-7 (e)

Title page art: Carol Hartmann

Book 1—Where the Wind Blows — The Sound
Book 2—Where the Wind Blows — The Call
Book 3—Where the Wind Blows — The Halls of Faith

This is a work of fiction. Any resemblance to actual events, people or circumstances is accidental and not intentional.

SPOILER WARNING: This biblically based fiction series quotes Bible verses and discusses biblical teachings. While some characters in real life would utter curse or swear words, these types of words are not used in this novel.

DEDICATION

THIS SERIES IS dedicated to faithful believers; may we continue, resting in the power of God.

But he said to me, "My grace is sufficient for you, for my power is made perfect in weakness." Therefore I will boast all the more gladly of my weaknesses, so that the power of Christ may rest upon me. —2 Corinthians 12:9

Abbreviations
and Definitions

A&O — Arrival and Orientation Unit. This is where inmates who are new to a federal prison are evaluated for placement in the general population.

ATF — Alcohol, Tobacco, and Firearms

BOP — Bureau of Prisons. This is a federal agency under the Department of Corrections that runs federal prisons.

CAF — Civil Asset Forfeiture. This is a seizure of personal assets from an offender by law enforcement.

CI — Confidential Informant

DEA — Drug Enforcement Administration

DOC — Department of Corrections

ED — Emergency Department, formerly the ER or emergency room.

DU — Disciplinary Unit. One of the names for segregated housing in a prison.

FBI — Federal Bureau of Investigation

GSW — Gunshot wound

INDIGENT — Inmates who have less than $6 a month in their account. They receive basic toiletries and writing supplies.

NGO — Non-governmental organization

RICO — Racketeer Influenced and Corrupt Organizations Act

SHOT — Disciplinary measure

SHU — Special Housing Unit. Refers to both protective custody and disciplinary segregation. Also known as the hole, solitary or disciplinary unit (DU).

USP — United States Penitentiary. High or maximum security prisons run by the Bureau of Prisons (BOP).

PROLOGUE

Office of the Press Secretary
Homeland Security Press
For Immediate Release:

IN RECOGNITION OF the link between hate crimes and biased, inflammatory literature, H.R. 756 Hate Crime Literature was passed to deter hate crime terrorism and create an inclusive society welcoming to all. Possession of codified hate crime literature (HCL) will be classed as a felony.

In fulfillment of the mandate contained in H.R. 756, the Homeland Security Administration, in partnership with the Department of Justice, the Department of Health and Human Services and other agencies have identified HCL. Portions of many classic works have been identified as HCL. Books of particular cultural significance have been revised to comply with H.R. 756.

During the six-month phase-in period, classic editions may be exchanged at no cost for approved copies at non-profit centers.

Government-authorized Bibles, identified with green-tipped pages, will be released shortly at participating houses of worship. In an attempt to balance cultural heritage with the spirit of the legislation to foster greater inclusion, only a minimal percentage of the text has been altered.

The HCL Joint Task Force, led by the Homeland Security Administration, in cooperation with the Federal Bureau of Investigation will oversee the removal of hate crime literature and investigate organized groups disseminating HCL beyond the phase-in period.

CHAPTER 1

THE INTAKE PROCESS to USP Hannibal, a maximum-security United States Penitentiary, run by the Bureau of Prisons (BOP), was eerily similar to the one for the federal detention center with a strip search and digital fingerprint scans. *Maybe they doubted they have the right guy.* Tom followed the path bounded by the yellow line.

"Don't cross the yellow line," the officer shouted when Tom's foot veered near the edge.

At the supply window he received his issue. Once he had changed into his prison uniform—t-shirt, khaki pants and boots—his slim bag of personal items was returned feeling lighter. One glance at the intake officer's closed face convinced him to let it pass.

The officer led him through two secured gate sections. Tom worked at not jumping with the clang and thud of solid doors locking behind him. His mind replayed the bus driving through the double-walled perimeter topped with coiled strands of razor wire. Gates, fences, and looming guard towers blocked most of the sky.

He sucked in his breath, freezing his steps. The guard behind him pushed him forward.

"Grand Central Station, main hub for Building One. Don't cross the yellow line. Always go right." The officer nodded to the third corridor, "Unit Two, your new home. Cell 35. Get there, check in and be quick. You don't want to be out for the count."

Tom hesitated, but the glare from the officer told him that he'd just better do it. Joining the flow of humanity hustling to their cell blocks before count and mail call, Tom tried to match the pace. His mouth dry, sweat forming on his upper lip, he tried to set a neutral "I-belong-here" look.

Recalling the instructions about reporting to the unit officer, Tom located what he thought would be his desk, which was vacant. He froze when he noticed the triple-tiered cells with bars, ten on each side rising to the solid-gray metal ceiling. Six bolted metal table-bench combinations dominated the center area between the cells. Inmates were everywhere—even lounging against the upper tier railings; all eyes seemed to bore into him.

"Lost, Kid?" a tall, handsome inmate asked Tom.

"Unit Two, Cell 35. Where's the unit officer?"

"Maybe he's me," the inmate stated, grabbing Tom's assignment sheet.

Before he could walk away with it, Tom stepped forward and held out his hand. "I'm going to need that to report. I'm Tom. What's your name?"

The inmate grunted and headed to the first table on the left.

"So, you the new guy—66789 356?" an officer questioned as he entered the block.

Tom turned to face him. "Yes," he said, listening to familiar rules and restrictions with the particular Hannibal twists.

Tom stepped through the process of settling into his cell with his bedroll and belongings, including chasing down his bunkmate to receive permission to move in—one of the inmate courtesies he had learned at the detention center.

By the time they had the count, completed mail call and lined up for their turn in the dining room, the icy stares and refusal to greet Tom told him he was definitely unwanted in this unit. He followed the inmate in front of him to a table.

"Find another table," the inmate ordered, turning his back on Tom.

Tom sat at the first unoccupied table down the line.

"This is our table," a man said as he placed his tray at the end. "You new?"

"Yep, Tom."

"Well, Tom, you need to find your group, but you can hang with us this time. What you in for?"

Tom licked his lips, "HCL terrorist is what they called it." He turned to his food, praying there would be no follow-up questions. Trying to explain why he was in prison for owning Bibles didn't go over very well.

Others joined them at the table, and Tom let the conversation flow around him. Catching a name here and there, he chose a youngish inmate sitting at the end on his side to find out more about his unit. He followed him down the gap between tables, copied his movements for turning in the tray and called his name just as they left the room.

"Earl, hey, I'm Tom." He fell into step with him. "I just came through today and wondered what's up with Unit Two?"

Earl paused but didn't look at him. "Unit Two? They put you in Unit Two?"

"Is that a problem?"

"Get a transfer and get it quick—unless you want to be marked as a snitch." With that warning, Earl surged ahead and disappeared in the flow of Grand Central.

Tom looked about, almost stepping across the yellow line, but remembered in time. He walked around the perimeter before coming to Unit Two. Breathing in, he headed for the tables, directly to the one on the left.

"I didn't ask for this unit, you know. I didn't have a choice."

"When did you arrive?"

"Two days ago."

"What about A&O?"

"A&O?

"A&O—admissions and orientation—usually takes a month or more. Figure out where to put you. You didn't fill out the questions, sit through orientation?"

"Did that in Oklahoma."

"This ain't Oklahoma. You're in Hannibal. Each facility does things its own way."

The inmate waved over a stout man. "Mark, you hear about this?"

"Yeah, newbie gets my job, right out of the gate. Not like me—I earned it." Cursing profusely, he described exactly where Tom needed to go.

Almost used to the language, he nodded his head. "Fine, when can I put in a transfer?"

"Tomorrow. Better yet, tell Officer Curtis you don't want to work for him. Safer, if you get my meaning."

"Get the prison manual?" the other inmate asked.

"I read it the first day. Do I need to know anything else?"

"No, that's all you need." The inmates winked at each other and laughed.

"By the way. Who's Officer Curtis?"

"The chaplain. What does an HCL terrorist have to do with religion?"

"Word gets around fast—well…" he looked around trying to find a feasible answer when a tall inmate with curly dark hair and dark eyes walked over.

"You play ball?"

"Ball? What kind of ball?"

"Basketball."

"Yeah, in high school, but never made it past junior varsity."

"Well, we're short a guy this evening. Come on. We don't want to miss the activity count."

"But I didn't sign up."

"Don't sweat it." He added Tom's inmate number and name to the recreation list and waved him on. "Sal, by the way. You don't have to be good, just need to fill out the team for practice. Got to keep up Building One dominance."

Tom breathed again.

Chapter 2

THE NEXT MORNING, Tom tried not to think about what he would be doing for Officer Curtis and ignored the glares. Word had spread quickly that he had been placed directly in a coveted office job. He worked at keeping up with Mark.

The Admin wing looked nicer and felt warmer than the rest of the facility. Tom stepped through the chaplain's door. Mark sat down at his desk, turned on the computer and hit a buzzer near his phones. He crossed his arms, smirking. "What you got I don't got?"

"Don't know. They didn't ask. You have info on the job?"

"Yeah, it's for that new project he's been buzzing about—HCL garbage. You know about it?"

"Yeah—that's me; your very own *HCL* terrorist. Stands for 'hate crime literature.' The agencies decided to classify parts of the Bible as HCL. Meaning…" Tom stepped back as a heavy-set officer with silver-streaked hair and a tattoo on his upper bicep burst through the door.

"Meaning there's those who are law-abiding citizens—as commanded by God—and those that ain't."

Tom held his tongue.

"Let's see 'em." Noting Tom's puzzled stare, Curtis held out his hand, "Your papers." He looked at them quickly and set them on Mark's desk. "In order." Sizing up Tom, he said, "This is how you will demonstrate a reformed attitude suitable for good time consideration."

"What exactly will I be doing?"

"You will assist my clerk in exchanging approved Bibles for contraband editions, unit by unit. See those boxes over there?"

Tom spied cartons brimming with books, booklets and other printed material.

"You need to go through those for contraband and send the rest back to the units. We'll see if you can cut it." The officer retrieved a small booklet with the covers torn off. "You a Bible college graduate?"

"Did three years of a four-year program, sir."

"Didn't even finish," he smirked.

"The college closed due to the new law."

"And that didn't give you a hint maybe you should have turned in your contraband Bibles? You know the sections marked for removal?"

"Yes, sir." Tom rattled off the list of verses now missing in government-approved editions. "And one more thing, sir. With all due respect, I will not take this job."

Officer Curtis drew a deep breath and slowly released it as he stepped closer to Tom and leaned forward. "I am the gatekeeper for good-time approvals. I set the bar. Reform, true reform, is shown by demonstrating good faith efforts to become a law-abiding citizen. In your case, that means accepting the new standard."

"The Bible is God's Word. I will not participate in any enforcement efforts of a law I consider unconstitutional and against God's higher law."

"Is that so? You want a visit to the SHU? Ever been to the hole?"

"Maybe, not sure." Tom tried not to recall the first three weeks after his arrest.

"Well, you incapable of doing this job?"

"No, sir."

"You can't exist with 98 percent of the Bible?"

"It's the principle, sir." Tom wet his lips, framing the right response, but the officer had already disappeared into his inner office and had shut the door.

"What's he doing?" Tom asked Mark.

"Giving you a *shot*." Seeing Tom's blank look, Mark explained, "Writing you up for an infraction—disciplinary measure. Refusing a job assignment usually won't send you to the hole—the SHU—special housing unit. But that all depends on how he writes it. You can appeal if he bumps it up."

"I'll keep that in mind. Mark, you know the verses deemed HCL?"

"No."

"Get a Bible—a real one and an approved edition—with the green-tipped pages." Tom listed the verses on a scrap of paper. Bringing a chair close to the desk, he stepped Mark through the context of the verses, explaining the meaning of each passage.

When Curtis emerged from the office, he asked, "What you up to?"

"Teaching your clerk so he can do it."

"You won't do it, but you'll let him do it?"

"It's a conscience issue for me, sir." Tom rose to face the officer head on. "Those books have to be reviewed. Mark will probably be more objective anyway."

"Fine." The officer nodded at Mark and ordered, "Take him to the detention unit and be ready for your test when you get back."

"Test?"

Laughing, Curtis added, "Yeah, to see if our HCL terrorist can instruct."

Tom walked with Mark to the next wing.

"Officer Meggars is in charge of the SHU. I'll give your shot to whoever's at the desk."

"How long?"

"What, oh…," Mark glanced at the paper. "Sixty days, but there'll be an investigation." Seeing Tom's hopeful look, he added, "Don't get your hopes up. They're just documenting the charges. Once you're processed into the unit, they'll question you. No funny games. He doesn't like that."

"I thought refusing a job assignment wasn't automatic for the hole."

"He bumped it up—insubordination, swearing and jeopardizing the safe functioning of this institution. You can appeal. Like I said, most don't work."

Tom turned in his prison issue and received the familiar-looking orange jumpsuit. No one answered his questions about his personal items. Remembering advice learned in detention, he answered the questions asked, offering nothing further.

His hearing was held a week later. He had received enough counsel to write a rebuttal, requesting it be reduced to the lesser charge of refusing a job assignment. As coached by a resident on his Oklahoma detention block, Tom requested the officer read his statement. *It sounds good.* Praying, he hoped for another cell and job assignment. Even going through A&O would be better than the SHU.

Tom tried to keep his face neutral when Officer Curtis described his insolent curses and arrogant job refusal. The officers' faces looked bored. Tom prayed again. His hope almost picked up when Curtis called Mark as the only witness.

A buzzing started in his head and grew when he heard Mark repeat the officer's description almost word for word. He wanted to shout it was a lie or run over and implore Mark to tell the truth. At the end, Mark stared at him with a set, almost smiling blank face.

The rest was a blur.

They took him to a different cell. Once the officers cleared the range, Tom called out to hear if he was in the same range. A few answered. "How'd it go?"

"They lied."

"What'd you expect? Just a rigged show trial. They gonna do what they want."

Later in the day, Tom requested his indigent supplies along with some cleaning supplies. This cell was as filthy as the other one. He organized the area, making it as clean as possible. After a brief workout, he pulled out his stack of papers. They had also returned his personal item bag.

Indigent inmates, those with less $6 in their account, receive paper and writing supplies—Tom's key to sanity and organizing his memory verses. He had settled the issue while in district detention that reaching out to friends or family would only bring them to the attention of the Task Force. With no funds to shop in the commissary he depended upon the indigent supply to never forget the Word of God.

He began to sort them by books of the Bible. Not surprisingly, some pages were missing. Sitting down, he began to write out the gospel of John from memory; letting the hope, the truths, and the reminders of God's love seep into his soul helped raise glimmers of hope.

"My God shall supply all my needs," he said. "You came to this wicked earth. The sin You witnessed," Tom shook his head. His mind jumped ahead to John 15:18, *"If the world hates you, know that it has hated me before it hated you."* The Holy Spirit brought to mind other verses assuring him of help to know what to say in defense of his faith. He prayed God would use him, and it would begin in the SHU.

After the officers had retreated to their desks and TVs, Tom paused to listen to the conversations resounding through the hall between the cells. He listened, praying for opportunities. "Give me a mouth and wisdom as it says in Luke," Tom prayed aloud.

He spent more time listening than talking—learning their speech patterns, empathizing with their frustrations, contemplating their heartfelt needs. He didn't feel quite ready to jump in with advice. He didn't want to resort to worn-out platitudes or the typical religious words of comfort. *The answers they need will come in time as I live with them.*

CHAPTER 3

AFTER SIXTY DAYS they opened the solid door and called him out to process back to general population. An officer escorted him to Grand Central. Tom hesitated when they strode past the yellow line.

"Move it," the officer pushed him forward to the forbidden center. Tom felt all eyes on him. They were doing the change right before the 10 a.m. count. Out of the corner of his eye, he could feel the surge of inmates trying to get back to their units before the count.

"Unit Four, your new home." The escort nodded to the day officer sitting at the unit desk. "Your newbie. Enjoy." He disappeared around the corner.

Officer Ganse, middle-aged and medium height, scanned the assignment sheet. "This is your new guy, Bruce—another dishwasher."

A large inmate with pockmarked cheeks, black hair tied back and arms bristling with well-defined muscles and tattoos emerged from the group waiting for count. "What ya' all looking at? Count."

The men scattered to their cells.

Heading to the officer's desk, Bruce said, "A freebie for Wallie—like they promised?"

"I'll see they make it good." The officer sat back.

Bruce yelled at Tom, "Get up there, cell 60. Left top tier."

Tom stood, holding his slim bag. In the midst of the usual string of obscenities and descriptive phrases, Bruce's directions broke through the fog, and Tom sprinted to the stairs.

"No running," the officer ordered.

Tom power-walked to the end of the third tier, just before the communal shower-toilet area. He tried not to stare at the short inmate peering out of the last cell. The man disappeared into the top bunk when Tom drew close.

"Hey, I'm Tom. May I come in? You want the bottom bunk?"

"Wallie. Top bunk's mine. Leave me alone."

"All right." Tom barely cleared the barred door when it began to roll shut automatically.

"Stay clear of the bars," Tom heard.

"Thanks for the warning."

"Wallie, get out of your bunk," the officer yelled. "Count. Stand for count."

Wallie stood close to the bunks. Tom hovered near the far-right wall, waiting for count to clear. When the doors rolled open, Wallie shot out of the cell and down the walkway. Tom released a sigh and stowed his gear.

"Hey, 66789, get down here."

Closing the locker, he headed toward Bruce's voice.

"You're working for me. You are going to wash dishes. We have ten minutes to get in place or get another shot. Time's ticking."

Tom followed Bruce to the right, passing most of the wings. Almost three-quarters around the oval, Bruce headed down a wide hallway labeled "Dining." The first set of double doors had large windows revealing the dining area—metal table-bench combinations arranged in long rows.

Angling to the doors, he forced himself not to visibly jump with Bruce's barrage of insults. "Never go through there. That's for those who get to eat. Workers go through the second set and sign in or they don't eat. Capiche?"

"Yeah, I mean…" He would have corrected his answer, but Bruce had already surged through the second set of double doors.

With a nod to a clipboard on the left partition near the door, Bruce, the head orderly for the kitchen, surveyed the cooks at the stoves, the guys working on a center counter prepping the veggies, and swung around to the line where the food would be served.

An officer emerged from a small office on the right to look at Tom. "66789?"

"Yes."

"Sign in. It's on the wall." The officer returned to his desk and pile of papers. He barked out a request for the inventory, and an inmate replied, "Al's still in the cooler. Ya' want me to get him?"

"No," he snapped. "Hey, new guy." Seeing Tom turn, he said, "Yeah, you, 66789. Get in the cooler. It's that way." He pointed to the left. "Help Al finish the inventory. Got to get this request in if we want to have food next week."

Tom scrambled to the cooler. Al was balding, short and reaching for the boxes on the top. "I can help with that. Hi, I'm the new guy. Anyway, they sent me in to help you finish the inventory." Reaching the box easily, he set it down.

Al shoved the clipboard at him. "Mark it up."

In a short time, they emerged from the cooler. Tom laid the clipboard on the officer's desk. He looked about. Bruce was perched on a tall stool at the edge of the serving line near the cooking center. Everyone seemed busy. The dishwashing station ran along the left back wall. Just about to approach the team working at the machines, he jumped when Bruce barked at him.

"66789, new guy. Set up the serving line." Bruce turned him to the rack of warming trays. "Fill 'em up with hot water. Matt'll show you what to do."

"Thought I was washing dishes."

"Officially," Bruce bared his teeth, "but we don't need dishwashers right now. Short a guy for the line."

Tom followed Matt as they filled tray after tray and set it in place.

Then came the cold food section with trays of ice. "Ron's otherwise detained, so we're short. Only good thing about line detail is we get to eat first."

Almost without a word, the group set up the food and served their plates.

Matt showed Tom the serving size for his station, then the lines of inmates began to work their way through for two hours. Unit by unit, scheduled in shifts, the small dining room accommodated all of the residents of the large facility.

Tom periodically stole a glance without staring at the young and old, all shapes and sizes, some well-groomed and others with scraggly hair, stubble, or shaved heads, along with the ever-present tattoos. Most looked him over with cold calculation, some wore a hint of a smile, a few even seemed to be holding back jeers, but he didn't want to be paranoid. He sighed in relief when the last inmate cleared the line. "Clean up, clean up. On the clock. Let's go," Bruce shouted. "Kitchen's closed."

An hour later, Tom was the last one cleaning up. Seeing the lull of activity, he risked asking Bruce a question. "If you don't need me anywhere else, where do I wash dishes?"

Bruce stared at him with a withering gaze and finally said, "We don't need you, but we're stuck with you. You sit—if there's nothing else."

Tom looked down to the end of the large room. Mid-sized wheeled dumpsters took up most of the end by the third and last set of double doors. Clumped together on the right side were three tall wheeled racks filled with an assortment of cooking trays, grills, and large pans. "I can clean what no one else will. What about that stuff?"

Bruce leaned back, a half-smile smirk on his face. "You a wise guy? Where would you do it?"

"Those sinks." Just left of the last doors hunched a dust-covered double sink/counter combo in the same line as the dishwasher units on the left. He tested the taps. Water ran, a little colored at first, but it soon cleared.

"Drain's broke."

"I could use a pan to hold the water."

Bruce shook his head and made a sound through his teeth. "Better," he grabbed a bag, stuffed it with rags and jammed it down the drain. "Try that."

"It'll work well enough." Tom smiled, but it disappeared when Bruce didn't smile back.

"You want to wash that. Go ahead, but you do what I tell you, got it?"

"Sure."

The afternoon set-up crew arrived. Bruce went over the supper menu with the lead orderly before motioning Tom to follow him out to the side hall. They walked back to Unit Four without a word.

Few were about. Only those working in Building One who had finished their work details could return to the unit. The rest had to wait until time for count and mail call at four. He looked at the clock—just past three. He had time.

Tom walked up the two flights and strolled to his cell. *Will Wallie be there?* It seemed empty. Tom pulled his bag from the locker. He had just shoved it in during the morning's rush. Tall and narrow, the locker wouldn't hold much, but he didn't have much anyway.

A small metal desk bolted to the wall in front of the lockers had a bolted stool beside it. Tom saw no other seat in the cell, recalling the other cells had two stools. He poured out his papers on the desk and organized them quickly—Old Testament, New Testament, some doctrine pages he had started and finally, the sheet he was looking for—his diary.

Tom counted the days, licked the pencil nub and added another slash. That's how he would survive—one day at a time. He briefly detailed day one on his new job. Tom tilted his head, listening for the cadence of the voices rising with waves of warm air. The heat of an upper tier was welcome in the winter.

Leaning back, he sucked in his breath. *Just two weeks until Christmas.* He blinked away a tear, shoving down the sadness. He occupied himself with his papers, but his focus had vanished.

Yielding to the temptation, he locked away his papers and walked out to lean by the railing. An older inmate on the opposite tier nodded at him and disappeared into the adjoining bath area. He emerged not far from Tom.

"They're connected?"

"Yeah," the inmate extended out his hand. "Stan."

Tom smiled and shook his hand, "Tom." He leaned back on the railing. "Christmas soon. When do the letters start coming in?"

"My old lady has it covered." Stan smiled, revealing a few teeth here and there. His graying, frizzy hair framed a scruffy face. "Halfway through a 45-year stint. You?"

"Pulled five years."

"That's nothing," Stan whistled, looking down at the gathering. "You'd think they'd get the hint. Count first, then mail. But they wait until Bruce yells count. What a stampede! Then get on down there to get close to the mail guy."

"I won't be getting any mail."

"Ask for mailing supplies. Let them know you're at USP Hannibal."

"Thanks for the tip." Tom watched the unit scramble with Bruce's barked orders. He found his place by the right side.

Wallie slid in, hovering by the bunks.

"Is it my imagination or is this cell smaller than the others?"

"It is. Why this was supposed to be a single," Wallie said without looking at him.

"We can make it work. I don't have much. I'm indigent."

"So am I," Wallie replied.

The bars rolled back after count cleared. Tom stepped back and looked directly at Wallie for the first time. "You first, I have no mail coming."

"Neither do I." He retreated to his bunk.

Tom sighed, reluctant to bring out his papers as he had only a little time until they lined up for supper. Leaning over the railing, he watched men step forward as their names were called. He hadn't realized the time until he felt Wallie breeze past him to head down. Tom tried to follow.

A slim inmate near Bruce led the unit when their turn came to go the dining wing. Tom glimpsed Wallie a little bit ahead. Feeling someone behind him, he nodded at Stan.

Stan was still catching his breath from stowing his mail and coming back to the line, "That's Doug, the second."

"Second?"

"Unit 4 is Bruce's cell block. Doug's his second. He walks the block to chow. How it's done."

"Going the long way around?"

"Got to time it just right. They don't like us to congregate too long."

Keeping his eye on Wallie, he let Stan go ahead of him, copying his every move and sat near Stan. Wallie sat on the other end.

"Like the misfit table?"

"Guess so," Tom smiled. "Tom," he said to the others.

"We know."

Tom waited, but no one offered their names. "Word travels fast. No hiding places here?"

"Nope."

"You bunking with Wallie?" a younger blond-haired inmate asked.

Stan growled at him.

"Hey, Wallie, you like your bunkie?"

Stan unleashed a string of expletives, telling them to shut up.

"He's fine. I think we'll get along," Tom began, but he was drowned out with peals of laughter.

"Cool it," Stan warned. He leaned close to Tom. "Take a hint. Keep your distance. Give him his space."

"Okay."

"I mean it."

"I get it." Tom looked at Wallie at the end of the table hunched over his plate of leftover stew, hiding behind his shoulder-length hair. "I'll do my best."

The snickers died down with Stan's glares. Tom listened as they began to discuss their favorite ball clubs. He turned back to his plate when he noticed many were already dropping off their trays and lining up.

A familiar-looking inmate approached him at the counter. "You up for a game?"

Tom stepped aside. "Sal? I'm still in?"

"Still short a guy. Different one this time. You survived the SHU. You in?"

"Yeah, how?"

"Put your name down on the list in your unit and wait for the change over." He turned back, "I'll fetch you—just in case there are any issues. How's the SHU?"

"It's the SHU," he said, smiling this time.

CHAPTER 4

THE NEXT DAY Tom set to work scrubbing the dust and grime off the counters and sinks. It was almost nine when he arranged the racks of dirty pots, pans and sheets. He set the tall racks in a line along his left side, providing some privacy from the rest of the kitchen and the open serving line.

He thought he heard a bang but attributed it to air in the pipes, until a loud squeak followed a thud off to his right. The leading edge of a wheeled dumpster poked through the cracked double doors.

Tom scrambled to the nearest door and pulled. Seeing it bind, he angled it back and tried again. When the door broke free, he found himself looking into piercing blue eyes set in a shaved head.

"Who are you?" the inmate asked. He pushed the dumpster to the center of the back area.

"Tom. And you?"

"Todd, I pick up the trash and drop off the empty." The tall, well-built inmate surveyed Tom's area. "So Bruce got another dishwasher?"

"Yeah, stuck with me. Do what's left over."

"Yeah," looking back to the dishwasher's area, "Not surprised they're behind on the scrubbing. Softies can't do anything without a machine." Todd combined the trash into one dumpster, angling the empty at the back of the line. "What ya' in for?"

"Owning Bibles. They passed a law making original Bibles illegal." Just like that, he said it.

Todd nodded. "Their laws always messing up regular folk. Well, not many Bibles here." His eyes almost twinkled with a small smile. The cobra tattoo running along his neck and jaw line arched. His eyes narrowed.

Tom felt someone behind him and looked back.

Bruce scowled at them. "Get lost."

Todd disappeared quickly.

"You don't talk to that kind," Bruce stated.

"Really? What kind is that?"

"Didn't you notice?"

"What?" He'd seen many bald heads, tattoos and bristling muscles.

Bruce's eyes blazed. "He's number two in the top gang here. They're very serious about what they do and…" he drew closer, leaning over Tom, "they hate Christians." Crossing his arms, he stepped back. "Most Christians get sent here because they molested a teen or stole money from Grandma. What kind are you?"

"Neither. They found me with Bibles."

"You're dumb. Most educated folk are. Listen, cop to the weapons offenses. Maybe you're a bomb maker? Lead violent protests? Attack a perv? We all know how it goes. What's on the books is a part of what you did. It's not the whole story. So, spill what really pulled you a bunk in Hannibal instead of a cushy prison camp. You take a deal?"

"Yeah, took twenty-five instead of the fifty counts they charged me with. That's twenty-five counts of hate crime literature. The way the law was written, it's seen as equivalent to a shooting, a bombing or an assault."

"Well, everyone lies."

Tom watched Bruce return to the cooking area, barking orders as he checked the progress of lunch.

———— ◈◈◈ ————

The next day at 9, Todd entered Tom's little area in the back. "So, what's so great about a book you'd go to prison for?"

"It's not just any book. God wrote it, through men. It's His book to us on how to live. It says His Word is truth."

"You really believe that?"

"I do. God uses His Word to sustain me."

Todd glanced toward the cook's area. Not seeing Bruce near his usual perch, he met Tom's gaze. "We'll see about that. This not your 'hood?"

"Not at all. Already survived 60 days in the SHU."

"Well, it's not over yet. They don't call it hard time for nothing." Todd collected the full dumpster. "See you tomorrow."

CHAPTER 5

TOM NEEDED A few days to settle in to the routine. Tom hadn't considered other Christians would be in his unit. When he overheard one of them thanking the Lord for a letter from his family, he angled closer to the inmate during the supper line-up.

"Hey," he said quietly, "I'm Tom. You a believer?"

"Yeah, what's it to you?"

"So am I."

"Not by Officer Curtis. Says you're another Rob." Seeing Tom's blank look, he added, "A phony. They come in here all the time. Play like they're on the Lord's side, but running their games' all they're after." He leaned closer, "What's yours?"

Tom stepped back a little. "So, I guess I'm not welcome at the services?"

He scrunched his face. "What gave you that idea?"

Tom doubted he needed to remind him Officer Curtis had put him in the SHU for two months. "What's your name?"

"Bob." He turned his back when a slender inmate joined him.

Tom had seen them together. Following close behind, he said, "Hi, Bob. Can you introduce me to your friend? Another brother in Christ?"

"Rick."

While they let him follow, they made it clear he'd better pick another table. He joined his usual group. "Who's Rob?" The men at the table stared at him, except for Wallie who avoided eye contact with anyone.

"Who told you about Rob?"

"Rick, just that they needed to avoid me. So, who's Rob?"

"A con-artist, smooth talker." Stan leaned forward, with a glint in his eye. "Pulled the wool over Curtis. That he did. Even spoke up for him for his good time hearings, but then Meggars caught him in his hustle. Not sure what all he did, but they sent him up the river."

"Up the river?"

"To the super max. Never heard from again."

Tom couldn't tell if they were pulling his leg.

A few days later in their unit, Tom sat on the far end of the last table where Rick and Bob were hanging out. "You guys get saved in prison?"

Bob ignored him, but Rick nodded, "Got a good group here. The Christian unit's in Building Three. Len leads it." He smiled at Tom. "You can join us for Sunday service."

"Sure. Did it help? Getting saved? Make a real difference?"

"Yeah, it did." Bob turned to face Rick and Tom. "What does it feel like to sin against God after you claimed Christ? Why you're here, ain't it?"

"I broke none of God's laws," Tom said.

"Curtis was right. You're a snake. Won't even own up to what you did. First step is to admit your sin."

Hopes of witnessing vanished. The air was tense. A nameless dread balled up in his belly.

Tom headed to his cell when mail call began. Christmas was drawing near. While some rejoiced over their mail, others sat apart.

Wallie ran up the tiers with his letters. Tom stayed out on the ledge, trying to give him space. Soon enough they'd be locked in for the night. He leaned back on the railing, watching guys hide their treasures away in their lockers. At least he had basketball to fill his evenings.

CHAPTER 6

TOM HAD TAKEN a few weeks to regain his skills on the court. He re-mastered the art of stealing the ball to pass to taller teammates. Working out his pent-up emotions, he exploded on the court that night with several assists. The teams, vying for the holiday tournament, played at top level. Unit Two advanced to the finals that night and decided to keep him.

Tom returned to his unit right before count with no time for a shower. Planning on cleaning up in his cell, he stopped at the cell door. Wallie sat huddled over piles of paper, notepads and books spread out on the table. Various pieces of clothing, plastic dishes, cups, pencil nubs, small boxes and other items covered Tom's bunk and parts of the floor. "All that fit in your locker?"

Wallie raised his head and smiled at him. His hair tied back, his eyes bright, he spoke in fast, clipped phrases. "Buddy's back. Good to see you. Come in for count. Sorry about the mess, but I have to find it."

"Find what?"

"My letter," Wallie rattled on, speaking so quickly Tom strained to understand what he was saying.

He stepped in, waiting for the bars to roll shut. "We got to stand for count."

"Yeah. I know, just a minute." Wallie looked back at the top letter. He didn't move until Bruce's call for count rang out. Nearly exploding to the front of the cell, Wallie stood in position, twitching in place.

With one eye on Tom and his stuff on the table, he warned, "You don't touch my stuff!"

"I wouldn't think of it," Tom said. He glanced back at the piles on his bunk. Exhaustion from the game returned.

"She sent a letter. She sent a letter with a message. I can't find it," Wallie continued, talking nonstop.

Shortly after count cleared, Tom looked across to the other cells on the third tier. Every inmate with a view of their cell stared in his direction. Tom recalled the warnings to give Wallie his space. He looked across to see Stan and his cellmate watching with lips slightly parted. The hair tingled at the back of his neck.

"Could I help you, Wallie? I would never take any of your stuff. I promise."

"If you swear to God, I'll let you help."

"I do. In the name of Christ, I will help you and not take your things. Good?"

"Yeah, that sounds nice—like what my auntie sent me, and I can't find it." Wallie ran back to his locker and searched every cranny. "You sure you didn't take it?"

Tom opened his locker and pulled out his pile of papers. "No letters, but we can check. I'll just slide your stuff over, all right?"

"Sure." Wallie moved the clothes and smaller items. He put the large ones back in the bottom of his locker. Back and forth he moved his stuff, pacing between bunk and locker.

When Tom set the papers on his lap, Wallie sat right next to him. "I want to see."

Tom smoothed out the papers. Some were crumpled, some water-stained, but they were in order. "These are verses written out from the Bible. First are from Genesis, about how God made the world." Tom began reading Genesis one through three. Wallie was still for most of it, but then his fidgets returned. Tom showed him each page.

"Where's your Bible? How did you get all that?"

"It's in here," Tom tapped his head. "God challenged me to memorize the Bible when I went to Bible college."

"You memorized all of it?"

"No, but a lot of it. I write it down and review it so I won't forget."

Wallie's concentration shifted to his letters on the table. He went back to rifling through them, muttering.

"Let me know how I can help. We know it's not in my locker, but I could go through what's on the bunk."

"It's a letter!"

"Can I help you organize them?"

Wallie agreed. They made room on Tom's bunk and began to sort them by date. Some letters were over ten years old.

"She really wrote you. Your auntie. Did you live near her?"

"No." Wallie shook his head, trying to find the date on the letter in his hand. "She checked on us, tried to bring food when she was in town, but…" he looked at Tom. "It didn't help. It didn't help."

Hearing the distress in Wallie's voice, Tom said quietly. "No worries, I'll get them in order at the table, and you organize your locker. How did you get all that in there?"

"Wallie's good. Wallie knows how to do things." He turned to Tom. "And he took my job. Nivens didn't tell me, but I found out."

"Tell me about it. Who's Nivens?" Tom kept Wallie talking as he fought the urge to sleep.

"You look tired."

"I am, but there's stuff on my bunk."

"I'm working on it. Give me a chance!"

"No hurry. I'm still working on your letters." Tom asked, "Wallie, do you have any brothers or sisters?"

Wallie shared his story of a drug-addicted mom and multiple half-brothers and sisters.

"Let's go through the letters. They're in order now. What are you looking for?"

"Aunt Margaret told me how to get better. I have to get better because I don't want to hurt people anymore. I wasn't supposed to have a cellmate. Bruce promised. Bruce lied."

"This wasn't Bruce's idea. Someone else did this."

"They don't like you. That's why they bunked you here. Said I could kill you, and it wouldn't count. Free—as if it never happened, but God would know, wouldn't He?"

"Yes, He knows everything, but Jesus loves you and will forgive you if you ask Him."

Wallie shook his head. "Too bad. Too bad."

"Let me tell you a story." Tom was tempted to ask Wallie to sit down, but the man seemed calmer when he paced. Gazing out across the unit, he noticed most had retreated to their bunks. "There were two vicious robbers who were crucified with Christ on the cross. Only the worst people were crucified. At first, they joined in and called Jesus names and made fun of Him. Then one of them realized Jesus was innocent. He reminded the other robber they deserved their punishment, but Jesus had done nothing wrong. He asked the Savior, 'Jesus, remember me when you come into your kingdom.' Jesus said he would be with him in paradise.[1] He had been forgiven by God. Jesus took your punishment on the cross, Wallie. Just ask and He will save you."

Wallie looked at him for a moment then resumed his pacing.

Tom didn't get any more opportunities. Once the lower bunk was cleared, Tom fell asleep, but woke up frequently with Wallie's pacing throughout the night.

As soon as morning count was cleared and their cells opened, Tom said, "Follow me." As they passed Bruce's cell, Tom said, "Skipping breakfast for morning recreation. I'm taking care of Wallie today." They breezed down a sparsely populated Grand Central.

Wallie laughed. "You skipping work? Bad. Bad."

"Yeah, but the pay's so low, I'm still indigent, so no sweat. Your job? Low pay?"

"No job. Officer Nivens gives me the jobs the guys who have the jobs can't do."

"I hear you on that one. They pull me to do the line serving. I hear that pays well, but I don't get that pay."

"Why you not mad about it?"

"I pray about it. Give it to Jesus. Just stuff I can't take with me when I die."

They headed for the basketball courts and ran laps. Tom helped Wallie dribble the ball. He set up some drills, anything to keep him moving. Seeing the other guys were leery about a game with Wallie, Tom kept him on the back side of the court. They headed back to the unit for mid-morning count.

Wallie walked slowly and fell silent. Bruce met them at the unit and walked up with them to their cell. He said to Tom, "Wallie'll be tired for the rest of the day. It helps him if he's bundled tightly. First, you have to keep him awake until count's done."

"Shouldn't he go to the infirmary?"

"What, and let them put him in the SHU and pump him full of drugs that'll mess him up even more?" Bruce told Tom what to do.

After count Bruce appeared and helped Tom get Wallie in his bunk. He promptly fell asleep.

Tom walked with Bruce to the kitchen. "How often?"

"Don't know. Holidays are the worst. It goes in cycles. You did good."

CHAPTER 7

WALLIE WAS NOW his friend. The other inmates stayed away from both of them, but they were still welcome at Stan's table. Tom had enough energy to go to basketball the next evening.

Sal intercepted him. "Listen, Tom, nothing personal, but the guys aren't comfortable having you on the team."

Tom saw how the team looked at him. "No hard feelings. Thanks for letting me play. You still in the playoffs?"

"Last game's tonight."

Uncertain of where to go or what to do, he saw Vince, the recreation orderly, at the far end. Tom eventually cornered him at the bench. "I need a team, Vince. I showed up, ran your drills. I can play. Not one team has an opening?"

Vince didn't look at him. "Give it a rest for a few weeks. I'll check into it. Once they see you're fine, I should be able to get you on a team, but not till after the holidays, you copy?"

"Yeah." Most avoided him because he wouldn't play cards, gamble or join in, but now he was a pariah. *Will Todd still talk with me?*

The next morning, he leaned against the sink and returned Todd's smile.

"Friends with Twitchy. That's a first. Upped your rep. Most'll think twice about taking you on now."

"A mixed blessing. You'd think I'm contagious."

"What I don't get is how words on a page helps you in here." He tapped his chest.

"God gives His Holy Spirit to all believers. Since God wrote the Bible, it's the Holy Spirit who helps us understand it. God uses His Word to strengthen us, warn us, and shower His love upon us."

"Well, my ex's writing about the Bible this and the Bible that. She makes it sound like it's real, this Jesus thing."

"He is real. Jesus Christ is both God and man. That's why He could pay our sin debt to God."

"Then why's the world such a mess?"

"Cause we're all trying to do it our way. God can show us how to straighten things out if we let Him. The Bible says all of us have missed what God expects of us. Romans 3:23, *'for all have sinned and fall short of the glory of God.'* It's like trying to leap across a chasm and not having the strength to make it to the other side. We're not what He created us for."

"Which is?"

"Set apart for Him, living right, doing justice, speaking truth, fulfilling His love in our lives—that's how we walk with God."

For a moment Todd's face softened, his eyes wistful, then his set lips pulled back. "When hell freezes over."

"Nice talking with you," Tom said to Todd's retreating back. Pumped with the opportunity, he turned to his sinks.

"Ya think it'll work."

"What?" Tom faced Bruce standing with arms crossed at the edge of the third rack.

Bruce pointed his chin to the double doors. "No one leaves that family."

CHAPTER 8

Two days after Christmas and before New Year's, Tom sat with Stan at the last table with Rick and Bob. Stan nodded at a new inmate to the unit.

"Hear about our new resident?" Rick asked.

Seeing Tom's confused expression, Stan said, "Word from A&O says he's a player. Bank robber or drug dealer?" Stan said.

"If I weren't a Christian, I'd place my bet he was dealing drugs. Probably thought it would be cool to sell to his friends so he could drive a fancy car," Bob explained.

"He looks really young," Tom noted.

"That would be selling to his high school friends." Rick laughed. "In the beginning, crime does pay, especially drugs."

Tom noted the kid's swagger as well as the scared look in the back of his eyes. For an instance, his heart went out to him.

After count and during mail call, Tom and Wallie waited by the back table. "No mail for you today?"

"They'll let me know," Wallie said. "Thanks for being my friend. I've not had one in a long time."

"No problem." Tom refused to think about losing his spot on the team. He tried to pray about it, but Stan joined them.

"Name's Justin. Rich kid with connections. Hope he's not setting up to deal in this unit."

Bob sat down with his mail. "Bruce won't put up with it. Word is newbie's already buying. Hope he can pay his bills."

"How they lose it."

Rick joined the group. "He won't make it to February."

"I doubt he'll see the new year if he doesn't stop talking," Stan declared.

Tom tuned out the gossip. Always chattering about someone doing something. Most of it went nowhere.

After supper Tom hovered by his locker. He could walk to the gym to watch the games, but winter's cold had settled in. He looked at the pile of new paper—fresh, unmarked. He had an idea for a different sheet, but he didn't want to spend more time in his cramped cell. Heading down to the commons, he placed his papers on the back table, examined the blank pages, and wrote SOT on the upper corner. He wrote verse references down the left side, stepping through soteriology, the doctrine of salvation. Even if he didn't have a group to teach or would never be the pastor of any decent church, he could still work through what he had learned. It might be useful someday.

Justin came over. "Just hanging out, huh? What you working on?" He reached for Tom's papers.

Tom rose, blocking his pages. "Just writing down some verses."

"Like Bible verses? Yeah, they talk about you, choir boy. But they know you got a secret. What is it?"

Tom folded the papers and tucked them behind his back. He gripped the short pencil in his left fist.

Justin's eyes were red-rimmed with constricted pupils. His clipped, fast-paced speech almost resembled Wallie's on his worst days, but Justin had a hard, dark edge about him.

Angling himself in full view of the camera, Tom said, "That's what the feds said." He knew better than to ask if Justin was a snitch. He prayed the guy would leave him alone. For an instant, he considered sharing the gospel, but Justin began to trash talk him, Wallie, Bruce, Stan and the rest of the unit.

Tom prayed to stay calm.

Justin's eyes glistened. He turned his tirade to the officers, cops, and the justice system.

Finding a break, Tom said, "Bruce runs a good unit. We all keep to ourselves and don't get into other people's stuff."

"Yo, you got the biggest kleptomaniac at your table, dude. You blind? I heard about Stan day one. Day one! You can't say you haven't had stuff missing?"

Tom could not refute the statements. "Just little things, and if you let him know you really need your stuff, it often reappears in your cell. He'll be good to you, if you show respect." Showing respect made the difference in surviving.

"Yeah, I get the respect thing. Just a bunch of cowards. You hit hard, and they'll leave you alone. That's my rule." Justin looked at him closely. "So, choir boy, you got game?"

Tom stood his ground. He noticed the rest of the unit had gone stone quiet. Bruce approached silently and whispered in Justin's ear, "Twerp, Tom's got more game then you'll ever have. Keep to your own business and don't bother him."

Justin tried to hide his surprise. "Calling me twerp, now?"

"32358, you're just a number. You earn the right to be called by your given name—Twerp. Do your own time and don't let me catch you messing with my guys, got it?" Bruce, head and shoulders taller and almost double his size, stepped forward.

Justin stepped back, "Yeah, no offense. Just trying to have a civil conversation. Like, yeah, I need to take a shower."

After he left, Bruce said, "Even if he throws the first punch, when you get in a fight, you all end up in the SHU. Got it? And, 66789, you just got here, and you already been in once. If you're in too often, they might send you up the river…capiche?"

"Yeah, I get it. He's been like this all night."

"High?"

"High as a kite."
"Hope he can pay his bill."

CHAPTER 9

THE COLD PENETRATED even to the center of Building One. Tom smiled at Rick and Bob sitting at the back table after supper, but they turned away. "Having a good day?" he commented, hoping to get some conversation going.

Bob glared at him. Rick half returned the smile.

"You got nerve acting all nice since it's your fault we didn't get our books back."

"What books?"

"The ones in Curtis' office," Rick said. He motioned to Bob. "Took his Bible study books, especially *Managing Anger God's Way*,[2]—the one he really needs back."

"I showed Mark how to do it."

Bob snorted and rose. Before he turned to the stairs, he let loose. "You prissy little choir boy. Thinking only of your stand for the faith. You're the only one who could get Curtis to give 'em back, and you're sitting here with your new friend." With a wave of his hand, he stalked off before Tom could reply.

"Is he serious?"

Rick laughed. "You're blind hiding out in your little cave. Curtis makes sure we all know who's not cooperating here."

"I should go make things right with Bob," Tom said.

"You're dumber than we thought you were. He went to his house. When he's ready to get right, he'll find you. Work for Curtis. It's that simple. Mark's not a believer, and there's a lot he doesn't get."

"I can't confiscate Bibles, and I don't think Curtis is the type to let me pick and choose what I can do."

"You'd think a real Christian could figure out a way. You know what the Bible says. A righteous man will be at peace even with his enemies."[3]

Tom started to state the reference and quote it accurately, but Rick cut him off. "And that spouting verses with the address all the time is getting old real fast. Showing off your bona fides like you're God's gift to Hannibal. Well, you ain't."

Tom watched him walk away. He retreated to his cell early. It was warmer in the third tier.

The next day Todd smashed the far door with the dumpster. Tom started to help until he noticed the glare on the man's face.

"Your God's a piece of work!" he spat through his teeth. "Likes of you sitting pretty and the strong ones getting stomped."

"What happened?"

"Now you want to know what happened—like you care? Come on. Go sit with your choir boy pals and sing hallelujah in lalaland. That's the good your religion's gonna do you."

Tom knew he couldn't connect with empty platitudes. "Was he your friend?"

"Friend?" Todd stepped forward. "Not friends—business. Had potential, talents, would've been an asset." He wheeled the empty to the nearest open slot and locked the wheels. A glance down the line showed no one looking their way. "You only kept because of him." He shot his chin in Bruce's direction.

Tom started to speak, but Todd approached. "Got no answers? Got nothing for why the best die and the scum live?"

"God sets our days. He's in charge. He decides, but…"

"Well, I hate Him, and you'd better stay away, or I might not keep my self-control."

Tom stepped back and watched Todd angle the doors open. An edge of the dumpster caught a cloth hanging from Todd's pocket.

He picked it up, along with a small picture. Tom heard a faint sigh. Straightening his shoulders, Todd wiped his brow. Tom thought he saw a few tears along his cheek. His prayers for Todd rose to heaven.

"I want you gone," Bruce said.

Tom whirled to face him, his back against the sinks. His mind raced through the many steps for a job transfer. "Make it happen." Tom pulled the next rack off the cart. "I'm not giving up my day job."

"This isn't your hood, and it's not your God's either."

Tom faced him. *"Where shall I go from your Spirit? Or where shall I flee from your presence? If I ascend to heaven, you are there! If I make my bed in Sheol, you are there!"*[4] Sheol's hell. God's everywhere. No one can get away from Him. He is here with me in Hannibal. No law, no force can keep Him out."

"Well, you're going to get yourself killed and lots of us in trouble." He stepped closer. "And it will be your fault. Todd's number two in his gang. If they knew he was talking with you, you'd both be dead."

"Then don't tell. I won't."

"You're a fool. You won't see it coming."

"And do not fear those who kill the body but cannot kill the soul. Rather fear him who can destroy both soul and body in hell."[5]

Bruce blew through his teeth and set lips. He muttered, "Hopeless."

Tom breathed again when he heard Bruce turn his attention to the soup cook.

CHAPTER 10

A BLIZZARD PUT the facility on lockdown. Bruce pulled Tom for food service delivery to the other buildings. Tom was glad for the chance to get out of his cell until he realized he would be carting food through unheated tunnels connecting the buildings. It took him hours to warm up.

The night was restless, and the unit echoed with swearing, cursing, and calls. Sleep eluded him. Heavy-hearted, Tom tried to pray, but his inner peace had fled weeks ago. Running through his verses didn't even work. Too tired to remember where he had left off, longing for release, he huddled on the floor by the bars. Sleep came too close to first call.

When the buzzer for first count came, Tom's eyes burned. *Did I run a marathon in my sleep?* Many in the unit were in no better moods. Tom hung back, trying to stay out of the mess of line up after count. A ball of dread filled his chest matched with a haunting doom. Wallie sped away as he often did in the mornings. Tom couldn't keep up with the flow and found himself left behind. He didn't notice the group congregating up ahead.

The cameras couldn't cover the section of the second bend. Tom saw without noticing a group of three push Justin to the blind inner curve. The first pinned him to the wall, the second shoved up toward Justin's right chest, the third slashed open his left carotid artery. In an instant they were gone, with not a drop on them as they vanished before the spraying blood could mark them.

Tom saw the light in Justin's eyes burn, flicker and fade; the look of stunned disbelief followed by utter terror ran across his face. Tom knew if he'd had time, he could stop the bleeding, but Stan, right behind him, pushed him past.

"Don't look. Not your business. Get off the walk and to your station. Don't tell anyone you saw the hit. Move."

Like a mirage, Stan moved on. Tom followed the instructions mechanically. The alarms sounded shortly after he reached his sinks. Tom grasped the rounded steel countertop, his eyes refusing to focus.

Right behind him he heard, "Who?"

Not turning to Bruce, he said softly, "The Twerp. Do I have to report it to the officer?'

"No. You heard the alarm. They know. If you tell him, he has to tell Meggars who has to drag you to Admin for interrogation. Whether you can ID 'em or not, they'll put a hit on you too."

"I don't think I could. It's…" he closed his eyes, trying to stop the images replaying in his mind.

"Stay here," Bruce ordered before returning to the cooking area.

Frozen, he stood motionless, gripping the counter for an hour. Trying to shake the dread, he forced himself to the coffee urn. Downing half a cup, he retreated to his sink and opened the spigots. Tom turned to the racks on his left. His mind in a daze, it took fifteen minutes to decide what to scrub first—a cooking tray halfway down the stack. Larger pots and a beat-up skillet sat on top of it, but he knew they needed the trays. He pulled. It caught. Angling it sideways, his anger flared up and he tugged, bringing down the pots and a jagged edge of a skillet on his inner arm, slicing it deeply before they crashed to the floor.

Tom watched the blood drip from his arm. His mind reeled with visions of the blood running down Justin's side and neck. He saw the blood ooze out of his arm and onto the floor. *It isn't pulsating,* one part of his mind noted. Bleeding out would take a while.

Bruce rushed over with a towel. "Tom, get with it. Stop the bleeding," he ordered. He returned with the first-aid kit, looking for bandages. Bruce ordered, "Hold it together."

"Thanks. Do I have to go to the infirmary?"

"No, not when you're like this. They'll stick you in isolation."

"That's the SHU. It's all the same—discipline's same as protective custody, same as isolation."

"And they'll pump you full of drugs to mess up your head. Get it together. Where's that God of yours? He put you in here. Why isn't He helping you?"

Bruce stood by the back door when Todd arrived for his pickup. "Get your stuff and get out."

Tom washed a few items. Exhaustion consumed him. Despite remembering the warnings, he slept after lunch. Bruce's question ran through his head—why wasn't God helping him? Slowly, the question changed. *Why am I not letting God help me?*

Hadn't God promised He would never leave or forsake him? Where was the deep inner joy—the peace that had sustained him through earlier trials? *How am I messing this up?*

The ball of dread returned anew when he rolled from his bunk to sit on the floor. He should shower, but he'd have to change the bandage. He didn't have any more bandages so he couldn't shower. The cycle of hopelessness enveloped him.

He barely heard Wallie come in until he sat beside him on the floor.

"You having a bad day, buddy?"

"Yeah. I saw the hit this morning, but I wasn't doing well anyway." Tom smiled at Wallie. "Thanks for asking. Thanks for caring. It's like they would have drunk his blood. One more thing to do—take out the trash, make your bed, show up for work. Wallie, there's a lot of evil in this world. How did He do it?"

"Who?"

"Jesus lived on this wretched planet for thirty years, and He couldn't do anything about it. He didn't perform any healings until He began His ministry. I guess He was doing something about it. He conquered our sin. Someday there will be no evil, sin, suffering or pain. He conquered it on the cross. So, if I know this, why am I having such trouble?"

"Count soon. You're going to have to get up."

Tom heard the guys returning to the unit. He made it through count, mail call, and supper.

He retreated to his bunk right after. Thoughts of pulling out his papers to go over his verses were not strong enough to propel himself out of his bunk and to his locker. The feelings of despair wouldn't lift. He dozed.

Wallie woke him for last count. He felt rested until he tried to stand.

After count he pulled out his papers and sat at the table, but the light was dim. Angling near the bars to catch the glow of the night lights he reviewed verses, skimming some quickly and pausing at others. A few hints of hope rose up only to vaporize like mist before a rising sun. He stopped at Corinthians.

"There it is. The answer."

"What answer?" Wallie asked.

"I've been trying to do this in my own power and strength. You know, do it for Jesus. Be strong. I, I, me, me. I missed it. Listen to this: *'Finally, be strong in the Lord and in the strength of his might.'*[6] That's Ephesians 6."

"So?"

"It's *God's* might, His power—*not mine*. I know the best verses." Tom set down his papers. "Paul wrote many of the books of the Bible. God gave him the power to perform healing miracles, but even he had a problem. We don't know what it was. The Bible never tells us, but he called it an affliction and he asked God to remove it. Maybe he thought he could do more for Christ without it, but God said no. In fact, God said, 'My grace is sufficient for you, for my power is made perfect in weakness.' If even the apostle Paul needed to be weak, so God's glory could work through him, I need to learn how to do this too. When Paul understood, he wrote, *'I will boast all the more gladly of my weaknesses, so that the power of Christ may rest upon me. For the sake of Christ, then, I am content with weaknesses… For when I am weak, then I am strong.'*[7]

"That makes no sense."

"I know it sounds backward, but if I have the strength to do it myself, I'm doing it—not God working through me." Tom turned to Wallie, "You see when we get saved, God the Father, God the Son and God the Holy Spirit dwell within us and will work through us when we yield to them. But when we can do things on our own, we tend to rely on ourselves. I can try to work really hard to be the best Christian I can be, but I'm doomed to fail if I don't let God walk beside me in here."

"In here? You mean, He's in here with you?"

"Yep. He's in here with a lot of the guys—Rick, Bob, even Officer Curtis."

"And Officer Nivens?"

"He's a Christian too?'

"Yep, since I can fix anything, he sends me to fix what the other guys can't fix or messed up. He told me if I could work regular every day, he'd find me a slot with a real job and some pay. Not much, but more than indigent."

"Are there many Christian officers?"

"Some, but they don't always act like it. Why is that?"

"Christians are sinners saved by God's grace. Each day we have to decide to follow God or our old ways. If we don't keep our eyes on Christ and ask Him to help us follow Him, it's easy to return to bad habits." The verses flowed. Tom recited passage after passage. They retreated to their bunks late in the night.

The glow, the feeling he could get it together if he remembered to let God in lasted until shortly before Todd appeared with the dumpster. Reviewing the Corinthian verses, he repeated them over and over in his mind. *Be weak in Christ. Let Him be strong through me.* Leaning against the sink, he dropped his head. He was forcing it again. *What blocked it?* "Oh Lord," he cried wordlessly counting on the Holy Spirit to fix his prayers.

Todd crashed his dumpster against the full one, laughing when Tom jerked. "Back from the dead?" One look into Tom's eyes, he whistled quietly. "You tight. Better find a way to let the steam out or you'll explode in front of the wrong people."

Tom went to shake his head, but one part of him knew Todd was right. He looked about. The three mostly filled racks blocked the view of the other kitchen workers and narrowed the vision for the guys on the line—his little oasis in the fishbowl. He met Todd's gaze. The guy was talking to him as if his outburst days before had never happened.

"Better figure it out fast cause it's a long hard winter to get through. Then it's the summer's heat." Todd's hard laugh caught in his throat. He glanced down the hall. Bruce didn't bother to interrupt their little morning chats anymore. "Well, got a schedule to keep."

"Yeah." Tom's mind was blank. He found himself staring at the door long after Todd's back had disappeared.

After mail call, Wallie joined Tom at the third-tier railing. "I'm glad you're my buddy. You can pray for me. Help me out."

Tempted to correct his bunkie, his mind froze. Tom focused on the throng down in the common area. Soon they would line up for supper. Walk back. Walk up the tiers. Stay in the narrow cell and do it over again day after day. A raw hunger rose up—to feel the wind in his face, to drive down an open road, to walk into a store, and to know he had a home and friends and a place. Shaking his head, he followed Wallie down the tier to join the end of the line.

CHAPTER 11

LIGHTS FLIPPED ON to flood the unit. Tom felt the thud and heard the tier shudder under the weight of a fast-moving squad. As he began to roll onto his side, the cell door rolled back, and a team of black-shirted officers pulled him from the cell. Two suited men approached.

Tom's heart skipped a beat. "Agent Trainer, Agent Cooper?"

"Remember us? We got you dead to rights. Where are they at?"

"What?"

"Your Bibles. CI saw you with them. We can do this quick. Tell the officers where to look. You're not getting away with it this time."

"What Bibles? CI?"

"Confidential informant. Give it up. You're not getting out of this." Noting his blank look, the Task Force agents nodded to the officers. "Rip the cell apart."

Tom watched them pull Wallie from the cell. "He's done nothing wrong."

"Yeah, well, he's bunked with you. Maybe he can tell us where they're at. Maybe he's smarter than you are. Take our guy down to the commons. We'll be down shortly." Trainer smiled at Cooper.

The officers pushed him down on the bench between Bruce and Doug's cells. Voices, plastic cups and plates falling on the hard floor, and the swish of mattresses pulled aside echoed across the cell block. Tom couldn't make out the words. Sometime later they brought Wallie down.

"He can bunk with me," Bruce said to the head night officer.

"Who's your contact?" Cooper said, leaning over Tom, pushing him back against the table.

"Contact?"

"Your uncle's network. How does he communicate with you?"

"I get no letters or phone calls. Have no visitors. There is no network, no underground organization."

"That's not what our sources tell us." Trainer leaned closer, drawing his hand from an inner jacket pocket. Cooper positioned himself to the side, nodding in Officer Curtis' direction.

Tom jerked to the side with the searing shock of the small Taser in Trainer's hand. Their eyes locked. Memories of weeks of interrogation in a closed room exploded in his brain. Tom stood up and wrenched free of Trainer's grip on his shoulder. Spinning around, he said, "Stop!" Holding out his hands, he repeated, "Just stop."

Cooper rushed to his side to grab his arm. He kicked at Tom's legs, but Tom pulled back against the bars.

Tom repeatedly broke free. In the back of his mind, he noticed the officers standing with crossed arms, watching the agents try to take him down. He said again, "Just stop," but the agents charged one more time. Shortly after, Tom heard a sharp whistle.

The nearest officer grabbed his arm, pulling him off-balance. Another kicked his legs from under him. His side slammed into the hard floor. His head buzzed. The multiple blows pulsed shock waves up his spine.

In a few minutes they trussed him up and carried him out of the unit. Agent Trainer stayed with the crew searching the cell. Cooper followed the officer to the kitchen.

A few hours later before the cell doors opened, Wallie sat up, still clutching the blanket Bruce had given him.

Bruce continued his complaining. "And why'd your bunkie mess things up like that? Why did he bring that stuff in here?"

"What?"

"The Bibles," Bruce spat, the words flowing.

"He got no Bibles. Not the kind you hold in your hand."

"Oh, yeah? You blind now or just covering for him? The guys heard him. They told me he read from his Bible the other night. So, Wallie," he leaned forward. "You can tell me. I got no need to snitch."

"He has no Bibles. He knows it by heart."

"What does that mean?"

"He knows it without the Book. It's up here." Wallie tapped his head.

"You're not fooling with me?"

"No, Wallie wouldn't do that. You gave me space. Kept me out of the SHU. I would never do you wrong, Bruce. You know that."

Bruce nodded. "So, what's all those papers about?"

"He writes it down, so he won't forget."

They stood to their feet when the bars rolled open. Subdued chatter filtered down as inmates walked along the tiers and down the stairs to line up for chow.

Doug approached Bruce. "You going to stand by and let them get away with that?"

"With what? Our Christian's just another hypocrite. Now we know. Like Curtis said."

"Not like Curtis said. Didn't you see?"

"See what? I ain't blind."

"I saw the Taser. He didn't fight back until they started in on him. One agent blocked the camera, and Curtis let 'em. He knew. We going to stand by for this? What if they can get away with doing that? We going to take it?"

Others backed up Doug's version.

Doug folded his arms. "You going to report it?"

"Me?" Bruce glared at Doug. "I got nothing to report. I didn't see nothing. That's on you, Dude."

Doug nodded. "Yeah."

Bruce headed to the kitchen.

His officer was already there. "They took his area apart."

CHAPTER 12

LIEUTENANT MEGGARS ASSEMBLED his lead officers. "These reports correct? Curtis let in federal agents?" He brought up the case file and checked the attachments. "Where are the warrants?"

"Curtis had actionable intelligence from a CI concerning contraband in Unit 4."

"What type of contraband?"

"Bibles."

"Bibles?"

"The unauthorized ones. The CI told Curtis he saw 66789 with illegal Bibles."

"And why didn't our staff investigate? Who signed off on this?"

His officers exchanged glances. Presson spoke first. "He let them in, uh, as a courtesy."

"Due process does not stop with these walls." Meggars noted his officers' nods. "How many did they find?"

"None yet."

"And let me remind you. I made this clear to Curtis as well as the DU staff; we do not pursue Bibles. Not going there. If they parade them around in general population, they can be written up, but we have more serious issues to deal with here. Going unit by unit to confiscate Bibles is not on the radar. Authorized copies are available through the chaplain's office upon request, no questions asked. That does not constitute grounds for a search."

"Yes, sir," Presson said. "We had no part in this action."

CHAPTER 13

B<small>Y THE TIME</small> they reassembled for early count, Bruce walked up to the third tier. Wallie and Officer Nivens were already installing a used table and chair unit in the cell. He said to Wallie, "You'd better pray for your bunkie. Curtis has a transfer order ready to go on him. You think they'll let you bunk single after this? You ready for another cellmate?"

Wallie stared at him. Bruce walked down the tier before Wallie could answer. He looked at Officer Nivens. "I can't pray yet."

"Just ask. He won't turn you away."

"Will you pray for me?"

"Wallie," the officer stepped into the cell. "I'll pray with you, but you have to pray for yourself."

Wallie nodded his head, trying to remember what Tom had told him. "He sounded like you, Officer Nivens. God will take me? Even me?"

"Yes, Jesus took your place on the cross. He died for you. Ask Him; He will forgive you."

"And He'll send His Spirit to help me, the way He helps Tom?"

"All who call on Him to get saved have the Spirit within them." The officer listened to Wallie's prayer of confession and repentance.

Wallie lifted his head, wiping his eyes. A brilliant smile crossed his face. "It worked. I know what we have to do." Wallie's eyes glinted as he continued, "It's going to take two of us, but I need to go to Unit L."

CHAPTER 14

TOM SHIVERED IN the thin orange jumpsuit. After medical cleared him, they shaved his head and hosed him down. Another set of shivers ran up his back. Tom tensed when the door swung back, and agents walked through followed by officers. He heard their yelling, but the sense didn't make it through. Tom focused on a dark spot on the far wall. He had nothing to say they would believe, and he would not lie.

"All right. We're not getting anywhere," an officer stated. The room grew quiet. "Officer Curtis, take your agents to the media room. See what they find in the video feeds." The officer returned with a cup of coffee.

Tom wet his dry lips. His throat stuck together. He stared at the cup. "Will I get a trip to the toilet if I need it?" he asked.

"What kind of question is that?"

"Well, if you let feds in here to Taser me, I don't eat or drink unless I'm in a cell. Otherwise," he met the officer's gaze, "you…" His voice cracked, remembering his time with the agents. "You…"

"We got CIs saying they saw you with a Bible."

"Did they find any in my cell or my work area?"

"If you think that proves your innocence, you got another think coming. The smart ones, and you're probably in that camp, know how to hide stuff with their friends. When we search, we never find it, but we know you got it. So, do we have to do it the hard way?" Seeing Tom's furrowed brow, he said, "That means searching the whole unit. Or you could tell us where they are."

Tom shook his head.

The officer laid out Tom's papers, page after page of handwritten verses. "Oh, those. I did those from memory to make sure I don't forget it."

"Forget what?"

"The Word of God. I memorized everything they taught me in Bible college." He shifted his weight in his chair and squared his shoulders. "I don't need to have a physical Bible to write it." He sighed, "So that's what happened."

"You going to fill me in?"

"Your CI's must have heard me quoting verses to Wallie. A few nights ago, we talked a long time about it. He had questions. Please don't rip up the unit. I have no Bibles."

"Then why does the Task Force think you do?"

"Because of what my uncle did, only they won't tell me what he did."

A tall, well-built officer stepped in. "Officer, I'll take it from here." He faced Tom once the door closed behind him. "I'm Lieutenant Connors. I run the SHU."

Tom ran through the information. He thought Lieutenant Meggars headed up the DU.

Connors sat down and set a Bible on the table. His mouth smiled, but his eyes bore into Tom. Breathing in, the officer sat back and flipped open the Bible. "Okay, whiz kid. What's Leviticus 18:11 say?"

"What?"

"You say you memorized it. Here's your chance to prove it. Ecclesiastes 8:20," he paused. "Prove you know the Bible like you say."

Tom brought up Ecclesiastes in his mind, recalling the structure for the eighth chapter. Before he could recall the chapter, Connors snapped, "Wrong! That chapter doesn't have 20 verses." He flipped through more pages. "Zechariah 9:9."

Tom recited the verse. He began to relax until the officer barked at him.

"Not how this Bible says it."

"You're reading from a different version, but the sense would be the same. I'm sure they match up."

"That's not good enough!" Connors shouted out verse references without a break.

Tom sat as far back in his chair as he could.

"What? Got nothing to say, choir boy?"

"Do not give dogs what is holy, and do not throw your pearls before pigs, lest they..."[8]

Connors stood up and shoved the table, pinning Tom to the wall. Two officers rushed in. As he walked out, Connors ordered, "Find him a fitting cell in Wing 2."

The two officers unchained Tom from the chair and pulled him to his feet.

He struggled to find his footing and keep up with the officers. They headed through three sets of locked doors, down two sets of stairs and along a narrow subterranean passageway. After walking up a full flight of stairs, they paused at the dark metal gate secured with bolts and braces. Eventually a buzz sounded, and the officer swung the door open.

Dense, stale air with scents of mold and mildew hit his face. Tom tried to shut his nostrils. Some of the lights flickered. Dark shadows hugged the corners. The sounds of chains merged with the sharp *ting* of keys on the officers' belts. Tom tried to lift his chest to take in a breath, but the tight belly chain bit into his tender sides. Shifting rotated his hands, and the cuffs, not locked in place, ratcheted down on his wrists. His brain nearly shut down when the next door opened, and light streamed into his eyes. He stumbled and nearly fell into the nerve center of Building Four.

The officer sitting at a bare desk swiveled his chair to face them. "He been sentenced yet?"

"No, still investigating. He ticked off Connors. What's open in

Wing 2?" The officer tapped his foot while the officer set his newspaper down and woke up his computer. "Got a bunk?"

"Yeah." He smiled. "Just the one. This the inmate who picked a fight last night?"

"Yep."

"You'd think they'd learn crime don't pay." He grabbed Tom's arm. "Been in the SHU before?"

"Yes, sir," Tom said, trying not to mumble.

"Behave or you'll be in X wing. That you don't want. Don't cause any problems."

"Sir, I need my indigent supply."

"Later. Get you in first."

In a short time, he was standing in front of a solid door with a small trapdoor halfway up. Holding his breath, he waited for the officers to release his chains. He stepped through.

On the lower bunk a rolled-up blanket balanced on a thin pillow. Stacks of worn novels leaned against the end wall near the door. Before he could ask the officers, he heard the door slam shut and the lock *slide-click-click* into place.

Tom focused on the problem at hand. He would not be alone in this cell. Tom settled on the small stool closest to the toilet-shower area to wait.

His chest throbbed. When he shifted his arm for better support, his right shoulder sent waves of pain down his arm and up his neck. Tom forced himself to breathe through it.

CHAPTER 15

SOMETIME LATER, HE heard muffled voices and footsteps on the range, probably residents returning from exercise. Cell doors opened and closed with the telltale *slide-click-click*. Tom held his breath when his door opened.

The stout middle-aged man took one look at Tom and pounded on the door. "What? Ya' don't bring in a new cellmate when I'm out."

Tom heard a muffled "Deal with it."

He swallowed a small laugh. "I'm Tom. Probably temporary. Just needed a place to put me until they could do a little more investigation."

"Sam," he said, "and get off *my* stool. This is my house, my rules. Don't sit on that stool. It's mine. I get bottom bunk. You keep your junk off my space, do the dishes and mind your manners. What happened to you?"

"Picked a fight with two feds."

"Well, you don't look that bad for doing something that stupid. Did it in front of the officers?"

Tom nodded and headed to the toilet. His urine was pink.

"Medical clear you?"

"I think they did." Tom turned to survey his new cellmate. Something about him was familiar. He sat down on the stool near the door. Tom eyed the top bunk, wondering how he'd get up there with his cracked ribs. Every muscle ached.

"Your stuff?"

"Don't know." He heard the officers walking down the range. Thoughts of banging on the door and calling for his indigent supplies circled in his brain. He barely heard Sam's questions.

"Great, I got a zombie." Sam rolled out his pad, adjusted the pillow, and pulled out his latest novel.

Ten minutes later, Tom focused on Sam. "I would have cooperated if they'd stop yelling at me."

"Now I got a cupcake. Yo, they yell when they're not hearing what they need to hear."

Tom nodded. "I guess they'll yell." His eyes shifted to a dark upper corner, his focus fading in and out.

"What they want?"

Tom refocused on Sam. He worked at formulating an answer. With no info on this large man, he guessed at the safest answer. "Contraband."

"Well, don't bring it in here. I'm trying to get a transfer. Need a clean record."

Tom eyed the top bunk again. It was tempting, yet a high mountain. He tried to rise, but the pressure on his rib cage sent him back on the stool. "How long?"

"How long what?"

"You wait for the transfer. When it's going through?"

"Five months. And no, it's not scheduled, not that they'd let me know." Sam sat up. "Someday around 2 a.m., they'll barge in here and expect me to be packed in fifteen minutes. So," he nodded at his bagged items stuffed under the bunk. "Don't even think of taking a peek."

Tom shifted his head. "Lunch soon. Sounds the same here as in the other halls." He heard the muffled calls of the others along with the familiar sound of clanging metal—the food cart.

"Set the table." Sam stood behind the last stool just in front of the toilet, sink and shower area. "You get that one. Your half of the table."

"Set the table?"

"Not much to it, but I expect you to be present like a civilized person."

Tom grabbed the plates as they came through and set them on the table. He sat on the hard metal stool. Everything was hard. Even softer sounds reverberated down the range. He met Sam's gaze. The piercing blue eyes looked familiar, but the broad face and short, dark brown hair of an almost middle-aged man didn't match anyone he knew. "Do I know you?"

"Doubt it. How long you been here?"

"In Hannibal? Almost three months. I'm indigent, and I don't think I'm getting my stuff back." Hearing the officers walking down the range, he called out through the slot. "I need my indigent supplies."

He heard a faint "Yeah, yeah."

"They don't do maid service."

"I'll keep reminding them."

"You upped your rep—taking on the feds like that."

"Yeah, I get that. Like when I became Wallie's friend." Tom half smiled, "For the most part my only friend."

"Twitchy? You made friends with Twitchy?"

"He is, or was, my cellmate. Hope he's okay."

"Twitchy? You're worrying about Twitchy? You know how many guys he put six feet under? If he's your friend, no one'll touch you now."

Tom nodded. "But I trashed the rep that counted."

Sam arched his brow. "Spill it. You don't make a comment like that without giving the rest of the story."

Tom locked eyes with Sam. "I'm a Christian. I'm in here for keeping my Bibles." He explained the HCL law.

"Yeah, you're going to need Twitchy as a friend. L block…they got your back?"

"No. Officer Curtis got 'em convinced I'm a fraud. Bad Christian. Now they know." He nodded his head. "I lost it—lost control."

"That's a mistake. One thing you can't do here is lose control." Sam set down his spoon. "But you don't have to do it yourself; just make it happen." A distant smile crossed his face. "You need someone gone? You get the guy two doors down to do it, and you've solved two problems."

"That's not an option for me."

"Probably not." Sam picked up his spoon. "You keep your religion to yourself. I know all about that religion stuff. My old man went to church and beat us at home. My mom even got it— made no difference to Dad."

"Going to church doesn't turn a person into a Christian."

"Ya figure?" Partway through Sam's description of his family, he stopped. "You going to eat?"

"I'll try, but…" Tom stomach turned again as the mushy potatoes and starchy gravy clumped in his mouth. The bread looked hard. Pain cascaded down his neck. "Food wasn't this bad the first time through."

"We're in the part of the SHU catered by the prison camp in this complex." Sam laughed. "That's what all the food used to taste like until they made Bruce head orderly for the kitchen. He knows how to make a crew serve good meals. When the repeats come back, if they can do eggs or fry chicken, they get their top jobs back." He lifted his chin to Tom, "You cook?"

"Nope." Tom started to laugh until his ribs reminded him. "Scrub the racks—stuff no one wants to touch. Keeps me busy." He knew better than to mention Todd.

Sam propped himself against the bunk end, opened his novel, and watched Tom do the dishes. He tried to find his place on the page, but the clang of the range door opening broke his attention.

"Getting guys for appointments?"

Sam rose and shifted his head to the top bunk. He watched Tom scramble up to his ledge. Sam bent his ear against the door. When the hard boot steps paused near their door, he stepped back.

Chapter 16

"3 1247?"

"Yeah, what's up?"

"Cuff up."

The two officers led Sam through the passageway to the DU Administration Interrogation Center. They secured him to a table in a narrow room.

Sam surveyed the room: one chair on his side, two on the other, no camera visible, but a large one-way mirror occupied the opposite wall. Sam sat up and maintained his best poker face when Lieutenant Connors stepped through—number two to Lieutenant Meggars, head of the SHU.

Connors pulled up a chair and slapped a file on the desk. "Looking to transfer. It's been…" he perused the file.

"Five months. Five months, sir."

"Seems you are persona non grata with some units here."

"It was a delicate situation."

"I imagine you'd like to get on with it."

"Reclassified for good behavior like I requested. Maybe a prison camp closer to home."

Lieutenant Connors curled his lip. "On the books, looks like you've behaved yourself." Their eyes locked. "Here's an opportunity to demonstrate cooperation." He pushed the file aside. "Did your new cellmate tell you where his Bibles are?"

"No."

66

"He just arrived, so…" Lieutenant Connors leaned forward, "help us out, and we'll expedite your transfer to that prison camp near home. Deal?"

"Sure. No skin off my back. Bibles, huh? But I got to ask, what did he really do to get in here? He said he pulled five years. Usually don't get this classification for just five years."

"Hate crime terrorist; he established a network here. Need to nip this one in the bud." Connors rose. "Do we have a deal?"

"Yeah."

CHAPTER 17

SAM HEARD HIS new cupcake cellmate snoring lightly when the door opened. He swallowed his laugh when Tom jerked awake, nearly falling off his bunk when the door slammed closed.

"Had a meeting?" Tom asked.

"My caseworker."

"Not scheduled?" Tom positioned himself to get down the easiest way.

"Forgot about it with the excitement of meeting my latest roommate..." Sam smiled. "You born a Christian?"

"My family was not religious." Tom settled on his stool, leaned against the wall and hugged his arm close to his side.

"How you get into the Bible thing? Become a terrorist?"

"Just because that's how they labeled me doesn't mean I am one. It's a long story."

"We got the time. It's hours 'til supper. So far, I've done all the sharing. We're going to be together for a while. Curious about how you did it."

"Did what?"

"Connect with your underground church buddies."

"Thought you wanted me to keep my religion to myself. My story's full of it."

"Why not? If they outlawed your Bibles, how'd you get them past the guards? Made your connections already?"

"All right, why so curious all of a sudden?"

"Well, uh..." he stuttered.

"What'd they offer you for getting me to talk?"

"You calling me a snitch?"

"No, Sam, I'd love to help you. I get you need to see your family. You have kids."

"My two boys are growing up without me. Ann, my wife, is strong, keeps 'em in line, but I know they're missing out."

"Listen, Sam, even though they're convinced I'm working with an organization, they're mistaken. It's not possible for their CI to have seen me with any Bibles. I haven't held a Bible since the day of my arrest when they took everything I owned and put me in here."

"So, you can't help me out?"

Tom shook his head. "I can tell you my story. Maybe you can get something useful out of it. My father and uncle ran the family business. Right when they were ready to expand, my uncle became a Christian and sold his shares to my dad for $1. He left for seminary to become a pastor. Devastated, my father told my mom to throw out all the Bibles."

"Did she?"

"No, she hid them. They removed any trace of God in the house. Some of my friends would invite me to youth group or vacation Bible school, but my parents always said no. I was curious how a book and a God no one can see could make my uncle do something so crazy. It felt like half the family had died, leaving just the three of us."

Tom smiled. "A few summers later, my parents went on this cruise to Alaska. I stayed with friends while they were gone. Their son Tony and I had a great time. My parents were strict and had always kept me busy with chores or helping out at the store. Tony and I rode bikes down to the community pool and hung out at the ice cream shop. A few days later, we found a bunch of kids hanging out down the block at a VBS."

"VBS?"

"Vacation Bible School. Tony noticed they had cupcakes, candy and soda. The leaders let us stay if we helped—even though we were technically a little old for the sessions. I heard how God sent His Son to earth to rescue us from sin. He was the only person who had ever lived a perfect life, earning the right to go to heaven. Instead of keeping it to Himself, He died on the cross to pay for the sins of the whole world—for all people for all time. I could know God, and He would save me. I didn't have to pay anything. I couldn't earn it if I wanted to. I just had to ask. It took me another day, but the story leader answered my questions, and I asked Christ to save me. I had become a Christian like my uncle.

"Once I felt the love of God and experienced His peace and joy in my soul, I began to understand why my uncle left the business to be a pastor. I remembered how he had pleaded with my father to forgive him. My uncle tried to help his brother understand God's calling. He wasn't trying to hurt us. Our family didn't have to break up. That was my dad's decision."

"Now you bought it," Sam said. "You walk out on them too?"

"Not at first. I had to wait; I was 12. I found some Christians at school who could answer my questions and helped me find verses that said I should obey my parents."

"You hid it?"

"Sort of. I reached out to my uncle, and he told me I was doing the right thing. I prayed every day for God to save my parents, but when I turned 21, I knew I had to follow God."

"By going to Bible school?"

Tom nodded. "Telling them was excruciating. I left the car keys on the table, told them I loved them and wanted to stay in touch, but God had called me to be a pastor. My dad was furious. Mom cried. I wrote a letter with my new address, but they never wrote back or called. I did reconnect with my uncle—watched him preach at his church, had a place to go for the holidays. It was great. His son Larry was older than me, and Karen was still in school. They were a fun family."

"They help you out now?"

Tom shook his head. "Uncle Al's in Leavenworth. He pulled 20 for HCL. Agents killed Aunt Sallie when they assaulted the farm. She was the sweetest person; she baked the best pies and always had a kind word." Tom looked up. "No, two years in at Mt. Zion Bible College. Over a year ago, my uncle called to let me know he couldn't help me with my college bill. He explained the HCL legislation and told me not to call, write, visit, or contact him. I hadn't heard anything about this. I'd been too busy working my way through college, along with all the memory work. He told me to burn anything with their contact info, as well as any lists or names of other Christians I knew."

"Your uncle usually that paranoid?"

"Never! The warnings didn't sound like my uncle. I lost my apartment and ended up living in my car for three weeks until I found an attic room to rent from an old, bitter, stingy woman."

Tom stared at the left far corner.

"I think God used my stay there to teach me how to love others even when they're not easy to love. I took her trash to the curb, helped her with some errands. Near the end of my third year with one year left, my best friend asked me if I could graduate with the extended summer courses.

"I didn't have a clue what he was talking about." Tom looked at Sam. "The administration decided to close the college because of the new law. Some were able to finish their degrees with the summer classes, but I had a full year left."

"The law was that bad?"

He met Sam's gaze. "I finished my third year, packed up and reconnected with my parents. Dad let me come home if I worked at the store and finished my business degree. I agreed and slid back into my old life."

"How long did that last?"

"Two months." Tom stared at the nearby bunks with their thin mattresses and no pillows. "Sam, how's it supposed to go when you're arrested? They get to take you somewhere for a while before they charge you?"

"You never been arrested before?"

"No."

Sam rubbed his hands. "Well, some take you to a back lot to rough you up on the way to the police station. They have to charge you in a few days or let you go. What did they do to you?"

"Those feds who came here, Agents Cooper and Trainer, took me to a building that was no police station. I don't know what it was, but I was there three weeks."

"You sure?"

"I didn't realize how much time I'd lost until I heard the date at my hearing. I'd lost track of three weeks. When they came in here and began to Taser me, I remembered. I don't know if it qualifies as torture, but they withheld food and water, kept me chained up so I couldn't take care of myself, stripped me, hosed me down. Made it too hot, then too cold. Kept me awake for days, besides the constant yelling with hours of loud noise in the dark or blinding lights. By the time they took my mugshot and fingerprints, I didn't feel human."

Tom traced the edge of the table. "I think that's why I snapped. It all came back. I don't think I can go through that again." He looked at Sam. "Can they do that here? Can they lock you away without food and water, naked and…?" The words caught in his throat.

"Not and keep the BOP rules. Warden Foster's done a good job of weeding out officers who do stuff like that. Some of it happens, but if you file a grievance, they'll look into it."

"They lied at my hearing for my first 60. They'd really investigate a mean guard?"

"The warden really surprised 'em when he first came on. They transferred right quick or were fired. Some lost their pensions."

"I'll write that up for my hearing. I wasn't going to, but then if they don't believe me, it's on them."

"What'd your uncle do?"

"Don't know. They didn't tell me. Just tried to make me tell them what he did, but he was smart. I didn't know where the Bibles were."

"Didn't they catch him with Bibles?"

"Yes, quite a few. He took the fall for all the Bibles in his church." Tom leaned forward. "They don't simply want to arrest people who keep their original Bibles. They want to know where all the Bibles are so they can destroy them. I don't know how many, but they had records that my uncle had purchased a large number of Bibles." Tom smiled. "I guess he gave them away. That's what Christians do."

"They think you have connections to a network with access to Bibles."

Tom laughed. "How would I accomplish that? No one visits me. I get no mail. I wouldn't risk ruining my friends' lives by contacting them. Those agents promised they would hunt down every friend I had."

"Did you get rid of your lists?"

"I did after I learned the college was closing, and I read the law. I destroyed my old phone and computer and prayed every day for God to shield my friends. Most of them are married with beautiful wives and little kids. Risking their lives for the sake of a few bucks in my commissary account would be so wrong."

"Well, they're probably on some other list."

"Not because of me. I'm glad I never dated. Don't have a family." Tom stopped.

"Ain't your momma crying because you messed up?"

"My folks disowned me when I left for Bible school." He stared at Sam. "No one's going to cry when I pass on."

"Well, I got those who do care. Help me out. Who has contraband Bibles?"

"Not going there, Sam. If I wouldn't put away my Bibles or turn in my friends, what makes you think I would rat on Christians in Hannibal? My life is basically over. No one's going to hire an ex-con pastor. I have no interest in caving now to earn a little good time."

"So, were all those years at school a waste?"

Tom wanted to say it wasn't, wanted to believe it, but his throat shut, his eyes burned, and the fire rose. He stared at Sam. "No," he said through clenched teeth. "I know God sent me here. I know He can make some good come out of all of this."

Sam pounded the table. "If you were a good Christian, you'd help me. Tell them anything. Sure, they got Bibles, but it won't make any difference. Most of them are already lifers. What can the system do to them for having a Bible? You want to help me? Help me. My boys need me."

Tom rose, never taking his eyes off Sam.

"You're a hopeless piece of garbage. Get in your bunk and out of my sight."

Tom climbed up. His right side hurt worse than his left. The dull ache on his left flared with memories of the Taser held against his side. A ball of fear squeezed the air out of his lungs. Hot tears rolled down his cheek. He began to raise his arm to wipe away the tears, but pain exploded in his sides.

No one cares if I die. Rage boiled up. *How could God have done this to me? What a joke!* To have thought he could have what his uncle had—a nice church, a pretty family. His thoughts froze—an easier life.

Tom blew through his lips, hanging on to the only verse he could remember, *"For the joy that was set before him endured."*[9] Nothing surfaced past that Scripture. Tom hung on to the one phrase as waves of darkness descended.

Chapter 18

OFFICER NIVENS HEFTED a tool chest onto the maintenance cart. "So, Unit L's finally going to get their lights upgraded."

Wallie nodded. He surveyed the cart, running through what else they would need. "The supports? The bolts?"

"All there. Let's go."

Wallie pushed the cart into the freight elevator. He watched the officer secure the door sections and press LL2 for the lower tunnels connecting the five buildings. "How's Officer Curtis a real Christian if he can do this to another believer?"

"He's the chaplain, the officer in charge of programs and a Christian. That's a balancing act." Nivens met Wallie's gaze. "He believes he's doing God's will by enforcing all the laws."

"How can this be a good law if it outlaws Bibles?"

"Just part of it, but even that's not right." Nivens sighed. He held unto the cart as the elevator jerked to a stop and gave its little recoil bounce as it settled. "You ready to make things right with the guys in L?"

"I have to. We can't let them send Tom away."

"All right, let's get 'er done."

Unit L in Building Three was mostly empty. The unit officer nodded in their direction and returned to his paperwork. Wallie retrieved the tall ladder from the building's maintenance locker.

Wallie and Nivens strung the cords, secured the supports and new light fixtures with few words. Every other unit, apart from the SHU in Building Four, had been upgraded. The *old* Wallie would never have thought of entering Unit L.

The bell sounded for the controlled movement before late afternoon count and mail call. Officer Nivens winked and smiled at Wallie who stood close by his side right in front of the unit officer's area. He had signed out of Unit Four under Nivens' count log.

The numbers grew; first those coming from the nearby shop building or recreation areas. Len, the unit leader, arrived a short time later. None went to their cells but clumped in groups in the open commons area.

Len noticed the good lighting. He smiled and turned to talk to a nearby resident when he recognized Wallie and Officer Nivens. "What's this?"

Wallie felt Officer Niven's encouragement. He stepped forward, looking over the group to set his gaze on Len. "I believe. Jesus saved me. I'm forgiven, and I am here." He turned. Officer Nivens nodded. "I came to ask you to forgive me for killing and hurting your friends and family. I need you to pray for Tom, so they won't send him away."

"We know all about that shark."

Officer Nivens stood by Wallie's side. "You only heard Officer Curtis' version. Wallie will tell you Tom's side. He's a fellow believer who's trying to walk with God in this place. He's shown by being Wallie's friend that he's a genuine Christian."

Wallie relayed Tom's story and the incident in their unit. Silence hung in the air. Wallie looked at Nivens, "I guess it proves Christians are still sinners." He turned to his cart and packed up the last few things. He heard rustling behind him.

Len patted his shoulder.

Wallie twirled around, ready for anything. He dropped his hands when Len reached forward and gave him a hug. "Forgive us for not believing God could save you." He wiped his eyes. "Guess it took a Tom to do it." He looked at the guys. "Come on. We have to forgive. Christ demands it. Let's pray."

CHAPTER 19

T HE NEXT MORNING Sam walked Tom through writing the statement for his hearing. "Don't forget to mention they Tasered you."

He set down the pencil.

"You got to report it. They don't hand out Tasers to outsiders. Someone helped them. You know who?"

"Not for certain."

"Tell it anyway. It's about time they were held accountable for treating inmates like they treated you."

"I will, but..." his eyes glazed over, "our word's no good here, is it?" He remembered his first hearing.

"Better say your prayers."

Heat rose in Tom's heart from the depths.

"I said, 'Say your prayers!'" Sam rose.

Tom leaned back against the wall. "How do you know I'm not?"

"Doesn't look it to me. Unless," Sam leaned closer, "your God's not really there, and it's all mumbo-jumbo just to keep you in line. What do you think about that?"

The statements—*my God is real*, and *I know it*—swirled in his mind, but his mouth remained closed and the breath locked in his chest. He finished his last sentence and tucked the form in his locker. He stared at Sam but words evaporated. Tom stepped up to the bunks and swung into his, biting back any groans of pain.

The officers came for exercise time. Tom had no interest in being locked in an oversized dog run for an hour with other inmates. He'd made that mistake his first time in the SHU.

They came the next morning. "66789. Cuff up," Tom heard through the door. A chill ran down his arm, but he slid his hands out the small hole. Cold iron nipped his skin. He held back a shiver. One part of him realized this process was becoming routine.

The freight elevator creaked and groaned up to the next level. They walked down a well-lit passageway lined with pairs of doors. A guard opened the second of a pair in the middle of the corridor. The officers secured Tom to the lone metal chair bolted to the floor. The door closed behind them. He surveyed the spare room. Switching to his other senses, he felt vibrations run up his feet, heard the higher pitched tick of hard-soled shoes float past. At first, they were single or maybe pairs. Once the footsteps increased, he lost count with the shutting of heavy doors without the *slide-click-click* of the lower level cell doors.

Tom wet his lips. He listened to the steps of those who could come and go freely. He shifted in the seat to reduce the pull of his arm on his broken right side. The uncertainty stretched the moments into an eternity of waiting. His life was suspended in limbo; his past, a distant mirage, his future dark and bleak. All the busyness, the ceaseless activity—classes, course work, helping with the youth ministry, stitched together with part-time jobs—evaporated with a knock on the door and hands cuffed behind his back. The raw anger returned.

Tom started with the door coming open. Two guards walked in with a portable table and chairs. The door slammed shut again, momentarily deafening his right ear, but he counted the footfalls of several going through the paired door. Tom stared at the very center of the large mirror. He visualized the growing crowd in that room. *How many pairs of eyes are studying me in this cage? Is Officer Curtis there? Do I have to worry about Lieutenant Connors badgering me with questions?*

A stocky officer with graying temples followed by two officers came striding in. The two stood just behind Tom. The hairs on the back of his neck tingled. The new officer pushed the table to Tom.

Instinctively, he braced for the table to be driven into his chest.

The officer's eyes scanned Tom. He placed a binder on the table, pulled up the chair and sat down. "66789?" With no response, he said, "Are you 66789?"

Tom sucked in his breath. *I am **not** a number.* He nodded.

"I am Lieutenant Meggars. I am giving you a chance to redeem yourself." He opened the binder.

Tom spied his papers in the center.

"You claim you don't need a Bible to recite Scripture, yet you were not cooperative with Lieutenant Connors. This is your chance to prove your claim."

Tom nodded.

"John 3:16."

"Let's back that up to John 3:10-22." Tom recited the passage. "It gives the context for the verses, revealing God's plan to rescue us from the beginning, tracing clues laid down over centuries. From the beginning all the righteous trusted in the Redeemer—Job, Abraham, Jacob, and Joseph, to name a few. Moses walked and talked with Him. Elijah, Jeremiah, Ezekiel and Isaiah revealed God's plan to save the nations through a servant who would suffer to save us all."

Tom nodded to the top paper. "That one, with SOT in the right corner, lists the verses for salvation."

"Where did you write those?"

"That page in Unit Four. Some of the others I started in Oklahoma lockup."

Lieutenant Meggars picked up the first sheet. "Okay, tell me what it says."

Tom recalled the verses listed, stopping to recite some of them in full. He described the knowledge of sin, the work of the Savior and the way to faith. Meggars pulled out another sheet with verses from Isaiah written out. Tom recited those as well.

"Hmm, and HAM?"

"Hamartiology—the doctrine of sin."

"Why did you fight with the feds?"

"They Tasered me. I was trying to get away from the shocks."

The lieutenant studied Tom. He nodded to the other officers. "Change up."

Tom watched him leave the room, heard the door close and the next one close as well. Steps grew louder. Officer Curtis stepped into the room. Their eyes locked.

"Why'd you do it?"

"Do what?"

"Memorize everything? That's above and beyond the usual requirements. Most remember long enough to pass the tests."

"Most? Many of us were there because God called us to minister. We studied the teachings, the Bible knowledge, all of it, so we could faithfully teach the Word of God. This was only the beginning of unlocking the Bible's secrets. How to study a passage and discern God's truth—those skills we sharpened in Bible college, but the journey to learn more of God and His ways will never stop." Tom paused. The answer didn't seem to satisfy the officer. "The day I walked on campus God challenged me to memorize the Bible. It's a huge set of books. I started with the verses relating to my coursework and my daily struggles."

Officer Curtis matched his gaze. "Exodus 20."

"The Ten Commandments." Tom recited the chapter.

Curtis called out verse after verse. Tom recited them. The officer did not check them with a Bible but nodded with each reference.

"If you have such a good grasp of the Bible, why won't you take the approved versions? Most preachers never reference or refer to the excised passages."

Tom hesitated. "While Genesis 18 and the Romans 1 verses do

come up, it's the principle. You know the primacy of the Word of God to a faith walk with Christ. You understand following God requires true knowledge tested and proven by studying the Scriptures themselves, as the Bereans did in Acts 17. If they can get away with these few, more verses will be removed. Bible stories and instruction showing the devastating consequences of sin demonstrate God's love for us. You have to know you are sick before you will submit to a doctor's treatments. Without the Word, we are a mere religion, made of man, subject to the winds of change."

Tom watched Curtis' retreating back, followed by the flanking guards. His mind replayed some of the verses and others rose up as reminders of why he had left his family to go to Bible college, the assurances of helping others with the Word of God at his church, the chances to share with Wallie and Todd.

A pulse flowed through him when the images of others ran through his mind—Justin, Doug, Mark, and Stan. He had not talked with them about the most important thing. His heart smote him, remembering Justin's last look in his eyes when he died. He prayed. *Lord, show me Your better way.* A calm assurance took shape. God's people were in Hannibal, and he had been sent to share the message.

Officers came to remove the table and chairs. After more waiting, a pair came for him.

Once back in his cell, Tom noticed the bundle of clothes and the indigent supply on his end of the table.

"So, you're back. Hearing go well?" Sam asked from his bunk, peering over the top of his paperback.

Tom looked at him. He wordlessly prayed for opportunities to share with Sam. "No. They're still investigating. Officer Meggars asked some questions."

Sam sat up. "Could be a good sign or a bad sign. Which was it?"

"Don't know, but I showed them I could recite those verses without a physical Bible."

"Strange case," Sam shook his head.

"When's lunch?"

"You missed it."

"Thought so." Tom arranged his pile and pulled out a clean short-sleeved orange jumpsuit. He shivered. At least they had also issued the standard thin blanket. Tom headed for the shower. When he emerged, a used pair of long johns lay on top of his pile. He glanced at Sam.

"Can't take everything with me."

"Thanks." *Does this break the rules?* One inmate was not to give something of value to another, but the thermals were worn and would have probably ended up in the trash. He was reminded of a prayer earlier that day. "Thanks, God used you to answer my prayer."

"Just one? That's all the thanks I get?"

Tom narrowed his eyes. "I can't pay you back. I'm indigent."

"Just joshing with ya. Take 'em or throw 'em out. Your choice."

"Still an answer to prayer." They had not returned his papers, but he had fresh pages to fill. Tom licked his pencil and wrote down the days' events since his last entry. He could collate it all later. He paused. *Where do I start?* Forty days the Holy Spirit drove Jesus, the Holy One, to the wilderness to fast and pray. Tom visualized the facts—forty days with no food, in a desert with little water, harassed by Satan himself. With no complaints, showing perfect trust in His Father, Christ passed the test. Writing out the accounts from both Matthew and Luke, he shuddered inwardly and repented of his bad attitude. He wrote out Hebrews 12:1-2. He had not striven so against sin. Quickly he laid down Isaiah 53 and added the last few verses of chapter 52 to the poetry of God's ultimate love gift to all mankind.

Tom retreated to his bunk to continue his prayers. *Let me do better,* he said silently. *Help me remember to fix my eyes on You.* His mind recalled Philippians 4.

CHAPTER 20

T HEY CALLED HIM forth three days later. An officer had collected his statement a few days before.

"Good luck," Sam said.

Tom nodded. They led him down a flight of steps, through the tunnel and up two flights. The lights of the Admin section for the DU momentarily blinded him. His nerves jumped with every clink of the shackles and the tug on his waist from the belly chain.

The long narrow room overflowed with officers filling every spot behind two long folding tables. Lieutenant Meggars sat to the right, Lieutenant Connors stood behind him flanked by Officer Curtis. He recognized his case manager on the left but knew none of the others.

Tom requested the day officer read his statement. The officers' faces were impassive, almost bored. He caught his breath when he recognized the day Unit Four officer with Doug standing out in his general population cream brown issue. Tom realized he must be the peacock in his bright orange.

The center stage officer read the charges and nodded to the day officer to read Tom's statement.

Meggars, leading the hearing, said, "The witness may speak."

Doug stepped forward. Tom set his face.

"Tom's telling the truth. The agents went at him with Tasers. The wrong man's up on charges. My unit buddy, Tom Hutton, didn't attack those agents. It was self-defense. Officer Curtis gave 'em the stunners, let 'em know where the cameras where and coordinated the attack on Tom."

Doug stared at Meggars, "If you think we all goin' stand by and let this continue without pushback, you're drinking the wrong Kool-aid."

A buzz rippled through the officers standing along the far wall. "Carry on," Lieutenant Meggars said. The lead officer stepped through the procedure.

His mouth still open, Tom saw Doug wink with a hint of a smile. The officer ended the hearing. Within moments the room emptied, and the guards marched him back through the tunnel to the SHU. Tom sighed in relief when he recognized he was back at Sam's door.

"Well? Fall on your sword?" Sam laughed. "You see a ghost or something? What gives? Get five months or six?"

"What? Oh, I didn't hear. Not sure," he stopped. A smile spread across his face. "My unit showed up for me. Doug backed up my story and laid it all at Curtis' feet."

Sam set aside his novel and took up his place at the small table. "Spill it...every word."

At the end, Tom shook his head. "I was so surprised I didn't hear anything else." He stared at the far solid wall—not even a window on this range—recalling the last moments of the hearing. "Yes, I was charged, and I pleaded guilty, but then Meggars ended the hearing, and they brought me back." Tom shrugged his shoulders. "What does that mean?"

"Yeah, smile. This is big—Curtis is going to get his packet. What we call the binder from the warden detailing possible charges, demotions, even loss of pension if he doesn't transfer to another facility," Sam laughed, "or retire." He slapped the table, "You won. Where's your happy dance? About time that weasel Curtis got his. Pushing his religion with his programs and ruining good-time packages for a lot of guys. He had it coming."

"I thought..." Tom met Sam's gaze. "I mean he and Meggars questioned me last week, upstairs. I thought I could work with him. We made a connection."

"Yo, cupcake. They're the *them*—the enemy. Never forget that. You got to know who your friends are, and a weasel guard can never be trusted."

Tom crossed his arms. "There are no friends here. Bruce taught me that."

"True 'nough. Given the right incentive or threat, I've seen close buddies betray each other. But, it's not so different on the outside. This is the world your God made?"

"Not in the beginning. We wanted to do it our way. The world's mess we did to ourselves—one evil deed at a time. The love of God is the only real solution."

Sam muttered under his breath and returned to his reading.

"When do I get my sentence?"

"When they feel like letting you know."

Chapter 21

Officer Curtis knocked on Warden Foster's door. The executive assistant ushered him in, and he stood to the side of the warden's gray metal desk.

"We have a matter of the statements brought up at the hearing for 66789. You care to elaborate. Did you, in fact, provide the Tasers?"

"No. I had no idea."

"Why didn't you bring the CI info to our investigators? Do we not investigate and deliver offenders to justice for further sentencing? Do you work for the HCL Task Force or the Bureau of Prisons?"

"I thought the CI was credible. I believed." Curtis shook his head, "I didn't know he'd memorized the Bible."

"Officer Curtis, you are free to transfer to this joint operation you seem so fond of. The enforcement side is run by Major Kincaid, is that correct? He's former Marine, as you are, right?" The warden rose and walked up to Curtis. "This is a warning. You do good work heading up the chaplaincy, education and release programs. I'd hate to have to dismiss you for something like this."

"I wouldn't want that, sir."

"Then drop the witch-hunt. Our mission is to keep our residents alive and maintain order. As long as the Christians don't break the rules or cause problems, they're not to be disturbed, including 66789. Activities that do not lead to chaos or bloodshed are not to be pursued to the same extent. If they do not make an open display of illegal Bibles, we will not go hunting for them. Understood?"

"Yes, sir."

"Keep me abreast of flagrant violations or smuggling attempts, but I do not want any more witch-hunts, especially any having to do with Tom Hutton. You are dismissed."

"Yes, sir," Officer Curtis replied.

CHAPTER 22

THE NEXT WEEK the officer for the range handed over Tom's personal effects and an envelope. He glanced at Sam.

"That would be your sentence."

Tom pulled out the paper and tried to make sense of the words. "I don't get it. I pulled another sixty."

"That's a win. What'd you think? Because some agents weren't nice, you'd get a pass? They couldn't let you get by without any punishment. You fought with agents in front of a squad in full view of your block. Sixty days in here, that's a gift. Your loss if you don't appreciate your blessings."

Tom nodded and retreated to his bunk. Another 60 days in the SHU. His whole body ached. It seemed to take forever for his ribs to heal. Having to climb up to the top bunk didn't help.

The cycle of hopelessness pressed upon his chest, taking away his breath. *Why was I so stupid?* Just because the agents had a Taser didn't mean they'd be allowed to repeat their performance in Hannibal. *I'm a failure here and on the outside.* Bringing Bibles to his parents' home had led the Task Force right to them. They had to take out a restraining order against him to keep from losing their home and family business because of CAF—civil asset forfeiture.

He had to stop thinking this way. *Have to fight it.* Tom scrambled down, pulled out his bag from his locker, selected his papers and laid them on the table. He set them in order, reading over the verses and theology notes. *"In the world you will have tribulation. But take heart; I have overcome the world,*"[10] Christ said to His apostles in the upper room before His arrest. Tom prayed. *Where is my victorious overcoming?*

He longed for release. *Where is my escape?* Hadn't God promised a way out in 1 Corinthians 10:13—a way of escape to endure temptations? The defeat, the years, the sixty days swirled in his mind. Now his world consisted of four walls and a locked door.

He thought of Sam without looking at him. No cracks in that armor had opened up, no magical moment where Tom shared the life of Christ and salvation broke forth. Sam would not let him pray for him. Not even Wallie, with all the verses he had shared, had believed.

He reminded himself Christ saves. He was only the messenger, leaving them without excuse on Judgment Day.

He dropped his head in his hands. "Stop it!" he told himself. "Think on the good things." To distract his train of thought, Tom selected his Isaiah pages and wrote down, verse by verse, where he had left off last time.

The days stretched out. He kept count every day, but found he had to number each day at the same time to keep it straight. Sam would return from exercise with rumors and gossip, but Tom gave them little credence. Officer Curtis had not lost his position. Nothing had changed. No programs, no call outs to his case manager, no letters.

He finally read his sentence: 60 days in the SHU and six months loss of commissary, phone and mail privileges. "Ha," he said with a little laugh.

Sam glanced his way, raising an eyebrow. Tom read the loss of privileges, and they both laughed.

"They don't have a clue, do they?"

Tom nodded. In that instant, he knew he would survive Hannibal. He was learning to fit in. He could read their micro gestures and respond. The Spirit reminded him. With God's help Tom could fulfill the work God set before him—but it would be on God's timetable and in His way.

CHAPTER 23

"CUFF UP," THE officer called shortly after lunch. "66789, come on. We don't have all day."

Tom looked at Sam, who shrugged his shoulders and returned to reading his latest mail.

They headed through the tunnel almost blocked by a clump of ladders and carts. Tom recognized a familiar face. Wallie beamed a brilliant smile in his direction. Surprised, Tom was halfway down the section before he could respond. He had never seen Wallie smile like that. A glimmer of hope began to rise until they took him to an interrogation room and chained his hands to a bar on a metal table.

His case manager came in, tested the cuffs and walked out. Tom heard a nearby door open and close. He stared into the large mirror on the other wall. The blood pounded in his jaw.

Two agents in dark blue suits with leather cases walked in and sat down on the other side of the table. The man on the left pulled out a small digital voice recorder.

Tom did not recognize the first agent, but the second one looked familiar. "Ma'am, were you on the team that arrested me?"

"Yes, Tom. I'm Task Force Agent Worden, and this is Investigations Manager Masters. We have a few questions to ask you about statements you made concerning Agents Cooper and Trainer. Would you be willing to clarify your statements?"

"Of course."

Masters flicked on the recorder. He stated the date, time and location of the interview. "Inmate 66789-356, HCL offender, Thomas Hutton. You stated Agents Cooper and Trainer had Tasered you before the incident. Is this correct?" Seeing Tom's nod, he said, "We need verbal confirmation for the record."

"Yes, sir. They did this and more for three weeks."

"When, exactly, did they do this?"

"The day they arrested me." Tom relayed the details.

"But that's not possible." Worden read out his official arrest date.

"That's the day they took me in for booking. They arrested me three weeks before. I remember the date of my last day at work, my last day of freedom before they seized everything. Check the records at the store. I didn't realize I had lost so much time until I heard the date read at my hearing. It was a month later."

"Why didn't you file a complaint in detention?"

"I had never been arrested before. Didn't know that was not the way things usually go. It might not rise to the level of torture, but it felt like it to me. I was so shut down, I could hardly function."

"I remember you were barely coherent," Chris Worden said.

"Yet you negotiated a plea deal, reducing the counts to twenty-five from fifty without representation," Will Masters stated.

Tom looked at the man in his thirties. "Self-preservation kicked in for that. Fifty counts of hate-crime literature when I only had five Bibles? Really? Twenty-five was too much, but I felt I'd better take the offer while it was on the table. Five years in a maximum-security facility? Your agents pulled strings to get that classification. Now I know no one with just five years ends up here."

"Didn't you realize your connections with your uncle would implicate you? The law states possession of HCL is considered a violent crime at the same level as an assault, bombing or attack," Agent Masters stated.

"And how did I network with my uncle since he cut off all communications years before?" Tom relayed Uncle Al's warnings.

"What date did you last speak with your uncle?" Agent Worden asked.

Tom counted back the time. "It was around the summer, shortly before my first payment to Mt. Zion Bible College for my third year." Tom gave the year and the month.

"That was more than a month before the bill passed Congress. The texts hadn't even been selected and codified by the committee," Worden said to Masters. She looked at Tom. "That was a year before the law came into effect—before any public announcements. How did he know?"

Tom laughed lightly. "Uncle Al was the marketing genius, networker and deal maker in the family business. He negotiated the buyer contracts, networked with suppliers and freight companies. He understood what our customers wanted and found it for them at affordable prices. Before he left the family business to become a pastor, it was ready to go national. He knew how to lobby state and Congressional representatives. He would have had no problem getting inside information on pending legislation."

"What were his plans for the Bibles?"

"Never mentioned it. He knew better than to bring me in on it. He was trying to protect me. The agents never told me exactly why a 20-year sentence in Leavenworth wasn't sufficient or why they had to go after me."

"Have you seen a Hutton Bible?"

"No."

Agent Worden pulled out two Bibles.

Tom sat back. "Are those real Bibles? I'm not going to get more time for being in the same room with them, am I?" He stared at the agents, thinking it through.

"Of course not." Masters pushed them closer to Tom.

He rotated the books to make sure the pages were not green-tipped. Tom smiled and picked up the newest looking one. He felt its heft and breathed in the aromas of ink and leather. The binding creaked softly as he opened the front cover and looked at the first few pages.

Tom reached for the second Bible. Its dark-blue leather cover with curled corners yielded to his touch. It looked loved and cared for. The imbedded silk bookmark had a frayed end. He flipped to the facing page and read the inscription: "To Betty on your graduation. With love, Aunt Charlotte."

"This one is new; this one is not. That's a puzzle."

Agent Worden nodded; Masters sat back.

"Your agents told me you had evidence of large lots from publishers. I forget the number. That's what they wanted to know. Where were all the Bibles? But this one's not a recent edition. What makes it a Hutton Bible?"

Masters pulled out a rectangular package with a soft fern-colored wrapper encased in plastic.

Tom laughed. "When did they pick the color for the pages of approved Bibles? You have any idea?"

The agents exchanged glances. "Colored pages?"

"All approved versions have green-tipped pages. You know real Bibles; the more expensive ones would often have gold-tipped pages. How did he know what approved ones would look like?" Tom sat up. "You know, it seemed strange that it happened so fast. Almost as soon as the law passed, and there wasn't much news about it, the regulations were set with announcements released overnight. I hadn't thought of it before, but maybe this was all decided a long time before they trotted the bill through Congress."

With the agents' nods, he reached for the package, pierced the outer plastic shell and carefully slid his finger along the crease on the end. He peeled back the first cloth covering, straightening out the folds. Tom leaned forward to catch the scents of orange and tea tree oil rising up from the inner wrapping. He rotated the bound book and carefully removed the second layer. Clear plastic sealed a used mauve Bible.

Tom released the book and pulled it forward. There was no gift note in the front but notes and Bible references were neatly scripted in the margins.

"Hutton Family Furniture Stores prided themselves on providing top quality furniture at affordable prices." Tom glanced at the agents. "We also had a select line of exceptional pieces padded with exquisite silks, only many didn't survive the hot, moldy warehouses and six months in ocean-going containers. My dad and Uncle Al tried everything they could think of to preserve the pieces from the elements, molds and mildews. Military grade anti-microbial solutions were the worst. When Uncle Al went to India to network with our suppliers, he discovered natural substances that not only did the job but added the special scents of the Orient." He tapped the coverings. "I see Uncle Al put his knowledge to good use."

A small sheet of paper fluttered to the table. Tom read the note aloud. "You hold in your hand God's gift to the world. His Word guides us in truth and righteousness. It holds the answers to our most important questions: who am I, why am I here, is there purpose in my life." Tom stopped. His eyes teared.

He sat back and looked away. In his mind he heard his uncle's voice. The words were very familiar. He had heard them at their kitchen table. The last few months before the phone call, his uncle had become passionate about God's Word.

Tom looked at the agents. "I know what he did and how he did it. I also know why. Shortly after I arrived at Mt. Zion Bible College, Uncle Al began collecting used Bibles to ship overseas to countries where English is the national or trade language. Many in these places could not afford to buy such Bibles, or they would be hard to obtain. We're swimming with Bibles in this country. You'd be surprised how many editions are in most homes. Many Christians have multiple copies. Even my mother had two tucked away.

"Being the promoter that he is, Uncle Al activated his network. He collected so many Bibles, they filled his two equipment sheds. Aunt Sallie was concerned the lawn tractor wouldn't make it through the winter, but my uncle promised he'd get them shipped out soon. Then it went quiet. When I tried to find out what happened, he told me the promised container fell through." Tom glanced at Chris. "Were his barn and outbuildings empty?"

Chris and Will exchanged glances. "Completely empty," Chris said.

"Even the farm equipment?"

"Farm equipment? Don't remember seeing anything like that—not even a lawn mower."

Tom picked up the small note card and tract. "Looks like he was planning for this law to be in effect for a long time." He traced the worn edging of the blue Bible. "I believe he seeded preserved copies of the Word of God throughout the United States. In the future, after..." Tom cleared his throat. The thought of the HCL Task Force destroying every Bible they could find took his breath away.

"God will preserve His Word. God the Son, Jesus Christ, is called the Word of God. His Words have power and might. The Holy Spirit, who lives within every Christian, reminds us of God's Word. This book tells us to study it, meditate on it and memorize it. I have laid up the Word of God in my heart."[11] He stared directly at the agents. "If you want to take away my Bible, you will have to remove my head from my body."

Chris looked at Will. She leaned closer to Tom, "It's not a capital offense."

"*Not yet.*"

They heard a quick tapping on the window. The agents exchanged glances. Masters spoke into the recorder, "Interview completed."

"Agent Worden," Tom said, "I'll answer any questions you have about the Bible and the Christian faith. I will receive your letters and put you down as a visitor, if you'd like me to help you understand it." Agent Masters scowled in his direction. "You as well, Agent Masters.

I understand it can be an overwhelming Book, but it will help your investigations."

The agents packed up the Bibles and recorder. They were out of the room in moments. Tom noticed Connors standing in the hall.

CHAPTER 24

LIEUTENANT CONNORS SLIPPED Will a note. Masters tucked it away. "Is our meeting with the warden on?"

Connors nodded. "Come this way." They stepped through to the DU office area and a small conference room.

Warden Foster, thin and wiry with sandy hair shook their hands. "Please sit." He surveyed the agents. "Agent Masters, you have quite a record, especially your RICO work. You transferred often—ATF, DEA, FBI?"

"All with the FBI. I worked large organized crime cases by liaising with other agencies. Pooling our Intel and resources helped crack a number of cases."

"And your ties with Major Kincaid?"

Will glanced at Chris. "None before this Task Force."

"I encouraged Will to apply for the Investigations Manager position. We were siloed, and I felt Will's ability to reach across to other enforcement teams would enhance our efforts," Agent Worden added.

"Does Kincaid think he can run operations through the BOP?"

"No, of course not. Our job is to arrest them, justice prosecutes, and the BOP sees the sentence is carried out according to the law. I don't usually pursue cases behind the wall unless your officers report crimes or an active case discovers an inmate directing criminal enterprises from his cell," Will answered.

"I see we agree…in principle anyway." The warden leaned forward. "Due process does not stop for our residents when they are delivered

---

to our care. Your agents are to have no access to any of our facilities. You can rest assured I will be filing a report with the DOC about your agents' behavior. I expect all visitors to proceed by the book. Any requests beyond public record must provide proper warrants."

"My apologies, sir. I was under the impression the Hutton case had been closed."

"Don't Agents Cooper and Trainer report to you?"

"Yes, sir."

The warden rose. "I recommend you properly direct them in the matter of dealing with the BOP."

Chris and Will stood and shook his hand. "Thank you for your cooperation in this matter. We appreciate the interview with Hutton and will pursue disciplinary action with these agents. We strive to engender mutual cooperation and regret any disruptions to your facility," Masters concluded.

An officer led them out and past the walls.

"What did Connors want?"

"Butch Connors," Will said. He unlocked the car. "He's former ATF, a good investigator. We worked together on a few joint operations." Will entered the address into his phone. "Has a tip for us. We'll meet him at a local restaurant after his shift. Guess he knew the warden would give us the gentle kick out the door."

"Considering everything—not the worst outcome."

"Did you know they were still pursuing Hutton?"

Chris shook her head. "Bad lot, those two. You really need to file an action against them. This is why I'm glad you're on board. FBI protocols and structures will help clean up this unit."

"Hope so."

CHAPTER 25

Tom STEPPED INTO his cell. He smiled at Sam hunched over a pile of papers on his end of the table.

"What you grinning about? I almost thought they'd up and moved you to X wing."

"What's X wing?"

"The *real* hole in here…and you don't want to go there. Them's that go there get Connors' special treatment. So, what you a Cheshire cat for?"

"Found out why I'm at Hannibal." He sat down. It almost felt like home. Tom shared what he had learned from the agents. Pockets of inner joy broke forth. "The joy of the Lord is my strength," he said.

"Now you're really daft."

"That's Nehemiah 8:10. My uncle gave up his life to preserve God's Word. Looking at it that way, I don't have it that bad."

"He got 20? How old is he?"

"58 or so."

"He'll die in there. Leavenworth's worse than Hannibal."

"You been there?"

"No, this is my first and hopefully last time with BOP."

"May I pray for you? Any other requests?"

"Me?" Sam bundled his papers together and headed to his bags. "You leave me out of that."

The range was quiet. He went to his bunk to rest. Some nights it was so noisy, he barely slept. Tom shifted, but his aches re-emerged and danced around his belly. "The joy of the Lord is my strength," he repeated, but the cloud returned, and sleep fled.

Tom gave up. He scrambled down and pulled out his memory verse papers to review again.

"Hey, get back up in your bunk," Sam yelled. "I got to put away these papers. Need to pull my stuff out."

Tom retreated to his bunk. His side hurt too much to slouch and sitting up was out of the question. He held up the notes to find something, anything, to help make it through. "The joy of the Lord is my strength," he whispered, trying to focus on the words in the shadows cast by the bare bulb in the ceiling. Another verse came to mind before he recalled its address. *"For I have learned in whatever situation I am to be content. I know how to be brought low, and I know how to abound. In any and every circumstance, I have learned the secret of facing plenty and hunger, abundance and need."*[12]

A deep rage returned. Tom centered his breathing and inwardly cried out to the Lord. The seconds stretched out to eternity. A decision rose up.

I will not give in to defeat. Tom focused his whole being and will. *I believe in the living God. I choose to thank You for*—he had to list it. He ran through his situation in Hannibal and the hole, thanking God for all of it. Names came to his remembrance—Curtis, Sam, Cooper, Trainer, and the rest. He thanked God for each one and prayed for them. The anger melted under the love. The dam burst forth. He had found his center in Christ once again.

"Yo, cupcake, count and supper."

Tom jerked awake, and aches turned into stabbing pain. He scrambled down.

"You don't have to stay up there all the time. You started snoring again. Didn't anyone ever tell you it's bad business to sleep during the day?"

"Yeah, but it's hard to sleep at night with all the yelling."

"You'll get used to it. Got two months to do that."

Tom ate his supper deep in thought. He prayed for direction, a purpose, his marching orders. His mind ran through the possibilities. Ideas began to form.

CHAPTER 26

WILL FOCUSED ON the traffic.

Butch Connors was waiting in the lobby. Once at their table, he slid a note to Will. "That group cult run by the Right Reverend Hawsley needs to be taken out. We tried, but they were too careful. We never could gather enough Intel for probable cause to get the warrants. But they are a church, at least according to their fancy building in town. If you could find illegal Bibles in their possession, you might get a crack at the mother lode."

"Explain."

"We all know criminals eventually end up in the same place—drugs, weapons, human trafficking or money laundering. No matter how pure and righteous their cause is, they'll do what they have to and, in the end, break the law. A sad case. Lots of brainwashed people including young girls." He tapped the note. "This is what HCL was all about, right? Giving us another tool to stop the bad guys? I understand guys like Tom are caught, but stopping criminals makes it acceptable losses. That's the contact, insurance agent, Asa Shirring. Seems the Right Reverend brainwashed Asa's wife and daughter. He keeps them at his ranch several miles out of the city."

"How many?"

"Thirty, maybe more, but we couldn't infiltrate. They always caught on. Asa's got good ideas, but nothing worked. It would be risky for whoever goes in. They're smart, I'll give 'em that. Have to go in clean. No wires."

"How were you planning on monitoring?"

"Dead drops and listening posts in the backwoods but ran into issues with the neighbor." Butch sat back and finished his steak. "It's one of the ones that got away that wakes you up in the middle of the night."

Will nodded.

"So," Butch looked over, "what did you think about that 'take-my-head-from-my-body' line? Shows you just how dangerous that bunch is."

Chris spoke, "What about the right to free religious expression?"

"Always been subject to more fundamental principles of human rights," Will said. "Why is it illegal to yell 'fire' in a crowded theater when there's no fire if we have freedom of speech? No right is without limits. We can all think of religious practices that are de facto illegal."

"Don't forget the Bible commands everyone to obey governing authorities," Butch added.

Chris pursed her brow. "It takes more looking into, especially with Acts 4."

Will and Butch said in unison: "Acts 4?"

"The book of Acts in the Bible, chapter 4. After Christ ascended to heaven, He told His followers to spread the good news which the authorities had declared illegal. They told the religious leaders they had to obey God."

"Don't forget it triggered their death sentences. This kind of thinking will get many in trouble with us, and rightfully so." Butch sat back. He nodded to Will, "Maybe the Task Force needs their own prisons. Not totally unheard of. Then they wouldn't be infecting the general population. The last thing we need is another set of inmates we have to segregate. It's a real headache keeping the inmates alive until their sentences are up. We spend a lot of time making sure we don't put the wrong bunch in the wrong cell block."

Chris sat back and listened to them plan how things should be done then segue into reminiscing about the good old days when they put away the bad guys.

CHAPTER 27

BACK IN HER unit, Chris surveyed the open case whiteboard. Hutton was off the active list. She smiled when she read Will's note at the bottom—"No contact with Huttons." Her eyes scanned the latest case and smiled. She was the lead for the Hawsley investigation.

"Meet me in my office," Will said on his way with a full cup of coffee.

Chris went to retrieve her laptop and entered his office soon after. "You finally have a proper office. Who's on my team?"

"Lyle, Benson and Briggs to start with. You can request specific agents when you have a plan filed. I'll upload it today." Will rocked back in his chair. "Anything else?"

"Kincaid's assigned me to the library and NGO outreach. I can delegate some of it. Don't mind that one, but the IRS data mining project yielded few leads."

"How so? I thought it was a good avenue. All churches have to file 990s and list every church donor."

"Yeah, but that law didn't come into play until this year. Unless they have a fiscal year end, their filing date's not due until April, or later if they extend. My sources tell me many are dropping their non-profit status and canceling their 501(c)(3) determination."

"That's a filed form. We can chase those down when the data's available," Will noted.

"That still leaves us with the problem of tracking down their membership. If they behave like Hutton, there won't be any records. Anyway,

I want to conduct the initial interview with Shirring next week. Fits in well with my outreach schedule. Walzer's scheduled to go with me, but who from the team would be a good fit?"

Will pulled up the duty roster and assignment grid. "None next week. Two still tied up in some big cases, but Briggs will be available by month's end. He's good for testimony in the courtroom. Lyle will need some handholding as he's green."

"He'll do fine. He's sharp and pays attention to details. I trained him with the Secret Service. I wrote Tom, but he never responded."

"He's in the SHU. He might have lost his mail privileges."

"Never thought of that. Oh well, I glean bits and pieces from the church leaders we encounter, but it's slow going."

"I could forward some online study aids I found. Haven't had much time to go through them. Funny," Will chuckled, "we have to study the Bible to learn how to catch them."

CHAPTER 28

A FEW WEEKS later Sam said, "You praying about your next cell, buddy?"

"What do you mean? Going to ask for a SHU transfer?"

"No, choir boy; it's the three week change-up. That's right, they bunked you single in the VIP quarters in the Admin wing. This is the real thing. Get all your papers together. Make sure everything's packed."

"How do you carry all your stuff?"

"You leave it for them to search, and they're supposed to return it all. Then they scramble all the cell assignments. Change up every three weeks."

"Can I pray for you now before we're separated?"

"No. I'm looking forward to having a normal resident to bunk with—not someone who's scratching away at papers all day." Sam pulled out his bags from under his bunk. "Now where did it go to?" He went from one to the other. "I'm going to prove you wrong when I find my Bible."

"You have a Bible?"

"My grandma's Bible." Sam pulled out his last bag and dumped it on his bunk.

Tom stared at the pile of books and papers mixed in with clothes. "What happened to it?"

Sam sat on his stool and leaned on his hand. He eyed the mess. "You put it back and check for me. Maybe I missed it." He watched Tom reassemble the bag and slide it underneath with the rest.

"Check the others."

Tom sat across from Sam. "When's the last time you saw it? When you packed up for the transfer?"

"Mine didn't go that way. Ran into a tight spot, and they had to get me out quick. Walked straight from the infirmary to here. The officers had to bag it up. I never thought of checking. Who'd steal an old lady's Bible?"

"Not *stolen*, Sam, *confiscated*. It's probably in a box in Curtis' office with the other seized Bibles."

Sam paced and returned to his seat, tracing the cracked edge of the table along the side. "My grandma, a tough lady, took us to Sunday school when we were little until my dad put a stop to it. My mom sort of believed, but we're a hard family. Even after my first time in, Grandma wrote, put money in my account. She died while I was here. Ann got them to send me her Bible. It's all I have left to remember her by."

"I'll find a way to get it all back—for all the guys. You want it as a keepsake. Would you care if the illegal sections were redacted or pages removed?"

Sam shook his head. "You going to work for Curtis?"

Tom smiled. "Volunteer. I can work in the kitchen all morning and volunteer in the afternoon to go through the boxes. Describe the Bible and the markings on it so I'll recognize it."

"Easy, it's stamped with my number with the covers ripped off."

Tom almost winced but kept a straight face. He pulled out his papers and wrote out a request. When he heard the officer on the range, he yelled and passed the paper through the slot.

"What's that?"

"A request."

"Lost commissary for six months, remember?"

"This is no commissary request."

—⟨∞⟩—

A green-tipped Bible accompanied lunch the next day.

"What's that?"

"A Bible. A legal one." Tom flipped it open and read a few verses. "Not a bad translation." He slid it across the table.

"What? You asked for it, not me."

"I figured it would be safer if I put in the request." He shoved it closer to Sam. "Check it out. Prove me wrong."

Sam eyed the book. He reached for it, feeling the hard-cardboard cover. "All right." He narrowed his eyes. "That garbage about," he mimicked Tom's cadence, "it's not by works and all that nonsense. Everyone knows we earn it. Every day we earn our right, and yeah, some's farther along, but in the end, we all get a chance. Not God's fault we blow it."

"Fair question. Ephesians 2:8-9, look it up." Tom would have helped, but Sam waved him away with a scowl.

"I know how to navigate a book." He flipped through the early section. "On and on about their translation. Here it is—the table of contents. Ephesians?" He ran his finger down the list, didn't see it and started again.

"In the second section." Tom smiled at Sam's glare.

"You ain't going to be smiling for long, cupcake. I found it." He thumbed his way to the book of Ephesians. "The reference?"

"Chapter 2 verses 8 and 9."

Sam read, *"God saved you by his grace when you believed. And you can't take credit for this; it is a gift from God."*[13] He looked at Tom. "That's just one verse."

"Go back to Titus 3:5."

"He saved us, not because of the righteous things we had done, but because of his mercy. He washed away our sins, giving us a new birth and new life through the Holy Spirit."[14] Sam threw it on the floor. "That's why Dad and Grandpa were death on your religion. All a bunch of loafers and leaches looking for handouts. We earn it."

Tom picked up the Bible and turned to Revelation 20. "Listen to what you're earning. Revelation 20:11-15," Tom said and read the great white throne passage. "Sam, we're all born into Satan's family. None of us have to learn how to lie, cheat and steal. It comes naturally. If we die in our sins, we've earned our spot in the lake of fire forever. But Christ paid our sin debt to God. He offers us the gift of salvation. When we accept this gift, our names are written in the Book of Life. We will never go through that judgment. There is no condemnation for us."

"Then how is that fair? Just get saved and you get a pass?"

"Not at all. When we are translated from death to life, from darkness to light, God adopts us and disciplines us as the perfect father. That's in Hebrews chapter 12. We will face a judgment—but one of reward and placement in God's future kingdom. If we mess up, we lose out, but we cannot be condemned to hell." He closed the Bible and slid it to Sam. "Keep it. You can read it later, if you want."

Sam tucked it away.

CHAPTER 29

"MOVING DAY," SAM announced after breakfast.

Tom nodded. His few belongings were in a bag in his open locker.

An officer knocked on their door. "66789, cuff up."

Tom looked at Sam who looked equally as puzzled.

"Hurry up. Don't got all day."

The door opened, and Tom recognized Officer Parks, the head officer for the first floor. Parks grabbed his elbow and marched him down the range, around the central hub and to the inner office section. He left him in a small holding cell.

"Stay here. Don't cause trouble."

Hearing the muffled voices and boot steps, Tom settled down for a long wait.

Hours later Parks led Tom to a small office. He placed a sack lunch and a cup of coffee near Tom's seat. "Bathroom's in there if you need it." Tom managed with his cuffs on. At least he'd get lunch. He sat down across the table from the officer.

"You just had Bibles, right?" Seeing Tom nod, he asked, "This going to happen to other Christians?"

"Who'd you have in mind?"

"Regular church folk."

"They're taking out the leadership first—if this law doesn't get shut down. Any news about the arrests, any pushback?"

"Nothing. Real quiet. Our church pulled the pew Bibles. Most had it on their phones or notepads. Wonder how they're going to enforce that."

"It's already done. The Task Force agents bragged—to stay in business the publishers and printers had to hand over their invoices and customer lists before the phase-out period ended. All the digital Bibles have been updated. Check Romans 1. It used to have 32 verses. It now has 23."

"When I get a chance." He bit into his sandwich. "How's it going with 31247?"

"You mean Sam? Very well. He's a good bunkmate."

"Nothing you want to tell me? Here's your chance."

"No, he helps me keep it together."

"So, those feds aren't going to go door to door for the church members? We had to submit the membership list to keep our non-profit status."

"I doubt they have that kind of manpower. I suspect they're trying to scare the rest into giving up their Bibles or risk paying the price. Are most of the churches still open? Things going along like usual out there?"

Officer Parks laughed. "Well, factor in the churches who've already made accommodations; this isn't much of a stretch. I remember seeing an ad for a large church downtown promoting their Bible recycling program. Where'd Curtis send the Bibles, anyway?"

"Looks like they're in boxes in his office. Why he wanted me to work for him in the first place, but I couldn't agree to confiscate Bibles."

"We knew. Why your first 60 was in the Admin wing." The officer leaned forward, "This is Connors' territory, and you don't want to cross him—not again. Make sure this is your last time here."

"My plan." Tom nodded.

"How'd you pull a level five?"

"They were trying to get me to flip on my uncle."

"I saw the interview. Lots like him?"

"Don't know. I just went back home and kept my head down. It didn't work, and now I know there was no way I could have avoided this."

"Except give up your Bibles. You know, I don't know of any pastors in my town who went to jail for HCL. Does that make them bad Christians?"

Tom met his gaze. "I'm not God. I'm not going to sit in judgment on a fellow believer. Turning in my Bible was never an option for me. Each of us needs to pray for direction and how He wants us to navigate these times. Only God knows the heart. We are to bear the crosses He sends us. I don't remember any verses telling us to create our own."

Officer Parks pushed an opened letter across the desk. "Those feds are asking questions. You really going to answer her?"

"Of course." Tom pulled out the papers. "Good questions. May I? Thought I lost my mail privileges."

"There are exceptions for official letters." The officer smiled, "And it's going to be read before it's mailed."

Tom returned his smile. "Thanks for the notice. I'll make sure it's complete."

"Here's paper and pencil. Take the letter, and I'll set you up in a room. Don't dawdle. We have to get everyone back in place before afternoon count."

A different officer collected his letter to Agent Worden and led him through the officers' wing to the central monitoring hub. They rounded the next corner. Tom counted less than half the cells in this range near the officer's wing.

The officer opened the first door. "Home sweet home."

Tom surveyed the cell. He was in first. "Hey, cleaning supplies," he requested.

The officer brought them with his bag of personal items. Tom cleaned the cell from top to bottom and settled in. Even with the distraction of chores, he squirmed with the wait. He prayed he could get along with his newest cellmate.

Heavy boots walked past the banks of the computers and monitors in the hub, but none entered his range. He was almost thinking he was going to be alone when footsteps approached. The door swung open. He stared into piercing blue eyes. Tom smiled, balancing on the stool near the shower, facing the door.

Sam whirled and would have yelled, but the officers offloaded Sam's bags from the cart and slammed the door shut. "Well, ain't you sitting pretty?"

"My house, my rules," Tom said. "I had a good teacher. This is *my* stool." He looked at the bags piled against the wall and around Sam's feet.

"I get the bottom bunk."

Tom nodded. "You get the bottom bunk. No way you're stowing your stuff under mine."

"I can't eat with my back to the door."

"Fine. I'll set the table, do the dishes and eat there, but this is my stool rest of the time."

"Well, serves me right." He heaved his bags under the bottom bunk. Tom moved his bedroll to the top bunk.

They settled down to their usual routine. Tom wrote out his verses; Sam read his novels or sorted through his bags. Each day Tom had an easier time getting into the top bunk.

"You not going to exercise?"

"Not sure it would be a great idea. I exercise when you're gone."

"Yeah," they paused when the mail cart stopped by their door. Sam picked up his letters and opened Ann's first. He laid out the pages, resisting the urge to smell the paper. He smiled with the news from home. "Ted's doing well in the sixth grade. He just might graduate to seventh."

"Your oldest?"

"Middle, but can be scatterbrained, distracted. A daydreamer." Sam sucked in his breath. His eyes widened. "Now she's done it." Sam threw down the letter and paced the area in front of the door.

"What?"

"Read it. She's going to divorce me. I know that's what's she's going to do."

"Why?"

"She done and got saved. Now she's really going to be done with me." Sam twisted his hands above his head.

"Sam, sit down. Everything's going to be fine."

"What's your God book say about that, huh? No mixing light with dark. No unequally yoked!"

"But she can't divorce you unless you tell her to go away," Tom said, "If any woman has a husband who is an unbeliever, and he consents to live with her, she should not divorce him. That's 1 Corinthians 7:13. Sam, do you agree to dwell with Ann as your wife now that she has Christ?"

"It really says that?"

"Check it out."

Sam found his Bible in the third bag. He made his way to the chapter and read it over and over again. "Just like that, we can," he looked away.

"You're so close, Sam. Hang in there. May I pray for you?"

Sam looked at him. "I'm not ready yet." He read 1 Corinthians. "Boy, they had problems."

"They did, which is why God told Paul write this book— to help us two thousand years later. Pretty neat when you consider many of us have some of the same problems today. You going to write her back?"

Sam glared. "I'll do it when I'm ready."

CHAPTER 30

A GENT CHRISTINE WORDEN approached the narrow door in the right front corner of a white clapboard building directly behind the Shirring Insurance building. Muted tan carpeted stairs led to a short hall. "Second door on the right," Asa's note had said. She nodded at Joe, her first pick for this undercover operation, pulled the door open and blinked with the light pouring in through the bank of windows facing the quiet back street.

Asa rose from a folding table, partly obscured with files, bankers' boxes and various office supplies. "Agent Worden," he extended his hand. "So nice to see you again."

Chris made the introductions. Asa directed them to a long table parallel to a mobile whiteboard.

"It's better if passersby can't pick you out sitting in the front office." Asa leaned forward. "They get a whiff you are connected to me, we might as well pack it in."

"About the plan I mentioned..." Chris would have continued, but Asa shook his head.

"With all due respect, the agents who go in have to go in clean—no wires. We have to convince them you are vulnerable and available. The best option is a failing marriage with a damsel-in-distress scenario." He sat back, "And then there's the Bible knowledge. Did you study the files I sent you?"

Seeing their nods, he said, "Joe, tell me how you became a Christian."

The young agent cast a glance Chris' way to see her reaction to their CI telling them how to run an operation.

"Proceed, Agent Lyle. If we can't make it with Asa, I'm sure we won't get past the front door."

Lyle stepped through the cover details. He did fine until Asa's next question. "Why should my God let you into His heaven? What works have you done?"

"Well, I read the Bible every day. Have it well hidden." His smile froze. "I confess my sins regularly?"

Asa shook his head. He looked at Chris.

"We are saved by the grace of God and not anything we've done," Chris said, meeting his gaze.

Asa asked, "Where is that in the Bible?"

Chris pursed her brows. "Ephesians 2:5 to 6?"

"Close, Ephesians 2:8-9." Asa narrowed his eyes. "They lost two undercover agents the first time. It will take the right ones." He proceeded to ask Chris more questions before launching into more details about the church in town and the ranch.

When it was time to go, Asa took Chris aside. "I'm very comfortable with you, Agent Worden, but Joe doesn't make the cut. They'd discover his deception and alert them to your investigation. Do you have any other prospects? The risks are too high with this group."

"Now that I know what you're looking for, I'll try to do a better job vetting them before the next meeting."

CHAPTER 31

Tom sorted his papers and tucked away his Bible verse pages. He kept out the page on the Bible, going over the list of verses on the left. Something was missing—yet nothing came to mind. Sam would return soon from exercise, and he didn't like a mess of papers out.

Tom waited for the footsteps, wondering which Sam would walk through the door—pensive, angry or not too bad. Sam was never light-hearted.

Sam's fixed look almost appeared angry, but he grabbed his change of clothes and began to shower.

Tom moved over to catch the lunch and set the table. The Word of God—the light to our path, the guide, the promises, our portion, our delight. He couldn't write all of Psalm 119 on the summary page. He needed to put down the most important verses.

"I'm ready," Sam said, standing before him, still dripping from the shower.

Startled, Tom looked over. "Ready?"

"You can pray for me now." Sam quickly dressed and sat down.

"Great!" Tom smiled. "Don't hold back. Dream big. Ask for the world."

Sam met Tom's eyes.

"Don't be afraid. He delights to answer our prayers. Name it."

"Level one, get transferred to Woodward Prison Camp. It's close, and they give guys who can keep it together home visits. They'll let the boys visit me." Sam wiped his eyes. "That's it."

Tom prayed. He prayed for Sam, that he'd get his level one classification, and that he could keep it together no matter what happened in exercise or during transfer. He prayed for the prison camp near home, family visits, and good-time hearings with early release on reasonable terms. Then he prayed for Ann and the boys, for the family and his friends.

"Just like that?" Sam shook his head. "No fancy thees and thous and pretty quotes?"

"Prayer is talking to God. When Jesus Christ died on the cross, He opened the way for us to come directly to God. It says, '*Let us then with confidence draw near to the throne of grace, that we may receive mercy and find grace to help in time of need.*'[15] We are His children, and we can ask Him to meet our needs. He wants us to ask Him in prayer."

"All right, cupcake. How do you explain how bad He's been to you? God sent you here. You said that. Maybe He's just as undependable as everything else in this world."

"He meets my needs."

"He does?"

"Yeah, my long johns."

"That I would have thrown out."

"Right, that's still meeting my needs. Listen, Sam, I did have a problem with accepting being here, but if Christ was willing to leave heaven to live on this earth to suffer and save us, I can be willing to come here to talk to you. He's still in control. Don't ever forget it. He is the only One who can turn disasters into triumphs if we choose to walk with Him. That's the hard part—figuring out how to do it."

"Got it all figured out, huh?"

"Some days are better than others, but I'm making progress."

"Bunch of bunk." Sam threw himself on his bed and read.

Early the next day—2 a.m.—they heard the pounding on a door

across the hub to the other range. "Lenny's transfer came through," Sam said and rolled over.

Tom heard the officers assemble in front of their door the following night. The pounding reverberated through the metal bunk. "31247," the officers yelled.

"What?"

"Transfer in 15 minutes."

Tom scrambled down to help. Sam quickly dressed and felt about for his belongings. Tom checked the lockers. "I think you're fine. You've been packed for months."

"Half a year." Sam teetered on the stool, the blood pounding in his chest. Their eyes met in the dim light. "You been a good cellmate, but I hope I never see you again."

Tom laughed. "Same here. I'll keep on praying you get home to your family."

"I got to do it different. I got to say I love 'em. I got to be there. You going to pray for that?"

"I will." Tom stepped back when the door flew open. He helped push the bags out the door. It slammed shut, and the lock mechanism closed. He sat on his stool, praising God. Songs poured forth. He had been singing praises quietly, but now the dam burst. He sat back to catch his breath. *Give me Your vision, Lord. Help me find Your people here.*

CHAPTER 32

CHRIS TRANSFERRED HER outreach duties to a pair of capable office assistants and reviewed her prospects for an undercover partner. Benson had a little better grasp of the verses than Lyle, but his inability to grasp fundamental concepts meant he could only spout verses and memorized phrases. He was incapable of responding appropriately and intelligently with Christians about their faith. Briggs couldn't hide his hostility toward Christianity.

She sighed and knocked on the frame of Will's open door. His desk was piled high, as usual. In spite of the physical disorganization, his mind kept everything in place. "Kincaid approved this workspace?"

Will laughed. "Barrie lets me know when to clean house before Kincaid's due in." It helped Kincaid spent more time in the Capital than in the office complex almost an hour away.

"Well, he does do unannounced inspections. He's especially known to wander the halls at midnight."

Will nodded. He'd seen the results—messy desks swept clean with everything on the floor in a disorganized pile, a warning placed in the personnel file, and a nasty email. "Yeah, day's mess gets piled in the credenza—out of sight, out of mind. What's up?"

Chris closed the door and sat in the corner, as far from prying eyes as possible. "Kincaid's big on order and discipline in some areas but lacks rigidity in assignments."

"Meaning a managing lead could step in for an undercover assignment without having to run it up the ladder or prove necessity for operational effectiveness." Will studied her pert nose and drawn lip. "I take it no one on your team passed muster with Shirring?"

"Have any undercovers I don't know about who could?"

Will shook his head. He shifted, noting her direct gaze. "Who do you have in mind?"

She smiled. Light laughter filtered past slightly parted lips. "We make a great team. You know this. Ready to visit Asa?"

Will couldn't hide the excitement in his eyes while he pretended to fret about having the time.

"Get over it. You run an efficient ship. Delegate the lower-level tasks. You can file your monthly reports from any location. Budgets and quarterly strategy reports were just submitted. This is the best time."

"I'll take it up with Barrie."

"Let's see if you pass muster with Asa first."

Dressed casually in jeans and short-sleeved tops, the couple entered the unmarked white building and ascended the stairs. Chris and Will squeezed to the right when two young men walked down. They passed a young couple on the landing, made eye contact and exchanged greetings. "He's in there, but you missed the session."

Chris smiled easily. "Just a follow up on something. Sorry I missed it. A good session?"

"Of course, but he can give you the notes."

"We'll be sure to ask for them." Will nodded his head. "Shall we, honey? Don't want to keep him waiting."

A middle-aged woman with a teen in tow added back through the open door, "You've got visitors, Asa. Behave yourself."

Will heard an object turning and the click of closing cabinet doors before a smiling Asa greeted them. "Come in, come in. Make a cup of coffee. It's on the far table along with some donuts."

Chris noted his fast, short breaths and flushed face. "Sorry to be a little early, but for once the traffic behaved itself, considering the time of day."

"Miracles do happen. Make yourself comfortable while I retrieve my notes."

Chris' eyes scanned the room. The back of the whiteboard faced their table. Just under it she could see a row of cabinets. Will caught her gaze, pointing to the same area with his chin.

Tempted to see if even Christian CI's would lie, Will framed his opening salvo.

Laying a gentle hand on his leg, Chris shook her head. They smiled in unison when Asa emerged from a small inner room.

"Leia and Arnold for a little counseling? Did I remember that correctly?"

Chris nodded and jabbed Will under the table. "Yes, we," she glanced his way while Will played the part of the uncomfortable estranged husband, "I thought this could help."

Will snorted under his breath, glancing at Asa sideways.

"You're not wearing wedding rings?"

"Well, we'd like to again." Chris moved to reach for Will's hand. He tucked it away before they made contact.

"They left out of lot things—a lot of things I would have liked to have known before we tied the knot, but, you know, for the family…" He locked eyes with Asa. "I'm here."

"Good start. Marriage is God's gift, but it's not easy. All marriages take work." His eyes slid away to the door thrust open by a young man.

"Next one same time and place?"

"Yes, could you lock the lower door on your way out? This is a private meeting."

They heard the assent and released held breaths when the wall shuddered with the closing door and the lock clicking into place.

"Didn't mean to interrupt."

"No worries. They're a good bunch. Your secret is safe." He locked eyes with Will and began the questioning.

Will continued to act the part of estranged Christian husband trying to save his marriage. He shared his faith story, their love for one another.

Chris swallowed, one eye tearing slightly when Will looked at her with loving compassion and reached for her hand, caressing her ring finger. "I can't imagine life without you, but…" He dropped her hand. "Most days we just argue."

Asa fit well into the role of counselor, probing for details, listening to stories, helping them build their cover.

After an hour Asa paused and sat back. "This is great. It'll work, but more than likely Chris will be going to the ranch alone, if all goes well."

Will didn't want to hear that. "How are we going to protect her? I heard the neighbors didn't let the other team set up listening posts."

Asa smiled. "Seems Hawsley decided to seduce Everson's fifteen-year-old niece. He's ready to tango and wants to see action taken. I'm working hard to keep him from making too much noise. A good visit from you would help, but make sure it's an unmarked car that doesn't scream agents."

"No black SUVs?"

"Exactly. And I want assurances you'll get the hostages out. Don't forget many at the ranch are brainwashed pawns, duped and unaware of his other activities."

"Which are?"

"He finances his doomsday guns and supplies with drug dealing and some money laundering. It looks like he's getting in deeper as the months go by. Money has its own draw."

"Typical."

"But only the top guys know anything about this, and…" He looked at Chris. "Watch out for his mother, Janya Hawsley. We suspect she runs the show. He's just a spoiled momma's boy at heart."

"Any illegal Bibles at his downtown location?"

Asa shook his head. "If that were the case, this group would have been taken out a year ago, and you, my dear, would not have to go in."

Chris nodded. "That is what we heard from ATF. On the surface, this group appears to be law-abiding. We can't get the warrants without probable cause." She leaned forward. "We'll have to find another way if there are no illegal Bibles at the ranch."

"I'll warn you. Getting in is half the battle. The other will be gaining their trust for access to sensitive areas." Asa added, "My sources have seen real Bibles at the ranch, which is what I'm counting on."

"I know how to pick locks."

"Every inch is covered by cameras. Some areas even have listening devices."

"Then I will have to get in and inform the team for a quick strike." She looked at Will. "With the strike team close, they'll be busy responding to the assault." They had discussed this, planned for it. She knew what she needed to see for probable cause; a district judge had been prepped and ready to issue the warrants. If all went as planned, she'd walk away without a hitch. That was the question. Things rarely followed the script—no matter how meticulous the planning.

"The hostages have to get out alive," Asa stated firmly.

"That is and always will be our top priority, sir." Will rose and shook his hand. "We in?"

Asa rose, looking between the two. "Yes, you'll do just fine. How soon can you start?"

"It will take some time for set up and coordinating the teams." Chris looked at Will. "We'll let you know."

"Make it as soon as possible. Some of the other families are getting anxious. I'll try to hold them off, but I don't want to tip our hand. Information can flow both ways. I have every expectation Hawsley has at least one plant in our little group."

"Of course."

Back in the office Chris set up the Hawsley team's assignments. Usually the lead agent did not go in undercover, and the investigations manager would never participate directly in any case. Both Will and Chris agreed New Hope Fellowship warranted exceptional treatment. If sources could be believed, the case would lead to serious federal charges including the RICO laws (Racketeer Influenced and Corrupt Organizations Act). She had gone over the coordination of these types of cases with Will, his area of expertise, and pulled up her list of contacts with ATF, DEA, and FBI.

Eventually, she pulled up the link to the open case board for their unit. Chris returned to the dashboard and opened the last item listing individuals and groups marked for no further attention. Since Will had joined the Task Force, they had been clearing small groups not actively disseminating HCL contraband even if they were not fully compliant. She scanned the latest editions to see if any of her active cases were listed.

Chris leaned forward. Asa Shirring's name appeared. Fearing there was another case she didn't know about, she headed for Will's office.

"My, my, aren't we busy today?" She sat down, gestured to the departing agent to close the door. "Is there a case on Asa that I don't know about?"

Will sat back, a broad smile on his face. "No, no one is messing with your lead informant. Think about it; he's not directly involved in any of Hawsley's doings, his wife and daughter have been out of contact for two years now. Why is he the only one we're talking to? Come on, Chris. You're not blind. What is he, in fact, doing in his back building?"

"Yeah, we knew Asa's been the only one brave enough to work with us. He is well placed with the group of families trying to get their loved ones back. You just said it; he's not facing prosecution. Why risk outing him like this?"

"He's already on our radar, and several have applied for the sweet assistant executive director's job. You know what I'm talking about. How's your application coming?"

Chris shook her head. "I'm talking about Asa. You really want to take him off the table?"

"We've both struggled with our mandate, seen churches and families broken up only because they kept their Bibles. Creating the no-go list helps direct our resources to criminal enterprises like Hawsley's. Leveraging HCL for what it can do—give us one more tool to penetrate RICO organizations. Do you think Asa would ever engage in any activity that would harm anyone?" Will sat back. "I thought more would be like Hawsley, but the ones most likely to keep their Bibles were solid, upstanding citizens before this law."

Chris laughed. "You're right. He's more likely to love his enemies. Kincaid agrees with the no-go list?"

"He did. I talked to him about the need to prioritize cases to better manage our resources."

CHAPTER 33

THE OFFICERS ROUNDED the center hub and separated the inmates to their ranges. Tom listened to the familiar cadence. His cellmate was at the end of the line this time. He prayed for wisdom.

The door swung open; his cellmate stepped in. The door began to close. Quick footsteps sounded along with a shout, and the door swung back.

"66789," a voice shouted.

Tom rose.

"Get your stuff."

He turned to his locker, stuffed his belongings in two bags and scrambled past his bunk mate.

The officers' closed faces kept him from asking what was up. They marched down the tunnel and up the stairs. Tom breathed the dry air of the Admin wing. They led him through a set of doors and to a short counter.

"Here are your papers. Look for the callout for your appointment with your caseworker."

"What's this?"

"You're being released."

"It's not been 60 days."

"Time served," the officer behind the counter said. He looked at Tom's paperwork. "Son, when they release you from the SHU, you don't argue."

"Yes, sir." He waited for his prison issue. "Does it say where I'm going? Did I lose my bunk?"

"Doesn't look like it." The officer smiled. "Been a busy week and we got lots of customers going to Building Four. Thank your lucky stars."

Tom nodded. "I will praise the Lord."

"You do that."

The process dragged on with the large group being released. Tom tried to sit still on the bench along with the others. In time, they marched them out to Grand Central Station.

Tom headed to Unit Four. He could see Bruce going over the assignments with the day officer.

"You escape?" Bruce asked.

"Early release. Does that mean I have to find a parole officer?" he asked, trying to make a joke. They just stared at him. Tom stood motionless by the officer's alcove.

"You're still in 60 with Wallie. Guy's hanging in there, but he gets more nervous every day." Bruce and Officer Ganse looked at him with their usual "get-lost" looks.

"I have a request." Tom licked his lips. "I need to volunteer for Officer Curtis. How do…"

They burst into laughter. Officer Ganse sat back and wiped the tears from his eyes. "He doesn't get it."

Bruce shook his head. "You want back there?"

"I can't work for him, but I can volunteer."

"66789, they're not letting you within 100 feet of that officer. No way, not with the history you two have." Ganse turned back to his papers. "Get settled in your house. Count soon." He glanced at Bruce. "Think you can set him straight? He pushes this, and he's out of here."

Tom tripped over his feet turning to the stairs. His head buzzed until he remembered to pray and trust. "Well, Lord, let's see You pull this one off."

It took longer to stow his items—some were gifts from Sam.

Tom leaned against the railing and scanned the faces of the residents walking in. He smiled when he saw Stan head up the other staircase. By the time Tom walked through the shower area to the opposite walkway, Stan was already in his house.

Tom knocked. "May I come in?"

Stan nearly dropped his book, caught it and shoved it under his mat. "Of course, but you're early."

"I was so good they had to let me out," Tom said with a laugh. He sat next to Stan. "You know, I prayed for you the whole time. God didn't let me forget you."

Stan nodded.

"Stan, would you like to know the Lord?"

"I would." Stan looked at him. "Do you have a word for me?"

"I do." Tom smiled. "God says if you are a thief, quit stealing, but work hard with your hands for so you can give generously to others in need."[16]

Stan nodded. "I like that. I like that a lot." He furrowed his brow.

"God will help you. He'll give you a living heart and a desire to give, not take."

"That sounds wonderful. Pray for me."

"Pray for yourself. Stan, do you want Jesus to save you and make you a child of God?"

"How do I do that?"

"Talk to God, tell Him. He will not turn you away."

Tom listened to Stan's prayer. The tears rolled down their cheeks. He heard a rustle behind him.

"He's here! He's safe! My bunkie's back!" Wallie grabbed Tom in a bear hug. He let go and bounced out to the walkway. "Jesus saves, Jesus saves," he sang.

Tom stared. "Wallie repented? He been like this the whole time?" he asked Stan.

Stan nodded.

Tom heard a tenor singing "Our God Is an Awesome God." He stepped out to the walkway. Rick sang along with Bob and Owen. Tom and Stan joined in.

"Count," Bruce's call rang out.

Wallie laid a gentle hand on Tom's shoulder. "I knew I needed God, so I could help you. And He did it. Brought you back." They passed through the shower area. "Stan wouldn't pray with me. He waited for you."

"I sense a conspiracy here," Tom said. They found their places in number 60. "Owen's a Christian too?"

"Yep, transfer from another prison. They remembered what you said—be in the world but not of it. Hannibal needs us to be salt and light out in the blocks. I know Christ is real. I have to tell everybody, so they'll know. I'm clean because of Jesus, washed white. I'm new on the inside. I'm forgiven, and they all have to know." Wallie paused. "Stan asked a lot of questions. I answered as many as I could remember. Can you teach me more?"

"It would be my pleasure, Wallie." Count cleared, and the bars rolled back.

Tom headed to the last table during mail call. When the noise died down a little, he said, "I need your prayers to get permission to volunteer for Curtis." He looked at Bob, "To get your books back." They shifted and looked away with funny smiles. "What's the problem? Officer Curtis wanted me to work for him in the beginning."

Wallie shook his head. "They think you're just trying to get close so you can get even."

"Oh."

"It's hopeless," Bob said.

"All the better to see His answer. We pray in hope and faith, even if we can't see it."

"Yeah? Well, I pray for what I can get, then I don't get mad."

Tom spied Bruce watching them from the table closest to his cell.

He would have to follow up with Bob later. "Don't forget to pray. I'd really appreciate it." He skirted the crowd around the mail cart and headed for Bruce.

"Hey, Bruce, I still got my job back? I'm not giving up my day job." Bruce stared at him and nodded in the direction of his house. He ushered Tom in and hovered by the open bars. "Yeah, no one wants your job. What'd you have in mind?"

"I work mornings in the kitchen and afternoons I sort through the books Curtis seized and get them back to the guys."

Bruce peered down the open commons. Rick, Bob, Owen, Wallie and Stan smiled as they talked. "This ain't gonna be a Christian unit, you know." He looked back at Tom. Bruce stepped in. "Listen, if you want to risk it, talk to the warden on the line at noon. Only way it's going to happen. Most weekdays, usually Monday through Thursday, the warden and at least two of his lieutenants and executive officers stand by the line for lunch."

"Thanks."

"66789, this goes bad, you're back in the SHU for plotting against an officer, or they transfer you."

"That's up to God, isn't it?"

Tom headed back to his area the next morning. Something was different. Most of it looked the same, but new drain levers poked out from the sinks. He went looking for his scrubbers and cleaners. Tom pulled the latest rack of dirty trays around to his left side.

He plowed through the cooking trays. Just about to reach for the pots on the shelf below, he heard the left door squeak and screech open. The edge of the dumpster poked through. The kitchen crew along with Bruce were busy discussing the best way to cook the meat for the day.

"Heard you're back." Todd thrust his chin in Tom's direction. His thin lips stretched across his face. The eyes as well as the nose were the same as Sam's.

"Hope it's the last time I'm in there, but it worked out. How you doing?"

Todd narrowed his eyes. "Different worlds…different worlds and now I got a sister-in-law on me about the faith."

Tom laughed. "Questions?"

"Yeah," Todd began with the first one. Tom answered and the next and the next.

"You got your footing. Most don't leave the SHU looking happy."

"The joy of the Lord is my strength. I had a lot to work through, but I finally figured out how to walk with God in here."

"Not goin' to be all roses."

"That's true, but God is good."

"And all the time God is good. That's what I get every letter."

"It's true, Todd. It's true." He couldn't tell him about Sam. Wouldn't tell him, but he prayed.

Too soon, Tom was back at his sink with an eye on the clock. Praying again, he reminded himself not to worry about what to say to the officers. God would give him the words and move the warden's heart to agree to his request.

When the warden and his officers appeared just past the dining room door, Tom headed out to the hall. Officer Curtis stood at the far end of the row. Tom focused on the warden.

When his turn came, he said to the warden, "Warden Foster, I'm Tom Hutton, and I need to volunteer for Officer Curtis so the residents can have their books and courses returned."

The warden looked at Curtis. "Do you know what this man is talking about?"

"The items collected," Curtis cleared his throat, "last year when we handed out the new Bibles."

"I see." Warden Foster stared at Tom. "Why you?"

"I went to Bible college. I could identify what can be returned."

The warden paused a moment and said, "Your number?"

"My number?" Tom's mind went blank. "66789," he heard Officer Curtis say. "Right, 66789 356."

"The first five are sufficient." The warden nodded at the officer standing off to the side taking notes. "66789, you may work for Officer Curtis, but my eye will be on you."

"Volunteer, sir, in the afternoons. I can't give up my day job."

"Your day job?"

"I wash dishes for Bruce. Can't give that up."

Warden Foster set his lips. "Report to your case manager to write up the order. I'll sign it. It'll be on your record."

"Yes, sir. Thank you, sir."

CHAPTER 34

THE NEXT SUNDAY Tom walked with Wallie to the chaplain's wing. "Officer Curtis at the first session before count?"

"No, Len runs it. He has to look up everything."

"That's fine, Wallie. As long as he understands what it says and knows where to find it, that's what counts."

"But he doesn't say it like you."

"I'm not him; he's not me. I'd expect that." Tom slowed as they neared the double open doors. He saw chairs with desk sections off to the side and a ring of folding chairs occupying the middle. "A classroom?"

Wallie walked over to greet Rich. He beckoned Tom closer. In a few minutes, Wallie introduced Tom to the half-dozen men assembled.

Len hovered by the doors and headed in their direction. "Well, it's about time." Len shook his head. "Was praying you'd show. Been a year since they took the Bible studies, and I've been working through this book here." He handed Tom a book by McDowell. "Not like it used to be."

"And how did it used to be?"

"They let us bring our Bible study books, and we'd go over the questions, check answers, stuff like that. Roland led the class, but he transferred out, so..." Len shrugged his shoulders. "They're stuck with me." Len looked at Tom. "You know this book?"

"I do." Tom ran his fingers over the smooth cover. "Didn't rip off the cover?"

"Curtis ordered it from the publisher."

"Pretty meaty apologetics, defending the faith. What chapter?"

"I bounced around. Skipped the first two." Len reached for it and opened to the second section of the first chapter. "Maybe you can tell 'em why it's important to know some university guys say that the Bible is God's Word. I just read my Bible and know there's a God talking to me. Every day I find something. But," he nodded at the group listening to every word, "some of 'em want to hear about this."

"Of course." He glanced around the room. Everyone had a Bible in his lap, all the same size and color. "The Bibles, are they?"

"Yep, government issue." Len swallowed his spit. "No one carries books around the prison anymore. Not allowed. Especially not Bibles."

They joined the group. "Let's pray. Len, would you do the honors?"

Simple, direct, and forthright, Len prayed for the men, the study and for the peace of God.

Tom surveyed the class. "When Jesus was in the garden praying to His Heavenly Father, He said, *'Sanctify them in the truth; your word is truth.'*[17] Tom reached for the Bible on Wallie's desk. "How do we know the Bible is God's Word and the truth to which Jesus referred?"

Carl said, "Peter said in 2 Peter 1:20-21, *'knowing this first of all, that no prophecy of Scripture comes from someone's own interpretation. For no prophecy was ever produced by the will of man, but men spoke from God as they were carried along by the Holy Spirit.'* This passage tells us they didn't make it up."

"How was it tested and proven it was real?" Tom rebutted.

Owen said, "It was written by eyewitnesses soon after the events happened. If it had been a lie, everyone would have known it."

"First proof—written close to the time these events took place. Do you remember any verses talking about this?"

"Luke's books—the gospel and Acts."

"Very good." Tom checked the first chapters in the book and continued to work through the main points. The discussion turned to sharing the Word. Bob brought up the importance of sharing the faith with Bible verses.

Tom noticed the time. "Let's wrap up. During the week, think of verses about memorizing and sharing your faith. Why would it be important not to just say it with our own words? I will end with 1 Peter 3:15 telling us to be able to share our hope in Christ. Look at the verses around it."

Matt closed his Bible. "You think we not up on this? We face opposition every day. Don't need no preacher boy from the burbs to tell us how to stand for Christ in here."

Wallie retorted, "You didn't see them attack Tom. You didn't see them throw him up against the tables or almost trip him down the stairs, rip up his mattress or scream in his ear. He's taken it too. What you against him for?"

Tom said, "Let it go, Wallie. This is a hard place to be a Christian. That's why I want all of you to think about 1 Peter 3. Persecution will come. How we handle it is what matters." He nodded to Carl. "Could you close in prayer?"

As they were waiting for the movement bell to sound, Len took Tom aside. "Coming back? You want this class?"

"Sure. How do I request it?"

"I'll deal with that," Len said. "I didn't want to talk to Curtis till I knew you were willing to take it. Not all of us are cut out for teaching."

Tom walked with Wallie to their unit. He watched Matt head to his building. Matt ran the serving line and was always curt when Tom had to help. "He's rough, but he's trying to make sure I understand. Things are different here."

Wallie said, "I won't let him disrespect you like that."

They found their place and waited for the bars to close. "Don't forget we are to be kind, especially to other believers. At the Last Supper Jesus told His followers, *'A new commandment I give to you, that you love one another: just as I have loved you, you also are to love one an-*

other. By this all people will know that you are my disciples, if you have love for one another."[18]

Tom prayed for Matt even though he was thankful he did not have to tussle with him during a meal. It was hard enough to stay clear of him in the kitchen.

That afternoon Tom pulled out his papers, looking for his page on Bibliology. He realized he would have to start one. Wallie paced back and forth, muttering under his breath. Tom pushed aside his papers. "Wallie, sit down."

Wallie continued to mutter.

"What's up?"

Wallie tried to sit, but his leg bounced. "I got to keep you safe. Help you out."

"Be careful. You need to stay close to Jesus. Being mad at Matt— you don't want to go there."

"You said I was a new person in Christ. It's all good."

"The Bible warns us that Satan's a lion trying to devour us.[19] Yes, we are new in Christ, but our sin nature still wants to follow the old ways. We have to be careful and guard against falling back. The Bible tells us to be watchful, alert, on guard."

Wallie sucked in his breath. "I don't want to go back. I need to go forward, like you said."

"Get a Bible from Officer Curtis and read the book of Romans chapters six through eight. It lays out our struggle and how to stay close to God."

Wallie shook his head. "Can't read." He jumped up and paced. "You tell me."

Tom recited verses from Romans, trying to explain the walk with Christ. "When we are first saved, it's wonderful. But then it's easy to return to our old habits. You don't have to defend me. God will take care of Matt."

"I'm not doing what I used to do. You said I'd be different."

"You are. Listen, my uncle had a friend who couldn't read before he became a Christian. He said the letters jumbled in his brain, but after his salvation, he prayed and asked God to heal his mind so he could read God's Word for himself. And God did! He often read the Scripture during service."

"Could I ask for that?"

"Sure. Pray and ask. I'll pray with you."

Wallie prayed. He glanced at Tom. "I'll be back."

Tom watched him walk toward the shower area. He pulled out his papers and looked at his mostly empty page. He caught movement across the way and watched Wallie enter Stan's cell.

Wallie returned just before count. "I'll ask for a Bible tomorrow. Officer Nelson will help." He smiled at Tom. "I like that God will fix me so I can read."

Tom licked his lips. "Listen, Wallie, sometimes God works slowly, so be patient with yourself. When did you stop going to the GED classes?"

"Long time ago."

"Have you changed since then?"

"Sure. I was crazy from the drugs and all. Everyone thought they could take advantage of me, so I had to fight back. Once I started, I couldn't stop. And they gave me these drugs when I was in the SHU that really scrambled my head." Wallie nodded, "Then Officer Nelson learned I could fix things. That helped. Bruce talked them into letting me stay in 60. It wasn't a cell before, but Nelson turned it into a small one for me."

"Maybe your brain has recovered. Maybe you can try again. Don't forget to ask the others to pray for you."

"I asked Stan. He prayed with me."

Monday morning Tom struggled to answer Todd's questions. He

was in a combative mood. Torn between shutting it down and trying to make headway without responding to the insinuations and jabs, Tom considered requesting a different job for the first time. *If Curtis offers me a position I can do in good conscience, I'll take it.*

Wallie appeared happy through lunch. When he returned for afternoon count, he stuffed a book in his locker and shoved it closed.

"Got a Bible?"

Wallie glared at him.

"What happened?"

"They're making me go back to the reading program. Great idea to ask for a Bible from Curtis. Nivens made me. It's his fault. I could have gotten one from my caseworker." Wallie tapped his head. "I know these things, but Nivens tricked me; he did." Standing near the bunks, Wallie twitched.

Tom hugged the other corner. Wallie was melting down. He started singing, "Jesus Saves." He relaxed a little when Wallie joined in. "Don't be afraid, Wallie. Let's ask the Lord to be in charge." As the bars rolled back, Tom prayed, "O dear Lord, give Wallie peace about what You have for him. If this class is bad news, give him a way out of it. If You are going to do a great work through him, help him lean on You. Give him peace and joy." Tom smiled and recited Psalm 23. "We all go through dark valleys, but He's right there with us. Never forget that."

Wallie nodded. "Thanks; it's just those classes. I flipped out and don't want to go back."

"You're a different person now, Wallie."

Each day Tom listened to Wallie's successes and complaints. Some evenings he skipped ball to help Wallie with his homework reading Bible passages. Each week he could see Wallie's progress.

Two weeks passed before he received the signed work order. Tom prayed for a job offer if he was supposed to leave the kitchen. He knew

Todd's gang was in the midst of a violent shakeup. The guy had good reason to be on edge, but Tom wouldn't miss getting distance from the gang leader. Memories of Sam returned. Maybe Todd was terrified his Christian wife would reject him. That didn't seem to fit. It felt like Todd was looking for reasons to prove Christianity a sham and a path only losers would walk.

CHAPTER 35

MONDAY, TOM APPROACHED the chaplain's office, his mouth dry. Standing just inside the Chaplain's office, it looked the same. *Looks like nothing has changed.*

Mark, sitting at his desk, flicked his eyes to the wall on Tom's right. "There it is. Have at it. You work afternoons five days a week." He filed Tom's work order.

Tom glanced at Curtis' closed door. He rotated to the two-boxes deep piles of books and papers. "Is there a small room or space where I can organize it?"

"No." Mark walked over. "And don't block the doors."

"Is there a computer I can use?"

"No."

Tom pulled over a folding chair. "Paper and pen. Where do I store it at the end of shift?"

"With the boxes." Mark laughed. "That'll keep you busy for a long time."

He nodded. "They sorted by units?"

"Sort of, but some got mixed when it began to pile up, and I had to consolidate."

Tom found the inmate markings stamped on the back or inside the first page. "Can I get a current list of where the residents are now?"

"Give me their numbers, and I'll give you the location. Why do that?"

"I'll sort the booklets by units as I work through them to make it easier to distribute."

"Just put it through the mail."

Tom pulled over a box, picked up the first study guide and sat down. "I talked with my case worker about the mail service. Warden told him this can't add to their work load or cost."

"Clear it and ship it."

"I thought of that, but what if a resident has more than one book? I'd like to personally return the books to a unit at one time. That way they all get their studies back together."

"You'll be out of time if you do it that way."

"We'll see. If it takes that long, then I'll rethink the process."

Tom pulled out his list of proscribed verses. He flipped through the first study. It was clean. He wrote down the name of the booklet, tagged the item with the owner's number, and started another list for Mark.

The time went quickly, and his pile of cleared books filled two boxes. The recycle box held fewer items. He left his list of residents with Mark. "Please ID their unit and location. I want to start organizing them tomorrow."

Officer Curtis emerged shortly before the afternoon bell. "This his list of inmates getting something back?" He scanned the papers.

"Yes, sir. He wants their cell blocks for sending them back."

"Do it in the morning. Make sure it's ready when he gets in. You have next month's schedule?" Curtis checked it over, made some corrections and additions. "Fix it and turn it in before you leave today."

Back in his cell, Tom had planned to work on his Bible doctrine sheets, but his eyes burned. Bruce was lounging in his cell. Tom knocked on the upright.

"You again?"

He smiled back. "Me again. May I?" Seeing the nod, he sat on the near stool.

"What no scribbling on your pages?"

"Just spent hours speed-reading books." He leaned back. "Yard's open for ball? Warm enough?"

"Yeah, it's nice out there today. Put your name down on the recreation list." Bruce narrowed his eyes. "No fireworks? Just go in, do your job and leave? Did ya see the man?"

"Nope. I guess it'll be a short assignment, but at least the guys will get their books back. Take it one day at a time."

"Still won't give up your day job?"

Tom met his gaze with a slight smile. "I have my reasons."

"One, anyway." Bruce narrowed his eyes. "What happened in the SHU that you got it together?"

"I had a lot of attitude to get adjusted." Tom laughed. He paused at the opening. "I had to see it from God's point of view. It's just," Tom shook his head, "not the life I'd imagined nor the way I thought it would go, but God is in control."

"You sure of that?"

"I am."

CHAPTER 36

T<small>HE</small> H<small>AWSLEY CASE</small> was ready to proceed—teams were selected, other agencies read in, gear and tactics in place. Chris and Will had visited a smattering of different churches to familiarize themselves with typical Sunday morning services.

The next Sunday Leia and Arnold walked through the doors of the open area of New Hope Fellowship. With vaulted ceilings and multiple skylights, the sun's rays focused on a rough cross seemingly hanging in space from the peak of the large foyer. "Impressive," Will muttered.

The couple paused, looked at each other and joined hands. Many flowed by them on their way to the sanctuary, but a middle-aged couple paused.

"It never fails to take my breath away," the man said. "What He did for us," he raised his wife's hand to show her diamond ring, "makes marriage possible. I couldn't imagine trying to do it without the Lord."

His wife smiled. "Is this your first time?"

Chris nodded. She focused on the couple and not Will who had tucked his hand in his black jeans the moment they approached.

"Welcome to our church. Feel free to stay for coffee during the fellowship time after the service." With sounds of the praise band warming up, the couple waved and headed toward the four open double doors.

"Shall we?"

Will nodded, "Into the lion's den." Ahead ushers with wireless earbuds stood sentry at each double door.

Chris cataloged their micro-gestures. She and Will tracked to the left, but a handsome usher in his late twenties approached, handed them a church bulletin and gestured to the righthand door. "This way, folks. Your first time?"

"Yes."

"The bulletin includes a visitor's card. Please fill it out and place it in the offering plate. New to the area?"

Chris began to answer but stopped seeing Will shake his head. The usher didn't wait for a response but escorted them down the slightly angled righthand aisle to an open pew near the front.

"Never saw that before."

Chris glanced his way. "What? Be herded to a special section?" Her eyes scanned the larger midsection and far left area. She settled into the padded seat. "They do it in style."

Will's eyes scanned the rows in front of them. During a pause of the band, while the music leader arranged his music, a pair of ushers escorted a gray-haired woman to the front row in their section. "Ms. Hawsley, I presume," he said under his breath.

Chris nodded. She glanced adoringly at her partner and said, "The left-most crowd seems to interact freely with each other."

Will nodded. "The inner circle."

"The midsection doesn't get the escorts and seems isolated."

"Not-so-regular attendees."

"So, we get the newbie treatment." Will held her arm while all rose in unison at the start of the praise and worship time.

They sang along with the words projected at the center and above both wings of the platform. In spite of herself, Chris clapped with the congregation. Will looked uncomfortably about the auditorium. She glanced his way and whispered in his ear; he resumed singing with the rest.

"We're singing Scripture. Notice any outlawed verses?"

Chris shook her head. "If it was that easy, they would have been shut down before this."

The leader gestured for all to sit while the band performed a solo number. Chris let the words sink into her soul.

With a final prayer, he presented their fearless leader, Reverend Hawsley. Clapping and cheering filled the auditorium with a crescendo as Hawsley took the podium.

The pastor masterfully wove verses into his sermon, drawing out application and life principles. Will began to wonder if Asa had exaggerated the man's threat, despite Connor's warnings. Hawsley connected with his audience, working the congregation with a charismatic smile and silken voice. Then his eyes focused on their section, their row, and particularly on Chris' beaming face with her golden hair and perfect smile.

Will's heart skipped a beat. He'd seen looks like that before—the look of joy, delight and *lust*.

Chris pulled her hand free from his grip. "Arnie, you're hurting my hand."

He came to himself. "Sorry, we have to talk about this."

"Of course, but shh." She didn't want to miss a word.

Will met the preacher's gaze the next time the man's glance lingered on Chris.

After the message during the fellowship time, Will tried to steer them out the door. It didn't make sense to risk blowing their cover with too much chatter. However, his attempts to keep Chris away from Hawsley failed.

The man rounded an adoring group and headed straight for them. Will faced him squarely. After all, it would be natural to want to greet the pastor. The man barely acknowledged him. His eyes were fixed on Chris.

"Pastor, what a wonderful message," Chris gushed. "It was great! Right, honey?"

"Very good," Will said stiffly. "I can see why you wanted to check this out."

"I'm so glad you did." Hawsley extended his hand.

Will grasped the preacher's hand. "I'm Arnold, and this is my wife," emphasizing the word, "Leia."

Hawsley stared into Leia's eyes and grasped her hand. "So glad you came. How did you hear about us?"

"A friend." Chris glanced at Will. "She said your church was very helpful for couples."

Will sucked in his breath. "It's just our first time here, Leia. We wouldn't want to bother the reverend with our problems."

"Helping…" Hawsley tapped Arnold's upper arm affectionately, "… is what we do here. Couples' group meets twice a month—this Thursday, in fact." He pulled out a business card, jotted down the date and time and handed it to Chris. "It's a great group. Can I count on you to be there?" He crinkled his eyes, "Remember all marriages take work, especially those, shall we say, with challenges."

Chris nodded and smiled; Will matched the man's gaze. He grasped her elbow. "Time to go, honey. We have that date you set, remember?"

She furrowed her brow but nodded goodbye to the pastor and let her partner guide her through the outer doors. "Arnold, Arnold," Chris said, "slow down." She tried to hide a smile when a backward glance revealed two suited ushers watching their every step. "They're watching, so make it look good."

Will approached their small Toyota, opened her door, waited for her to glide gracefully into her seat. They both breathed after he started the car, letting the air conditioning begin to cool down the interior. Putting it into gear, Will said, "You can't go in alone." The car rolled out the drive with the others and turned left toward the town's center.

Chris glanced at Will. "Asa said there's no other way."

"We'll see about that." Will navigated to the south side and a small neighborhood with winding streets, sidewalks, and small parks. Asa, also a real-estate agent, had selected a house that had recently sold to a couple who would not be moving into the area for some time. Their cover had to withstand scrutiny. Some of the ushers carried themselves like former military or law enforcement. Will assumed one of them was checking out the new couple to ensure they were exactly what they appeared to be—a young couple with a troubled marriage.

He drove up the short drive and opened the garage door. They waited until evening before leaving as if to go out for supper. Once certain they had not been tailed, Will parked the car in a rented storage area in a nearby city. They walked to their parked cars a few blocks away. Will didn't want to start an argument, and Chris remained quiet as well. He appreciated that about her. She didn't have to talk every minute. "Be safe. Are you going to that meeting?"

Chris nodded, "I was thinking about going."

"We'll talk more Wednesday when I'm back in the office."

"Going with Kincaid to one of his regular meetings at the Hill?"

"Something like that."

"Looking forward to hearing about it."

Will followed at a distance to make sure she safely reached her car. He didn't care if she knew. Even trained agents can be jumped.

He drove directly to Asa's house, donned a pizza-delivery vest, grabbed an empty pizza box and rang the front bell. He entered the small ranch before Asa could finish his invitation. "She can't go in alone."

"You saw it too?"

"That he's a sexual predator? It's unmistakable."

Asa nodded, sighed and gestured to the small table in the kitchen area. "I didn't recognize it in time. Not like you." He poured two glasses of water and sat down. "I gather you've seen his type before." He shook his head. "If there were any other way, I would have never suggested it, but…" he leaned forward.

"Yes, she's trained. She is very capable of defending herself, but he's…" Will's voice caught.

"You'll have time. He's patient. He'll work to win her trust, bring her into the fold at the ranch, groom her." Asa looked away. He'd heard the stories from others who had eventually found a way to leave. "My wife is there. It breaks my heart. I don't know what's happening to her or my daughter. I try not to dwell on it." Asa rubbed his hands as if to cleanse them. "I understand your concern." Their eyes locked. "The sooner she can get in and find the evidence you need, the better."

Will had to agree. "Pizza-delivery guys don't linger too long in a house. Is the mother involved or clueless?"

Asa walked him to the door. "She makes the final selections and gets them ready. She's definitely a part of this."

"Did the earlier teams include local special-victim units?"

"You saw the ushers. In the initial stages, this has to be done without local law enforcement or social workers. The city's agencies and organizations are riddled with his sympathizers. Remember, he's a hero—a local guy who made good and is building a national audience."

"He personally invited us to the next couples' study. Should we go?"

"Well, it would be better if you missed it, but attend next Sunday. Play a little hard to get."

Will nodded and donned his cap, looking at the insurance agent. "I agree." He didn't have too much time. A good undercover operation against a well-orchestrated organization could take months—time they didn't have. Kincaid had no patience for drawn-out cases. He wanted results. "Pray it doesn't take too long."

"Daily."

CHAPTER 37

Tom surveyed his lists of inmates by number and name, which had been organized by unit for each building, taped to the wall above stacked boxes. Building One only had Units Two and Four. What happened to Three, not even Bruce could explain. The unit names in the other buildings didn't seem to follow any clearer logic. Building One had a partially filled box.

Buildings Three and Five had the most. The inmates presently in Four, the DU, had their own box in the corner, sitting next to the four-box-high pile of confiscated Bibles. The next project would be to find a way to redact the Bibles, including Sam's.

Officer Curtis paused before going into his office. "Close to finishing?"

"Getting there." Tom rose. "Did you get a chance to go over the list of books I put in last week? They don't mention any of the outlawed verses. Did you want to review the items? If you had any questions, I could…"

"No." Officer Curtis scanned the neat lists taped over the boxes of wrapped books for each inmate. "As you were and see it through." He turned to Mark.

Tom went back to sorting the last few boxes. Most of the remaining books could be quickly categorized and sorted now that he had identified the few books that could not be returned. He couldn't help but listen to Curtis.

"53142," Curtis started. Tom knew it was a bad sign when the officer addressed Mark by his number. "Thought you said we were out of communion cups. Now I find a case on the other side, and you never finished numbering the shelves. No wonder we run out or order too much." Curtis looked at his phone. "Ren says we double-booked the third classroom. He needed it for a hearing. Did you forget about Roger's A&O class?"

Tom surveyed his area. There would be room for another desk after the items were returned and the rest sent to recycling.

He approached Mark after Officer Curtis entered his office. "I can help with the inventory."

"Good luck with that." Mark stared at him. "Curtis had me organize that closet four times last year. I don't get why they can't just let us put the stuff on the shelves where it's sat for as long as I've been here."

"Well, I'll make the offer once the boxes are delivered. I need a pass to the mailroom to coordinate deliveries."

Mark handed Tom the form.

"Thanks. I'll hand it in maybe the end of this week. Do you think he'd want to oversee the deliveries?"

"No."

CHAPTER 38

SATURDAY CHRIS DROVE up to their undercover house and chatted briefly with a neighbor walking their dog about returning from visiting her sister. Will parked a borrowed semi minus a trailer on a side road and entered the house later in the evening. They camped out in the kitchen.

"Game plan? We fight, make a scene?"

Will nodded. "Kincaid'll give us to the end of the month or we move on."

"My, he's impatient or is there another reason he doesn't see this as a worthwhile investigation?"

"You got me. He was on board when you presented the case. Now he's on to his next issue of the week. Some of the ex-cons Larry's team rolled up last week had been with Hutton in prison."

"Tom?"

"No, his Uncle Al. Those Bibles of his are showing up all over the country in regions we didn't think he'd ever visited."

"Remember, Tom said he had connections. Sounds like he had his own Bible network."

"That's not funny. It took me a while to keep Otis from sending a team back to Hannibal to talk to Tom again."

Chris groaned. "We both know that's not happening. Anyway, we make a scene, you storm out of church and leave with the car. Let's see who comes to my rescue."

Sunday morning Will didn't bother to shave. He topped off his t-shirt with a sleeveless leather vest. Chris preened in front of the mirror as if she were going before a camera crew. They winked and drove to church.

In the parking lot, Chris slammed the door and avoided his hand as they walked in. The ushers led them to the same section. Will acted as if he would bolt any second. "I told you, we have better things we can do with our morning."

Chris glared at her partner and glanced over nervously when she saw that others were watching them. "Keep it up. It's working," she whispered.

They made it through the worship time. Pastor Hawsley glanced their way frequently during the message. Chris watched him with rapt attention while Will stared at the far wall, refusing to be drawn into the message.

The congregation was still singing the last song when Will grabbed Chris' arm and pulled her up the aisle to the exit.

"Arnie, what are you doing?"

"Leaving. We've heard enough."

"But…" Chris cast a panicked look at the nearest usher who tapped his earbud and spoke into his sleeve. They were mostly through the foyer before one of the assistant pastors could intercept them.

"So nice you could join us for a second week," he began.

Chris wrenched her arm free. "Arnold, let's stay. It wouldn't hurt to be friendly." She leaned in, "They can help us."

Arnold stepped toward the young pastor. "We don't need your help. We're doing just fine. Time to go."

"The lady wants to stay." The pastor took a small step back when Arnold drew closer.

"Please, Arnold, can you get a coffee?" Leia pleaded.

He tried to grab her arm again, but she moved away. "I'm not ready to leave. I'd like you to stay."

Arnold looked between the two—his wife and the young assistant with a pale, scared face. "Fine, you stay. I'm leaving." He stomped to their car and drove away.

Leia's hand shook.

The pastor reached over to quiet it. "Let's get that coffee."

She glanced over and saw Pastor Hawsley watching. Leia nodded to the assistant and sat at the table while he brought the drinks. Her story poured out—high school sweethearts, she'd given up college and career to marry her husband despite her parents' warnings. They'd made a go of it until they moved away from family and friends. Alone, confused, she shared her heart's desire for things to be better, for their marriage to work.

After the service and an intense session with Pastor Hawsley in his office, she agreed to go directly to the ranch. "I don't have anything with me."

"Not a problem," Pastor said, "You'll find everything you need there. You'll be safe—right where God wants you to be."

Chris nodded, dabbed her eyes and ran through her options. They had not expected to advance this quickly, but she was now in. She trusted her team would follow the plan. Even though she knew Will led the overwatch team on the neighbor's farm, her heart pounded, and butterflies fluttered.

A phalanx of ushers moved Hawsley down a back corridor. One of the women who accompanied Janya greeted her warmly as she stood by the pastor's office. "Come with us," she said, following Pastor's mother. A side door led to a large garage with waiting SUVs. They formed a convoy and drove to the countryside with wooded, rolling hills.

Once they were underway, Janya Hawsley looked back from the front passenger seat and smiled at her.

Chris smiled back, rehearsing her cover story and the facts she had already shared.

"My dear, I hear you are in some difficulty. Do you have any children?"

Leia shook her head. "We tried. I always wanted to have kids, but I miscarried." She dabbed her eyes. "After the last one, I felt so lost and defeated. My heart was broken, but someone told me my children were in heaven. That thought gave me hope."

"You became a Christian? When?"

"Last year…" Leia nodded her head. "It helped, but it didn't fix everything."

Ms. Hawsley narrowed her eyes. "Sometimes it takes finding the right man."

"No, it was my problem—not Arnie's."

"Do you like children?"

"Yes, almost became a teacher, but…" She looked out the window, testing, trying to grasp a sense of this woman.

"Did you finish school?"

"Not college. Was interrupted by family plans and then the move. Arnie wasn't a truckdriver when we wed. Now he's gone so much."

The woman focused on the winding, wooded road. "We'll be at the ranch soon; it's a safe haven for the chosen." She smiled condescendingly. "I'm sure it will feel like home."

The vehicles turned again and again before stopping at a paved driveway bounded by brick walls with a grillwork gate blocking the entrance. The lead vehicle stopped, and the driver entered a code in the keypad. The gates swung open. She noted the multiple cameras. Chris tamped down her inner shudder when she felt as well as heard the gate latch close behind the convoy.

The woman on her left grasped her hand. "You're going to find the ranch a blessed retreat."

Leia nodded and forced a small smile. "Arnie."

"You find your center in Christ, and then Pastor will help you reach out to your husband. Before you know it, you'll both be in the fold and part of the family."

"I know Christ has a plan for us. Hard to see right now."

Looking back, Janya said, "Pastor Hawsley will lead the way. He walks with the Savior. You have nothing to fear, Leia."

The driver crossed a bridge over a babbling brook. Through the windows Leia saw a two-story building of dark wood set into the hillside. Porches wrapped around two sides on both levels. The lower deck extended out to a firepit circled by rows of benches. The small valley held additional buildings behind the main house, surrounded by evergreen, birch, maple, oak and pine trees.

The sun poured down on the stream making its way along the right side. Leia breathed in the fresh air, smelled the scent of flowering bushes, heard the songs of birds, and watched a butterfly flit from flower to flower.

"Home…" the woman nearby said. "It can be your home, if you let it. Let him in. Don't be afraid."

Janya gestured for her to follow them around a paved walkway sloping up the hill to the front entrance. She grasped Leia's hand and escorted her past the ushers, the assistant pastors and the women who had accompanied them. The matron placed Leia's hand in Hawsley's smooth palm.

He beamed at Leia. "Many are called, but few are chosen. Welcome to New Hope. May it be your new home as we prepare for the new world."

She nodded, smiled and stepped with him into a large room.

"The Lord bless you," the pastor said to a waiting group of men, women and children. "Welcome Leia—a visitor and perhaps a new member—Leia."

Several women walked up to greet her. Some were shy, teen girls. Leia bent down and shook the hands of three youngsters hovering near a young woman.

"Are these your children?" she asked.

Leia sucked in her breath when the young woman merely nodded and silently herded the children along.

"You're not afraid of young ones?" a woman asked. She extended her hand. "I'm Fran."

"Nice to meet you. I did my time babysitting, but it's been a while." She looked at Fran. "We don't have our own children." *This could be Asa's wife. The photo had not been recent.* "Do you have children?"

Hearing a commotion in the kitchen, Fran turned her head. "Sorry, I have to go, but let's talk later."

Janya's ladies called her to their table. "Join us."

A friendly blonde sitting next to her described how most of the meal had been grown and prepared right on the ranch. "Natural food. Natural living. It's so healthy."

Leia nodded and asked, "Do you jog?"

"Jog?" the woman asked.

"Exercise, that's another part of healthy living."

"Oh," she laughed, "we get plenty of exercise. We keep very busy. You'll see." She leaned closer. "We always welcome another set of hands to help get the work done."

Leia smiled and let the conversation flow around her. In no time, people finished their meals, dropped off their dinnerware at the counter and headed back to the front room.

Leia positioned herself closer to Fran who seemed eager to talk to her.

Fran led her to the front room. Quietly, she asked, "Are you visiting?"

"Well," for the first time Leia hesitated spouting her lies. "I was at the church, and my husband walked out on me. We've been trying to get things right, but they keep going wrong. Pastor invited me here to clear my head, find my center. I'm just visiting."

"We'll see. Follow me."

Folding chairs surrounded a podium. A young man handed her a large Bible. She sat next to Fran as everyone moved to the innermost seats and filled up the chairs without jostling for position or any fixed grouping she could discern—as if well trained to sit in the next available spot with no gaps in the center. All sat with Bibles unopened on their laps, eyes front and center on Pastor Hawsley.

A few in the front began to strum their guitars. In unison, the group sang as one. Fran pulled out a songbook tucked in the back of each Bible and pointed to the words. Leia thanked her and tried to sing along, but the tune was not familiar. The song spoke of a new world, a new hope, a new life. Her mind returned to the pastor's words of greeting to her.

"Fewer visitors have dropped by; we are getting ready for the time to come, and it is close, my beloved, my friends." He leaned forward, warmly embracing each one with his eyes.

When he looked at her, a tingle ran up her spine. She felt as if he could look into her soul. She stilled the thought, settled her breath and focused on the plan, her cover, the lies she had to utter.

"Turn with me to Romans 1." All opened their Bibles. Chris was thankful for Asa's admonition to memorize the order of books in the Bible. No one had to rescue her to find the passage.

The chapter contained 32 verses. She held an illegal Bible in her hands. Buttoning down her excitement, she whispered to Fran, "What version?"

"The Authorized King James."

"The full edition?"

"Of course."

Pastor started with verse 18, adding brief commentary as he stepped through the descent of a culture into darkness. "Given over by God after rejecting His truth. Turning from the Creator, Savior, Redeemer, He gives them over." Pastor read to the end of the chapter and paused.

"Think on this." He lifted his Bible. "I hold what our government considers contraband. Are we afraid?" He paused, scanning the room. "No, because our God is the Most High God. His Son is the King of kings and Lord of lords. Can any rule of man stop the working of the Holy Spirit?"

The group shouted, "No!"

"Can they purge the true Word of God from our soil?"

"Never!"

"That's right." He nodded his head. "And these laws prove we are near the time. Proof God will come and put down the wicked ones. Put down the injustice. Remove the unrighteous laws. When a society calls evil good and brands good…" He lifted his Bible again, "…*as evil, we know His coming draweth nigh.*"

Pastor Hawsley laid out God's plan, verse by verse, from Genesis to Lamentations, from Isaiah to Matthew, from Zechariah to 1 Timothy, weaving in the duty to lay up a community and prepare a bride for Christ—ready, spotless, waiting for Him to come. He ended with, "This is our hope, why we are at New Hope, waiting for our King to come again. As I, His lowly shepherd…" he placed his hand on his chest, then lifted his arms as it to embrace his congregation, "make you ready for heaven."

Leia's head spun. She caught a few of the references, but most was a blur. She had no idea if the pastor's timeline agreed with the Bible. "Do you understand this?"

Fran patted her knee. "Don't worry. You'll hear it every day." She looked at Leia as they rose for the final hymns. "You like kids?"

"Sure."

"Want to help with the nursery and early grades?"

"Sounds better than an empty house."

CHAPTER 39

THE GROUND LEVELED out into a plateau behind the building before climbing again near the wooded areas. She knew the team waited a half mile away. They had surveyed the area, but from this side, the hill seemed so high.

Fran described the buildings. "That's the Main or Big House. We hold chapel there Sundays after dinner." She pointed to the right. "That's the hall and work areas. We meet first for chapel each morning in our own buildings." They took the path jutting to the left. "And those are the living areas. The center one is for the nursery and young ones." She continued walking. Leia matched her strides.

"Why are you here, Leia?"

Chris paused only for a second before retelling her story.

"Why are you really here, Leia? Did Asa send you?" She headed toward a path running behind the nursery and a landscaped playground. They stopped behind tall bushes. Chris assessed the middle-aged woman. For the first time, she prayed and felt the urge to answer. "Yes, I am here to rescue the hostages."

"They would deny they are captives."

"Obviously, but…" she searched Fran's face. "How did you know?"

"Your eyes are not glued on the reverend. You're looking at us—not his eminence."

"Are you ready to leave?"

"Yes."

"Why do you stay?"

"I'll show you." They rounded the play area. Leia copied Fran's example and picked up trash and downed branches. Leaving the refuse in the appropriate areas on the left, she followed Fran into the center building.

The foyer had shelves for outdoor shoes and hooks for coats and sweaters. On the left, carpeted play areas ranged from toys for toddlers to play kitchens and monster truck racing tracks. She watched four boys running their minitrucks with the appropriate sounds along a printed map on the floor.

One towheaded youngster headed their way. "Grandma," he said running to Fran.

She embraced him in her arms and looked at Leia.

"The father?"

"One of the young men—not the ones you would have seen at church. Pastor Hawsley pairs them off." She hugged her grandson and set him down. "Play nice, and I'll tell you a story later, but first, I have to check on your sister."

Fran adjusted her sweater and nodded down the hall. "This way," she said in low voice. "They try to discourage playing favorites with your own flesh and blood. We're supposed to be one big family."

Fran knocked on Door Seven and stepped in. A young woman sat in a rocker, cradling a newborn in her arms. "How's she doing today?"

"Finally settling down." The young mother wrinkled her nose with a smile. "Someone new? It's been a while. Prophet said more would come." She laughed lightly. "You the next best thing?"

"Guess I am." Leia stepped closer. "I'm Leia. Just for a visit. She's beautiful. How old?"

"One month already. Everything all right?"

Fran nodded and reached for her granddaughter. "Leia volunteered to help with the children. Isn't that nice, Heather?"

"Definitely." Heather worked to stand up. Leia stepped forward to help her.

"Thanks, this delivery was harder than the first."

Leia noticed the worried look on Fran's face. "I'm sure your mom will show me the ropes. Where will I sleep?"

"I'll set that up." She handed the baby back and leaned forward to place a quick kiss on her daughter's cheek.

Leia helped Fran with her chores until Emily came to assign a room and basic supplies. Fran accompanied Leia to a small room with bed, stand and chair. Leia rested her hand on the large Bible on the stand.

"She ready?"

"More than before the baby."

"The father?"

"Not sure, but he might want to stay with her. They seem close, but it's hard to tell in here."

Leia nodded. "Do they have any runners, athletic shoes? I usually run a few miles around the end of the day."

"I might have a pair. We can see if they fit you. The supply room has standard lace-up loafers. Will that do?"

"Better than the pumps I'm wearing now. This was so sudden I didn't have time to pack."

"It can go that way." Fran looked as if she wanted to say more, but she shook her head and went back to the hall. "Your best bet for that run is right now. Curfew's in a little while with evening sessions and prayers."

Leia followed Fran to her room on the other side of the building. "This is larger."

"Been here long enough I'm sort of a shift supervisor. I do what I can to keep things moving. At least I don't work the fields or gardens. Not my thing."

Leia found a pair of shoes that would work. Following Fran's directions, she exited the building from the side doors, skirted the playground, stretched to warm up her muscles and headed down the trail. Once deeper in the woods, she found the path as Fran described it and worked her way up the hill and over the ridge. She threw some dirt on the electric fence—sparks flew with sharp sizzles. The fence was active.

Chris dug out a hidden miniature phone. She found herself praying again she could get a signal. Nothing. She followed the fence trying again and again until she made a connection and sent the text. She had little Intel on locations of weapons, contraband Bibles or where other hostages could be. Maybe it would be enough that she had seen Bibles and suspected they had hundreds on the property.

CHAPTER 40

THE NIGHT WAS uneventful. Chris rose with the dawn, found coffee perking in the small kitchen near the nursery, stated she was going for a run and exited the building. When she reached the spot, she smiled when Will's answering text loaded, stating the time of the assault.

Leia tossed the phone over the fence; hoping eyes had seen it and could recover it for the photos she had managed to shoot the evening before. Heading back, she found herself praying again for safety for all, especially the little ones. As much as she wanted to warn Fran, she knew that would not be wise.

Two men found her on the path not far from their building. "Where you been?"

"Getting my run in."

"Been looking for you."

"Well, I jog two times a day. Now it's time for a shower."

"Hold up." The first one said, blocking her path. "They need to see you in the Big House."

"Thought I would work with the little kids today. Fran said they needed the help."

"Ms. Hawsley makes the assignments. She's looking for you."

Leia fell in step between the two.

They ushered her into what appeared to be the Hawsleys' suite of rooms. Janya sat upright in an overstuffed chair with an open Bible on her lap. "You're quite the athlete, Leia."

"Good morning, Mrs. Hawsley. It's for my health. I haven't had a chance to shower."

"Don't want you to miss morning devotions. Now," she patted a chair on the other side of a small table, "tell me everything about you."

"Not sure what you mean, Mrs. Hawsley. I'm a stay-at-home wife. For the past few years my husband has driven truck. He's gone most weeks."

"Does he help with the family?"

"Well, we lost the babies, so I was trying to figure out what to do, but it's complicated."

"I'm sure it is." She nodded. "My son is a wonderful counselor. Once you find your place in Christ's kingdom, everything falls into place. You turn away from the past and what held you back. You reach forward to the future God lays before you. I believe your being here, Leia, is all part of His plan. Do you pray for more children?"

"It's not possible. We'd have to adopt, but…" she looked aside.

"Yes, you need stability, guidance and a godly man to lead the family."

Leia sat up. The woman's tone bit into her soul. Janya looked at her closely, as if she were assessing, judging, weighing. She felt as if she were a specimen on a lab bench. "I found God last year after the last miscarriage. I don't know a lot about the Bible or how God leads, but I want to learn and find that center in Christ you've talked about."

"You do know all of His children have the Holy Spirit, don't you?"

The breath caught in her throat. She remembered reading something about that. Her unease subsided when Mrs. Hawsley continued in a monotone.

"Christ baptizes us into His body when we surrender to God and take the free gift of salvation. We are baptized with the Holy Spirit and experience *the unity of the spirit in the bond of peace*.[20] This bond between believers is stronger than family, greater than earthly ties. All believers comprise one family."

Leia breathed when the older woman sighed, sat back, glanced far away and then smiled at her. "They usually don't teach this right away, so it's not unusual for you to be unaware of this. It explains why we can feel close even if we have just met."

The woman rose and extended her hand. "Let's join the fellowship. No one will notice or even care if you haven't had a chance to freshen up. That's the old world. Let us live today in the heavenlies—the new world, our new hope."

Chris followed, conflicted. One minute, Janya sounded like a monster, the next she felt like a sweet lady. Her mind reeled with Pastor Hawsley's warm greeting. He wrapped her in his arms and hugged her closely. She worked at not stiffening her body.

"Have a good run?"

"Yes, I did," she answered. Finding a seat, she tried to ignore the stares of the other women.

Regular, daily concerns along with prayers for the nation were spoken and prayed for. Pastor read, prayed through and made some parting remarks from Psalm 139—we are never far from His presence.

A smaller group ate in the main dining area. Two younger women shadowed her, directing her to the Hawsleys' table. "They want to get a chance to know the newcomers," the brunette explained. "We had your items brought around to a room here. When it's time, you can transfer back to the Middle Building."

Leia nodded and listened, feeling the ebb and flow of the place. Later that day when she went to put on some running shoes, Pastor Hawsley approached her. "There has been some movement along the roads. For your safety, Ed and Russ will be your guides for your run."

"Thank you. That is a very thoughtful offer, Pastor, but…"

"It's not an offer. I insist." He stepped closer and squeezed her hand. She perceived Janya's scowl and heard a few brief words between them before the three exited the central room.

Leia didn't wait for them to pick the path. She set a fast pace and was deep in the woods before they could turn her. She hoped if the team waiting in the next farm spotted her running with guards, they would understand why she couldn't make the agreed check-in. She tried to settle her swirling thoughts with the knowledge the team would descend on the ranch early the next morning in about ten hours or so.

After the run she helped in the kitchen and was seated with the Hawsleys for a second meal.

"I think I've cleared my schedule so we can begin, Leia. You up for an early evening session?"

She asked, "Can we begin without Arnold? I've not had a chance to let him know I'm okay. Could I have my phone back?"

"That can be arranged later." He extended his hand. "But first, a session with you to lay the groundwork. Then we can invite your husband to join us—if you think he'd be willing to come."

"I'll ask him…if it's important enough to him." She looked away. It took little effort to look lost and abandoned.

"We can continue this later." He ignored the warning looks his mother sent him.

After supper Janya took her son aside. Leia could not make out the words, but it seemed heated.

A young man fetched her from the kitchen shortly after and led her to a large study with an inner door. Pastor Hawsley sat in a comfortable chair near a small table. He pointed to the tea and coffee service.

"Coffee or tea, or maybe herbals? Caffeine doesn't bother me this time of day, but it does some."

"I don't have a problem with it, but usually only drink it in the mornings."

He smiled and handed her a dainty teacup. "Jasmine." He sat back. "My favorite—sweet just like you." Bending his head to sip from his, he looked away for an instant.

Leia shifted, pretended to take a sip, and set the cup down. "Need to let it cool. So, Pastor, where do we begin?"

"I'd like to hear your testimony and how you met your husband."

"We were high-school sweethearts. Everything seemed possible. College didn't work for him, but he did manage to get his CDL. I worked odd jobs through high school, but he wanted me to stay home to raise our children." She reached for a tissue and blew her nose. "That's when things…" She glanced his way before adding, "losing the children drove us to the Lord. We found God, but it might have been too late."

"You both became Christians?"

"Yes."

"Who saw the light first?" His broad friendly smile captivated her soul for an instant, but the inner warnings persisted.

"I did."

"You did." He leaned forward, his voice gentle and warm, "Was it genuine? Or did he go through the motions to keep you?" Hawsley pulled his chair closer to Leia's.

"I don't understand. He said he believed. We've prayed together, shared verses."

Pastor leaned forward and gently grasped her right hand. "Leia, I have seen this countless times. They pretend interest in God to keep you." He stroked her hand. "Was it real? I saw how he was at church."

Leia pulled back; a chill ran down her spine. She shook her head. "No, I don't believe it." She looked aside and blew her nose. "I don't know."

The smile that spread across his face told her she needed to act.

"Pastor," she said with an open, waiting look, "if I could call him, we might find out. I have an idea. Shall we?" Leia extended her hand confidently.

"I'll be right back." The pastor emerged with her cell phone.

"This is such a good idea." She found herself praying. The ringer sounded three times before the call picked up. "Arnie," she said, "you done driving for the day?"

"Yeah, Babe. What happened?"

"You left me."

"Leia, you know me better than that. I waited around the corner for you to come out. I had to get out of there. Where are you?"

"I'm safe." She glanced at Hawsley. "I'm at the church's country retreat." She nodded and mouthed, "Everything will be fine" when he began to scowl. "The Pastor wants to help us, just us. When do you get back? Tomorrow?"

"Oh, Leia, I hate to tell you, but the office added another delivery to this load. It'll be the day after tomorrow."

"That's fine. I'm making friends, and I have so much to tell you. They've been so kind, praise the Lord. I never realized a church could feel so much like a family. How about you? Do you think God wants us to let them help? We haven't been doing well on our own."

"Listen, Leia, I'll pray about it. Maybe we can try one session the day after I return."

"Arnie, are you glad you're a Christian?"

"Believe me, if I wasn't, I would have stormed that place and dragged you out of there Sunday—no questions asked. You know this."

She nodded. "I do. See you soon. Love you." Leia looked at Hawsley but couldn't read his expression.

He extended his hand for the phone. "We like to disconnect, so we can focus on the eternal."

"Of course. Maybe Thursday at the church? I've known Arnie for a long time. It's real. You wouldn't want to have faced him before he met Christ."

"I can imagine." The pastor took the phone to his office and returned with a Bible. "You became believers after you married. Have you considered God doesn't automatically expect you to stay together? Perhaps He has annulled your marriage. You," he held her hands, "are a new creation in Christ. Your former husband has changed as well." He paused when she pulled back. "We at least have to consider this possibility." Hawsley glanced at the closed doors. They were alone in his suite. "Drink your tea. It should help."

"I don't drink this late in the day." She smiled. "Too many evening trips to the bathroom ruin a good night's sleep. She rose. "Pastor Hawsley, I made a promise before God and my husband to remain faithful to him. Until he decides to end this marriage, I'm committed to make it work and welcome your help. Now, if you'll excuse me, I promised Fran to help with the children's devotions this evening." She turned and walked out of the suite. He did not stop her.

Emily stood near Ms. Janya and held out her bag. Janya smiled, "Good night, Leia."

"Thank you. It's been a pleasure getting to know all of you. Is my room still available in the Middle Building?"

"Definitely."

CHAPTER 41

LEIA BREATHED MORE freely once she cleared the threshold and saw Fran's welcoming wave. Will had told her the assault was delayed. This gave her extra time to scope out the other buildings.

She made her way around the assembly of young children, mothers, and older women to join Fran near the back in front of the kitchen serving counter. Leia glanced at the line of young men waiting by the back section.

"They're waiting for free time before lights out; for some it's the only time they can spend with their families," Fran said.

After the storyteller wrapped up the session and they sang their last song, a lanky young man who looked barely twenty approached Heather and reached for the baby.

"That's Simeon. His mother brought him with her years ago."

"Where is she?"

"Dead." Fran whispered, "They're not great on getting medical help when you need it." She added, "Heather has still not recovered from her last pregnancy." Fran glanced her way, "Had your session with the pastor? Was it what you expected?"

Leia smiled. "I cut it short."

"Good for you. You can have the same room. Don't venture out before dawn. They're very strict about that."

The groups separated, making final preparations before lights out. She helped Fran clean up the kitchen and play areas.

The next morning Leia was halfway through her first cup of coffee when Ed and Russ entered.

"There she is. Up already, I told you," Ed said to Russ. He glanced her way. "No jog today. Morning assembly at the Big House."

"After breakfast?" She glanced at the few early risers filling their bowls.

"No, now. Where's the head boss lady?"

"You mean Fran? I haven't seen her yet."

"Well, find her, unless you want us to."

"Relax, fellas, grab some coffee. It might take a while to get everyone up." Leia headed for Fran's room and tapped on the door. Hearing no response, she looked in. The bed hadn't been slept in. She tried Heather's room and entered when she heard a quiet reply.

Fran rocked the baby and gestured toward Heather still in bed. "Had another rough night. The baby did fine."

Leia relayed what the two men said. "Something up?"

"Definitely. What do you think we should do?"

She ran the possibilities through her mind. "Stall." *Something must have made Will execute the hit today*, Chris reasoned.

Fran rose, handed her the baby. "Wait here. Is it Russ?"

"With Ed."

"Those two I can handle." Fran winked at her, "I've not met a man yet who could resist a hearty breakfast."

Leia sat in the rocker. She felt a rumble in the little one's diapers, and her nose confirmed her suspicions. Trying to recall her distant babysitting days, she approached the changing table. *Have the teams been discovered? How can I keep the children from being used as human shields?* Chris found herself praying again.

Heather stirred and sat up. "How's she doing?"

"Almost done." Leia zipped up the onesie, bundled her in the small quilt and handed her to Heather. "I'll check on your mom. She's entertaining Russ." She noted Heather's dull eyes and lack of interest in anything she had said. However, the young mother's eyes were only for her baby.

"How old are you, honey?"

"Nineteen last month."

"You hang in there."

Leia's pace quickened to the communal area when she heard a distant bullhorn. She resisted the temptation to peek outside and looked for Fran.

The woman had Ed and Russ distracted with their latest hunting stories. She winked at Leia. "Our top hunters. We can't grow venison." They seemed not to have heard the noise. She was pondering how to advise Fran when Ed's radio squawked with an unclear message.

"Take it outside," Fran said. "Probably need both of you. Your breakfast will be waiting for you."

Once they left, Leia asked, "Can you lock all the doors from the inside?"

"Yes." Fran ran to the doors, secured the crash bars and placed a metal bar across the entrance. Leia followed her to the side door.

Fran paused at the double doors leading to the cavernous storage area. "If we can't secure the outer storage doors, we can block this one, but it's not the best. You in contact?"

"Not today, but I heard a bullhorn. That means the perimeter's in place."

"You'd better be right, or we're in real trouble."

They paused, hearing the pop-pop of gunfire. They pushed through the double doors and ran to secure two side doors. Fran turned to the large barnlike door at the end. They froze when Ed pushed one side opened and yelled.

She grabbed Fran's arm, and they ran back to the living areas. "Secure the inner door."

The women worked at catching their breath, leaning against a side wall. "Will it hold?"

"For a while. Now what?"

Only a few were up, and they seemed unaware anything was different.

"Keep things as normal as possible. Need a hand with the cooking?"

A few hours later Leia heard Will's "All clear." She unbarred the doors and stepped out. SUVs, assault vehicles and the mobile command center occupied the central plateau. She could see at least two lines of suspects kneeling in front of agents. Their jackets sported letters from various agencies—ATF, DEA and FBI as well as HCL Task Force. Her assistant brought her jacket and kit. She donned her firearm and other items, pulled out her badge. Her three leads followed her into the building.

She caught Fran's gaze and nodded. "Everyone, your attention please. I am Task Force Agent Worden. Remain calm and cooperate with the agents. Answer their questions. Once you are cleared, buses will take you to the Fredrickson Community Center where your families are waiting for you."

Chris gestured for Fran to join her. She gathered her staff together. "This is Fran. She is our local contact and can answer any questions." She took Fran aside. "Have the families sit together and help guide them to the agents for interviews."

"What about the young men?"

"We know many are not directly involved in the criminal activities here. I'll go check on their building." She added, "It might take longer to secure their release, but we will do our best to identify the real perpetrators and clear the others."

Later that day she toured all the buildings, some hidden back in the woods. The lead agents from ATF and DEA, along with her staff, discussed the teams to collect evidence.

Once plans were made and Chris handed out their assignments, Will took her aside. "Time to go. You hit gold, girl, with that meth lab in the woods. You did good. Think you'll bump me for that promotion?"

"Don't even go there, Slick." She smiled. "This is what we do."

"Amen. See you back in the office."

"Maybe next week." Chris had booked a suite of rooms in a local hotel to keep tabs on the case. "Will, had I misunderstood your signal? I expected this tomorrow—did something happen?"

Will nodded. "Warrants came through late yesterday. Good thing too—we picked up chatter they knew about the raid. Thankfully, they thought it would not be today."

"Probably through the community center. Asa knew this was a risk. But we did it with no collateral damage."

By the end of the day, the last group had lined up for the bus. She followed it to the community center and entered the large open room. Asa sat at the registration table. He stepped around a few others. "It's happening. After all this time. Are they?"

Chris nodded. "Fran has a few surprises for you."

Asa didn't wait to hear. He ran forward, reaching out to Fran with open arms. "My love," he said.

Tears streamed down Fran's face. "I don't deserve you anymore. I..."

He drew her close. "You are completely forgiven." When Asa saw Heather, his eyes grew wide.

Fran wiped her face with the tissue Chris offered. "There's a lot to tell, but first, we have grandchildren."

Not wanting to intrude on their moment, Chris stepped back and surveyed the main room, looking for the director.

"Leia, no Chris, wait up." Fran pulled herself away. "Don't be a stranger. Do you have our address?"

"Yes."

"Drop by anytime so we can thank you properly."

"Of course." Chris turned toward the director making his way to her. She scanned her latest text messages. She had other teams to connect with and files to manage. It would be a long night—many of them.

CHAPTER 42

TOM NEEDED TWO more weeks to work through the boxes. Mark helped him make the deliveries in Unit 2, and Tom hand-delivered packages to Rick and Bob. Doug and a few others had items returned.

The next day Tom loaded his cart and followed the mail team to Building Three. The fine weather meant they could scoot across the sidewalks. The building was almost cube-shaped, squat and fat, as tall as it was broad.

The first walkway on the right hummed with sounds of rolling bars and many voices.

"Yo, choir boy, deliveries for Unit G?"

"This is a unit?" Tom looked up the left wall to see three tiers reach to the ceiling. Large fans above the hall rotated lazily, but Tom could still feel the spring heat through the windows.

"Yeah. Showtime." The resident pushed his cart after the lead officer, yelling, "Mail call."

The day officer pulled him aside. "Set up here," he nodded at a spot his desk.

Tom looked about. He didn't recognize anyone.

"Start shouting the numbers. They'll find you."

Tom picked up the first package. He heard an inmate shout, "Hey, he's got packages." A small stampede headed in his direction.

Tom repeated the number.

"What gives?"

"Getting your books back." Tom added, "The ones they collected last year."

"Oh," the inmate said as he pulled back the envelope. "Yeah, thanks."

A smaller number hung around Tom's cart once the rest realized it was not mail. He worked through the items for the unit and searched for the orderly to escort him to the next one.

He delivered to three of the eight units the first day. Tom wanted to begin with Len's unit, but he had to follow the mail carts.

He saw Unit L for the first time two days later. Len greeted him near the entrance. Several shook his hand and thanked him repeatedly for the books. He knew many of them but worked at putting names to the faces he had seen on Sundays. "No problem. So glad I could help," he stated.

Tom watched the mail cart go on to the next unit, but he hung back with Len and the others. He had time with only three packages for the last unit.

"You really did it," Len said. "I thought we'd never get them back."

"I have the list of books that didn't pass. It's been forwarded to the mailroom. I'll give you a list on Sunday. Let the guys know."

"Yeah, you okay with Curtis?"

"Doing fine." He saw the mail carts wrapping up at the last block. "Got to go. See you Sunday."

"Or in the yard," an inmate called out.

"Yeah, see you tonight, maybe."

Tom smiled. Thanks to the first session class he had a small group of men he called his Second Timothy 2:2 guys—"*and what you have heard from me in the presence of many witnesses entrust to faithful men who will be able to teach others also.*" They were men who loved the Word of God, had a good foundational understanding and were thirsty for more. They played ball in the yard while he taught them meat from the Word. Everyone had different cell blocks, jobs, and meal schedules, but could gather in the yard. It was the best solution he could find.

Officer Curtis emerged from his office shortly after Tom reported the next day. "66789, report, and shut the door."

Tom followed the officer in and placed his feet on the two yellow imprints painted in front of Officer Curtis' desk, "Yes, sir?"

"You delivering to Building Five?"

"Yes, things went well with Building Three. "

"Five's the blacks. Keeps the peace if we don't mix things up." Officer Curtis met his gaze. "You stay close to the mail crew. Don't wander off like you did in Three."

"Just for Len's unit."

"You don't know the difference between friend and enemy. They smile just the same." Officer Curtis leaned forward, "You're almost done."

Tom paused. "I could help Mark organize the inventory. Did that for my family's business when I was home."

Officer Curtis scrutinized Tom. His bloodshot, dark-rimmed eyes narrowed. He almost began to speak but sighed and placed the clipboard on the desk. "Sure. Have at it." He raised his eyebrows. "You're dismissed."

"I was thinking, after the studies are delivered, I could find a way to redact the Bibles."

"Go on."

"Make them legal." Tom explained Sam's loss of his grandmother's Bible.

"And how would you ID the ones willing to take a redacted Bible?"

"Send a letter. Each resident would have to make the request. Sam described his Bible. I'd like to get it to him."

"Next week," Officer Curtis coughed, "we can talk more about this." He looked at Tom, "That's it for now."

Tom turned to go. "Thank you, sir. L Block was happy to get their studies back."

Tom began to sort through the Bibles and pondered how to organize the boxes. It would take a while to find Sam's. A glance at the clock reminded him it was time to load the cart for Building Five.

Tom followed two other mail carts along the walkway to the mammoth concrete cube building with a large 5 above the main doors. He licked his lips, his mouth dry.

The main corridor led to a wide hallway. The center commons had several tables. The tiers rose three high. "This one block?" he asked the other inmate with a mail cart.

"Yep. Biggest units in Hannibal. Stay close."

Tom paused, waiting for mail call to begin. A small group hung out across the commons. His eyes shifted away. Large groups descended on the regular carts. In an instant he realized the small group had surrounded him.

"You the prison preacher we heard about?" an inmate said.

"Sure," Tom smiled back. "What's your name?"

"Riser," the tall black man nodded to the guy beside him. "This is Jordan, our preacher."

"Glad to meet you," Tom nodded. He noticed some of the inmates folding their arms. He began to call out the numbers. The single-item packages were on the top. Guessing Jordan would have more, he reached for the larger bundle. "What's your number, Jordan?"

"78345. I'm the other HCL dude in here."

Tom handed him the books. "Was it hard? Getting adjusted?"

"Been in before. I'm in here for 8. Prior convictions, you know."

Tom nodded. "Pulled 5." He picked up the next package and called out the number.

"Hey, line up, say your number. Give him space," Riser said.

Tom retrieved the packages for each inmate. He noticed the other carts getting ready to go to the next block and handed out the last few packages.

Jordan held the cart. "Saw you playing ball in the yard. We can do a quick game some night. Don't be shy."

"Good idea. I'll keep an eye out for you. I'd better keep up, or they won't let me do this again."

CHAPTER 43

THE WEATHER HELD for evening exercise, warm with a breeze making it past the high walls. Tom sauntered over to his group—Carl, Jerry, Rick, Bob and Owen. The ball Bob had was soft and mushy again. "Challenging our dribbling skills?" Tom joked.

"Late to the box gets the duds." Bob winked at Jerry, "Now if you could remember to fetch the ball when you first get here, we'd be sitting pretty."

"Had an invite to join a game," Tom said, nodding in the direction of the left center yard.

Owen peered over. Carl grabbed the ball. "Careful it's not a setup."

"It's not," Tom said and headed over. Jordan emerged from a group and led them to a small half court on the near side. Tom made the introductions.

Riser joined them, surrounded by two other tall inmates. "We talking or playing?"

Tom noted the easy way they dribbled and passed. He winked at Carl when they drew closer. "Usual?" he said with a smile.

"I'm ready."

Jordan whispered to Tom, "Riser's been in the NBA."

"Not surprised to hear," he replied, setting himself up just behind Riser and caddy-corner to Jordan. Carl hung out on the left side, Bob and Owen were in position. Riser and his group made two quick baskets.

Tom drew closer now that he had their rhythm. Owen blocked Jordan who passed the ball to Riser. Tom ran behind Riser as he dribbled

184 | Dorothy Gable

the ball behind his back. Tom's arm snaked out to snag the ball. He was three strides away and passed it to Carl before the other team could recover.

Large and full height, Carl dribbled and lobbed the ball. It swished into the basket. The game was on. They played hard, only losing by a few baskets.

"Good game," Riser said. "No jokes; they take the game serious here."

Carl nodded.

"Ready for drills?" Tom asked. Riser lobbed the good basketball in his direction. Tom caught it and dribbled two times before sending it to Owen. *"For the wages of sin is death..."*

Owen dribbled the ball, *"...but the free gift of God is eternal life in Christ Jesus our Lord."*[21] He sent it to Jordan, *"For by grace you have been saved through faith...."*[22]

Jordan smiled, dribbled the ball and finished the verse. He sent it to another in their group. *"'I am not ashamed of the gospel...'* yo, Sylvan, look sharp."

Sylvan furrowed his brow while he dribbled, circling the group, *"for it is the..."* He looked at Jordan.

"...power of God for salvation to everyone who believes."[23] He passed the ball to Tom.

"These your drills?" Riser asked.

"Our warmup," Tom replied. He nodded, "Call a drill."

"And if you don't know it?"

"We can learn."

Tom launched into his latest topic with Jordan joining in. When the end of recreation drew to a close, Tom asked Jordan, "Why don't you join us for first session on Sundays?"

"We study in our units. Now that we have our Bible studies back, we can get going again."

"You're welcome anytime."

Chapter 44

THE SUMMER DRAGGED on, growing more humid and oppressive each week. Third tier could be an oven, and tempers were growing short. Tom slipped in after a cold shower right before last stand-up count. Something caught in the back of his throat, but he didn't see anyone behind him. All seemed clear until he heard Wallie's nervous clicks. The hairs tingled on the back of his neck.

After count cleared, Tom moved to his locker and Wallie jumped into his bunk, but he couldn't settle.

"Wallie, what's up?" He stepped to the bars when Wallie swung down to pace.

He muttered, "Not good enough. Never good enough." He slapped his locker. Wallie's eyes were glazed with eyebrows drawn down. He looked at Tom. "Wrong book. Wrong Bible. Not good. Bad Wallie."

"What are you talking about?"

"They told me my Bible's not the real thing. I'm not a good Christian if I don't have a real Bible. But I can't have one like they have and bunk with you."

"Who's they?"

"They mad at Carl and Jerry too. Said it's all the Word of God. They got Bibles like Stan and I."

Tom nodded. "Listen, we can't keep everybody happy."

"Others say the same thing." Wallie nodded. "There's the green-edge Bible group and the KV—what's-it group. Some say you have to have other kinds." Wallie paced and muttered.

Tom stayed near the bars. He watched Wallie twitch. The blood pounded in his throat. He tried to sing softly. His racing pulse settled out, but Wallie didn't seem to hear. Tom clung to prayer. He couldn't do anything else. The hours dragged by.

"Wallie, let's go over your Bible reading for the day. I think we missed it."

Wallie thrust his head toward his locker but kept on pacing. He looked at Tom. His eyes gyrated, looking side to side.

Tom wet his lips. "Wallie, Jesus Christ saved you. He's not thrown you away. You can't listen to them telling you how you're supposed to follow God. Remember? *'The* Lord *is my shepherd...'*" he waited.

Wallie turned and said, *"I shall not want. He makes me lie down in green pastures."*

"He leads me beside still waters."

"He restores my soul." Tears ran down Wallie's cheeks.

Tom pulled out Wallie's Bible and held it open at Psalm 23. Wallie read the verses. "Why'd they do that? Why'd they say that? I thought they were Christians."

"We're saved but still broken and, in our brokenness, when we're not walking close to Christ, we can mess up. I know when other Christians attack us, it hurts bad, really bad, worse than anything. But we have to forgive them and pray for them. Some are fooled into thinking they're helping God."

They talked a little while longer and finally settled down to sleep in the early hours. Tom thrashed in his bunk. A deep anger rose up. He had to set things right and show them God's better path. He reviewed verses in his mind even after they separated and jumbled in the descent into sleep.

CHAPTER 45

THROUGHOUT THE DAY Tom worked on the message. It had to be quick and to the point, but the guys had to understand that attacking one another was not the right way.

More than his small group hung around during the ball time. Tom shoved away a small uneasiness rising in his chest. *Wasn't the good turnout a sign from the Lord this was the way to do it?*

Once through the usual Bible drills, Tom stepped back to the fence and faced the throng. His eye caught movement in the facing guard tower. Three guards were talking and looking his way. Small groups of officers hung out by the two closest gates. He shifted his eyes away when they turned their focus to his section of the yard.

He had to act. A rising anger overcame his hesitancy, and he raised his voice. Tom began with John 13:34-35 concerning the love for each other before reciting from 1 Corinthians 1. His raised his voice again with the increasing noise.

Tom paused to summarize his first main point when whistles sounded, and he spied movement from the left. A squad of officers rushed his group.

He noticed his friend's panicked looks. "Go on. Slip away. I'll take care of it." Tom approached the officers.

"What you doing?" they asked him.

"Just talking."

"Find the wall," the yard officer yelled. Several inmates were lined up next to Tom. Pairs of officers pulled them aside for frisking.

Tom heard their questions but couldn't quite hear the answers in the hubbub. He tensed when three officers approached him. He clenched his jaw and set his feet. Fighting back this time would spell disaster.

"He's clean," the tall guard said. He spun Tom around and pushed him to the linked fence. "You starting a riot? What's the plan?" He paused and looked at the head yard officer when the five-minute warning bell sounded.

The guard approached Tom. "Spill it. You called an unsupervised meeting. You started this."

Tom paused. "I did. Let them go." No time for excuses or explanations. He knew that could come later. He could not let the others take the fall. *We were only discussing the Bible. How is that wrong?*

An officer spun him around against the fence and pinned his hands behind him. He could see them releasing his friends in small groups. Tom breathed again once the yard was mostly clear. They marched him directly to Building Four.

The officers put him in a small spare room right inside the door and chained him to a chair bolted to the floor. The lead officer started the questioning. "So, you admit you called an unsupervised meeting. What you plotting?"

"There was no meeting. I didn't tell them to meet. I didn't call them over. We were just discussing something."

"Oh, so you lied back there? 'Fess up. What's the plan?"

"There is no plan. We were discussing something that came up."

"It'll go worse unless you 'fess up. Why'd you start a riot?"

"I wasn't starting a riot. Just needed to tell them something."

The questioning went around and around. Another officer stepped in. Tom recognized him from the yard. He leaned over; his breath thick in Tom's nostrils. "Be straight with us. You been gathering every evening for weeks now. What you telling 'em?"

"How to live for Jesus Christ." Tom stared at the wall.

"Who's supervising your meeting? Who's the sponsor?"

Tom shook his head. The rules for not congregating or holding a meeting without officer supervision couldn't apply to a group simply discussing God's Word.

The officer wet his lips, motioning the others to leave the room. He pulled up a chair and sat down.

"You do most of the talking. They answer questions you ask. You direct the conversation. This makes it more than just an average conversation in the yard. We been easy on you since Curtis vouches for you, but we can't have you preaching in the yard." He stared at Tom.

He swallowed and looked away. "I'm sorry. I didn't mean to break the rules."

"You'll plead guilty?"

"To what?"

"To leading an unsupervised meeting."

"No charges for the others?"

"No, just you. You'll sign off on that?"

"I will." He had tried to show he was not a criminal by keeping all of the rules. He had ignored the little warnings from the Holy Spirit, Carl, and some of the officers.

An hour later an officer put him in a temporary holding cell for the night.

CHAPTER 46

H E SIGNED THE papers the next morning, and an officer led him down the hall. The color in Tom's face drained away when Connors with three officers stepped forward.

"What's the sentence?" Connors asked.

"Ten days."

"Ten days? That's not what I recommended."

"Done deal. Meggars signed off on it."

"That changes things." Connors nodded to his squad. They marched Tom down the corridor through another set of doors to an old freight elevator.

The large doors rolled open, up and down. A clinking chain released the linked inner barrier. The box, suspended on cables reeking of oil and grime, swayed slightly with the squad's steps. It lurched up. Tom lost count of the levels.

They spun him around to the opposite doors. The gate swung up; the solid doors separated. Heat poured in. "Welcome to X Wing—the hole."

Tom said nothing as the guards had him remove his prison outfit but let him keep his underwear. The blood pounded in his chest. Connors emerged from a side room with his arms crossed.

"Button him up, tight."

Two stepped forward and put the hardware back on. With a word from Connors, they pulled off his socks and ratcheted the shackles tightly around his ankles.

"Make it short."

They cinched up the connecting chain, shortening his stride to less than half a step. Connors surveyed the progress, nodding or shaking his head. They fastened the belly chain high up Tom's chest. Tom held his breath, but the nudges and shoves forced an exhale, and they cinched it tighter.

Connors force-marched him to the range. The stench of open sewers brought tears to Tom's eyes, but he focused on placing one foot in front of the other in rapid succession to keep up—he needed two strides for each of the officers. Tom glimpsed three inmates peering from small, square windows in solid cell doors. He prayed for words of wisdom. Perhaps God could rescue something from this mess, but they marched down the range to another door—solid, black, marked with dents and scrapes. It creaked open. The stale air, mixing with the range, brought bile up the back of Tom's throat. Connors pulled out a key and unlocked a thick door.

"The box," Connors glanced Tom's way, a slight smile on his face. "No one can hear you—not your screams, not your religion, not your propaganda." He pulled it open, pushed Tom through and held him against hot concrete walls. Connors brought up his right hand, flicked a switch and pressed a small device against Tom's side.

Jolted by the shocking current, Tom tried to pull away, but the hot solid bricks held him close. He clenched his jaw, turning only his head to still the waves of pain.

"That little stunt you pulled with the agents. Don't think you can do whatever you want in here, golden boy. This is my house, my rules. Ten days." Connors spat on the ground. "I'll make it feel like half a year. I know you and what you are. You don't fool me even if you've wrapped Curtis round your little finger with your volunteering. You're a con." He leaned in with more jolts to Tom's side. "A criminal. You're all alike. There's no difference. Religion's just another scam. Well, you're not with the sheep you can swindle. No," he laid in again and again. "No one's going to hear your garbage or be corrupted by your book in here, so don't even try."

The moments slowed to a crawl. Tom focused on Christ and drawing breath between the jolts. An inner strength kept him silent. He tried not to draw comfort in Connor's displeasure.

The man leaned forward and spat in his face before he left, closing the doors behind him. The *thud, thud* of the heavy doors reverberated through his skull as he fell to his knees, gasping for air. Sweat poured from his face.

He had heard of the box. Visible from the yard, it hung out from the top floor of the building like a concrete coffin. Guys in the yard had talked about it.

Heat radiated from the concrete. No air moved. Tom tried to rise, pushing up as he rocked back on his feet. He arched back, but the belly chain bit into his sore sides. Panic rose as his breaths came quickly, gulping for air. One part of him knew he would lose consciousness if he couldn't regain control.

Wordless calls to the Father above welled up. *Deliver me. Deliver me.* He focused his mind. *O Jesus, deliver me.* In time his heart rate leveled off, his breathing slowed. Tom looked about in the gloom. A small bulb ten feet up, barely lit the corners; a few stray beams seeped through cracks in the aged walls. They didn't provide enough light to see by, but Tom could use it to track the days.

He walked about, testing the rough floor with his bare feet, staying away from the hole in the center. In a far corner, he found a small pile of dust and spread it out with his left foot. With his big toe he drew ten parallel lines. Each day he would put a bar across it to mark the days. He prayed again. He had no illusions. It would be a long ten days. Today was Friday. Sunday would be the tenth day, but no one was released from the SHU on a Sunday. He had to hold on through two weekends.

Little by little, he framed the time—how to sit, how to lie down and still rise, how to eat and meet his needs. Only ten days. He could do this, and then the hope slithered away.

Tom latched onto the book of Isaiah and started with chapter 6—Isaiah's vision of the throne room of God. In the heavenlies now. *Let me know this in my soul,* he called out wordlessly, knowing the Holy Spirit would fix his prayers.

As the heat intensified and his pain increased, he sensed something beyond words—a task from God. The edges of the command hovered just out of reach.

Tom managed to eat and drink from the water bottles provided. Sweat soaked his t-shirt and the material adhered to his back, making it harder to stand, but he managed to make it up for each count. Was it only midmorning? Yet light faded from the wall soon after.

Tom worked to still his rising pulse and rapid breaths. Buried alive, dying alone, terror of the darkness threatened to overtake him, but the words, *My God,* repeated in his mind—over and over. He knew Jesus would add the rest.

Moments passed. Tom woke, but no light peeked through the cracks in the wall. He closed his eyes again. Countless times, he rolled, repositioned, and stared at the wall. Eventually, light began to form. Tom rolled to the wall, braced his shoulders and pushed up with his legs. He hobbled over to his lines and drew his toe across—day one.

Two days later, Tom drank the water early in the day. The guards only brought bread and water two times a day although the timing seemed to vary. He knew he should ration it, but the heat grew so quickly, he began to long for the evening's chill. He looked at his lines, but his vision blurred. *Is the light fading?* Panic rose. *Have I lost track of the days?*

CHAPTER 47

BEADS OF WATER clouded his eyes. Tom jerked with the biting sting of water digging into his back. Cold water fell from above and ran around his prone figure. His eyes focused on pink streams among the colorless liquid swirling as it disappeared down a drain inches from his face. He noticed the raw marks on his left wrist.

He heard from behind him, "Is he coming around?"

"He's getting there." The sound of a faucet closing matched the streams of water lessening. Raging thirst overcame his nausea, and Tom rolled to suck up all the water he could before they put him back in the boiling box.

Hands pulled him aside and dressed him in dripping wet underwear. One part of his brain registered the fact this would keep him cooler for a brief time. His matted hair clung to his cheeks, but he could not clear his eyes. They put the chains back on, but Tom could feel they were not cinched as tightly this time.

"Where does he go?" Tom heard.

"The box."

"But, sir, the thermometer's broken, and the rules…"

"Stow it. He goes back in the box. That's an order."

By the time they marched him to the box, Connors was gone. His mind worked to remember what he was supposed to do, but his focus dissolved with the wall of heat engulfing him.

The evaporation cooled him for a short time. Again, he felt the heat overtake him as well as a growing rage. He couldn't get through this if he yielded. Searching about, Tom began to sing, "Thank You, Lord, for saving my soul. Thank You, Lord, for making me whole…" The tears fell, hot and burning, but the joy of the Lord enveloped him. Moment by moment, if he could keep his eyes on Christ, he could.

The next day Tom remembered his lines. *How long has it been? How many days have I lost?* He hobbled over but saw only scuff marks. He walked the perimeter and back to the wall where he thought they should be, but they were no more. Anger and rage tried to return.

"No," he said. "I will trust God. *'And this is eternal life, that they know you, the only true God, and Jesus Christ whom you have sent.'"*[24] Tom's mind wandered, but it returned to John 17 again and again. He did not know how many times he repeated the same phrase as he clung to the words.

A distant voice yelled, but Tom did not move. His mind tried to place the sounds with their meanings, but snakes slithered up the walls until he felt a blow, and he saw the officer.

"Eat your bread now."

Tom felt his thick tongue. "Water."

"Here."

He grasped the bottle and drank it all, feeling his cells open up with the moisture. He took the bread and nibbled on the edges.

"He still alive?"

"Yeah." The officer turned back. "You eat it all."

Tom stared. *What more can they do to me?* He said nothing but drank in the light pouring in from the open doors. A slight breeze worked its way in, and Tom leaned into the little blessing. The box was a few degrees cooler until the guards closed the doors, and it rose again.

That night heavy rains pounded and saturated the hot air. Tom felt like he was drowning. He stared in the dark, waiting for some light to appear, leaning on John 17, praying for God's glory to seep through his soul in the darkness.

<hr />

Beyond space and time, Tom felt the water clog his throat. He rolled and gagged, spitting out vomit and phlegm. Like the first time, he stepped from the shower and put on damp underwear, but Connors stayed watching.

Tom looked at him. "I forgive you," he said.

The young officer jeered and mocked, but Connors stared at him before walking away. The officer replaced the hardware as tightly as the first day. He yanked the belly chain. Tom sucked in the stabbing pain and focused on remaining upright.

Once back in the box, he leaned his ear against the outer wall. The vibrations of the yard in summer during evening exercise seeped through. His mind filled in the images between the sounds. Each one who came to his mind brought along a list of prayer requests. Tom's thirst to share the living Word of God and make a difference rose up.

His reality set in. *How can I go forward?* His 2 Timothy 2:2 group lived in different units, never saw one another in the dining hall and worked different jobs. He shifted left. *How can I continue to teach them without breaking the rules?*

Tom rose and paced to try to settle his nerves, but the shackles cut into his ankles, leaving a thin trail of blood. He jerked aside when the door came open. Tom sucked in the slightly cooler air that flowed in. The guard called him out. He turned, focused on not falling, and lifting one foot after the other, inched forward.

"Against the wall."

Tom turned his head to keep his nose from being slammed into the wall, but the officer pushed gently. He breathed out in relief when the belly chain came off and the shackles were removed.

"Turn around. Now," he leaned in, "you behave, and we can make it through the night. I'll bring more water and a meal. You eat it. I'll leave the outer door open unless you get noisy, understand?"

"Yes, sir, and thank you." Tom walked back into his cell and heard the officer close only the barred door allowing a slight breeze from the fan at the end of the range.

The officer returned with the provisions and clean socks. "Today's Sunday. You'll get a shower before you're released tomorrow."

Tom nodded. The officer left the range before Tom could thank him again. Even this little bit of mercy and kindness brought tears to his eyes. He almost felt as if the Lord was telling him, "I have a plan," but Tom could see only darkness.

"I will trust You, Lord," he said and tried to sleep.

CHAPTER 48

MONDAY DRAGGED ON. It seemed as if it must be time for mail call, but judging the time was impossible. The other officer arrived and marched him to a changing room with no shower. His uniform was dirty and torn. After protests, the officer arranged for another set.

The officer took him down to the first floor, placed a pass in his hand and opened the door to the yard.

Tom stared at the sky and breathed in fresh air. A few inmates worked pigeon detail, scrubbing white blotches from the walkways and paved yards. A bored officer walking his rounds looked at him and seemed to head in his direction before heading to Building Five.

Tom identified the gate to his building and stepped out—relishing the stretch of full strides. The sun beat down, his mouth was dry, but he kept at it one step at a time.

A little hunger nibbled his belly, but it dissolved when he spied the day officer's desk and Officer Ganse bending over his reports. "Pass," he said without looking up.

Tom handed over the slip of paper.

Officer Ganse stared at the bony arm and looked up. "You're back." He studied Tom's gaunt face. "So, the rumors were true. You learn your lesson?"

Tom nodded. "Can't go back to the yard for a while." He wet his lips. "Any changes I need to know about? Still in 60 with Wallie? Still working for Bruce mornings?"

"That's your caseworker's business. You need to get square with him."

Tom nodded.

Ganse pulled up the paperwork on his tablet. "Everything's in order. You know, they won't go as light on you next time." He slipped the pass in the day's lockbox. "You look like death and stink like the hole. Clean up."

Tom turned toward the left staircase. He saw Bruce stride in with three others. *Was it that late already?* He nodded at Bruce and would have continued on, but Bruce thrust his chin toward his cell. Tom rotated and followed Bruce to his house.

They stared at each other across the small metal desk bolted to the side wall. Bruce shook his head. "You look terrible. In the box? Kept the door shut the whole time?"

Tom nodded. "Except for last night." He looked away as Bruce cursed and swore.

Bruce leveled his finger at Tom. "You got to report this."

"I forgave him."

"Okay, you forgave him, but you have to file a report." Bruce leaned forward, "This isn't the first and won't be the last time, and rules say no one in the box when it's too hot. It was blazing hot all week." He leaned back. "How many times they pull you out?"

Tom raised two fingers. He waited for Bruce's tirade to end. "I forgave him. I said it to his face. That settles it."

"No, that doesn't settle it." Bruce wagged his finger. "You don't report him, and he kills someone else in there, that's on you."

"No, that's on him." Tom leaned forward. "Believe me, Bruce, God can take care of Connors." He sat back. He hadn't intended to name his persecutor, but Bruce probably already knew.

"Oh, really? Your God's so great and mighty He can reach down and stop Connors from abusing and killing inmates? You ready to bank on that?"

"I am."

"You're an idiot." Bruce began another tirade.

Tom rose and started to leave.

Bruce coughed and stood up. "Still glad to see you made it even if you're an idiot. Better get a shower or not even Wallie'll want to bunk with you."

Tom nodded and headed up the three tiers, his mouth dry and legs like rubber. Few were about. He could take his time. He doubted he'd have the energy to go down and back up for supper. First, he needed water, a shower, and then his bunk. Maybe he could get a better night's sleep.

Once clean and in a fresh set of clothes, he sat on his stool and leaned against the wall. Everyone else would be arriving soon—stand-up count, mail call, supper—which he decided to skip. He resisted the urge to lie down. Tiredness came in waves, his sides ached, the cuts on his ankles and wrists stung, and it was still hot in the third tier—but not as hot as the box.

Wallie walked in just before count. "You're back! My bud's back!" He rushed in and stopped by the first stool, taking in Tom's sunken, darkened eyes; pale face; and translucent skin outlining his bones. He sat down on his stool. "We prayed for you—that you'd make it." He turned when Stan stuck his head in after a polite knock on the outer upright.

"Hi, Stan," Tom said to Stan's retreating back. He smiled at Wallie. "I could feel your prayers. They made a difference." Stan returned with a small package of nuts and an orange.

"Thanks, Stan. That'll help."

"We prayed for you every day." Stan added, "We couldn't lose you. You know that, don't ya?"

Tom nodded.

"Every minute of every day," Wallie said.

Tom smiled. "Knowing you were all pulling for me made a difference." He wet his lips. His mind shifted to what to say, not wanting to break the rules again.

Stan scattered when Bruce called count.

After count Tom looked at Wallie perched on the edge of the bunk staring at Tom. "Any news? Classes go okay?"

Wallie smiled. "I help the others." He rattled on about the latest member of the unit and the ones who transferred out. Tom nodded and tried to listen. *It's good to be back in my place with my bunkie.*

The gang appeared—Owen, Rick, Bob, Stan and Cecil. Rick handed Tom a chocolate candy bar.

Tom's eyes brightened as he consumed it. "I never thought of chocolate as good food. Didn't realized I had sold it short. Thanks."

"When you filing the report?" Rick asked.

Tom explained. "God told me to forgive him, and I did. It's done. Can't take it back." They tried to argue. "Listen, guys, God calls us to forgive."

"But that crosses the line."

Tom listened to their arguments, but the call to line up for supper cut it short. He hung back.

Owen said, "Better come. Don't start skipping meals or they just might force-feed you, and that's no fun."

Tom waited until everyone else was gone. He looked at Wallie, "Can I make it down and back?"

"Yep, I got your back."

Tom nodded. He took it slow and ate lightly. As soon as he returned to his house, he brushed his teeth and started to lay down. He needed real sleep, and the few hours when many were in the cooler yard might be the quietest hours of the evening. Bob walked in without a knock and sat down on the outer stool.

"Got some nerve not backing us up. Lots of guys hurt bad and never get it back. The warden and the officers listen to you. Meggars'll believe you. Don't you think God wants you to stand up for us?"

Tom moved to his stool and looked him in the eye. "What if the kindness and mercy of God in the face of evil is the way to demonstrate God's love? I'm not God. I don't know everything, but I do know God had something for me to do. Every day, even during the worst days when I could barely string words together, I knew God had something for me to say. And when the time came, He gave me the words and the strength to say them. Connors heard it." Tom shook his head. "The weapons of our warfare are not of this world. We're not fighting guards or other inmates, but the powers of darkness. They're just captive pawns. If we understand the guards without Christ are prisoners to Satan and sin, pray for them and forgive them, they might come to know the peace of God."

Bob listened without arguing.

"When we become a Christian, we experienced peace with God, but it shouldn't stop there. We can have peace with others when we forgive, especially those who have hurt us the most. When we can be thankful to God for everything, we can begin to rest in His love and grace. That's when the chains of bitterness and anger can be cast off."

"Some things are just too hard to forgive."

Tom nodded. "I know it's hard, and God calls us to do things we can't do of ourselves. Believe me, I've wrestled with the anger, raging at God for putting me here and taking away everything." He sucked in his breath. "I'm never going to have a family, a normal life, or pastor a church—not after this. But I have to trust God knows what He's doing, and, in the end, He'll take me to His heaven." The words caught in his throat. The memory of coming to on the shower floor in X Wing was too raw.

Wallie entered shortly after Bob left.

Tom perched, unmoving, on his stool, staring at his bunk. "Hey, dude. Why am I so tired?"

Wallie shook his head. "Just the way of things." He studied Tom's lowered head and sunken eyes. *"To live is Christ...."*

"To die is gain."[25] Tom met his gaze.

"To live is Christ. Choose life, Tom. We need you here. That's why God hasn't taken you yet. It's just not your time."

Tom's leaden gaze slid away. "I will. I'm trying." He looked at Wallie, cast aside and locked away by society, life, cruel happenstance and neglect, yet rescued, redeemed, and made new in Christ. His eyes filled with tears. "I am glad I met you."

"I'm not ready to let you go. I need you. Can you make it?"

Tom nodded. "In Christ, if I can stay sane in Him, yeah." He stared at the ceiling, remembering why he had ended up in the box. Tom said softly. "But I decided to teach in the yard. That's on me. How do I teach my guys and keep their rules?"

Wallie started to speak, then shut his mouth. "Talk to Curtis tomorrow. You don't have to do it all on your own, Buddy. Come on. Last count's coming up."

Tom reported for work the next morning. He walked past a glaring Bruce to the kitchen officer. "You up for this?"

Tom nodded. He walked back to his sink. The only evidence he'd been gone was a slight covering of dust on the sideboards. The racks weren't as full as he had expected. He turned when Bruce walked up.

"Officer's making them pull their own weight. We gonna work you out of a job, and you can hang with your wishy-washy Christian buds all day in the office."

Tom didn't respond. Bruce was looking for a fight, and he wasn't willing to tussle. He found his next item and filled the tub.

It was good to be back, but a helpless dread would not go away. He longed to see his group grow in Christ. *How can I do it?*

"You a zombie now?" Todd asked, laughing when Tom jumped.

"No, but you got me." He turned and leaned against the counter.

Todd made a face. "How you survive that? It was blazing hot all week."

Tom wet his lips. "Guess it wasn't my time. The first time they pulled me out, I was disappointed I was still in X wing and not in heaven."

"You're really not afraid to die, are you?"

He studied Todd. "Not much of a contest—heaven or Hannibal. Just got to live through it day by day."

CHAPTER 49

MARK LOOKED HIM over when he walked in. "Go on in. He's waiting for you."

Tom drew a breath and prayed for strength. When he stepped into the office, Curtis pointed to the chair against the desk and pushed a cold orange juice toward him.

"Thanks."

Curtis eyed him closely and pulled out a form.

"What's this?"

"Make a report. You got the goods on him. It's the right thing to do."

Tom set the paper down. "Normally, I would, but I can't. God told me to forgive him, and I did."

Curtis nodded. "Well, then, what's the plan?"

Tom sighed. "I don't have a clue. I tried to keep the rules, but it's hard when you don't know you're breaking 'em until after the fact."

"You were warned. Thought you were smarter than that. What's the plan?" Curtis met his gaze. "When, besides the yard, are the guys together?"

"Never, not..." Tom narrowed his eyes. "Sunday, but I teach the class."

"There can be two. Delegate. Who takes your entry-level class so you can teach the advanced? Carl ready?"

"Jordan. He'd been mentored by a good pastor."

"Breaking the color barrier. Think the guys are up for it?"

"Sure. We've been doing it in the yard."

Curtis laughed. "And boy, the officers didn't like that. Made 'em nervous. That's not the only group ticked either."

"I tell the guys this week?"

"Already told 'em." Curtis sat back with a smile. He passed a list across the desk. "There's your advanced class. What'd you call your guys?"

"My second Timothy 2:2 group—the ones who are open, honest, and thirsty to learn about God and His Word."

Tom studied the names. He glanced at the officer. He scanned the names. "Bob and Matt?"

"Bob's making progress. He knows it. Just needs help connecting the dots."

"Matt can't say three words without cursing, and that includes reading from the Bible." Tom shook his head. He left unsaid Matt's critical spirit, sharp tongue, and the fact he dreaded working for the guy when he had to help serve the line.

"He's a diamond in the rough." Curtis leaned back. "You think I picked this ministry when I went to seminary? Back in the day, I was like Matt, thinking I had all the answers—telling everyone else how to live." He sat forward. "It took a patient, godly officer to show me the way. Don't take his guff; let him know your expectations, but don't give up on him. The growth starts when they find Christ. I think Matt's ready."

Tom nodded. "Pray for me. I'm going to need it."

Curtis nodded. "I think you're ready. What were you so fired up that had to be said in the yard?"

"Wallie nearly killed me the night before the incident. After all the Lord's done here, the guys started dividing over their Bibles." Tom described Wallie's complaint. "I was so mad, I felt I had to do something about it."

Curtis nodded. "When'd you go off the rails?"

Tom blew out his lips. "You know the Bible's really true." He laughed and shook his head. "The wrath of man never produces the righteous-ness of God."[26]

"Never does—even when we think it will."

"Knew I wouldn't have much time, so I went right to 1 Corinthians 1 and 3—I'm of Paul, I'm of Apollos."

"That's it? Could you get a sermon out of it?"

"Sure. Had ten days to think about it. I would begin with that but move on to the kind of love God calls us to have for one another—John 13:34, I Corinthians 13. Then wrap up with reminders of what God's done for us and why we're here."

"All right, you preach this Sunday."

"Really? You'd let me have your pulpit?"

"Yep, and if you do okay, I'll put you down as my relief pulpit sup-ply. You square?"

"Yeah, that's great."

"Now, Wallie's doing great in the reading class. He's a natural teach-er and knows how to help others who are struggling. Think he'd want a job doing that? He'd have to give up his maintenance work for Officer Nivens."

"He'd love it. He's always complaining about not having a paying job. Last night, he kept talking about how great it was God could use him to fix people. Said it was better than fixing machines."

"You'd work for him from time to time, help with the SHU visits. You handle that?"

"Sure. He knows how to talk to the guys. He's right for the job."

"Good. It's settled. Mark'll finish processing the order, and we'll let it filter through his case manager. Not a word to Wallie."

Tom nodded.

"You have a desk now. Work on your sermon, and then you can get back to the Bibles." Curtis pulled out a memo. "Warden signed off on your Bible redaction idea. I'll review your letter, and you identify inmates who might want their Bibles back."

"And the ones not claimed, where do they go?"

"The recycling center," Officer Curtis looked away; his brows knit together. He wiped his forehead and turned his chair to stand.

Tom rose. "Thank you, sir, and if there's anything I can do for you…"

"Yeah, I'll keep it in mind."

CHAPTER 50

THEY CELEBRATED IN their cell after lights out the day Wallie accepted a paying job working for Curtis in the Chaplain's Office. Wallie split a soda, and Tom shared some of the chips and candy the guys had given him. Warm air surrounded them as they huddled over the small metal desk.

Wallie leaned back, dim light catching his smile. "I have a job."

"Going to lose your indigent status. Can you live with that?'

Wallie shook his head, sending his hair twirling. He wiped his eyes and sat back. "God's real awesome."

"The awesomest."

"The awesomest awesomest."

Calls for them to be quiet floated up the range and along the tier.

"Now they want us to shut up?" Wallie rose and broke into song. He paused. "I'm not going to let them ruin it." Wallie flung himself on the stool. Knitting his brow, he said, "After all, they keep us up listening to their songs and cussing."

"And you know what that feels like." He matched Wallie's gaze.

"All right. I get it." Wallie walked to the bars. "Hey, just wanted to share my joy in the Lord! He gave me a job today. Me, Wallie! And if He can do something with me, I know He can do something with you."

Catcalls flew up. "How long you think He's gonna put up with you?" "What's really different now?"

Wallie looked back at Tom, smiling. "Help me out here." He turned back. "'I can do all things through Christ who strengthens me.'[27] "How's that? That's what's different. I am a new creation in Christ Jesus, the one true Lord and God and King of kings and Lord of lords. And if you think you can avoid Him by spitting on Him down here and hiding out in hell, well, guess what? Everyone, and I mean everyone, will bow to Him as the awesomest, most wonderful Lord of the universe. That's right. The very God you despise and fight against is going to judge you and sentence you to hell. You know what's better? He made a way for us to be with Him in heaven. That's one promise I can bank on."

Wallie leaned back against the wall. "I got it right?"

Tom smiled. "You sure did."

"Anyway, thanks for listening, 'cause if you're yelling at me, I know you are listening. Just want to say I'll be praying for you tonight. And praise God for His great love because He is the only One who can rescue you."

Wallie and Tom sat at the inner end of the lower bunk, sharing verses, stories and praising God. The catcalls died away, and the block settled down with the night.

Tom turned his ear to the hard wall. "It's quiet. If I pressed my ear to the outer wall in the box, I could feel the crickets. Even heard an owl a few times." Tom leaned back, blinking away a few tears.

"Even though I'm never getting out of here and don't deserve to, I still never get over wanting to be outside, like walking in a field or splashing through a stream." He patted Tom's knee. "But that makes heaven even better."

"Sure does."

CHAPTER 51

C URTIS SQUINTED AT the page, took off his glasses, wiped his brow and cleaned the lenses before putting them back on. He looked at Tom over the top of the pages.

"Would it help if I printed it instead?"

"No, it's legible enough, just," he laid them down and glanced at a pile of pages clipped together and jutting out from the top of his in-basket. "Got SHU interviews to complete for Admin—medical, stuff from their caseworkers, and still not ready with the program report. Warden's also asking for next year's schedule." He handed the top pile to Tom. "You and Mark know what to do. I think you two can handle it. I'll have a decision on this when you get back."

He watched Tom rise and take the papers. "Remember—don't lose track of the time. Oh, Tom, one more thing. The officers supervising the Sunday classes and morning service are doing it for the overtime. I deliberately pick 'em," Curtis smiled, "so they end up having to listen. Anyway, you'll probably recognize some of them from your time in the SHU last week. You good?"

"Absolutely. Thanks for the heads up."

Sunday came quickly. Tom pulled his sheet from his pocket—a sketchy outline for his first advanced class. In the yard it'd been informal questions between half-hearted basketball drills or short games. He had to admit he'd not really followed a list of topics but began with a question he had been thinking about that day. Their answers, or non-answers, picked the route, sometimes revealing the destination in a few moments. Now it was one class a week—he had to make it count—with a different mix of guys. Often Jordan had kept the conversation going or suggested a fresh topic when the pace lagged. He prayed the new mix of guys would get along.

The desk chairs were in neat rows. Owen followed him in, and they pulled the first few rows into a circle. Tom picked up his notes and nodded at Carl who stood by the desk near the door, handing out approved Bibles.

The guys drifted in, some arriving as the final movement bell sounded. The hum from the air conditioner filled the quiet room. Tom sat last. He ignored the officer standing with crossed arms by the door, making this officially sanctioned. The officer, who had worked X-Wing, avoided his gaze.

"Thank you for your prayers. I could feel them when I was in there." He nodded at Carl, "Please open us up in prayer."

After Carl, Tom said, "This is our first official class, so let's introduce ourselves with a brief testimony how Christ found us. Owen?"

"Cornered us is more like it." Light laughter floated in the sun's rays and mixed with the dust in the air. Owen glanced to the side. "I thought I could talk anyone into doing anything, and I did."

Everyone nodded. Tom listened to the ultimate con-artist describe his marks and his biggest wins. The handsome man with brilliant blue eyes, black wavy hair, an athletic build, easy smile, and silken voice always charmed. His face fell. "But it was so hollow. I took and never cared. Always had to be on the lookout for what others would con out of me. There was no love, and the fancy clothes, jewels and cars could vanish in an instant. I started over so many times." He described his arrest and the shock of prison. "And I didn't just have to mess up to land in prison. No, I had to do it, so I'd end up in a federal prison. That's a whole different level."

"I can't take all day. At Oklahoma, you've all been there." Everyone nodded. "They say everyone goes through Oklahoma, you just look at the guys locked in that little space with you and know it's all over. God got a hold of me before I could find the exit—and you all know what I mean. For the first time in my life, I was ready to listen. Found a Bible course and read it. Knew I'd found the truth. I read the Bible cover to cover before I made it out of A&O."

Everyone thanked him for sharing. Tom nodded at the next resident who gave a brief version of his salvation. Some were longer than others. Carl's was by the book, hitting all the main points: knowledge of sin, understanding hell would not be a fun party place, God's offer and his acceptance. His was a little distant, but they all thanked him. Bob shared a brief version, naming the course he had taken when he surrendered to Christ. Everyone looked at Matt.

"Yeah, all the same—we're bad, God's good, I accept it, I acknowledge I need a higher power to live right and learning good habits so I can do it better this time." He stared at Tom.

"Thank you, Matt. With Christ as we yield to Him, we can." His reply felt lame. A gulf lay between them. Tom relaxed when the next one shared his story. Then it was his turn.

"I guess you could say I was a goody two shoes. Did what Mom and Dad said, worked at the store, earned good grades." He leaned back. "I didn't even have parking tickets or library fines." Laughter filtered through the room. Tom described his salvation, the cost to go to Bible college, the change in his uncle and his moving back home when the college closed. "Honestly, I didn't have a clue what was going on. Things were quiet. I slid right in as if I had never left, but inside God was whispering a change was coming." Tom licked his lips. "God called me to shepherd other believers. Always thought it meant a nice little church with a nice family—like some of my friends." He looked at the group. "I never regret having a chance to share and live Christ with all of you. And that's why we're here. When we get saved, God could whisk us up to heaven, but He leaves us here to touch others. He allows us the privilege to share this message. Just saying it is not enough. We have to live it. If it doesn't work for us, how can we expect them to buy in? Who knows 2 Peter 3:15?"

Owen recited the verse.

"Look at the context—its neighborhood, the surrounding verses. Carl, please read verses 13 through 16." They had a few moments left before the 10 a.m. bell. "Think about the topics you'd like to cover and bring your list next week."

Tom felt the folded paper in his pocket outlining his upcoming sermon. He prayed he would let God work through him. He couldn't imagine doing it alone.

Curtis was standing before the raised platform in the auditorium when Tom followed Wallie to a seat. The officer motioned him to come forward. "You ready?"

"As ready as ever. Been over it a number of times, but you never know what God's going to do." The worship band started the service. Tom licked his dry lips. He had to get it right this time.

After Officer Curtis' prayer and a brief introduction, Tom walked up three worn steps to a narrow podium. His single sheet refused to lay flat. Tom scanned the sea of faces. His mind went blank. All his opening remarks vanished.

He prayed aloud for guidance, direction and faithful representation. "God draws us to Himself with the cords of His love. Little by little if we accept, He shows us more until we understand who we are—wretched, utterly lost and alone in our sin. And He still loves us, reaches out to us so we can be one with Him. One day, for some, we will surrender our lives to Him so we can have His life flowing through us. Not of ourselves, but all of Him. And we owe Him everything.

"He chooses to keep us here to share this wonderful message with others—that a loving God cares for us. We can't hold it back. On Jesus' last free night on earth, He said our sign to the world is our love for our brothers in the Lord. He commands us to love one another, not the old way—a hit for a hit. Not even as we love ourselves, but as He loved us and gave Himself—He died for us. That's a whole new level of love we can't do on our own. But we can with God's help." Tom recited John 13:34-35.

"The apostle Paul wrote a letter to the believers in Corinth who had forgotten how to love one another. They were dividing into groups and quarreling."

He recited 1 Corinthians 1:10-12.

"I heard some of you are dividing over the Bible a brother has. What should we do if we see a brother stumble? Warn him? Yes. Attack him? No! We help him in love. For how we love others, especially our brothers in the Lord, fair or not, is a reflection to this world of God's love. He calls us to love one another as He loved us."

Tom walked through 1 Corinthians 13. "Love is patient, kind, not jealous or envious, proud or rude. Love seeks the other's benefit over our own. Can we live this kind of love here? Can we? With God's help, with the Holy Spirit leading us, we can.

"For if we do not, we are no different from the others. We can expound on the Bible and dazzle others with our brilliance. We can have the best voice and delight people with our music. We can do great works, but if we have not love, we are nothing—what we do is nothing. Love first, the rest follows. Yes, we can warn, but in love—speak truth with love."

He was running out of time. He touched on the spiritual battle—in the spiritual realm. And the call to do in love the good deeds God lays before us.

His final glance rested on Matt—the one he avoided. When in the kitchen, if he saw Matt, he went the other way. He knew he had to show the love he had just described to Matt in the kitchen.

CHAPTER 52

C HRIS FOLLOWED U.S. District Attorney Russell, the lead prosecutor, into the conference room for the federal district detention center. The final holdout would be brought down shortly. She
was there as a favor to Attorney Russell. She glanced at the aide who
positioned her at the end of the table. If necessary, she would say her
piece. If not, she would get one last look at Hawsley.

Three guards escorted him directly to a lone seat across from the
prosecutor. He'd managed to slick back his hair and was clean-shaven,
but his suit was a full set of chains over an orange jumpsuit. Hawsley
surveyed the lawyers set against him and the woman he had met as
Leia. He stumbled but detected no hint of mercy in her eyes.

Chris met his gaze. She turned her attention to the prosecutor
when he opened the session. They were here to convince the man that
his best interests lay in signing a deal and avoiding a public trial. Earlier recordings had shown him defiant and eager for a public forum to
showcase the persecution of Christians in America and to warn of a
coming apocalypse. One part of her hoped he was ready to deal. The
other almost welcomed the public flogging he would receive with his
sins publicly portrayed for the nation to see.

When the prosecutor presented the deal, Hawsley almost smirked.
She watched the prosecutor, a career professional hardened by dealing
with many criminals, maintain his neutral gaze. Eventually, he nodded
in her direction. Sitting at the end of the long table, far from the defen-
dant, she rose holding a slim file.

"Mr. Hawsley, where are your attorneys? With your assets you could not retain even one?"

He glanced at her sideways, not granting her the honor of his full attention. "You, Ms. Worden, are well aware all assets have been seized."

"Yes, because your case rose to the level of racketeering, also known as RICO." She stepped closer.

"Your HCL laws created this monster, Leia." He looked her full in the face. "You engaged in deception; your office entrapped me." His voice almost descended to a whine.

She resisted the urge to smile. "Mr. Hawsley, I understand you wish to send a message to the citizens of our country with your trial—that your group was driven to these crimes."

"You have outlawed our faith and trampled our First Amendment rights. You are closing churches and sending pastors to prison to die. You do it quietly with your backroom deals so this debacle can continue out of the public eye."

She would not debate that point. "When it comes to matters of faith, Pastor, people look at the totality of the evidence. Perhaps if we had violently shut you down as you printed the Holy Scriptures or performed other acts of faith or if we had lined up your followers and shot them, perhaps you might gain some public sympathy. However, that is not how we conducted our operation and not what we found at New Hope Retreat."

She continued with her opening salvo. "Minimal force was employed on our part; your hostages were rescued without harm. We found illegal weapons," she displayed the glossy photos showcasing the grenades, launchers and heavy armament. "We found 500 pounds of top-grade marijuana," a glossy photo slid across the table, "one hundred grams of meth," she produced two more photos, "and a meth lab hidden in the woods…" Chris leaned forward, "putting your members at risk. All of these violations of the law will be paraded before the public—every gram, every round, and every sexual victim you drugged and raped."

Chris paused, her face a hard mask. "I don't think you will raise any sympathy at all, but instead add to the damage you have already brought to the name of Jesus Christ—whom you claim to represent."

The leering gaze and his rank perusal of her form in her suit made the hair tingle at the base of her neck. Her eyes locked with his. "I don't have to show you photos of the women ready and willing to testify of their evenings in your suite." A glossy fell to the table and slid before him. "The ketamine, your date rape drug of choice, as well as those willing to testify of members who died at your ranch due to lack of medical care…" She splayed an array of pictures of the graveyard by a pair of oak trees. She leaned on the table. "for all the world to see, to hear, and to know what you are really all about, Mr. Hawsley."

She straightened, letting her denunciatory words sink in. "Mr. Hawsley, the deal takes into account the gravity of your offenses but is measured to give you a chance to repent." Chris froze with the look on his face. To distract him from her poor choice of words, she faced the lead attorney. "U.S. District Attorney Russell, please state the years he could be serving if the jury finds him guilty of all counts."

"About three hundred years."

She tilted her head. "That's multiple life sentences. Yet, the offer on the table today is fifty years with a possibility of early release for good behavior with participation in selected programs as outlined in this deal. Think about it. This deal will only be on the table for a short time. If all goes well, you could be a free man someday." She resumed her seat. "Or you may face the full wrath of the court and the judgment of a jury of your peers." She deferred to the prosecutor who walked through his final summation of the deal.

Hawsley looked at his hands and took a breath, staring out the window. He asked, not looking at anyone in particular, "Will I be permitted to make a public statement?"

"You are required to recite your crimes and your acceptance of the deal in district court. You may make a statement at that time."

"I accept."

Chris wanted to ask how a Christian could have betrayed his faith and how he could, in good conscience, consider he had served God with his actions. But she couldn't. The question could not be asked while appealing to him to take a deal. Now she could not bear the thought of having to be in the same room with him. At least they were spared the grueling months of work to prepare for trial—one she was confident they would have easily won.

She stayed for the formalities. The court date was set. The only thank you was a brief nod from the lead prosecutor. She knew by reputation the gesture was high praise indeed.

The letdown after a big case concluded, especially with no jury trial, sucked her dry, leaving her bone-weary in the middle of the day. The drive back to the office would take at least an hour. With no other required tasks apart from informing her team of Hawsley's deal, she headed for the Shirrings. They deserved to know there would be no public trial. She assumed they would be relieved not to have to face him and maybe answer her question: how could a Christian do what Hawsley had done?

CHAPTER 53

THAT AFTERNOON CHRIS submitted the final paperwork for her transfer, and Kincaid signed off on it. She had anticipated he would not make any effort to convince her to stay. No one at the office had a hint of her plans. She was almost done with the Task Force.

The next day followed as the rest. She reviewed her open cases, not too many anymore as her direct supervisor gave more to the other agents. Promotion and awards would be presented at one that afternoon in the third-floor conference room—the upper rooms of Kincaid's inner circle.

Chris opened an email from Otis' assistant. It was an invitation to the event. She suspected Will was behind this. Chris texted back when he asked if she would come. She'd go for his sake but suspected what was coming. She had done a good job and didn't need anyone's congratulations.

A large sheet cake dominated the center of the long mahogany conference table pushed to the front of the top floor conference room. The bank of windows overlooked a pond with lilies, geese and swans, surrounded by acres of grass bordered by flowering bushes. Chris had assumed few from her lower level would be in attendance, but she spied several agents from her division.

She stepped back, watching to see who stood next to whom. Will entered with three others in tow, joking lightly. Thankfully, she was at the other end of the room and made no move to join him. Instead, he purposefully walked over to stand by her side. "Are you sure you want to be seen with me?"

"What? The hero who talked Hawsley into signing his deal?" Chris lifted her eyebrow.

Otis and Barrie shadowed Kincaid as he headed to the front of the room; agents and staff stepped aside. The man's suit had a military cut, his hair high and tight, his bearing ramrod straight.

"You all know that I'm former Marine." He looked about the room. "Some even still call me Major Kincaid." He puffed out his chest. "When Marines promote, they do it right." A few voiced "hoorah!" Kincaid accepted the compliment and pointed in their direction.

"While we are no longer military, we are still in the service—the public service." He looked about the room with pride. "The talent I see here, the aggregate years of serving our country—and I know you all could be making more in the private sector—humbles me. That is why I am going to recognize your achievements and honor your promotions."

He nodded to his executive secretary in high-heeled pumps and a tight skirt. She brought the first envelope. "In recognition of your service, dedication, and passing of the qualifying exams," he added the last bit with a smile and paused for the laughter, "I promote the following agents to Task Force Agent." He read off the names. One by one, they walked forward, accepted their new name badge and a small envelope. Kincaid ran through four more promotions. He paused.

"And for the acknowledgment of closing the Hawsley Case and outstanding performance overseeing our Investigations Unit," he looked about the room, passing over Chris to Will. "I promote Investigations Manager, William Masters to Assistant Executive Director of the HCL Task Force. Assistant Executive Director Masters, please step forward."

Everyone clapped. Chris set her face. He would fit the role well. She was glad Cooper had not received it. She barely heard Kincaid's remarks.

The secretaries cut the cake and handed out the party favors. Chris took a small piece and turned to leave.

"Chris," Will called to her, "our favorite place, a little later, perhaps sevenish?" She paused at the door and watched him draw near. "I have some things I want to ask you. This will work out for both of us."

She couldn't refuse him. "Of course—seven then." She wouldn't call it a date; they were just friends, nothing more.

Their favorite Italian restaurant, nestled in a small strip mall, served bread made daily with grains from the fields of Italy, sweet Italian sausage, lasagna and the sweets to go with them. Chris arrived a few minutes late and was surprised to have the waiter seat her at the back booth. Will rose to greet her with a kiss on her cheek.

"My, you're still flushed from drinking the rarified air of third floor. How is it inhabiting the upper levels?" She laughed with the question to let him know she held no bitterness or resentment.

"Chris, I'm sorry. I'll get it straightened out about the Hawsley case. I heard you were brilliant. He signed the plea deal after five minutes with you?"

"You exaggerate, but Will," she rested her hand on his arm, "open your eyes. I knew what I was getting into with Kincaid at the helm of this Task Force. He doesn't see women qualified to do more than answer emails or serve coffee. But it was my best shot at getting back into investigations. I was ready to leave the Secret Service. Tolson told me they needed former FBI to help steer this ship in the right direction— networking across agency lines, supervising HHS and DHS personnel. It's been a good challenge."

"Been? You have a future. And now you really have a chance. Your name is on my list. I get to pick my staff."

"Then you'd better take my name off and select someone else. What about Walzer or Lyle?"

"What about them? They can't hold a candle to you. Why would I not include you on my team?"

"Think about why he gave you the credit for the Hawsley case. He knows I was the lead, but he can't admit I worked it and not you doing the heavy lifting for me. Why was not one female agent promoted? Why did he sign off on my transfer back to Secret Service without a second glance? If you want to make a difference on the third floor, you can't start looking like you promote the sisterhood."

"You're leaving the Task Force? You're bailing?"

"I'm leaving it in good hands. I hope you can be a good influence."

"This isn't about the other reason?"

"It's all about the other reason. You know the truth. Hawsley's group is an anomaly. Don't minimize the damage this law is doing. I have to warn you. He's still Major Kincaid at heart—a compartmentalized, siloed, rigid, black-and-white thinker. He won't hesitate to running black ops with one team and sending out boy scouts like you to the Hill for plausible deniability. I've heard rumors of others who were coerced to stay, threatened with criminal indictments if they didn't pursue certain persons of interest. Watch your back, Will. I'm sorry I asked you to join the Task Force. Don't overstay your time. Get out the second an opportunity arises. You still have friends at the FBI. I'd started putting out feelers for lateral transfers to other branches." She sat back.

Will stared then chuckled. "Relax, the Hawsley case has been on your back for over a year. I thought you'd enjoy the shift to your other cases."

"Actually, I've accepted a management position. I'll be in the head office, not traveling or working nights. It's still a lot of hours, but in one place." She didn't voice her other plan.

"It's been hard. In some instances, the punishment doesn't fit the crime. But, Chris, isn't it time for Christianity to join the twenty-first century?" Will saw in her eyes that she was done with the debate. "Lasagna, your usual?"

"Plain old spaghetti and meatballs." Small lines crinkled around her eyes with her smile. "Reminds me of Grandma's kitchen table and her warm, buttered garlic bread."

Will slid his hand over to hold hers. "You did great with your cases, all of them—well-coordinated, well-planned, well-executed and handed to justice on a silver platter. Your percentage of successful prosecutions, most taking a deal, is up there with the best of Kincaid's top agents."

"I don't need a Marine to tell me my business, but it sounds great coming from you. Do us proud. I know you will."

CHAPTER 54

SOME WEEKS TOM helped Mark or Wallie do the routine SHU visits. Tom glanced up from his box of Bibles, searching for the one requested by an inmate. Curtis stood at Mark's desk and told him to make the rounds that day with Wallie.

"Need to see you," Curtis said with a flick of his head.

Tom followed him into his office. "What's up?"

Curtis caught his breath and mopped his brow. "You're going to help me do the notifications."

"Notifications?"

"When a close family member dies at this facility, the chaplain gets the honors. So, you game?"

"Of course." He followed Curtis out to the Admin hall.

"Most today are from general population, but when you do 'em in the SHU, insist they put 'em in a room. Can't do this through a door." Curtis glanced at Tom. "Some don't show nothing; some fall apart, but they all deserve a chance for a little privacy."

Tom nodded when the officer paused before the first door. "You listen today. Heard you swapped Sunday message with Jordan. Didn't have it in you this week?"

"No, he wanted a few more weeks to wrap up his series. You taking in services at your church?"

"Yeah, the wife likes the company," the officer smiled. "But don't get used to it. I'll be starting my fall sermons in a few weeks."

The days melted into weeks. By late fall the last of the games finished up in the yard with just the final tourney matches left. Out in the yard, he took his place on Riser's misfit team. The man had cobbled together a ball team that could hold its own against the rest. Riser's growth in Christ came through with each practice and tough game.

Tom caught the ball and dribbled, waiting for Carl to get into place or Mouser to find his magic spot under the basket. For an instant the way cleared, and Tom drove to the left, feinted and passed it to Mouser who swished it in the basket. Over and over, evenly matched, the pace quickened with the drive to win. Fouled, Carl had his chance, but missed the free throw. Tom drove through for a layup, but the ball circled the rim and slid off to the side. He shook his head. He was off. He traded places on the bench at Riser's call.

"You tight, man. What's up?" Riser looked closely at Tom.

He tried to avoid the sharp gaze. He wet his lips. "Case manager's pushing a package on me—got to find a job, reserve a bed at the halfway house."

"What's to think about? Do it, or do you want to serve the full sentence?" Riser stood up and called the next play.

Tom slid away. The game was almost over. They still might win but not with his help. He joined Wallie for the walk to their unit, sneaking a sideways glance at his cellie. "They say I won't be here much longer."

"You're getting short. About two years, right?"

"That's short?"

"In this system, they transition you down to lower levels." Wallie looked at him as he asked, "That is why you got to get a good-time package started. It takes time."

Halfway through the next afternoon, Tom felt more than heard Curtis thrust his office door open and stride to Tom's desk. He turned his head from the piles of Bibles covering the right third of the gray desk.

"66789, report." The officer spun on his heels, slapping his leather shoes on the hard floor.

Mark grinned. "What'd ya do now?"

Tom shrugged. This was not unexpected. He followed the officer and stood on the yellow footprints painted front and center in front of the desk.

Curtis grunted and the chair creaked. He pulled it around and leaned forward, resting his arms on the polished wood. "Was I not clear? Were the instructions too hard for you to understand?"

Tom shook his head. Before he could respond, the officer continued. "Fill out the forms. Finish your résumé. Write your family. Let them know you're coming home." The officer narrowed his eyes. "What? Afraid they'll kick you out?"

Tom studied the ordered shelves of books and manuals just past Curtis' left shoulder. He breathed, prayed silently and said, "Can't go home, sir."

Curtis rocked forward, the thud of his fist hitting the desk echoed through the spare office. "That's not going to fly with me, felon." He placed his beefy elbow on the arms of his chair. "Yeah, I know your number, and it's not Christian charity. Those excuses you spout—got to protect your folks from the consequences of your own actions. Not happening—not in the real world, con."

Tom's eyes flicked over, and he met the officer's gaze for an instant.

Curtis leaned forward as if to rise. Instead his elbows landed on the facing edge of the desk. "You're no different from the rest—just terrified of facing the review board. Deny it. Prove me wrong." He sat back. Tom could feel moisture well up in his eyes. He blinked it back.

Curtis watched Tom's shoulders slump, his body sag like a popped balloon, collapsing inward. His eyes revealed a deep despair. The officer had seen others on the edge. His heart smiting him, he tendered his tone a bit.

"The shame follows, but in time you'll win 'em over—just like in here." He longed to step past the barrier and embrace this earnest young man in his arms and encourage him, but outside his office Tom had to live the reality of general population. "Dismissed."

Tom left without a word. One look at Mark's set face let him know this was not a day to approach him either. The redacted Bible requests were all caught up. Neatly arranged and marked Bibles filled two boxes. Jordan would not wrap up his sermon series for another two weeks. It would be at least four weeks before he'd have to develop a message.

Tom entered the storage area. With a sigh, he shelved items strewn about the small room. Mark was definitely messy.

The impossible swirl haunted the rest of his day. After final stand-up count, he slid down, curling up against the hard wall. He peered through the bars, his eyes shifting in and out of focus. The cool of the week settled in. After a series of shivers, he reached forward and pulled his blanket to wrap around him.

Wallie plopped down on the lowest bunk. "What's up, cellie? Quiet today." He poked him.

Tom rolled his eyes to glance his way. A wall of exhaustion enveloped him like a shroud.

"You got to let me in, bro."

He froze, face toward the bars. "I had no idea. I brought them to my parent's doorstep and into their home." He shook his head. "If I had known, I would have stayed near Mt. Zion Bible College; they would be pushing to release me there—instead of home." He looked at his bunkie. "I've seen the halfway house where they want to send me. I was there during the ribbon-cutting ceremony. Dad helped finance it, along with the county EMS and ambulance corps, and now they want to send me there."

Wallie nodded. "I don't know what's that like, but I've seen enough guys come back 'cause it's hard to make it work on the outside when you've been in."

"Yeah, and to think I didn't have a clue when I was there so long ago."

"Guess you're just going to have to trust God." He recited verse upon verse—the ones he'd learned from his friend.

"I get it. I know I'm crashing right now. Thanks for caring, buddy. Thanks for listening, and keep praying for me. I really need it."

"That's obvious." They both laughed.

The spell broken, Tom rose and hugged his roommate. They ran through their Bible reading and prayers—the usual evening routine.

"Moon's full tonight," Tom said, staring past the cell's upper corner.

"Naw, it's silver crescent, waiting to get bigger." Wallie laughed. "I saw it on Ganse's calendar. He left out the one he hides in his drawer. I know things, you know."

"Yes, you do. So, it's crescent."

"And when you leave, each night, look up with your special God-given, x-ray vision and know we're seeing the same moon; we'll be together in spirit. Don't forget now. I'm counting on you."

Tom met his gaze. "Meet you on the other side, bro."

"Guaranteed—it's sealed—thanks to the blood of Christ applied."

"Amen."

CHAPTER 55

THE WEEK OF Halloween, an officer pulled Tom from the kitchen. They marched across the center straight to Admin and the chaplain's wing. The young officer flung the door open. "Here's 66789 as requested."

An officer was seated at Mark's desk. "You inmates run this show?"

"Sir?"

Mark emerged from the supply room and stood by Tom's side. He whispered, "Curtis had a heart attack. They've been here all morning."

"No talking, or you'll both go down." The officer rose. He angled his piercing black eyes at the two inmates and launched a series of questions—who taught the classes, who did the SHU visits before listing the Sunday activities performed by Tom and Jordan.

"Sir, he supervised all the programs, GED and reading classes, anger management, victim resolution, administered the good-time program recommendations, as well as prepping for the next few years of programs. We…"

"That *we* again. Thought he had civilian assistants."

"He chose to handpick and mentor residents for our development, sir." Mark glanced at Tom. "We maintained the standards. Tom went through all the material, ensuring we were using currently approved courses and books. Yes, we helped with the visits, but he always checked up on it."

Wallie came through the door from the class area—his face clouded and closed. "The class is ready for the debrief, officer."

"What is that?"

"Officer Curtis' debrief—the guys share what they have learned and how they will apply it this week. That's what he called it," Mark explained.

"Not regulation. Hand out the test," he ordered. He raked Wallie with his eyes.

Wallie disappeared.

The officer leveled his gaze at Tom's desk. "What's this?"

"Sorting the Bibles to be returned to the residents. Some aren't clearly marked."

"Contraband Bibles?"

"Yes, sir, but…"

"Send them to recycling." The officer stepped forward, spit flying from his mouth, "That's an order, inmate."

"Yes, sir." Tom stepped to the desk and carried the boxes to the back of the supply room. Later he'd take it up with Ganse or his case officer. They knew the warden had signed off on this.

Lieutenant Connors stepped into the office, studying the scene. He pointed at Tom. "I need him. He's mine."

The officer started to speak but wilted under Connors' sharp gaze.

Tom breathed easier when he emerged from the stifling office.

"Blowing things up, huh?"

"You could say that. Sir, Curtis did his job. He didn't shirk."

"Relax. We know that. I'll speak with the Warden's Exec. He'll clear things up. This heart attack caught us by surprise."

"How is he? Will he make it?"

"In open heart surgery right now and no, we don't know—just your God, I suspect. Do any good to pray?"

"Always. But he's been sick for a long time—just hid it well."

"I can imagine. Anyway, you do notifications?"

"I do."

Connors handed Tom a stack of envelopes.

"They set up?"

"Waiting on floor two. Remember floor two?"

"I do," Tom smiled, "but this time I'll be on the right side of the table."

"That you will. Here's your pass. Get there. I got business."

Tom watched Connors head to the warden's wing. He had two ways to go—through the cold yard or down through the tunnels. The thought of the dank musty corridors sent a shiver down his spine. He headed through the yard to Building Four, praying as he walked.

The first two were stoic, almost stone-like in their acceptance of the news. Their hollowed eyes hinted of other hurts and losses—just one more to pile on top of wounds festering deep within.

The third cried. Tom held his hand while waiting for the torrent to subside.

He lifted his face and stared at a far corner. "Mom lived too far away to come. Didn't have no one to take her and…" He blew his nose.

Tom looked about the spare room—no tissues in sight, not like in the Admin wing.

He met Tom's gaze. "Can't help in here. Can't visit, can't do the little things she needed doing."

Tom listened, nodding. Being locked away and unable to render aid added to the pain of the loss.

An officer pounded on the door. Tom yelled, "More time."

"Naw, I'm good. I'm gonna be crying for a while."

Tom nodded. He rose and knocked on the door. He turned to the end stairs leading to the yard.

"Hold up. 66789?"

"That's me."

"Bringing one more in." The officer nodded at the second door down. "Will be here soon. Wait there."

Tom found his place, running his hand over the slim letter with only an inmate number printed on the outside. It looked familiar, but he couldn't place it. Knowing guys by their given names had been more important to him.

Todd stepped through. "Tom?"

"Hi, Todd," he glanced at the letter and back at Todd now sitting across from him. In the yard or away from their back corner in the kitchen Todd had to play the part of gang leader. He relaxed when Todd smiled back.

His eyes focused on the envelope. "Is it Sam?"

"I knew he was your brother, but I…"

"Good thing you didn't let on. Were you with him in the SHU just before his transfer?"

Tom nodded. He slid his finger under the lip and pulled out the paper, opening it on the table.

Todd read it. "Had stomach cancer. Wrote me, told me about God." Todd looked up. "Not surprised it was you that preached to him in Hannibal."

"Ann wrote to him about God. He had lots of questions."

"Yeah, my wife, Ann, and then Sam all pushed God." Todd shook his head, a slow smile forming.

"When did you…you know?"

"Jump ship, take the leap of faith?" Todd's blue eyes met Tom's. "More like a slow walk to glory, one step at a time." He spread out the paper, reading the sparse language aloud. "Knew, figured when Sam's letters stopped, and my Shirley wrote to say he'd been sent home on compassionate release." Todd scanned the far corner and looked back, "So, if it's true, I'll meet him in heaven, along with my mom and grand-mother—only a temporary separation, but…" Todd wet his lips. "But not like before, not like when we fought and couldn't talk. We occupied the same block but existed in different worlds." He met Tom's eyes. "To have your kin, your older brother, become an enemy hurt bad." Todd shook his head. "It's so different with Christ."

Tom smiled, listening to Todd share his hope and joy in the Lord.

They froze when an officer pounded on the door, and the ten-minute buzzer sounded.

Todd rose first. "Got to go."

Tom slipped the letter in the envelope and handed it to his friend. "Praying for you always—no matter what."

"We still not friends out there."

"I know."

"I have to hide it, for now. He cool with that?"

"Ask God yourself and do what He says. At the right time, remember, the one to truly fear…"

"Yeah, not man, but the one who can throw you into hell or welcome you into heaven." He stepped forward and hugged Tom, enveloping him in his long arms. "Thank you."

Tom stood back and watched him leave. He waited a short time and followed, making sure not to be seen together. His mind ran through the final teams slated to play after supper. Their team had been eliminated a few days before. He was glad he'd be a spectator tonight.

What just happened had to remain a secret, but he couldn't stop thinking about how nice talking to Todd in private had been—just the two of them not looking about and not having to hide. He prayed for Todd through supper and the walk back to their unit.

CHAPTER 56

WHILE THEY WALKED to the yard during evening rec time to see the final games, Wallie continued griping. "You can't believe how bad classes went today with the officers riding our case."

Tom nodded, trying to listen. He paused just a few strides into the yard. An inmate called him over to the walk from Building Five. "Just a minute," he glanced at his cellie. "Meet you at the bleachers. He's been asking questions for a few weeks."

"I'll wait up."

"It's up to you." Tom looked about. He knew the resident. His heart skipped a beat, but the guy seemed harmless enough. The man drew him farther down the narrow path bounded by two buildings. The walkway opened up to a small, tight courtyard, mostly out of sight of the nearest guard towers.

He would have turned away, but Todd appeared, surrounded by three guys covered in tattoos, some pierced and studded, muscles bristling and fists clenched. Their dead eyes bore into Tom, coldly assessing size and strength—marking the kill spots.

"That's your hit, boss. Do us proud." Tall and spare, lean muscle over sharp bone, the speaker stood just behind Todd's right. Tom recognized the stance from his high school wrestling days. *Either Todd or I will die today—who will be up to Todd.*

Todd jerked his head slightly in the direction of the path and Tom's escape route. He winked and nodded imperceptibly. The plan carried by the micro-signals set Tom in motion. He whirled and ran toward the nearest guard post. With a quick look back, he saw Todd blocking pursuit.

Tom increased his pace, pushing through a group of stragglers heading for the bleachers. The usual guard hangout was empty. They were watching the games. Even the guards on the towers were transfixed by the contest. Tom plowed ahead and veered straight for the closest gaggle of guards.

"Hit! Hit!" he yelled, trying to overcome the deafening cheer when a basket pushed the pros farther ahead. "They're killing Todd," he yelled, not slowing as he drew near.

A guard to the side of his field of vision tackled him. Tom spun about, gathering his feet beneath him. "There's a hit. A hit. Killing Todd in the courtyard near Four and Five." Tom closed his mouth when they face planted him into the hard ground. He spat out the clods and yelled again.

The klaxons sounded. The dribbler froze. The forward couldn't stop in time and ran into him. Guards emerged from the crowds, some pushing the inmates to their houses and others running to the courtyard.

The nearest guard spun Tom around. "Get out of here," he said before joining the group descending on the site. "It's three on one," Tom yelled, but he began to breathe again when he counted more than six sprinting toward Building Five. The group he merged with divided along the paths for their units. He crossed into the first entryway.

A force shoved him sideways into the wall. Instinctively, Tom flowed to his right and wrapped around. He pushed back and paused to ID his attacker momentarily pinned against the wall. He stared into a chest and looked up. It was Bruce.

Tom stepped back, ready for either running or attack—but he stopped and tried to stand down. If Bruce was part of it, it would be the same as if Todd had decided to live and Tom had to die. He prayed. Bruce stepped forward, "Who else's the target?"

Tom met his gaze. "Me."

Bruce swore and spit on the ground. "You got to Todd and took the heart right out of him pushing your God on him. A lot of blood's gonna be spilt, thanks to you."

"How's that on me?"

Bruce grabbed Tom's arm and pushed him to the wall. "Todd's number two who should have taken down number one six months ago 'cause he's getting old and weak. But Mason's been vying to take over since he transferred in last year. Todd could have kept the peace." Bruce pushed Tom's shoulder. "Todd would have figured out a way to squeeze out McCall without blood, but you had to mess things up. The warden wants equilibrium. Why'd you think he lets me run the kitchen or Wallie bunk single or Nivens run his guys the way he does or Curtis? He doesn't like guys who disturb the fragile balance of this facility. That's why the agents got the boot and Curtis' Bible fixation was shut down. I want you out of my unit." He grabbed Tom and headed for the DU Admin section. "And you're gonna get gone."

"It's more than just this life, Bruce. There's so much more, and yes, maybe it looks like it causes too much trouble, but breaking through to life with God is worth all the hurt." He felt the grip tighten and pace increase. Tom put one foot in front of the other. They surged across the yellow line straight to the SHU.

An officer held his ground in front of the double doors. "Get to your unit."

Bruce tried to object, but the officer interrupted him. "You Unit Four? Any McCall's gang in your group?" When Bruce shook his head, in the next breath he stepped forward and gestured to their block. "It'll be safer than here. Get."

Tom ran to his cell and shared the news with Wallie. "How long do you think lockdown will last this time?"

"They usually get it stopped quick, but we'll be on lockdown for a while."

"Like winter."

"Just a different kind of storm."

Tom felt like saying his goodbyes, but second-guessed himself. Not knowing what to say, they sat side by side on the floor, staring at the ceiling.

"Guess the championship matches will be finished up indoors," Tom said.

"If they finish at all. Always another year."

"Our misfit team did good making it to the semi-finals."

"Riser's pleased."

"You playing next year?"

"Not unless you're around. Won't be the same." He met Tom's gaze. "I will never forget you."

Bruce pulled Wallie to help deliver meals. The black curtain of aloneness descended when the bars rolled shut.

CHAPTER 57

T HE SOUND OF their cell bars rolling open entered his dream as a thick metal gate closing off his only escape. The guards' yells pierced the veil, and the dream collapsed. Tom jerked, almost falling off his bunk. He caught himself, rolled to the floor and forced his heavy legs to push upright.

"66789, come out."

Tom stumbled in his long underwear. Before he could reach for his pants, they pulled him out and marched to the Admin interrogation rooms. Just days before, he had delivered notifications and conducted interviews for Curtis. Everything dissolved and disappeared. The dread of transfer rose up.

It felt like way past midnight. A glance at a clock showed it was three a.m. He shook his head to dispel the cobwebs.

The short officer's radio squawked, "Find 66789?"

"Yep, back in his unit, all tucked in."

"Bring him in."

"He's here. He a participant?"

"No, has info. Keep him in a room. I'll be over when I'm done with this mess." Tom's brain put a face to the scratchy radio voice; it was Connors.

Lieutenant Connors pushed open the door, still reviewing placement arrangements on his pad. He looked at the table—no inmate in sight—but bit back his outburst when he spied movement in the corner. "Rise and shine, Tinkerbell. Front and center. Now!"

Tom uncurled, half stumbled, half-walked to the chair.

"Coffee," Connors said to the officer. He sat down. They brought three cups. Connors kept two and slid one over.

Tom shook his head.

"You're going to need it. This is your wakeup call, Choir Boy. He's calling for you."

"Who?"

"Todd."

"He's alive?"

"Tough bird—amazed he lasted that long, but he's beat bad. Doctor's give him 40-60, and that's 60 percent he doesn't pull through. Just waking up from surgery in the medical complex. Doc thinks letting you see him might help him pull through. But before we take you there, and that's being generous letting you see him, you've got some explaining to do."

"You see the notification?"

"I did. How'd you meet?"

"During my first day in the kitchen. He delivers the empties and takes the trash every morning. Just enough time and out of sight to answer questions." Tom described how the relationship evolved.

"When'd he crossover?"

"Not sure, but I suspected. Maybe six months ago."

Connors nodded. "About when we started picking up chatter but couldn't ID the problem."

"What happens now? Do I have to live in the SHU, transfer to the prison camp in this complex?"

"Too close. That gang has a long reach. No, we'll send you as far away as we can, but the receiving camp will have to take you."

Tom nodded.

"Describe how it went down—every detail."

Tom did the best he could. "Hope that helps."

"We'll put it together. Every bit helps. Sit tight till we get a team to take you over."

Barely half an hour later, Tom rose when the door thrust open. It felt like reverse reception—they handed him an orange jumpsuit along with his bag of personal effects. The final insult was putting on a full set of chains before bundling him behind the wire in the back of an SUV for the short drive to the medical complex.

Todd was in a private room on a guarded hallway. He studied Todd's swollen eye, the multiple abrasions on his nose and cheeks, his bandaged arm and left leg cradled in a sling.

Todd's eyes opened. He reached for Tom's hand. Their eyes locked.

"Thanks for saving my life." He paused when Todd furrowed his brow.

Todd cleared his throat and tried to talk.

Tom held up the water mug for Todd.

He sat back. "Wasn't even an option. You'd never have survived that." Dark worry clouded his eyes. "I fought back. I thought I'd do it different, but…" He looked at Tom, "did I sin?"

"Ask the Lord. He's God. He allowed you to survive the hit for a reason. Don't look back, but forward and follow Him."

Todd glanced around the room. The nurses and aides were gone, the heavy door closed. He looked back at Tom. "Teach me."

"It would be an honor." Tom began with the assurance of God's love and care and to the call of salvation from the beginning of time, citing verse after verse. "In the womb, God formed your inner parts. You are fearfully and wonderfully made.[28] He has tasks for you to do that He planned before time began. God's plan in your life became active when you accepted Christ as your Savior. He will mold you, shape you, call you and provide what you need. He will never leave you or forsake you.[29] Our times of feeling lost come from our own fears, struggles with sin and conflicts with others. Never stop finding your way back to God in those moments.

"As we cooperate, work with God, accept His discipline, we will learn to live in His love. Wherever He sends you or what He calls you to do, He will be there by your side—enabling you, providing the strength." Tom shared his struggles with letting God be strong through him, being thankful and resting in the joy of the Lord—no matter what happened.

He paused, a settled conviction rising. Curtis was right. His resistance lay exposed as the terror of starting over in a new facility. "We must surrender and accept the changes and challenges God brings our way, or we will get sidetracked and miss out, not ready for opportunities He brings to us."

When Tom paused to take a breath, Todd launched his questions, long held back. Time froze. Tom marveled at the answers the Holy Spirit provided. With short, clipped sentences, he imparted the living truth as best he could.

When the guards would come to take him away, he knew he would never see Todd again. He shoved down the grief.

"Follow God, not men. He will provide you other teachers. Test what they say by the Word—nothing else. Sometimes our own hearts can deceive us. Even what we think the Holy Spirit is telling us—check it out by the Word. Read it—all of it. Know it. Seek out others who are able to rightly divide it." In answer to the questions in Todd's eyes, Tom expounded on the proper handling of God's Word. "Do not count yourself as not worthy—none of us are worthy—but a holy privilege to open up the Bible to those with open hearts."

"Honest answers to honest questions." Todd smiled. "The days you didn't answer, you knew I just wanted to fight, draw you out, but you never took the bait or reacted to the insults." A tear formed in his eye. "If God would use me the way He used you, it'd be an honor."

"It is. It was. Keep your eyes on Him, and He will." The door burst open, and two guards stepped through. Tom leaned forward and lowered his voice. "I'll meet you on the other side."

CHAPTER 58

TRANSPORT TO OKLAHOMA Detention Center took two days but felt like a week. They kept him separated, locked in the back of the bus, away from the others. His solitary cell in the detention center tucked away in a short, back, dim hall held echoes of bars closing and distant voices. He looked at his tomb—six by eight with a single bed, a metal shelf, a stool, and a toilet/sink unit.

Tom sat. With no clocks and no watch, he could only tell time by the daily routines. He tracked the days in his journal. His bags were still piled close to the naked bunk. The thin mattress with a pillow bump, a sheet, a towel and basic toiletries was still rolled up at the foot end. A settled tiredness washed over him, a reluctance to move except draw breath and grieve.

His world had been torn asunder; his dearest and closest friends were separated not only by distance but regulation—the day he left Todd's room they told him he was now a Level One and could no longer be in contact with any Level Fives.

Tom blinked back the tears. He could not go home; his family had disowned him. Turning to his Bible college friends would only bring the Task Force down upon them. An idea formed in his mind, but he rejected it outright.

Where was his hope? He didn't want to go back to pleading with God to take him to heaven. He'd been down that road before. He had to stand up. He had to face the frightening abyss.

Just about to gather himself, he heard a buzzer, felt heavy doors open and the high clink of a wheeled cart crossing the threshold to the range with metal trays slapping down on the shelves. He visualized the standard food carts making a SHU delivery; he'd done enough of them. The sounds were distinguishable even through the solid cell door.

He rose and waited, holding the flap open to receive the meal. It should be lunchtime, or at least that was his best guess. A simple sandwich, fruit and granola bar came through. "Is this supper?"

"Lunch."

"Thanks." He looked at the spare meal. No matter. He was barely hungry. The empty hours loomed before him. His heart's cry rent his soul. *Help, Lord.*

He knew he had to set his own routines. There would be no programs, no activities here. The guards had told him as much. They talked freely in front of him as if he were no different than a pound dog to be warehoused until he passed or time ran down. Flagged with being in gang activity, he doubted any facility would take him before he ran out the clock, and they would have to release him.

Tom placed the tray on the shelf in front of the stool. An inner urging sent him to his bags. He would pull out his papers and journals, move in, and arrange his items.

The third bag seemed heavy. More books lay below his extra underwear and long johns. Tom grasped two volumes: a Greek New Testament and a compact lexicon-concordance with the covers intact. *How?* He wiped away a tear.

Gifts from Officer Curtis. Mark must have slipped them in the bag. He prayed for God's blessing on the man God had used to mentor him at Hannibal. He knew what he had to do—study, write, organize and refresh his Bible memory work. The quiet days in isolation were not a punishment, but a gift for the days ahead, still bleary and indistinct. A glimmer of hope emerged.

CHAPTER 59

WILL TEXTED CHRIS again and stared at his phone, willing her to answer. It had been a long time, and he'd been too busy to stay in touch as they had discussed on her last day at the Task Force. Impatient to share the news, he decided to call.

"Hey, big brother. Still watching out for me?" Chris' laughter brought a smile to Will's face.

"Back at ya, kid sister, you not paying attention?" he teased back. "Got news. Same place, does Friday at 7 work?"

"How about Saturday? My weeks are pretty full."

"Sounds good. See you then."

Chris looked at her phone and thought of the Shirrings. She had neglected them as well. Their place was not that far from the restaurant. It was a pretty drive and a welcome break to her double schedule. She hesitated to call Fran in case something came up and she would need to put in a full day at the office Saturday. It hadn't taken her long to realize Saturdays were the best days to get certain projects done.

By noon, Chris cleared her desk and headed out the door. She wondered how much the grandkids had grown. Imagining Asa chasing the kids around the dining room table, she parked in front of the house. A swing set occupied the right side of the backyard. A few toys were piled along the side of the house. With three cars in the driveway, it looked like Heather was still living at home.

She rang the front doorbell and waited. Simeon answered the door.

"Hello, Simeon. It's Chris, just dropping by. If it's not a good time."

"No, it's great to see you," he looked behind him. "Come in." He disappeared, and she heard him calling Heather.

Chris entered. The house seemed dark with the curtains drawn. Reggie played with his trucks, and Cheryl toddled over to her. She scooped down and picked her up. "You're walking. Such a big girl." She beamed at Heather, drying a dish. "They're beautiful. I bet Asa's so proud."

Heather turned aside. Chris heard the clatter of dishes and a soft sound. The young mother emerged, her eyes red-rimmed, her hand fingering a tissue. "You hadn't heard?"

"No." Chris slid aside for Heather to sit by her on the couch.

"They arrested Dad." Heather glanced over. "We wondered why we never heard from you. I assumed you knew."

Chris glanced at Simeon standing in front of the side hallway. "I left the Task Force over a year and a half ago right after Hawsley took the plea deal." She rested a hand on Heather's arm. "I didn't want any of you to have to testify." She looked about the living room. "Where's Fran?"

Simeon gestured to the bedrooms.

"Whatever help I could…"

"They killed him."

"Asa? Tell me what happened."

A soft voice emerged from the dark hall, "The arresting agents took him to the detention center that day. When they dropped him off, they told the guards he'd raped some teen girls. He was found beaten to death in the bathroom two days later." Fran's wooden voice bore no emotion.

Chris rose and embraced her. The woman crumpled in her arms, sobbing.

"I'm so sorry." She thought back to the day of Will's promotion and Cooper's livid face. "I'll look into it. I'll find out…"

Fran stepped back and put an arm around Chris' shoulder. "No, please don't. It's covered by the blood." She walked her to the couch. "It's just grief. Some days are worse than others. It will pass." Fran grasped Chris' hand. "He's with the Lord—in a much better place. Whoever's to blame I have committed to the Lord—laid it at the foot of the cross."

Her mind swirling, Chris' breath came in ragged gulps. "I had no idea when I joined the Task Force, no clue what it meant." Her sobs rent the air. Fran reached out and held her. Chris reached over to Heather sitting next to her. "I'm so sorry. It's not what should have happened."

"How could your God do this to someone as faithful as Asa?" She turned, looking from one to the other. "How could He allow Hawsley to harm so many? And why did He allow this law if He is in control?"

"God's ways are not our ways. We know He works all things out." Fran paused, "Asa knew the risks with contacting you. For a while we thought it had worked." She nodded toward Heather. "The doctors said she had barely a month to live if your team had not rescued her and taken her to a hospital. We had Asa with us for over a year. He saw his grandchildren."

"I had a chance to get to know him," Simeon said. "All we like sheep have gone astray. We each have gone our own way, and the Lord laid our sins on Christ.[30] We can't see from here what God is doing, but we know He has a plan and a purpose for everything, even the hard things."

Fran nodded. "Chris, this is just our training ground for heaven. In the hard nights He has comforted me with these words: '*For I know the plans I have for you, declares the Lord, plans for welfare and not for evil, to give you a future and a hope.*'[31] This gets me through. I still live." Her voice caught in her throat. Fran swallowed. "I still have tasks He sets before me every day. And I will be with Asa in heaven when it's my time."

"You believe this?" Chris' eyes scanned the three. She didn't need to see nods or hear their assents. Their faith was evident—sorrow wrapped in faith, a deep river of strength upholding a small family in a common house on a back street. What they had appealed more to her than all the medals, promotions, prestigious awards or fancy halls. "I'd like to know God the way you do."

Simeon brought out a Bible. Chris could see it was a legal edition. Fran opened it to the book of Romans. "I know you've studied it, but faith is a gift from God." Fran began with the perfect world, God's design and plan to call out a people for Himself. She laid out mankind's sinful, lost condition, Christ paying their sin debt on the cross and the free gift of salvation available for the asking. She read the verses, gave the explanation and waited.

Chris took the Bible and turned to Ephesians 2:8-9. She bowed her head and prayed. A settled peace flooded over her. She read the passage again and looked at Fran. "I'm speechless."

"This brings me great joy, Chris, to see life out of the darkness. Christ works through all things."

She nodded, rose, staring sightlessly out the picture window. Chris turned. Simeon retrieved the truck Cheryl had pulled from Reggie's hand; Fran consoled and scolded the toddler; Heather looked at Chris with wide, soft brown eyes. As if she saw for the first time, Chris said, "lambs for the slaughter." Tears welled up in her eyes. "You are lambs for the slaughter." A settled rage rose up followed by the vision of her memories.

She turned, leaned against the windowsill. A cold breeze fluttered past her face, pushing the teardrops closer to her ear. Her head dropped in her hands; her shoulders quaked. She turned. "What have I done? How could He save me after…?" She melted into Fran's embrace and then pulled away.

"Chris, God knows. He was not surprised by any of this. He paid it already. It's covered at the cross. You are forgiven. It might look hopeless now, but God will make things right. He is our strength, our advocate. He will bring justice to all, and no one will be able to thwart Him."

She shook her head, unable to fathom or comprehend. As she sat on the couch, Simeon opened the Bible. "After the Jewish leaders could not refute Stephen's testimony, they stoned him. A man named Saul approved the execution and held their cloaks." He read, "But Saul was ravaging the church, and entering house after house, he dragged off men and women and committed them to prison."

Fran said, "Saul was struck by Jesus on the road to Damascus. He repented of his sin, accepted Christ, and authored many of these books."

Chris furrowed her brow. "Paul the apostle was Saul? He was the same man?"

"Yes, and God used him to bring God's wonderful news to the nations around Israel. None are born believers. We all have our pasts, but God has greater plans for us—for you."

Chris breathed deeply and sighed. She nodded. Her eyes noted the time on the wall clock. "Oh, I have to go. I have a dinner appointment."

Fran accompanied her to the front door after hasty goodbyes. "Chris, come by after your date. I'd like to show you some things. Stay overnight and go to church with us."

Tempted to say no, she stopped. An inner urging changed her mind. "Okay, but I have some work to do in the afternoon."

"Sure, head home after church."

"Thanks for everything." She embraced Fran, feeling the unity of the Spirit. Chris smiled, assurance once again flooding her soul.

CHAPTER 60

A s she drove to the restaurant, her mind swirled with what had happened. She had to tell Will, but questions reared up. Her understanding still scrambled and unsorted, she tried to plan what she needed to say.

Not seeing Will's car in the parking lot, she assumed she had arrived first. Chris started in surprise when the waiter led her to a smiling Will sitting in their favorite booth. He rose, hugged her warmly, and gestured for her to sit down.

"A new car?"

He squared his shoulders, adjusted his dark, sheeny $1,000 suit, and settled an erring cuff link. "Invested in my own hybrid." Will flashed his signature smile. "LS Hybrid Lexus."

"Aw, the brilliant blue Lexus parked in the lot?"

"Nightfall mica—I see it caught your eye."

"How often do you represent the Task Force on the Hill?"

"Regularly, sometimes daily. Makes sense not to have to depend on a ride service."

"Assigned a driver?"

"Really? I'm not there yet, but eventually it will be required. You know I enjoy driving myself." With that explanation, he requested the ordered hors d'oeuvres. Will reached for her hand. "I've ordered a special meal for two." His eyes surveyed the place, "wanted to make this special in a familiar location."

Chris sat back. *He isn't going to propose, is he?* They had changed.

Running through how to share her new faith, she noticed his intense gaze, his fervor, his joy. "I never imagined working for Kincaid would be so invigorating."

"It's what I get to do. How I am at the right place to shape the future." He gently rubbed her hand with his fingers and pulled back. "It's hard sending pastors and church leaders to federal prisons. It's not a good fit all around."

She swallowed.

"Some don't make it to trial."

Before she could break in, he said, "I am heading up the effort to locate, design, and structure our own prisons modeled after the best of the BOP. Working closely with top management, we're going to create safe spaces for those not yet ready to support the new initiatives. When they engage with Bible scholars and national leaders, they will find their vision to bring the church forward to the future."

They sat back for the calamari fritti. Will thanked the waiter and served their plates.

She dipped one in the sauce, waiting for an opening, but Will continued his monologue. Chris nodded her head in agreement.

Will described the massive effort to create their own bureau of prisons under the HCL fold—regulations, staff requirements, locations and facility layouts. He paused, watching her closely.

Chris shifted her gaze to the waiter bringing three large plates.

"The Tour of Italy dinner for two," the waiter said.

She licked her lips with the aroma. "You can't beat their sauce. I'll take a small lasagna, with more pesto please."

Will smiled. "I've saved the best for last." Once settled, he pulled out his notepad. "Here, it's a gem."

"What am I looking at?" Chris noted the dense evergreen forest not far from a somewhat pitted gravel/dirt road. A faded sign read "Rosemont."

"An abandoned Boy Scout camp in Minnesota, north of Minneapolis. It's tucked away in the trees but not far from major highways. He swiped to the next picture. "And this is what it will be. We inked the deal yesterday. Now it's game on, and we have a deadline."

"You always do." She studied the architect's rendering of what looked like a resort with running tracks, tennis courts, and small cabins. Chris handed back the tablet. "You certain you can make sure the residents are not abused?"

"If BOP can do it, we can too."

"Sounds to me like you no longer have any problems with the HCL mandate."

Will tilted his head. "It's not what you think."

"They murdered Asa."

"I know."

"You knew? Did you bring the agents responsible to justice or did you put another note in their files?"

"The name's changed to Hate Crime Laws Task Force. We strive for a holistic approach of enforcement, education and policy advisement."

"I've seen the ads." Kincaid had converted him. Will was on board—as much a proselyte as Barrie or Otis. Her resolve to share the gospel withered with a rising unease.

"What's up, Chris? You're lovely, as always, but you look tired." He leaned forward concern on his face under a half smile. "Thought you'd find a desk job with the Secret Service an easier gig."

"Don't laugh. We have our daily stress points, dealing with internal oversight to stay ahead of things." She paused. She wasn't being completely truthful—her step of faith earlier that day overshadowed all else; however, a reluctance to reveal she had joined the other side kept her quiet. Chris knew she had to give him a valid reason for her weariness.

"I'm going to night school to earn a law degree with Georgetown U. It's a six-year program."

"Really?"

"You finished yours shortly after you joined the FBI."

"I know you can do it, Chris. That's great. Five years left?" His eyes gleamed again. "Check us out when you're done. We need good lawyers on our team."

"I'll keep it in mind." The evening progressed from there. Chris listened, saying little, as Will shared his vision for creating a brave new world. She wished him the best. She really did, but clearly, they could not be as close as they had been in the past. They no longer walked the same path.

The house looked quiet, and Chris considered driving by. She parked the car. Fran turned on the porch light and waved.

"It's not too late?"

"I gave Heather and Simeon a date night. The kids are tucked in bed. I've been waiting for you."

The warm glow from the kitchen looked inviting. She saw the small books and Bibles on the table. Chris thirsted to know more. She followed Fran to the table and selected a tea bag. "A cup would be welcome." She watched Fran set the kettle on the stove. "It's not as I had imagined. God doesn't take over."

"He made us free beings. Each day we have the choice to walk with Him or follow our old ways."

"The old man," Chris said. The phrase stirred memories of something she had read. "I almost lied to Will. Didn't say what I thought I was going to say. It's still easy not to do the right thing—even after you let God in." She had thought about it during the drive back. "How do you not get trapped like Hawsley?"

"You guard yourself every day. Stay close to God, lean on His Word. It's easier to set things right before you go too far down the path." Fran paused and grasped Chris' hand, "but never forget there's always a way back."

"What do you have here?"

Fran started the first Bible studies—describing the gift of salvation, how to walk with God, deal with sin, and pray. "This is just the beginning. You already know a lot."

"But I have to understand it. Before much of it seemed unintelligible."

"Wait here." Fran left for her bedroom and emerged with a gift bag. "For you."

Chris pulled out a cherry keepsake box. "It's beautiful. A family heirloom?"

"His grandfather made it for Asa's mother. Lift the lid."

She lifted the lid, felt the soft red velvet, and removed the top tray. "I couldn't…" she started to say.

Fran reached over and pressed a bump in the lining on the lower right bottom of the box. With a click and slide, a drawer opened from the back. She rotated the box and pulled out the drawer to reveal a hidden slim Bible. She looked at Chris. "I know he would have wanted you to have this." She slid the drawer closed. "Push the box against a wall or a mirror, and no one will ever suspect."

Speechless Chris accepted the present.

"The days before you arrived, after Cheryl's birth, Heather was so sick. I couldn't lose her as well; the guilt rent my heart. It was my fault she was there. Finally, I prayed for God to send an angel to deliver us. I waited so long because I was afraid to face Asa after what Hawsley had done to me. He had defiled me. How could I have been so stupid?"

Chris handed her the box of tissues and held her hand.

Fran smiled at Chris. "You are the angel God sent. Thank you."

CHAPTER 61

Six months and three weeks later, Tom surveyed his fellow residents pondering the usual Tuesday noon meal or talking with their buddies. His eyes scanned the crowd scattered amongst the large open dining room. North Platte Prison Camp, in some ways, felt like a college campus, but it was still a prison, which the guards never let them forget. He recognized the distinguished-looking resident he was looking for—grizzled temples framed by a full head of dark brown hair, with wire-rimmed glasses and a ready smile.

"Officer Walpole's assistant, Ryan?" he asked.

The middle-aged man nodded with a smile.

"May I join you?"

"It's a free country."

"It is." Tom sat.

"You're Tom, right?"

"I'm flattered. I can't imagine how many newbies you process each week for Ms. Walpole."

"Not many transfers have to be sent to A&O. Amazed your last facility didn't catch that."

"A deliberate choice on their part." Tom relayed his first week at Hannibal. "They signed off on the classes. They used my college counseling courses as the excuse, but it was really to have me confiscate inmates' Bibles for the chaplain to satisfy HR 756. You aware of 756 or the HCL Task Force?"

"No. Did we miss something? How does this apply to North Platte?"

Tom turned his plate and selected a piece of fish to skewer with his fork. He paused to study Ryan. He explained the not-so-new law.

"And this concerns us how?"

"I pulled a five-year sentence for five Bibles and my Bible college books and notes. They put me directly in a Level Five penitentiary."

"That's hard to believe in this country." Ryan turned his attention to his pudding. He looked up. "My wife's a believer. She has Bibles and goes to church where everyone else has Bibles. She's never spoken of this law."

"They're keeping it quiet, going slowly; taking out the leadership first. Probably haven't heard of many pastors going to the pen for Bibles, have you?"

"I don't exactly keep up with the news, but Patty would have told me."

"It might also be localized. I was in Ohio when I was arrested—farther east. This is Nebraska."

"Maybe they don't know we exist." Ryan sat back. "I'll look into it. Patty might have heard but never said anything. After all, I'm not the Bible type."

"But don't do it over the phone. The Task Force aggressively monitors all public record communication. Does she visit?"

"Yes, we even had a few weekend visits."

"I imagine that's nice, but hard."

"Going through the pain of separation again." Ryan shook his head. "I almost didn't apply for the last one, but Patty pushed for it. She needed it." He looked off in the distance. "It was a more..." he would have said *difficult*, but he said, "intense time." He glanced at Tom. "You a Christian before prison?"

"Yes."

"Some of your records seem to be missing. No contacts, no good-time package. Even the applications were missing."

Tom stirred his veggies. He glanced over. "I had SHU time, spent six months in solitary at Oklahoma." Tom sat back. "Honestly, what are my chances of getting any good time?"

"None, if you don't complete the forms."

Tom sat back and glanced at Ryan. "I've got some issues about going home. Officer Curtis gave me a week to get it done, but then he had a heart attack and the hit came down." He focused on his half-empty plate, the ashes returning in his stomach. "Back to square one again."

He looked aside, remembering Curtis' surprise gifts. The assurance God had not abandoned him arose, helping him keep his cool despite Ryan's questioning looks.

"Did he survive?"

"I pray he did. He survived the attack and went into open-heart surgery. He'd been sick for a while—was glad to volunteer and help with the SHU visits. Did many of the death notifications for him." He looked over and back, trying to clear his mind of memories of those he had left behind in Hannibal. He had to focus on the now and his current predicament.

"You're pretty short, a year and a half? Going to run out the clock at this rate."

Tom shrugged.

"Good time gets you some help after release—a halfway house until you get settled."

"Yeah, that's the rub. We're now forever marked as convicts, criminals, but I don't have to let that define me. I tried to follow the rules to the best of my ability."

"You were in the SHU three times—two were sixties."

"Yeah." Tom glanced at the clock. Lunchtime was almost over. He had signed up for recreation; therefore, he was required to show up or get demerits. "There were reasons—some on me." He looked at Ryan. "It seems they're looking for any excuse to send me back to Oklahoma. Tried to get a code violation to stick, but it didn't go anywhere."

Ryan nodded. "I stopped that one before the officer embarrassed himself with Walpole. Showed me your papers, all those verses and the verse reference shorthand. I recognized that from my wife's letters."

"Walpole a stickler?"

"Fair, but firm. Doesn't have any patience for stupidity or baseless demerits."

"Thank you, then. I've been trying to keep the rules, but they seem to be majoring on minor issues."

"That's the biggest adjustment transitioning down to Level One. In a Five they can't afford to go after guys for not showing up for recreation, but it counts here."

"You got that right. They're trying to keep us alive until we complete our sentences. You show up for recreation or not, but you still got to be ready for count." He had a few moments left. "Is there a chance I could volunteer for the chaplain's office in the afternoons and do recreation after supper?"

"The chaplain's office is no more than a storage section for the various worship services. The day program officer keeps track of the schedule."

"There's no Christian chaplain?"

"Volunteer civilian. Sunday service's in the afternoon. He does a Bible study Thursday afternoon."

"Many Christians here?"

"Good group. Keep to themselves. Have their own study time Sunday mornings in their pods. Some of them finished online seminary degrees. They take it very seriously."

"Good to know."

"You've been here more than two weeks, right? Didn't check it out yet?"

"They put me in segregated housing the first Sunday, and I was tied up with the code violation the second. Looking forward to getting together with other believers." The warning bell for afternoon sessions rang through the hall.

Tom scrambled to get to recreation lineup in time.

———⌘———

The nest day Ryan joined him for lunch. "So, you want to volunteer. Can't get a paying job until you're done with A&O."

"That's fine with me. I'm indigent. Had no paying jobs in Hannibal. If you got nothing to take, harder for them to get to you." Memories of not even making bail because the Task Force had seized all his assets rose up. The blood pounded in his throat. Tom focused on relaxing and calming his breathing.

"I read your résumé. That did follow your file. Tell me about your EMT certification."

"Completed that when I was in high school. Was expected to work at the family business most of the time, but Dad invested heavily in the city's EMS and fire station. They had a big inventory problem. Instead of donating money to cover it, he sent me in to research the problem and install a state-of-the-art inventory management system. Got to hang out with the EMT's. Was fascinated by what they did, and they helped me earn the certification. I read through their books, they gave me hands-on practice, completed enough hours in ride-alongs and passed the online test. It was a grand time."

"A real accomplishment. Did you solve the shrinkage problem?"

Tom raised his eyebrow and glanced at Ryan. For an instant he almost forgot they were still in prison. "Yeah, there were three primary issues—a main supplier was shorting us. When I separated their bundled items and counted everything coming in through the door, the pattern was obvious. The EMT's needed better training on keeping track and logging the supplies that went with them. The training and supervisor follow-through took a little doing. The scanning system and inventory software we installed helped too."

"So, your family had a store. It wouldn't be Hutton Family Furniture Stores, would it?" Ryan noticed Tom's frozen look. "Relax, Tom.

Your secret's safe with me. I was hit with the usual scams they run in here if they think you have any money. I won't tell anyone."

"Thanks. Can't afford to mention things like that."

"At least you have a family who can support you when you get out."

Tom looked at the clock. It was early, but he didn't want to get into why he couldn't go home. "Have to get my stuff together for recreation." He looked at his plate, still half full.

"Tom, I might have a spot for you. I'll check around and get back to you."

"Thanks, I'd appreciate it," he said. He rose, scooped up his tray and left, walking swiftly. He had to find his center in Christ before he stepped on the court.

CHAPTER 62

THEY HAD MORE free time on Saturdays but spent a good part of it confined to "the barn"—his name for the large open area filled with cots and short lockers.

This was his first weekend not in the SHU or sitting in interrogation. He pulled his chest locker around, sorted his papers, ran through the day's memory verse drills and went to the first open page in his journal. Tomorrow he would get to meet other Christians. His mood lifted. He hadn't seen Ryan at lunch for two days. He tried to shake it off. He should be used to being alone in a crowd by now. His eyes scanned the cavernous room, taking in the groups huddled for cards, games or just hanging out. He would never fit, not really. It didn't seem so obvious in Hannibal with the cells and smaller groups.

Sunday dawned. After breakfast Tom retreated to his corner for Bible study. He was going to take another crack at getting a handle on Revelation. Using his Greek New Testament, he opened to chapter 6 and reviewed the margin notes for Old Testament quotes and references. The references ran from Genesis to Deuteronomy and most of the prophets. The contiguous thread running through the whole Bible, old and new, front to back thrilled him once again.

He glanced at the clock throughout the morning, but time seemed to drag despite his interest in the study. Tom tried not to daydream about fellowshipping with other believers. Tempted to doublecheck he was on the list for Sunday service, he sat back and recalled the Zechariah 14 passages to find the right reference.

Ryan did not seem to be at lunch that day either. It'd been a while, and Tom tried to push down his disappointment. He walked back to the barn and waited for the callout.

It came an hour later. A handful lined up, and they followed an escort—a full-fledged resident in brown. The newbies following wore brown pants, but orange tops.

They crossed the campus, following the paved walkways. Tom watched many making their way to the Admin building that also housed the meeting rooms. Today the main auditorium was a chapel. Tom's heart lifted with the sight of others carrying books, many looking like Bibles. He found a seat in the middle and smiled at the pair on his right. His eyes glanced down at their Bibles. They were all different, and many had Bible covers and other items with them.

"Hi, I'm new."

"We can tell; I'm Ron, and this is Chad. You are?"

"Tom. They got Bibles to hand out? They let you bring your own?"

"How else would they do it?"

Tom didn't answer. He nodded to the large Bible in Ron's lap. "That an approved Bible?"

"No, not KJV, if that's what you mean. The chaplain can help you get a Bible but have to get on the list. This is an NLT."

"Is it approved?"

"Like I said. It's not the authorized version, but these do just fine."

"They didn't take your Bibles? They didn't hand out the government-issued ones?"

"No." Ron looked at Chad.

"Listen, Tom, we can go over this with the chaplain later. The worship band's setting up. It's time to start."

Tom rose and joined the singing, but his eyes roved throughout the assembly, noting that most had their own Bibles. He didn't see one government-approved Bible in the hall. The blood pounded in his throat, but he reminded himself—he had not reoffended. They couldn't charge him for being in the same room with someone with an illegal Bible, but his unease grew.

Chad brought Tom up to meet Pastor Timmens. "Hi, Pastor, Tom's asking how to get a Bible. He's interested."

"I'm wondering if you have access to the government-approved Bibles."

"I don't know what that is, son. But we have donated copies. I can bring one next week."

Tom tried to explain the HCL law and what it meant, but Pastor Timmens and Chad exchanged glances.

"Son, that doesn't sound like this here US of A. A law like that would go directly against our Bill of Rights, particularly our First Amendment rights."

"I agree with you, sir; however, they consider hate crimes and speech laws trump our religious free exercise rights. It might seem extreme, but I received a five-year sentence for owning five Bibles."

"What else did you have, and did you accept a plea deal?"

"My Bible college books, and yes, I took a deal." His heart sank with the looks the pastor and Chad exchanged. His head buzzed when the pastor lectured him on owning up to his crimes and taking full responsibility. He felt like running when the pastor ended with, "And you went to Bible college. We all need to be good examples for others to follow."

Tom excused himself and headed for the benches by the back courts. His head fell into his hands. The chaplain's words with the looks of the inmates standing next to him swirled in his mind. He tried to stall the plunging grip of despair. Logical thought fled, and any reasoned solutions vanished as the memories replayed over again. He lifted his head, focusing on a distant line of trees bordering a closely cropped green lawn spreading out over the softly rolling area bounded by a simple chain-link fence.

A figure drew close from his left. He glanced over. "Hi, Ryan.

Missed you last few days." Tom turned his head to wipe away a few tears. He sat back, trying to affect a relaxed look.

Ryan's broad smile melted away. "I had a visit with Patty, but what's up with you?"

"Not hiding it too well, am I?" Tom tried to laugh it off. "They didn't believe me at Hannibal either. Not until the Task Force came in and ripped apart my cell and workstation in the kitchen. The warden kicked them out. No more fishing expeditions without actionable warrants." He glanced over. "Looks like I'm starting at square one again. Pastor and his band of Christians don't believe me."

"You can imagine, but from their point of view, it sounds crazy. Patty hadn't heard much about it, but she will look into it. I don't think we even had a delivery of those Bibles you were talking about." Ryan leaned forward. "But I did get you a hearing for a volunteer position in the infirmary. The medical supply inventory's a mess, and Nurse Hutchins is pushing for a civilian worker. The warden likes to utilize residents' talents to fill positions—helps with the stats." He patted Tom's knee. "Those all-important numbers give you an edge for the position. Just…" He smiled. "do exactly what she says, no questions asked."

"What's the problem?"

"Every resident I've sent over's not been cooperative or downright obnoxious. You might be the warden's last chance to keep it a resident position—if you know what I mean."

"Working the medical supply area sounds way better than laundry or kitchen duty…" Tom returned the smile. "…and cooler too. Is it air-conditioned?"

"You bet. I'll jump through the hoops to get Walpole to sign off on the position, be a super assistant to Hutchins, and you'll have a great job—at least in my book."

Tom nodded.

CHAPTER 63

Tom showed up at Ryan's desk after lunch. It took a few hours, but Ryan walked him to the infirmary during mid-afternoon count. "Good luck."

Tom nodded. He stepped through the door and breathed in the cool, dry air. The medical supply shelves extended back, filling the long, narrow area. A lone supply cart sat in the middle of the wall to the left of the main entrance. The short wall on the right sported a crowded counter covered with monitors, piles of paper and many-tiered in-boxes. A middle-aged woman perched on a stool hunched over the middle console.

"Ms. Hutchins," Tom said, trying to keep his voice from cracking, "I'm reporting for work." He froze, wondering if he should say it again.

The woman in the white lab coat held up her finger. "Just a moment."

Tom stood, watching the second hand advance the minute hand as it swept across the large face of the clock on the wall.

"All right," she called over her left shoulder. "All right already."

He started slightly and handed over his papers. The nurse uh-huhed and harrumped but didn't look back at him. She selected a file and printed a sheet. "Have at it. Count them."

"What?" Tom puzzled over the form.

"The first item to be counted. Find its location on the shelves. Get acquainted with the racks. You're going to be spending a lot of time here—if you make the cut."

"How many?"

"How many what?"

"How many times do you want me to count then?"

"Count as many times as it takes to get it right, and I'm not telling you the number. Count, find me, and if it's right, you can count the next item."

Tom nodded. "Sounds fair to me." He entered the stacks. The numbering system came back quickly, not far different from the EMS, but the layout was unexpected. Assuming the left door of the room went to the triage, waiting and treatment rooms, first-aid supplies were housed farther away in the far righthand rows. He did not have to go far down the left-most row to find his victim—a large, unorganized tub of one-time use needles—standard issue for vaccinations, insulin injections and many medications. *This will take a while.*

Tom made room and started to count. He doublechecked his numbers and headed to the nurse. She looked at the number and shook her head. He nodded and counted again…and again.

One look at the clock told him he was running out of time. "Nurse Hutchins, my numbers are finally settling out, but…" He showed her the number. He suppressed a groan when she shook her head. "I'd like a table or surface and a sterile cloth to cover it. I'll try one last time to see if we can get better numbers."

Nurse Hutchins sighed, nodded to a folding table and pointed to a drawer labeled sterile cloths. "Have at it."

Tom arranged them in groups of ten, fifty and hundreds. His last count had been the same. "So, at least we have a confirmed count as of today. How short is it?"

"203."

"When was the last count?"

"Last week."

"That's a lot. When's the next shipment?"

"Tomorrow."

"Can you hold it unopened until after lunch tomorrow when I can confirm the shipment?"

"Why afternoon?"

"Got A&O classes all morning."

"Ryan promised you weren't a newbie."

"I'm not. My facility didn't make me take the classes. Warden didn't accept their sign-off."

Hutchins nodded, "I'll put up with that for now, but you come back to receive the shipment."

"Thank you, ma'am."

Her eyes narrowed. "Don't call me ma'am. Nurse Hutchins will do."

Ryan met Tom after count and mail call. "Well? How did it go?"

"They're seriously short. Counted the needles four times, but we're working on a solution."

Ryan smiled. "I knew you could do it." He moved with Tom to the dining hall. "Now, as soon as you finish up with A&O, I have to start your good-time package. You have to fill out the forms, including contact information for your family."

Tom stopped, nearly tripping Ryan. "I can't go home."

"You can't *not* go home," Ryan laid a gentle hand on Tom's arm to get him back on track for the dining hall. "Don't want to be at the end of the line. You get released back to your city. Where you go after you're done with supervision, that's up to you."

Tom started to protest. Ryan looked his way. "It's not up for negotiation. What's the plan for the supply shortages?"

"I take it there's more? Well, count everything coming in. Daily counts for suspect items, carefully tracking what's out to treatment rooms and the crash carts."

"You'll do just fine. She okay with you just working afternoons?"

"I explained the situation. She didn't say much."

"Never does." Ryan added, "And don't call her *ma'am*."

"I already made that mistake."

He loaded his tray and followed Ryan to his usual table. Tom noted the Christians hung out tables away. He spied one Bible near a resident. They really hadn't taken him seriously.

"Hey, Ryan," Tom set his tray near his new friend. "You play basketball?

"Not really, but I run every morning."

"Have evening recreation teams?"

CHAPTER 64

Tom FOUND THE evening rec coordinator to get his name on a list. He had to stay busy or he'd go out of his mind. The next evening, he sauntered over to the outdoor courts after supper. Tom slept well that night.

The next day when he walked into his usual class, the training officer yelled at him. "Didn't you see your call out? Report or get written up."

He stared at the sheet thrust in his hand. It told him nothing but his caseworker's name and time of meeting. He was late.

Tom walked quickly to Admin and paused at Ryan's desk, catching his breath. "What's up?"

Ryan smiled. "You did so well, you're out of A&O. Hutchins has you full-time. Can you live with that?"

Tom smiled. "You bet."

"Don't you want to know?"

"What?"

"The pay?"

"Not really. Will it threaten my indigent status?"

"It's not bad for here, same as mine. In a month you're going to have an account."

"Don't see how that helps me."

"Decent shoes and clothes that don't go threadbare after three washings, that's what."

"Guess I'd better get my indigent supply before they get the message."

"One more thing." Ryan patted the chair next to his desk. "You have to get a haircut." He noticed Tom's frozen look. "What? They cut ya?"

"Yeah, cut me the whole time shaving me bald right in front of the guards."

"I'll take you over—my treat this time. This guy's good. It helps for the good-time hearings."

Tom rolled his eyes. "It's a useless exercise."

"How's that?"

"I won't take the Bibles."

"What Bibles?"

"The government-issued, approved Bibles that are probably sitting in the back of a shelf in the chaplain's office."

"That settles it. We're going to find those Bibles or prove you wrong after lunch."

Tom nodded.

The chaplain's office storage room was a disorderly jumble of items and boxes with minimal labeling. Tom headed for the boxes shoved in the back. Ryan helped sort through them. Eventually he spied familiar markings and opened the box—pristine Bibles embossed with a logo on the spine with green-tipped pages near the binding.

They carried a handful out into an open area in front of the chaplain's office. Tom flipped to Romans 1. "See, it's short."

Ryan pulled out the packing slip. "Shipped over two years ago."

"This would be the second shipment. Not the first." Tom turned back to storage and pulled out boxes jammed under the back right-hand shelves. He opened two more. The Bibles had green-tipped pages all around. "The first edition was not popular."

"I can see why."

"Can these be available for services? No one should be carrying their Bibles around."

"Not our decision, but we can let the officer know." Ryan knew exactly what to say to gain a hearing with the duty officer.

He listened, looked at the piles of papers flowing out of his in-basket and nodded toward a small table under a window. "Leave them there. I'll look into it."

Tom would have protested, but Ryan signaled it was time to go. "Now what? They have to be warned."

"Let's take a few to Walpole. She might have a better attitude."

Officer Walpole listened; her mouth drawn tightly over her teeth. "Sit." She perused the Bibles. "What's the law?"

"HR 756, Hate-Crime Literature. It's enforced by the HCL Task Force—a joint operation between Homeland, HHS, DOJ and FBI."

She entered the data and held her breath at the long list of HCL regulations. "Our lovely federal bureaucracy creates regulations as readily as we breathe air." She glanced at the two residents. "If we kow-towed to all of them, we'd have no time or money to do our job. This, gentlemen, is another example of red tape run amok." She leaned forward. "Do you honestly believe this Task Force is going to come in here and cite us for not taking Bibles and handing out these?"

"I do. Officer Walpole, could a notice be issued to the residents letting them know government-approved Bibles are available at the chaplain's office?"

"Oh, and who would monitor the transfer?"

"Transfer?"

"Confiscation of Bibles? Isn't that what you want us to do? You can't have a Bible so they can't?"

"No, ma'am, not at all. Best if they hand out the Bibles no questions asked. It'd be on them to decide what to do with their complete Bibles. I'd rather not have a list anywhere of who might have Bibles."

"Ryan, write up a notice, and I'll get it approved for posting. I don't want to hear any more of this from either of you."

Ryan rose. "Thank you, Officer Walpole. It'll be on your desk this afternoon."

Tom followed him to his desk.

"Help me with the notice, then I'll have her sign a pass." Ryan added, "At least she gave us a hearing, and they've been warned. She's right about the avalanche of regulations. BOP's got to focus on their main task."

As Ryan's fingers flew over the keyboard, Tom suggested some changes.

"We can't make it too long. That's going to have to be good enough."

Tom headed to the infirmary with his pass. It felt like high school— only there was no ride home at the end of the day.

Nurse Hutchins stared at the note, her brows drawn together. "I hope you have a good reason." She laughed after Tom's explanation. "You can't make this stuff up."

CHAPTER 65

A FEW DAYS later, Tom joined the supper queue. Not seeing Ryan, he took a tray and decided to check out the salad bar.

A stocky figure drew close as he hovered over the mostly brown lettuce. "You know about that notice they issued? The one about the Bibles?"

"Yeah," Tom glanced over. "Have we met?"

"I'm Terry. Saw you at church last Sunday. That notice about those authorized Bibles. They really taking Bibles?"

"Supposed to hand them out, no questions." He didn't want to know whether or not Terry had a Bible.

"Getting out soon. Can't afford trouble." Terry turned aside and walked to the tables where the Christians hung out.

Tom headed to the far left, sat with his back to the wall and studied the day's fare. He'd never say, but Bruce's kitchen had regularly turned out better food.

A tall Sioux Tom played ball with sat on the left corner. They exchanged nods.

"Ya know, you making 'em mad the way you play," Luke said between bites.

"I am?"

"Yeah, stealing the ball and getting in their face."

"Legal moves. How we played in Hannibal."

"You ain't in Hannibal," Luke said.

Ryan joined them. "Hi, Luke, Tom."

"What's up, Doc?" Luke laughed.

"You know each other?"

"My auntie worked with Nurse Hutchins at the reservation nursing center," Luke said.

Tom, still confused, returned to his meal.

Ryan sat across from Luke. "He's right, Tom. Some officers like to write up players."

Luke added, "The residents know how to get a person into trouble. The smart ones don't play ball when they're trying to get out early. Now transients, guys like you, transfer in, get your package and depart. Just like that. Not a good idea to hang out on the courts if you're trying to make your package stick."

"Listen to him, Tom. Some officers love to mess up guys almost ready to get out. Terry's not playing ball anymore. Ask him." Luke and Ryan exchanged knowing glances.

"Yeah, but there's no one to talk to in the supply room, and you don't make conversation with Nurse Hutchins."

Ryan nodded, "Jog with me in the mornings and go to breakfast after."

Tom looked over. He buried his first instinct to say no. "That's very generous. I make the change with my day officer?"

"Something like that." Ryan gave the details.

CHAPTER 66

I T TOOK ALMOST a week. Tom waited by the path bounding the camp. Small groups formed and headed out—some jogging, others walked. In the distance he spied Ryan walking quickly.

He worked to catch his breath. "They only want you running on the path."

Tom nodded. They started slowly.

Ryan cleared his throat. "You never asked why some call me *Doc*."

"Everyone's got their own reasons for being here. I suspect you're not the same person who came through those gates. I like to take people for who they are today. You've been kind, generous, helpful and honest. I don't need to know anymore."

"I appreciate that."

They turned the last bend before looping back behind the Admin buildings. "A guy in Hannibal said he used to get mad about pulling a 25 for a frameup job until he realized if he'd been convicted of all the crimes he had done, he'd be in for twice as long."

"Hard to imagine. Yes, I've changed. My wife as well. I used to be a doctor, a good one, until I hired the wrong business manager. Deep down I knew something was wrong, but he brought in the money."

"Oh, boy."

Ryan nodded. "He pled down to nothing and laid it all on me." Ryan shook his head. "Patty found God, liquidated our assets, and sold the house. It was hard to accept her making all those decisions, but it had to be done, and I didn't make bail. She fired the lawyer, found one willing to negotiate a better plea deal, and here I am, getting ready to leave."

"Things are going to be different on the outside."

"I've come to terms with it. She helped me find my first job on the outs and moved us to a different city."

"That will help."

"Anyway, you have to find a pod, and my pod mate's being released soon. You interested?"

"Yeah, but can it wait a few weeks? If by next month the Task Force hasn't shown up, then I'll make the move. They let me hang out in the barn a little longer?"

"You don't have two weeks."

"I will pray about it. I'd love to say yes today but would feel terrible if they noticed you."

"You know how that sounds."

"Paranoid? I get that. I hope you're right and they're done with me. If all's clear in a week, then I join your pod. By the way, where's Terry been?"

"Home now with his good-time release."

"That's great to hear."

CHAPTER 67

TWO DAYS LATER Tom, deep in the racks, heard his name called. Nurse Hutchins stood in the center area, in front of two DU officers.

Tom accompanied the officers to the DU and sat on the far side of a table in a spare room. The opaque mirror stared back at him from across the room. *They have come.*

Agent Cooper led a pair of agents to Tom's bunk in the open dorm. He tried not to scowl at the DU officers surrounding them. He felt cocooned and hemmed in. Things would change when they had a chance to dig into Hutton's area. They had him this time. He could feel it in his bones. "This it?" he spied the taut-made bed and spotless area. As he stepped forward, the nearest officer shook his head.

"We perform the search. You may only observe and note any findings. What are we looking for again?"

"HCL contraband. That would be Bibles or any written proscribed verses." He spied the pile of papers and notebook pulled from the locker. "We need to see that."

"File your search parameters, and we'll let you know if we find anything."

"Also, hidden cell phones or any other devices he could use to contact his network."

They nodded curtly.

Agent Trainer adjusted his sleeves before opening the door. "Well, finally decided to join the civilized world and get a haircut."

Tom stared at him. "Agent Trainer?"

"So, you remember. That's nice." He sat down opposite Tom. "This time we have warrants. We will find out how you've been doing it."

He sat back in his chair to keep his distance. "Doing what?"

"Communicating with the underground church." The nearest agent handed him a photo. "Your old buddy from Hannibal. How'd you lead him to a stash of Hutton Bibles?"

Tom recognized the inmate who had attended his seeker's class, but he couldn't remember the man's name. Sitting up, he held back a smile. "I'm quite a magician then—no mail, no phone calls or visitors, as well as indigent. How did I manage that?"

The agent smiled back, meeting his gaze.

As a pulse ran down Tom's spine, he forced his face to remain neutral.

Trainer sat back. "You never make this easy, do you? We'll get you in the end. We always get our man."

"You got me years ago. Wasn't that good enough?"

"You obviously didn't learn your lesson." He sat back and tapped his earbud. The agent near the door swung it open. As he left, he smirked at Tom. "Your uncle's not in Leavenworth."

"Where is he?"

The agent laughed hard and loud. "Buried in an unmarked pauper's grave. He died alone. No one claimed his body." He leaned forward. "That's what you get when you make yourself a criminal."

Tom sat back. *How is this possible—Uncle Al, the fountain of boundless energy and health?* Images of his uncle thriving at Leavenworth, living out the truths of God's Word, being an effective witness for Christ had kept him going.

In the seconds the agent held the door open before he walked out, Tom's brain registered the time on a distant clock—two p.m. A few seconds later he recalled the day—Thursday and Pastor Timmens' Bible study.

CHAPTER 68

L ATER AN OFFICER opened the door. "Skedaddle; need the room." Tom passed the officer and walked to the main intake area. He sucked in his breath. The benches were filled with many he recognized from the Christian group. Sounds of low talking filtered from behind him. Tom twisted slightly to catch a glimpse of Pastor Timmens sitting near Ron and Chad.

The middle supply room was quiet with everyone in the clinic. Steadying his shaking hand, he turned to the sameness of routine to find his center.

Tom was deep in the stacks and didn't hear the head nurse until she called his name a second time.

Perched on her usual stool, she stared at him.

"Yes, Nurse Hutchins?"

"What's all the uproar about?"

"They're here—the Task Force."

"Found nothing on you?"

He shook his head. "They're searching for the mastermind who's leading the Christians, but He is beyond their reach. He sits at the right hand of the Father in heaven."

"Our Father."

"Will this administration help them?"

"To a certain extent. We follow the rules here or try to, meaning they will probably add Bibles to the contraband list. Won't treat your kind any different than the drug dealers."

Tom nodded.

"Delivery counted and stacked?

"Looks good."

"Complete your list of the nurses and orderlies who had access to the missing supplies. I requested Intel from the video feeds. Maybe a few are making others look bad. The security officers will check the surveillance. I told them what to look for. Checking video feeds is not on us. We have enough to do."

"That's great to hear."

"Not a word about this. Understood?"

"Of course. They think I'm just counting supplies and loading carts."

Tom looked about on his way to the barn for afternoon count. No agents lurked in the main corridors or walkways between buildings, but he had no doubt they would be in the DU for hours. His area seemed undisturbed.

He entered the dining hall late and sat alone, not greeting anyone. Eating quickly, he returned to his cot. Tom's chest tightened when he looked inside his locker. His notebooks and papers were gone.

Tom sat against the concrete, feeling the sharp edges nip his back. He stared at a distant corner, his eyes drifting out of focus until he blinked. His uncle dead, his papers gone. Tom's head dropped to his hands resting on upright knees. Unbidden, the survey of his losses rose up. His mind saw the moon, traveled to Mars, imagined the retreating earth grow smaller. No escape. Nowhere to hide. Death, separation, the tearing asunder of all that was good. The tears welled up.

He watched four return to resume their card games. A group in the corner started their music. There was no place for him here—never would be.

Oh, Lord... His wordless prayer rose to heaven and a settled peace, an echo of joy passed by. "My hope is in the Lord, who gave Himself for me," Tom said softly and finished the hymn in his soul. He recalled an image of his aunt and uncle's anniversary photo. A tear fell, remembering their brilliant smiles, shining eyes and gracious home. He knew without a doubt they were home, together in heaven, and no agent or Task Force or system of man could reach them now. Someday he would be there too.

He hadn't lost his hope—just hadn't looked far enough. The Lord would see him through. He had experienced God's provision and blessing in the darkest places. If he could just hang on, keep breathing, take each day as it came, he could survive with his faith intact—as long as he remembered to fix his eyes on Christ and Christ alone.

The early evening light filtered through the large double doors. Tom's eyes followed the outlines of two officers approach the main desk and look his way. He rose, waiting for the inevitable.

One was an officer, the other a young agent. They escorted him to an Admin conference room next to the case managers' desks. His notebooks and papers were stacked at one end of the table.

Tom stood where they left him. The usual flurry of questions and answers followed—no, he had no Bible; it was all from memory. No, he had no contact with the outside world. They must have heard this before, but they seemed to enjoy asking the same questions over and over.

The agent skimmed his pages of handwritten verses. "Why?"

"How I keep it fresh. Scripture memory requires constant review. It helps to have it written down when writing sermons or teaching notes."

"These," the agent surveyed the cryptic pages. "Basic salvation, life in Christ, the armor of God."

"So, you know?"

He lifted his gaze. "Believers are commanded to obey the governing authorities."

"Except for laws that violate God's commands to read His Word, study it and share it." Tom recited the Acts 4 passages.

The agent rose. "We will be filing a statement with your case manager that while we can find no evidence you have re-offended, you are resistant to the law and not a candidate for good-time release." He nodded to the officer. "He may go."

Tom took a chance. "May I have my papers?"

The agent nodded. "We're done with them."

CHAPTER 69

Tom cradled his papers in his arms, walking quickly along the walkways. It would be time for last count soon. His other dormmates were filing back after their evening activities. The area slowly filled up with others graduated from classes still waiting to find a pod. Heading straight for his cot, he ignored the stares and catcalls.

Lee came over and sat on a nearby cot. "Hear they nabbed lots of guys."

Tom nodded, dropping the notebooks into his locker. "It's about the Bibles." He had talked to Lee about his before.

"They're not going to search everybody, are they? To think if I had gone to that study today." Lee shook his head.

He sat on his heels. North Platte seemed to be cooperating. "I don't know. Didn't ask. But if I hear anything, I'll let you know."

It took another day for the agents to collect the evidence and ship the offenders to district detention. Tom avoided Ryan and had unscheduled free time that evening. He set to sorting his papers, updating his diary and running through the next set of chapters on his review schedule.

Partway through the pile, he came to his sermon notes. He noticed a half-filled sheet—his unfinished sermon—the one he would have preached at Hannibal.

Tom read the title—"The Pearl of Great Price." He reviewed the parable of Christ's giving all He had for the hidden treasure and the pearl. He recalled his uncle's sacrifice, his own travails and hardships.

From the world's point of view, he should be devastated, broken, disheartened, but at that moment, the joy of the Lord burst forth. The privilege to stand for Christ before a dead world, to share the love of God to those abandoned and cast aside, to see God work in the darkest wing in Building Four, and to hear of inmates reclaimed and restored through Wallie's preaching lifted his soul with praise. He prayed ever more fervently that the North Platte Christians standing for the Word of God would know the same joy, feel the same love and testify to God's glory. He prayed for the agents to see God working in their midst, especially the agent who seemed to be a believer.

He took up his pencil and wrote down the verses flooding his soul—Christ's work to save the world, the great price He paid. Continuing on to His victory over sin, Tom rotated to the salvation He brought and the open door to God's throne room of grace. His hand flew over the pages, barely able to keep up with the verses pouring forth. The way of salvation, the joy of the Lord, the fellowship with God Himself—no longer alone, cast adrift without resources, tossed aside by a cruel world—was available to all who would follow the Lord and take the hidden treasure.

The next day Tom walked to the jogger's path until he reached the section bounded by trees and bushes out of sight of cameras. He stepped to the side and retied his shoes, praying for Ryan to come by. Three groups later, he heard familiar footfalls. He stood waiting by the closest tree.

Ryan stopped and smiled. "Let's jog."

"Is it safe? They gone?"

"Yep, keeping to routine and not lurking is the best way to avoid questions." Ryan set the pace. He glanced at Tom. "Some of the warden's lieutenants wanted to initiate a lockdown, execute a prison-wide search and hand over everyone with Bibles. Walpole and some of the others projected what this would do to the warden's stats. She's young and ambitious."

"I reckon the Task Force's having to show them how to enforce federal guidelines would not be a good career move?"

"Exactly. No extra searches, but they are going to enforce 756." Ryan laughed. "You should have heard the managers going on and on about Hannibal's using criminals to review materials for compliance. Don't even think of trying to get involved."

Tom nodded. "Who's coming in to do the services?"

Ryan shook his head. "Civilian preachers willing to come to prison are hard to find. They've contacted the state chaplaincies for volunteers, but that's going to take time."

"I could fill in until they get a schedule of volunteers. How should I make the offer?"

"I'll let you know."

"Are they going to monitor our activities now?" Tom added, "They going to record who I hang out with?"

"No more than usual. It'd probably be fine for you to resume your daily routines."

While they were alone on the path, he asked, "Ryan, I don't know if this is appropriate. If it would get you into trouble, I'll try a different way but, the agents bragged that my uncle died. He's under 65, was never sick. Could you find out how he died?"

Ryan held his hand. "I'm sorry to hear that. Nephews don't get notifications, but I don't have that kind of access. Ask for a callout. Maybe Walpole will be in a good mood and look it up for you."

CHAPTER 70

Tom WAITED A week to join the Christians. Ryan appeared to be gone for a visit. He walked toward the mostly filled table and plopped down his tray. "Hello." The conversation stopped. "I'm at a disadvantage. You probably know my name, but I don't know yours."

A grizzled middle-aged inmate sized him up. "Marsh. You here to gloat?"

"No, not at all. How are you all doing? Did they take everything?"

A young slender man with stringy blond hair nodded. "Officers said Bible study books are illegal too."

"Not true." Tom explained the law and how to navigate it. "Push back. They can't outlaw our faith. Tell your case manager all books that do not quote the proscribed verses should be returned."

"I'm Howie, by the way." He dug out a folded sheet from his pocket. "The list we got."

Tom laughed and shook his head. "Well, well, this is the one I created for the chaplain in Hannibal. Yes, those booklets and courses are fine." He handed it back.

Marsh narrowed his eyes. "If you're so pure and innocent, why'd you end up here on this side? You took a plea. Timmens said you were labeled a terrorist. Come clean with us. We don't want no pretenders—abusers of God's grace, charlatans taking advantage of the love of the true brethren. We fellowship with ones washed by the blood of Christ, who faithfully follow God and His commands." He leaned forward and added, "Who obey the law."

Tom nodded. "Listen to my story, and I'll leave it up to you." Tempted to walk away, go back to his small circle of acquaintances, some becoming friends, he was not afraid to walk alone. If they accepted him, fine; if not, no problem—he was just passing through.

He told his story, eyes focused on a point in the middle of the table, hanging in the air in the hot hall, smelling of bland grease, lukewarm food, and sweaty bodies.

Seeing their blank faces and silence, Tom shrugged his shoulders and stared at his food. The ashes returned to sink into his gut.

"You shall know them by their fruits," Marsh said. "We watchin' you—see how you do when delivered up to Satan."

Tom smiled. "He can dance on our chests all he wants in the darkness of the night and try to harass us with terrors, but God will never forsake us—not even in the silence." He met Marsh's eyes. *"Even the darkness is not dark to you; the night is bright as the day, for darkness is as night with you. For you formed my inward parts… "*[32] Tom's voice cracked, and he could not finish the verses from Psalm 139—too many memories from Hannibal sprang up unbidden. He began to rise, lifting his mostly filled tray. "When I had to leave Hannibal after three years, it felt like I lost my right arm."

"What? You booking out like a coward? Slink away like you got something to hide?"

Tom sat and met Marsh's hard look. "What's your pleasure? Can we be friends or distant brethren? I'm short, so decide."

Howie laughed. "Stranger and stranger, but sure, we can hang." He stared at Tom. "This really cost you."

Tom matched his gaze. "No way I'd have met any of you or the guys in Hannibal. Not my usual circle." He leaned forward, "But it was God's plan, and I had to accept it."

Marsh nodded, almost smiling. "Most of the guys reeled in are practically lifers. They not gonna be bothered by a few more years tacked on."

"Timmens is the one to pray for. They won't hesitate to threaten him with the destruction of his family—have no respect for small children or women. You get on their radar; they'll never stop hunting you down. I'd hoped I was wrong, but I wasn't. They followed me here. Sorry about that. Wish it was different."

"You get out of your head and into the game, young man," Marsh ordered. "Be strong in Jesus, no looking back. Follow Him, and don't think you be the only one getting the chance to suffer for Christ."

Tom nodded. "That's right. They told me my uncle's dead. Really got to me until the Lord reminded me where he is this very moment." His gaze grew distant, *"For I consider that the sufferings of this present time are not worth comparing with the glory that is to be revealed to us."*[33] He studied Marsh's grizzled black hair, cut short and inset brown eyes. "You preacher?"

Marsh shook his head. "Study every day. Read, pray and try not to mess up. Don't want to bring shame to Christ because of me. Lots that come out wishin' I could take back."

"True for us all." Tom gathered his tray. "We good? It hurts when there's something between the brethren. Don't have to be friends; just know you're on my prayer list."

CHAPTER 71

RYAN MET HIM the next day at the jogging path.
"Welcome back." He assumed Ryan had had another conjugal
visit. Ryan grunted and stopped to retie his shoes. He looked aside past
Tom.

"What's up?'

Shaking his head, he started out with a quick sprint. Tom worked
to keep up with him. "Anytime you want to talk about it, I'll try not to
interrupt."

They started the second lap before Ryan voiced his fears. "It's getting closer, and I don't know how this is going to work. Patty's so different. She takes control. She's…" he shook his head.

Tom searched for what to say until he remembered to listen. Ryan
tore into the details of his fears. Nearing the end, the only thing Tom
could think of was to encourage Ryan to remember the giant mon-
sters of what could be were often only shadows nipping at our heels.
"You've been together twenty-five years. She stood by you, man. She's
not walking away now. If you are both committed to each other, no
matter what, God will make a way."

He wanted to reach out and encourage his friend, but Ryan's face
was closed. He said without looking at him, "You preach this Sunday.
Get ready."

"Do I give you the sermon so Walpole can review it?"

"Are you nuts? They don't want your sermon notes. Just fill the time
slot. That's all they care about."

Tom watched him stride off the path, not looking back. He gave him his distance.

He had to the end of the week to complete the message. Tom refined his notes and committed them to memory.

Jumbling nerves dancing along his spine and down his chest continued through the day. *Why am I so uptight?* He'd delivered many sermons, but not here. Casting down imaginations, he tried to focused on Christ.

Half the chairs in the converted classroom filled up, mostly with the Christians. Tom knew some of them, but many he didn't. His eyes scanned the room for instruments, and he headed for Marsh.

"Who does the worship time?"

"Not many left. Paul can sing, Les plays bass, but our keyboarder's in detention along with the rest of the band."

Tom walked to Paul and Les. "Let's get started. Les, follow Paul's lead and don't drown him out."

"We don't lead."

"Well, you are provided the opportunity to serve the Lord by leading today. I'll be with you."

Tom opened in prayer. His eyes scanned the still crowd, staring at him blankly. Paul looked at Tom. "Let's start with some choruses. Anyone have a favorite chorus?" Silence hung in the air. Tom saw the slumped shoulders.

He shifted his mic and walked to the front. "Our God reigns in heaven," he said with lifted voice. "He's not dead in the ground, decaying, but sitting at the right hand of the Father in glory. Do we know this?" He waited for the yeses to float up. "Do we know this?" They answered back, some rising up. "We know this."

He nodded at Paul. "Our God Is an Awesome God!"

Paul led the chorus. They ran through it several times. Les shouted out the next praise hymn, and Paul sang it. The residents were now standing and singing. Tom's heart swelled with the sound of many voices praising God.

Tom motioned for them to sit. "Nothing can separate us from God and His love—no regulation of man, no bars, razor wire or steel doors." He looked about. "God reached past our chains, our walls, our prisons to our very souls. He reached down and saved us because He came and paid the full price of every sin past, present, and future. And when He entered our soul, gifting us with His love—complete, total, unconditional love—He made a new creation in Him."

The time to share his message had come—not necessarily as he wrote it or memorized it, but as the Holy Spirit directed. He preached the love of Christ and the amazing treasure He offered. Partway through he recited Isaiah 53—the rejection, the agony, cut off, but not defeated.

At the end of Marsh's closing prayer, Tom glimpsed Ryan's back as he fled the room. Praying once again for his friend, he greeted those who approached, learning new names, smiling at those he knew. Luke of few words nodded in his direction before heading for his pod.

CHAPTER 72

RYAN KEPT HIS emotions at bay. He would have collapsed if he hadn't. His heart skipped a beat when he realized he'd left his call card back in his room. Walking briskly, he retrieved the card and joined the line forming down the narrow hall. Sunday afternoon was primetime for calling friends and family. Time was ticking; stand-up count drew closer. He worked to keep his leg from jumping. Ryan scowled at a resident trying to cut in line.

Eventually, he cradled the handset. Willing his hand to be steady, he punched in the numbers and breathed when he heard the phone ring—one, two, three. His tension mounted, and he prayed for Patty to answer. *This can't be left to a voice recorder.*

Click. His heart stopped. *Has the line disconnected?*

"Hello? Hello," he heard Patty's voice, tentative and uncertain.

"Honey, I love you," he said. He repeated it again, louder this time, but no one looked about. The lines could be scratchy and noisy. The room buzzed with many voices.

"Ryan, I'm so glad to hear your voice."

Taking advantage of her pause, he said, "I believe."

"You believe?"

"I believe."

"You believe!"

"Yes, I believe in Christ, and I have to apologize for last weekend. I was in a bad place and…."

"Oh, Ryan, I've prayed for you—every day, every minute, with each

294

breath that you'd find Him and know His peace. If we have God, to-gether, both of us, I know He will show us how to do this. It's scary. I can't imagine what it's going to be like for you, but we have each other. Even better we have God who will never let us down."

Ryan leaned on the narrow counter, wiping his eyes. "It took a while, but God finally got through to this stubborn old man."

His time up, they said their goodbyes.

Ryan glanced at the clock. He could still make it. Striding quickly, he headed for the large A&O dorm. He nearly passed by the group lounging around the benches in the commons until he spied Tom in the midst of the group. He slowed, weighing his options.

"Hey, Ryan, join us," Tom called. "Just hanging 'til count." He laughed. "Cause we're all so anxious to go to the barn."

Ryan nodded. He longed to share his news, but this didn't seem the right time. "Yeah, well, nice seeing you all again."

Tom stood up, nodding at the group. "Yo, bud, wait up." He walked alongside.

"Something I forgot to tell you earlier." He stopped and looked back at the large steel building. "You up for bunking in my pod, with me?"

Tom's eyes lit up. "Yes, of course." Tom, tempted to shake his hand, brought it up to sweep his hair back instead when he spied a guard watching them.

Clearing his throat, Ryan said, "And I want you to be first one in here to know." He paused, then blurted out, "I believe."

Tom stared at him. "Your running from the service, that wasn't?" A broad smile spread across his face. "You had to call Patty. This is awesome, Ryan."

"Why did I wait so long?"

"I understand. We all do."

Ryan met Tom's gaze. "It's like I've been walking through life in my sleep, not really in control—just going from one thing to another. I like to help people, and my uncle was a surgeon. It seemed natural, then I took the shortcut for family practice. We wanted to settle down and raise a family." He looked away. "The kids—our kids—are in heaven."

Tom nodded, remembering that conversation.

The warning buzzer sounded. Tom reached out to Ryan. "You are new in Christ. It's going to be exciting to see what the Lord has planned for you."

"Listen, you'll be notified about the pod transfer. Be ready to move. They don't give much notice."

CHAPTER 73

ONE MONTH OUT, living with his family, Terry watched them eat supper together as if he had never experienced this before. He'd forgotten how busy life on the outside could be—too busy to really think things through. His son's Little League practices, his teen daughter with school and work, and Adeline's shift work at the hospital made it hard to enjoy a meal together.

He smiled at Clarisse—now a precocious eleventh grader. He imagined a slight smile on her face as she avoided his gaze. Cole winked back and smiled broadly again.

"You'd think you were back in fifth grade!" Clarisse said, nudging his foot out of her way under the table. "He's been home a month already." Her eyes swept past him to the clock hanging over the sink. "Listen, my ride'll be here soon. Can I escape already?"

Adeline nodded. "Young lady, you know what to do."

"Yes, Mom," Clarisse said, and gathered her dishes, rinsed them and put them in the dishwasher.

"A month already," Terry said in amazement to himself. Not once had he gotten into a fight, arranged an illegal buy or helped plot another bank heist.

"Staying home has its advantages." Adeline looked at him through her short bangs.

"Addy," Terry took in her new look—ten pounds lighter, hair bobbed short and colored a burnt orange. "It's going to work this time."

"We'll see." She glanced at the calendar on the fridge.

"You go to that meeting tonight. You said it helps."

"Yeah, yeah, support group for us prison widows. News flash—you're home."

"The others quit when their guy returns home?" He tamped down a smile.

Addy's eyes narrowed, her back tensed until she caught the glint of mischief in her husband's eyes. Two could play this game. "Get with the program, fella. It's 'significant other' now."

"Right." His voice softened, "I'd like you to go, Addy. I think it will be helpful. I've changed; the kids are growing. There are more adjustments coming."

Adeline studied Cole, her youngest.

"Mom, Dad's going to show me that muscle car he's been working on."

"Oh, that's it. Going to just happen to stop by Nana's too, I bet." She smiled and shook her head. "Bribery lives. It starts with the young learning to twist Granny round their fingers."

Terry joined the laughter. "Get out of here. Have a good evening. We'll do fine, and I haven't forgotten about bedtime."

After finishing up the last of the dishes amid Cole's groans, they headed out the door and down the alley. A block and a half away, "Dillard's Garage" hunched on the left—an odd collection of a converted block-and-concrete gas station with an attached steel building adding four more bays. The "& Sons" was still crossed out with the "s" added back after "Dillard." It had once felt like a trap, but now he found himself almost enjoying the grunt work.

He entered the combination on the entry pad and flicked on the switch. A few lights crackled, coming to life. He surveyed the possibilities—something else he could do—fix up the place and clean it out.

Cole brushed past him. "Whoa. Check out the red caddy."

Addy let herself in the side door; it creaked less than the front. She froze, sensing movement to her right.

Terry flicked on the light by the chair. "It's so quiet. Listen," seeing her head shake, he said, "Cole's asleep. Clarisse's not back yet. How'd the meeting go?"

She sat across the table. "Marsh's wife sent a text to Gert. That Task Force you talked about raided North Platte." She relayed the news. Her face hardened. "Your newfound religion going to bury us?" Addy pulled out a cigarette, her hand shaking.

He held her hand gently and patted the Bible on the table. "Honey, we got nothing to worry about. This is a government-approved edition. We're going to be fine."

Adeline pulled her hand away. "Next shift is at six."

"Tomorrow night?"

"The a.m. So, off to bed for this gal."

Terry wrapped her in a hug.

Two weeks later Terry had finished stowing the tools after the shop closed when he heard pounding on the back door. With the last bunch gathered together, he dropped them in the top tray and pulled the door open.

Cole almost fell in. "They're here. The cops, guys in suits, and they're looking for you."

Old instincts reared up. A strong desire to head for his old hunting grounds, Pat's Pub, on the other side of town burst forth. Terry turned away from the idea. "I'll be right there. Mom and Clarissa home?"

"Yeah, and…" Cole's voice cracked.

"Not leaving you to that. Let's go." He looked Cole in the eye. "If we have nothing to hide, we have nothing to fear." He hoped his voice sounded more convincing than he felt.

Two black SUVs, a state patrol car and a blue Toyota surrounded their small house, blocking the family van. His bike was back at the shop. He resisted the urge to flee, reminding himself what he had told his son. With wordless prayers, he paused. "Cole, go stay with Grandma and tell her it's just a routine check. See my parole officer's car? Can you do that?"

Cole cleared the far corner of the shop. Terry heard the back-porch door squeak open and thud closed. He breathed, prayed, squared his shoulders and walked home.

Addy was arguing with the trooper, demanding to see a proper search warrant.

Terry paused by Hartig, his parole officer. "They have one?"

Hartig said, "Not necessary. Had sufficient CI info to authorize this search through the parole office. This counts as your month's visit. We find nothing, they can't do nothing, and I'm out of your hair." He nodded toward Addy.

"Yeah, I get the picture." He caught her eye. "Sorry, Honey, it's part of the game with early release. Let them do their job."

She stomped out. He knew she was headed for her stash of cigarettes in the third outbuilding. All eyes were on him, especially the suits. The hair tingled along the back of his neck. He set his face and prayed, trying to look relaxed and unflustered, not flinching with the sounds of opened drawers and closing doors.

After an hour, Hartig disappeared down the back hall. Terry heard him talk to the agent. "You done yet? Either find the contraband or clear out."

The older agent emerged and pointed at a kitchen chair. The agents hovered over him after he settled his back against the wall. "Where they're at?"

"What?"

"Illegal Bibles." He leaned forward, inches from Terry's face.

Terry held the gaze, unblinking.

"Found it." The other agent emerged with his Bible book bag.

He kept the smile from his face as the agents pulled out the lone Bible, two study guides and notebook.

"Government-approved Bible, gentlemen, as you can see from the embossed seal on the binding. Study guides stamped on the inside cover mean they are compliant with HR 756, approved by the North Platte staff. You can check my notebook." Terry sat back, calm and collected, the assurance of God with him ran along the edges of his soul. The agents flipped through his notes, skimming the pages.

"Satisfied?" Hartig asked, exchanged looks with the state patrol officer.

The older agent sat across from him. "I see you are determined to take your place in society as a model citizen. Help us out. We hear many of your friends from North Platte are not likeminded. You understand this is for better communities, peace and security."

"I wouldn't know. Didn't ask. Didn't check. My Bible," he nodded to his copy on the table, "tells me there is no condemnation for those in Christ Jesus. It's not my place to play God in their lives. It tells me all men are sinners, and if they do not accept the free gift of salvation from Jesus, they will give an account at the great white throne judgment. Christ paid for our sins, everyone's for all time, but we have to receive it. Have you accepted the free gift of salvation in Christ?"

He kept a straight face. Hartig's jaw nearly hit the floor; the older agent's eyes glared at him. The younger agent picked up the Bible. "Show me."

"Glad to." Terry walked him through the Romans road. Even if the man was collecting info to entrap others, it was still the gospel. God could reach down and save these men—just as he had been saved.

He walked over and retrieved Addy and Cole from his parent's house. She finished up the beer and wiped her mouth. "You still here?"

"Still here, and it's past his bedtime."

"Mine too." She marched past, closing the door in his face.

After supper Terry headed to the door.

Clarisse followed him. "Going shopping? Can I tag along?"

"Sure," he winked at Addy. "We won't be long."

She clicked her seatbelt into place. "Is it real this time?"

"What?"

"This is not just an act to keep Ma from walking out? What you told the agent, you really believe that?"

"I do." He glanced over. "Honey, God cornered me, and I had to give in or…" He shook his head, blinking back a tear. "I saw where I was headed and who I was hanging with." He chuckled. "Once I really understood, it was the only thing to do. I started to pray and asked God to get me down at least to a Level Two, and it happened." He wiped his cheek. "He sent me to a Level One camp where Pastor Timmens and the group explained salvation and how to live the Christian life. It's not like I had never heard it before, but it began to make sense."

"Can you show me?"

"Love to Clarry. When we get back."

"What are we getting?"

"A burner phone. Got to warn the others."

"Mom's got a cell."

"Yeah, and her number's my emergency contact with Officer Hartig."

"Oh."

CHAPTER 74

MARSH JOINED TOM and Ryan for a late breakfast.
"You reformed now?" Ryan joked. "I've been telling him breakfast is the most important meal of the day."

Marsh slid over with his cup of coffee and Danish.

"Course it matters what you consume for the meal."

"At least it's not soda." Tom smiled.

"Don't think this is going to be a habit." Marsh looked about and lowered his voice. "Someone sang."

"I didn't hear any serenades," Ryan said.

Tom looked at Marsh. "What happened?"

"Task Force showed up at Terry's house—full-on search for Bibles."

Ryan looked between Tom and Marsh. "Could you explain this to me?"

"How did they know the names of the other Christians in North Platte they didn't catch in their nets?" Tom looked at Ryan. "Did Walpole or Smitty hand over a list of names?"

"Such a list doesn't exist."

"Correct," Marsh stated. "The only way they knew about Terry would be if someone nabbed last month cut a deal." He added, "They asked Terry for names, but seeing they had nothing on him, he couldn't be pushed. He shared the gospel with them instead."

Ryan's eyes widened, and he laughed. "That is rich."

Tom nodded. "The agents have to read the Bible to learn how to hunt us. I'm more than happy to explain the Word of God to any agent or officer who asks." Tom sat back, praying again for Agents Worden and Masters.

Ryan finished his morning routine and headed to his desk behind Officer Walpole's. He pulled up his task list and surveyed the day's events—slim intake with only three transfers and no newbies, follow up with unfinished questionnaires for five in segregation and two in medical isolation. He paused with the highlighted event schedule. Civilian chaplain was back on the list for Sunday service and the Thursday afternoon meeting. He glanced Walpole's way. She seemed approachable.

"Officer Walpole, have they found a chaplain for the Christian services?"

She didn't even look up from her email. "Timmens is back."

"But he was arrested."

She looked at him. "Must have been the Boy Scout we always knew he was. Not charged, and he wants back in. The lead agent put in a good word for him with the warden." She stared at him. "Hutton's done. You can give him the news."

"I'd be glad to." He resumed his station, his mind swirling with the details, but lacking experience, he shrugged his shoulders. He'd tell Tom first.

Tom missed lunch. Ryan waited to share the news during standup count before mail call.

"What do you think happened?"

"Not sure. Hard to tell. Guess we'd better ask him this Sunday instead of guessing."

"The guys'll be suspicious."

"I am."

"Do we tell them?"

"Yeah. These kinds of surprises we don't need." He took a half-step closer, "And all the new attendees, everyone that started coming after the arrests, we need to tell them to stay away from Timmens until we make sure he's not a problem."

Tom saw Ryan's puzzled look. "Listen, if they flipped him, he's coming in as a CI—confidential informant—to finger every Christian in this facility. We need to keep the new ones away, including you."

Ryan nodded, his face blanching. "How do I tell Patty to clear the house?"

"Very carefully, but not over the phone or through the mail."

CHAPTER 75

Sunday afternoon Marsh and Tom straightened the auditorium chairs and set out the stacks of Bibles.

Pastor Timmens arrived as usual—thirty minutes early. He smiled at Tom and headed straight to Marsh who shook his hand but sidestepped a hug. He looked at Tom. "Guess I owe you an apology, young man. Let's get properly introduced."

"Tom Hutton, Pastor Timmens. I've been holding your spot open here."

"He preached every Sunday. Didn't miss a week."

"No rain days," Tom quipped.

"Where is everybody?"

"Well," Marsh ran his fingers through his hair, "still in detention working through their charges and deciding on plea deals. How'd you get through so fast?"

The pastor's eyes slid to the left. "Gave me a warning. Told me about the new law. Since I didn't have any priors, they let me go at that."

Tom cleared his throat and worked at keeping his face blank. "You handed in your Bibles for approved editions?"

Timmens turned away and surveyed the stage. "Where's the drum set?"

"We have a singer and a bass guitarist who's filling in, but we manage." Tom smiled. "We praise the Lord in song with the tools we have at hand."

"Been working, been working. Anything you need, Pastor?"

"No, guess I'm good to go. See you have Bibles ready."

"New regs. No one walks around with Bibles anymore. Not allowed." Marsh studied Pastor Timmens' reaction.

"Good to know."

"Well then, we'll let you get settled and start at the usual time."

Marsh nodded at Tom. They headed for the foyer and out the door. "You buy they just let him off with a warning 'cause he's such a good boy?"

"Not on your life. I was a Boy Scout and didn't get just a warning." Tom stopped near a bench. "I think we have our CI."

"I think so too."

"When do we tell the others?"

"Let's see how he does today." Marsh nodded to a group heading for the program building and intercepted them. "Listen, fellas, not a good day to attend. We'll catch up with you tomorrow by the birch trees during evening recreation."

The first started to protest, but the shorter fella pulled him past. "Keep walking." They headed to the call and visiting center.

Tom and Marsh headed in shortly before the session started and sat at the back, keeping an eye out for latecomers.

Tom had only heard the pastor preach once months ago. He glanced at Marsh who dutifully followed along in a Bible, giving no indication of what he thought of the message. The pastor appeared nervous, ill at ease and uncertain. He tripped over the Bible readings, lost his place in his notes and continually scanned the room as if he were mentally noting everyone present.

After the service, the pastor headed for the few new attendees and appeared to be writing down their inmate numbers. Tom couldn't watch anymore.

He waited for Marsh to leave the building. "The coast clear?"

"Not yet. Sometimes he eats supper with some of us after service."

"He hangs around through count?"

"Yeah. He's also the chaplain for the officers, so he also meets with them." Marsh shrugged his shoulders.

Tom nodded. "We all need to act like we don't know Ryan."

Marsh nodded.

CHAPTER 76

Tom listened to harsh comments about Timmens the next day at lunch.

Ryan asked, "How could a Christian do this? Doesn't this violate the code?"

"The code?"

"Isn't there something about loyalty?"

Seeing blank looks, Tom said, "Christ said you can't be His disciple unless you hate your family, meaning loyalty to God trumps loyalty to family. We know God is good and loves our families more than we do, but we have to trust Him. This is new for us to have to decide between standing for God or shielding our families. The Task Force can be brutal. They are willing to send the parents to prison and take the kids. Pastor loses his secular job if he's marked as a convicted felon. Does his wife work? Can she support them?"

"No, she homeschools their six kids."

"You see how hard this would be. How many cases of Bibles do you think he had at his house? I received five years for five Bibles."

Marsh shook his head. "He saved his family at the expense of ours. Think what would have happened to Terry if he hadn't taken precautions. There are no winners here."

Everyone nodded.

"I'm not going Thursday or Sunday," Howie said. Others said the same thing.

Tom glanced at Marsh, "Timmens usually preaches that poorly?"

"Never—not like that." He leaned forward and grabbed his tray. "I guess his ministry's done here."

Tom nodded. In any other situation, he'd counsel them to keep up the charade that they weren't on to him. A known CI is easier to work around than the ones they didn't know about, but sitting through another sermon like that was too painful. He agreed with the decision to avoid Timmens. He looked at Ryan. "How do we teach? Can we get a sponsor for other Bible classes?"

"Why? Have conversations that just so happen to be about God and His Word."

"I got SHU time for 'unsupervised meetings'—that's what they called them at Hannibal."

"Not an issue here. It's not expressly forbidden in the violations code. North Platte doesn't see it as a problem."

"They major on other items," Chris said. "Going from Five to One can be a trick."

CHAPTER 77

THAT NIGHT RYAN reminded Tom to keep his appointment with Walpole the next day. "Your release meeting is set up. She'll go over it with you." Seeing Tom's stricken face, he added, "Relax. They don't bite."

"Not physically, but I hear they can be humiliating."

"Think of it as practice."

"I get enough every day."

Tom didn't let Ryan or Patty provide better clothes for the hearing; it would be on his record that they had helped him. He entered the spare room. Four suited men hunched over their files. The one on the left with a coffee-stained, poorly knotted tie passed a folder to the lead officer in the center. They did not look up or acknowledge his existence but talked amongst themselves like bees buzzing around a hive.

The day officer gestured for him to place his feet over the shoe outlines on the floor.

The lead officer with shaved head, a tight-knit shirt, and spit-polished black shoes glanced his way. Tom tried not to imagine a sneer of disgust on the man's face. Dressed in clean khaki shirt and pants, Tom looked down at his scuffed work boots. He still didn't have the credits in commissary for decent footwear.

"Is this the file?"

"That was the last one. Here it is," a young man on the right produced a file from his pile. "66789, HCL offender." He briefly glanced his way, bright-eyed and eager to please.

The leader read off the particulars—date of arrest, charges, plea deal, dates in detention, including his stays in Oklahoma. The file only listed his current job in the infirmary.

Tom began to add his volunteer work in Hannibal, but the day officer barked, "Don't speak until spoken to."

He worked at not reddening—wondering if the flushing was rage, embarrassment, humiliation or a swirling mix of all three. "Accepted in the beloved, a child of God," he reminded himself. 1 Peter 4 rose up in his memory. "If anyone suffers as a Christian, let him not be ashamed, but let him glorify God..." As long as he focused on Christ, his pulse settled out.

"Says here the Task Force does not recommend early release."

Tom thought it was another comment between the committee members.

"Well, what do you have to say about that? Why would they make such a determination?"

His mind blank, Tom said, "I suppose since I have not taken any approved Bibles." He wet his lips to outline his strategy for not reoffending, but they moved on talking amongst themselves as if he were not there. He longed to share his work in Hannibal, then realized that would be a mistake. God's rescue of many society had cast aside, and the joys of discipling other believers didn't need to be recorded for the Task Force's data trove. His heart ached again for lost friendships and camaraderie.

"Good recommendation from Nurse Hutchins," the junior member said. He dropped the matter with the leader's dismissive look.

The buzzing talk continued for ten more minutes. They barely waited for Tom to answer their questions, let alone give him a chance to explain.

He left the room feeling empty, almost raped. Ryan would ask how it went. He had no idea. One part longed for it to be over with—he wasn't afraid to serve the full 60 months. It would at least solve his issues with being sent back home.

Supper clogged in his throat, and he pushed away his tray with the plate half-filled.

Ryan said, "I'll have the report shortly. Look for your callout to Walpole in a few days."

Tom nodded and left the hall. He walked to the ball courts, grabbed a ball and threw several baskets, dribbling to various spots on the marked pavement.

"You playing?"

"Guess so." He rotated to the smooth, melodic voice. "Shoot a few?"

"Yeah, not seen you around."

"They told me to stay off the courts so I wouldn't mess up my package." He smiled. "But you have to have a package to lose in the first place." Tom passed the ball and watched him lob the ball through the hoop in two strides. "Game on."

It was an easy decision a few days later, sitting by Walpole's desk and hearing the not unexpected news—good-time release denied.

"Don't have anything to say, 66789?" Walpole leveled her gaze at him.

Tom didn't square his shoulders or raise his head. "No, ma'am."

"Get an appeal form from Ryan. Highlight your work at Hannibal. Do a better job describing your release plan."

"Officer Walpole, I don't want to appeal. It'd only be for a short time anyway."

"No halfway house, no help. What do you plan on doing?"

He met her gaze, unblinking. He could not state what he had in mind. Just hinting at it to Ryan had caused him to promise never to voice it, especially not to any officer. "I trust my God to make a way. King David said in Psalm 37 that he had not *seen the righteous forsaken or his children begging for bread.*"

"That's not a plan, but a vain hope."

"Then my first plan is to play ball."

She shook her head, muttered and dismissed him with a wave.

Tom wet his lips. "Officer Walpole, I'm not sure if you can do this for me, but I was wondering if you could find out how my Uncle Alex Hutton died in Leavenworth? The agent said he was buried in an unmarked grave. He had a son. Wouldn't he have requested the body?" Tom's voice almost broke. He looked away.

"Give me a minute." Walpole navigated to the BOP network. "You know his number?"

Tom shook his head and began to rise.

"Sit tight. I can search another way." She glanced at the inmate. "Who told you?"

"Agent Trainer."

Walpole shook her head. "Figures. Let's see," she scanned the lists. When that took too long, she tried a different search. "Ah, here it is. He had a heart attack, 59, body claimed by Larry Hutton."

"His son." His eyes saddened again, wondering if his parents had attended the funeral. Even his cousins had experienced losses. "Thank you; that helps."

CHAPTER 78

"You're not avoiding me, are you?" Ryan asked after final standup count.

Tom began to shake his head, but he sat down on his bed. "I guess. You disappointed with me too?"

"No, just sad. I see the ones who get good-time releases, and they can't come close to you. It's the system."

"It's God's way of making His will known."

"You really going to live homeless?" Ryan sat near Tom, speaking softly. "Patty and I would like you to come live with us. My supervisory period will be done before your release, so it's not going to get either of us in trouble."

"If you're on record for picking me up…" Tom left the rest of the sentence hang in the air.

"I thought of that and after seeing Timmens, I understand we have to be a little more creative."

"I'm listening."

"You can't be released into the community. They'll give you a bus ticket back home—that's Akron, Ohio, right? We'll be waiting for you at one of the rest stops. When you see Patty, you walk off the bus and meet us at the back of the store. We'll take you home." He patted Tom's hand.

"The guys told me they drop you off at the bus terminal in town early in the day. Some have to wait hours before their bus departs. They said I could sell my ticket and just happen to have someone pick me up."

Ryan nodded. "I'll check it out."

The next week Ryan said, "There's a McDonalds just around the corner. Meet us there."

"Wichita, Kansas, right?"

"Will that work for you?"

Tom stared into Ryan's eyes. "I'm so blessed that you're willing to do this for me. I'd stay with you even if it was in Alaska or Timbuktu. That's the most," his throat caught.

"Don't mention it."

Howie slurped his soup at supper and smiled at Marsh. "You should have seen Timmens' sour face today. Nobody attended the afternoon Bible study." He flashed a victory sign. "Bud and I intercepted the few clueless saps."

Chris said, "Looked like he'd been sucking lemons." They dissolved in peals of laughter.

Tom looked at Marsh. "The Bible tells us to never take pleasure in our enemy's troubles lest God decides to show him favor. He is a fellow believer."

"And how do we know that?"

"How do you know he's not? Did you doubt his testimony six months ago? We can't sit in condemning judgment of one another. We can discern those who act disorderly, but God commands us to pray for him to find his way back. Otherwise, we're no different than anyone else."

Marsh nodded.

Tom was mostly done anyway. He gathered his tray, thinking of his ball team and their improvements. He hardly thought about Pastor Timmens except while praying.

Tom dropped off his tray and turned to relax in his pod before the evening rec sessions.

"Yo, Hutton, listen up," an officer stated. He pointed at the loud-speakers. "You have a visitor. Need to report to the visitor center now."

Tom stopped in his tracks. He had not added anyone to his visitor list. The officer pointed toward the visiting area. Tom nodded and walked along the path and joined the line.

The officer led them to a bright, airy room filled with tables and stools after they were lightly frisked. Vending machines lined the left wall. He recognized Timmens in a few moments.

"This is a surprise. How'd you get on my list?"

"Professional courtesy. Take a seat. Not seen you at any of the sessions lately. Lost your way?" The pastor tried a small laugh, but he closed his mouth, seeing no response. "You made me?"

Tom nodded. "Not hard. They don't give warnings. My uncle pulled 20 years. No way you'd be released without charges."

"I told them it wouldn't work. Bad deal, you know."

"I can imagine." Tom still didn't smile. He'd be civil. He'd give him that. "I pray for you and encourage the others to pray for you as well."

"I appreciate that." He looked over.

"It's a Romans 12 thing." Tom said.

Timmen's face hardened. "Yeah, well, I think I have more to offer here. What can I do to convince them to trust me?"

Tom smiled. "Walk away from the deal and join us in here."

Timmens' face blanched, but he was not deterred. "You know, they're looking for that big underground organization that's keeping the church resistant to the new laws. They're just trying to bring our religion into the twenty-first century." Pastor leaned in and lowered his voice, "It really spooked him that guys you'd influenced in Hannibal are now part of the underground church."

Tom sat back and met his gaze. "No laws of man can stop God. He will build His church, and the gates of hell cannot prevail against it. We don't follow a religion."

Timmens rubbed his hands together. "Yeah, get that. Me too. But they're looking for the top leadership and believe you have the keys to the kingdom."

Tom sat back. "Did you tell them Christ is the head of the true church of God—not lavish brick buildings or fat associations claiming the name of Christ while denying Him with their beliefs and actions? Did you tell them Christ is at the right hand of the Father in heaven, and His Holy Spirit indwells every true believer? Did you remind them their own laws and enforcement efforts are creating the underground church they're so bent on destroying?"

"See here. Only a small portion of our Bible's illegal. That's all."

Tom rose. "And if you think they're going to stop with that, you're naive. Wake up. If they can get away with this and it looks like they are, the next phases are coming." He cleared the stool bolted to the floor. "I guarantee, they're already on the drawing board." Tom walked out before he said something stupid.

He found Marsh watching the ball games. "You'll never guess who tried to get some info out of me."

Marsh nodded, not taking his eyes off the ball. "Ciles' smoking tonight. Yeah, heard the rumors. Didn't think he was that stupid."

"Maybe they piggy-backed off his hearing aids."

"I've never seen him with hearing aids."

"Ah, so it was his last attempt to garner Intel."

"Well," Marsh looked at him. "What'd you say?"

"Basically, called him a fool—without the French. Maybe I said too much, but I didn't say a lot. Walked out before I lost it."

"Good call."

Most of the other Christians filtered back to North Platte, several with concurrent sentences. Tom networked with Ron and Chad, mentoring them on sermon prep and preaching. Ryan assured them they would find another civilian chaplain. Marsh let him know they were doing just fine. Tom noted the Task Force had not touched any of the Greek, Hebrew or Spanish volumes.

"Guess the law's just for us English dudes," Chad said.

Ron invited Tom to bunk with him after Ryan's release. Tom now had access to Ron's impressive library tucked away neatly under his bunk in boxes.

"When we doing the Revelation study?"

"Soon. I did tell you I missed the Daniel-Revelation classes, as well as Introduction to Hebrew grammar."

Ron laughed. "It can be a group study; we all learn together."

"This Sunday." Tom opened the Revelation study course Ron had handed to him. "Can you get more of these?"

"I'll try, but many ministries have shut down. Chad's running down another contact. We can start without everyone having a copy. Force 'em to read the Bible."

"Absolutely." Tom nodded. He had a year left to disciple this group.

CHAPTER 79

TOM WALKED INTO the convenience store and adjoining fast food joint. Worn plastic chairs lined a short hallway. The bus depot was a glorified gas station. His hopes of selling his ticket dashed, he passed through to the other side, took stock of his surroundings, saw the tall McDonalds sign and headed over. Just past noon, a line of cars skirted the red-brick restaurant. He sauntered past the front and squinted along the line of parked cars. He thought he spied Ryan's profile in a blue Corolla.

He tapped on the window. "Hope you haven't been waiting long."

Ryan shrugged his shoulders. "I remember. The wheels of bureaucracy work slowly. I'll let Patty know you're here." He looked over after texting. "Sell your ticket?"

"Chickened out. Realized it might attract attention."

"No gear?"

"Just my books and the clothes they give you on release. They took everything, and that was five years ago. I think I've filled out a little."

Patty emerged from McDonalds.

They headed for the highway. Patty leaned back to greet Tom. "We'll stop for a bite to eat on the way. It's so good to meet you in person."

Tom watched the scenery flow past as the car accelerated to cruising speed on the county highway. Patty was easy to talk to. He shared his family story, their history, and the family business. Ryan asked for updates on his friends in North Platte. "Ever hear anything about Timmens?"

Tom shook his head. "Some of the guys still wondering how Pastor could turn on them. It's the new way of things, I guess."

Patty glanced at Ryan. "We had the discussion. Caving to protect other Christians is similar to making ransom payments to terrorists. I'm as willing to pay the price as you are."

"It's just so much harder when they hurt the ones you love." Tom watched a large bird circling overhead—had no idea if it was a hawk, an eagle, or some kind of turkey buzzard. "It was easier on me. I have no one."

"You had no one," Ryan said.

"There it is, honey. Take this exit for the Perkins."

A growing unease rose up. Tom's eyes scanned the parking lot. He was in the open—no barriers. Smiling, he closed the door and nodded to Ryan.

"It's fine, Tom. Everyone's a little nervous when they first get out. I had them too."

Tom swallowed, not wanting to admit he was terrified of messing up and going back to prison. His senses stayed on high alert. Panic set in with the large multi-page menu sitting on his side of the booth.

Patty smiled. "So, Tom, feel like burgers or a dinner meal?"

"Burger." He copied her movements to the burger page. His eyes widened with the choices.

With gentle questioning, she helped him decide. Patty said in a lowered voice, "He had the same problem the first day."

Ryan looked like he was about to protest but flipped through the menu again. "Gets better with practice."

Tom couldn't imagine doing this on his own. "You can't begin to know how much…"

They both shushed him. "We know. That's why we're here. All one in Christ."

⌒⌒⌒

Patty and Ryan's modest bungalow nestled in a quiet neighborhood a little past the city center—mostly older homes with small yards and tree-lined streets. Patty led him to the guest bedroom and shook his head at his two bags of belongings. "I see we have to do some shopping."

He settled in quickly, learned the nearby streets, and headed off to the job center with his résumé and ID.

By mid-afternoon of the third day, Tom entered a convenience store, purchased a cola and a bag of nuts. He leaned against the building's ledge and considered his options. He had visited every place with a job opening he could fill—menial labor with few skills required. Many were rough with curt staff and foul-mouthed laborers. He tried to shove down the humiliation of being cast out of those places.

As in so many cities, multiple hospitals resided nearby in the crowded downtown districts. He rose, rolled the almost empty bag of peanuts into his pocket and headed for the nearest shining hospital complex.

Within the hour he was at the tall counter of the Human Resource Office. The young woman assured him they had housekeeping jobs until he told her he'd just been released. She navigated to another screen on her computer. "Oh, sorry. Looks like it was just filled." She wrinkled her nose, "Try again next month?"

Tom headed out of the office, looked for the nearest bus stop, pondering his fate. He recalled a large facility not far from his new neighborhood. The bus route often stopped at the complex. It wouldn't hurt to make one last try. This wasn't unexpected—he'd been warned. Even so, hope had vanished yesterday. The other plan, the one Ryan forbade him to talk about, might be his only option.

Tom exited the bus in front of the hospital's main entrance. The red-brick buildings, grouped together in a large complex, occupied several blocks. The digital LED signs with images of pretty faces, scrubbed nurses and smiling children mocked him. *Why would they make room for me?*

Tom squared his shoulders and headed along the walkway to the ambulance bays. *There is no condemnation for those who are in Christ Jesus,*[34] he reminded himself.

For I am not ashamed of the gospel of Christ. Tom walked through wide double doors, past the intake counter and triage area, noting the sparsely occupied adjacent waiting area. Midweek, late afternoon, one would expect the ED, emergency department, to be quiet.

He leadeth me. Tom breathed in the scents of cleansers, astringents, antibiotics and other medicinal smells. His eyes scanned past the digital treatment board, trauma bay rooms and waiting gurneys lined up along the long corridor to the right.

The hospital signs were fairly decent, but he still had to ask for directions to find the personnel office on a lower level in what appeared to be an older part of the complex.

The large room visible through the long, narrow side window appeared empty, yet the signs indicated this was the right place. A tall counter on the right faced a bank of small mini-cubes with monitors on the left. Signs listed steps to search openings, but he was reluctant to step through another fruitless exercise.

He panned back over the empty room. Short cube walls segregated four desks in front of a back office with the door ajar. Tom stepped closer to the counter when the door opened behind him, and a tall middle-aged woman breezed through.

"Well, well, seems you have to talk to me today, young man."

Tom smiled and fingered his small folder.

"The gals had some gala to get ready for. Took off half the day." Her smile was warm and friendly, not at all condemning. "It still hot as blazes out there?"

"Yes, ma'am."

"Nice to meet a polite gentleman. You walk? Orange or apple juice?"

"Orange juice would be great. Thank you." Tom watched her approach a small fridge along the back wall.

"You look a little peeked. Not used to the heat?"

Tom shook his head.

"If you're here to find a job, this is the place. Always needing to hire staff." She flashed a brilliant smile, "I call it job security, but some see it as the curse. Don't be shy."

"Yes, ma'am, before I begin, I need to let you know I was just released from North Platte."

"And that is?"

"A federal prison camp."

"You have any work restrictions or reporting requirements we need to know about?"

"No, ma'am."

"Tell me about it."

Tom furrowed his brow, his mind unable to divine what part of his past five years she wanted or needed to know.

Noting his confusion, she extended her hand. "I'm Evelyn Ohr; I run the Human Resources Department." She leaned forward. "We make sure your payroll's correct and that you are signed up for all the benefits. That's kind of an open-ended question, isn't it? Let's begin with what you were charged with."

His hand rested on the unopened cold drink. "I was…" He glanced over as beads of sweat formed on his upper lip. "They gave me five years for having five Bibles and my Bible college textbooks and notes. Have you heard about HR 756?" Incredibly, the woman nodded.

"What position are you looking for?" Evelyn scanned the one-page résumé.

"Housekeeping—here's a recommendation from Nurse Hutchins. I worked in the North Platte infirmary."

"What did you do there?"

He described his duties. "I had an EMT certification but never did the job. It was fascinating."

Evelyn nodded. "Can I keep these?"

"Yes."

"Have at it." She nodded toward the computers. "Create a login, apply for an opening, jump through the usual hoops."

"Ms. Ohr?"

"You can call me Evie. Complete the usual testing to make sure you're alive, have basic reading and math skills."

"Thanks. Thank you."

"Don't forget the juice." Evelyn slid the papers in her right hand and began to turn to her back office. "Call me if you have any questions." She glanced again at the name center top of the résumé—Tom Hutton. "You know an Alex Hutton?"

"Yes, he is…was my uncle."

"Was?"

"He died in Leavenworth a few years ago. Did you know my uncle?" Tom scanned his memory, wondering if he could have met this woman at any of Uncle Al's events.

"No." She met his gaze. "He's well-known."

"Do you know what a Hutton Bible is?"

"I do." She nodded at the computers. "Make your application, and we can talk. It would be good to get it done today." Her eyes scanned the empty desks.

"Of course." Tom reassembled his folder. "One more question, if you don't mind. Do some housekeeping positions get a chance to clean the ED bays?"

"Some." She wrinkled her nose. "We can talk further when your app is in the system."

"Great."

O ye of little faith. His heart sang with praise, kicking himself for ever doubting. Tom floated down the hall, walked up the stairs and headed down the street. After a few wrong turns he found his way to Bluff Street—not far at all from the hospital.

He sat at the built-in booth by the kitchen, smoothing out the papers before him—job offer, wage and benefit details, training schedule and start date. Mrs. Evelyn Ohr's cheerful face beamed with his affirmative response to working the night shift, swing shifts and cleaning any area that needed attention. She was impressed with Nurse Hutchins' wonderful recommendation, and he thanked the Lord again that Mrs. Ohr had not pressed for more references. The fewer names in his personnel record the better. He provided a mailbox storefront for his address.

He would have to open a bank account for direct deposit. Hearing the key in the lock and the side door swing open, he waited, a broad smile on his face.

CHAPTER 80

Tom's scheduling pad sounded an alert. He glanced around the outpatient operating bay. The room was almost done, but he had to check the message. The screen blinked a red high-alert message from the ED.

He mopped quickly to finish the room, leaving the wet floor sign behind and headed to the ED.

In the past he had cleaned various bays when the ED signaled a room needed more cleaning than the volunteers could handle. Tom reasoned working the night shift from midnight to 8 a.m., he had more ED calls than the day guys; few volunteers signed up for the graveyard shift. This was his first ED emergency.

Tom parked his cart in the housekeeping storage room and grabbed a fully loaded cart ready to go. He tried to tamp down his excitement. Yes, he was looking forward to being a part of this, but he had to remember he was not at North Platte with Doc Ryan. He was not certified to help fetch drugs or handle patient needs. Even so, he walked as quickly as possible without running or upsetting items on the cart.

The waiting room overflowed with people and the usually calm receptionist had a panicked look. She cradled the phone in her hand, covering the mouthpiece, "Turn over bays one through three STAT." She added, "large apartment fire. Some are being diverted here." Tom nodded. This hospital did not have a dedicated burn unit. The patients would be stabilized and transported over once beds were available.

Tom slowed down to avoid the nurses, assistants, and techs surging

328 | Dorothy Gable

past the long computer counter and whiteboard. He didn't have to glance at the board to know—he could hear it. He could feel it; he could smell it. Even in the waiting room scents of fire and blood accosted the nostrils, leaving an acrid taste in his mouth.

Tom mentally shut his nostrils and entered the first bay. Bandages, pieces of clothing and wrappings, mixed with blood and debris littered the floor. He'd been on the job for a month, passed the training tests and audit examinations. The routine of protocol kicked in, and Tom systematically cleared the floor and wiped away the blood.

"Anybody," a voice called out. Tom scanned the department. No one shifted or moved to the voice. He noticed the receptionist nodding to him and headed toward the voice. The head ED doctor stood at the foot end of a gurney. A small girl occupied only a portion of the bed. Tom watched a nurse attempt to place an IV.

Ches Asters, the head night nurse gestured him away. "Anybody but you, fella."

Before Tom could retreat, the doctor glanced his way. He countermanded. "He'll do. Find this girl's parents. We need a consent signed to proceed."

Tom nodded, read the name from the treatment board, washed his hands at the nearest sink and headed to the waiting room. "Anyone here for Sallie Carter?" he asked, scanning the faces—some still waiting to be seen or family and friends waiting for news. Tom began to work the room, asking each group. He approached the people sitting along the back wall. A young girl with braided ponytails leaned against an older girl who stroked her hair. Tom paused, hearing the girl's ragged wheezing.

"Is this your sister? Did anyone look at her?"

"I think so, mister," her dark brown eyes stared into his. "Bibi needs help now."

"I'll get someone to look at her again, but I need to find Sallie Carter's family. Do you know who they are?"

"Sallie's? Is she?" her eyes teared.

"Not sure, but are her parents here?"

"No, but Pastor Lincoln might know." She tugged on a pert woman sitting across from her, "Betts, Ms. Betts, the man needs to see Sallie-bee's mama. Know where she is?"

The middle-aged black woman turned to Tom. "Let's talk over there."

"Go to bay 6 and see Dr. Wilcox. He needs to talk with the family right now." Tom looked closer at Bibi. She slumped against her older sister. "I'm Tom," he said, kneeling by the girls. "What's your name?"

"Ginger."

"Ginger, let's get someone to look at Bibi again, okay?" Seeing Ginger's nod, he scooped Bibi up in his arms and headed for Head Nurse Asters.

"Ches," he said with intensity in his voice. "Please listen to this girl's breathing." He didn't want to voice what he thought he was hearing in front of her sister.

The nurse turned with a scowl but after a quick glance at Bibi, he positioned his stethoscope and walked over. He met Tom's gaze. "Get a gurney."

"I can clear Bay 1 in five minutes."

"Get the gurney."

Tom brought one to the edge of the first bay. Ches met him there and began to bark orders for supplies. Tom fetched them, winking at Ginger when he passed by her. "You can stay with your sister. She's going to need you, but do what that nurse tells you, Okay?"

Tom turned over three more bays and scrambled back to finish the outpatient OR's. He returned to the ED two more times before his shift ended.

He clocked out at eight and headed for the ED. The sun's rays streamed in through the wide double doors and windows lining the waiting room. Groups of chairs had been pulled around into semi-circles, empty cups and wrappers littered the tables and floor. He wondered how many had been transferred, how many could leave on their own and where they would stay.

Dr. Wilcox handed over a file and gestured to him. "What's with Ches? You violate his house rules?"

"He doesn't like ex-cons. That's me. The little girl, Bibi? She going to make it?"

"Yes, we were able to help her. Good catch. You done this before?" The doctor studied Tom's face.

Tom relayed his sparse medical experience.

"You help out with medical emergencies?"

"At North Platte prison camp. I worked with a doctor there when they were short." He looked over. "I'd heard that kind of wheezing before, and the guy at North Platte didn't make it, but he was in his sixties and dying of cancer."

The doctor nodded. "Who hired you?"

"Ms. Ohr. She was willing to give me a chance."

"Is your record why you started in housekeeping?" Wilcox shook his hand. "Good work today. Keep it up, and we'll find you a job here. Not everyone can handle the ED when it gets busy." The doctor stretched to release his tired back muscles. "Ches will come around. His brother was in and out of prison. He doesn't trust anyone who's been in jail."

Tom scanned the unit, but Asters was not in sight. He looked back at the doctor. "That's too bad. I saw many turn their lives around on the inside when they realized they had to make a change before it was too late. I left a lot of friends back there. Maybe I could talk to his brother."

"He overdosed last year. Easy to do these days with the synthetic drugs."

"Sorry to hear that. Will keep it in mind. Makes it easier when I have to pray for Ches." The doctor seemed to understand what he meant. "Need me to clean up the waiting room?"

"No, I already reminded housekeeping. You go home and rest."

Dr. Wilcox headed to Evelyn Ohr's office in HR after he had changed. He had to find out about the hospital's newest janitor.

CHAPTER 81

A FEW DAYS later just before his shift started, Tom read the text on his unregistered phone. He never used it near the house. His eyes popped. Evie Ohr needed him to report to HR. Forcing himself to stay calm and breathe, he tried not to imagine her reason for the summons. His pulse increased when the young woman at the counter sent him to Mrs. Ohr's office.

"Please close the door, Tom, and take a seat."

Tom perched on the edge of the padded chair.

"As you might suspect, I'm a Christian, and I wanted to invite you to our church. You could also bring some friends—if you have others who might be interested." She slid a piece of paper over with time and place. "Fair warning, the meeting's not in an established church building."

His interest piqued, he nodded. "Sure," as his mind tried to run through his schedule.

"I already checked. You're not scheduled then."

He memorized the info and slid back the paper. "You might want to destroy that if I understand you correctly."

She nodded.

"Everything fine?" Tom asked.

"Just need to fill out the life insurance paperwork. We can do that now."

He could hardly wait to tell Ryan and Patty he'd found a real live underground church. They had tried a few regular churches. Tom insisted on not attending together. He had even taken a free government Bible that sat on his nightstand—his memory verse pages and notes tucked away.

Tom avoided being with Ryan or Patty in public. Ryan put up with it; Patty thought he was this side of paranoid, but he knew the guilt that would haunt him if something happened to this couple who treated him like their own son.

"I checked where it is. You can drop me off."

"No, this stops here!" Ryan added, "We're going to trust God, and we already told you we're willing to pay the price. We have counted the cost. So, quit trying to protect us."

Tom nodded.

The day passed slowly. Tom rode the bus to check his mailbox, sauntered along downtown and headed back home. They were meeting at a residence on the north side. Following Evie's instructions, they parked around the corner, took the long way and knocked on the back door not far from a three-car garage.

A younger version of Dr. Wilcox opened the door. "I'm Caleb. Ms. Evie said some new bodies would be coming by."

"And we're breathing too," Tom quipped. Caleb furrowed his brow before a small laugh escaped. "So, you work at the hospital. I hear you met my dad, Dr. Wilcox. They're expecting you." Caleb chatted as he led them past the foyer area down a short hall to an open flight of stairs. "We built up and down on a narrow lot. Like two rooms per floor. We meet in sublevel 1," he said, lowering his voice. "You that Tom Hutton Mrs. Ohr's been talking about?"

"Guess so." He furrowed his brow and glanced a peek at Ryan who shrugged his shoulders.

"It had to come out sometime," Ryan said.

Tom faced front and followed Caleb around the half landing. The lower half of the stairs opened up into a large common area.

"This is level one's big room." Caleb raised his arms, sweeping back to the three behind him. "Hey, folks, meet the *famous* Tom Hutton."

Tom froze, tempted to run, but put on a smile and descended the last few steps. He didn't even try to remember names at this point—definitely at a disadvantage, they all knew his.

Mrs. Ohr worked her way through the crowd and introduced herself to Ryan and Patty. "So nice to meet you. Know Tom well?"

Ryan nodded; she didn't need to know they'd shared a pod at North Platte. In a few moments, he found himself sharing their current life in Wichita.

"Oh, Wichita is the best city, don't you think? Just the right size—not too large, not like KC, if you know what I mean." They nodded as she outlined the city's history, points of interest and best shopping areas.

Dr. Wilcox gestured to Tom. "I'd like you to meet our pastor, Pastor Hathaway. You have a few moments to get acquainted."

"They tell me you were in prison for 756?" Pastor asked. "Are you related to Alex Hutton?"

"Yes. He died in Leavenworth." Tom met his gaze. "He's graduated to heaven—joined his wife. It's over for him now."

"I see." The pastor looked at the young man tuning his guitar in front of the circles of folded chairs. "We'll have to talk later."

Tom found a seat next to Ryan. The praise songs started. Everyone stood to sing praises to God. Tom settled his nerves and tried to focus on the message and verses cited. Simple, direct, forthright, Pastor Hathaway's preaching felt like a mix between his uncle's and his last pastor near Mt. Zion Bible College.

The pastor looked his way after the message, but some older men approached, and they appeared engrossed in discussion. Tom didn't see Caleb until he was at his elbow.

Caleb pulled a chair over and plopped down. "So, what's it like? Going to prison for Jesus? See a lot of action?" He paused, noticing

Tom's dazed look. "Like, I'd think you'd have a real witness and all—you know. What'd they get on you?"

Tom leaned back. He relayed the barest details of the charges.

"This is an exciting time."

"You think it's cool to do prison?"

"Yeah, like for the right reason. Doesn't happen much in this country."

"It's happening now, and no, it's not cool, exciting, awesome or fun." He licked his lips. "I saw some get saved. I also lived with many who swore, cursed, ridiculed, just plain avoided me or wanted to assault me." Tom found himself trying to convey the terror of lockdown in a 6 by 8 with a known killer. "Some don't make it three weeks. Their skulls are shattered in the bathroom. Those are the lucky ones." He leaned forward, the phrases spilling out, but he had to sanitize the language. Years of listening to standard prison conversation had programmed his brain too well. "You don't want to go there, Caleb, unless the Lord sends you because guys like you." Images of the young ones assaulted and raped rose unbidden in his mind. Tom stopped, shook his head. "Following Christ is not a buzz, a high, or always fun."

Tom rose and headed for Doc Ryan. "Hey, we got to get out of here."

"Sure. It's getting late." They headed up the stairs and out the door.

Once in the car, he asked, "Do you think we can trust them?"

"Why not? They're obviously believers and love the Bible."

Tom tried again. "I mean, are they careful enough?"

Patty glanced his way. "It seems that way, but you'd have to get a chance to talk with the leadership."

"Well, the teen's not someone I'd confide in," Tom said. Ryan nodded. *At least he got it.*

CHAPTER 82

Pastor Hathaway's fellowship met every week or so—not always at the same time and never in the same place. He only saw legal Bibles, if he saw a physical copy at all. Many used their digital devices to follow along with the sermon. He finally admitted they seemed careful enough. The next meeting Dr. Wilcox cornered him before he could slip out. "Let's have a meeting." He handed a slip of paper to Tom.

Tom pocketed it without looking at it, his eyes scanning the crowd. He tipped his head and turned to talk to Caleb. They'd finally progressed to being able to converse comfortably. The outgoing teen loved to share his latest issues, victories or concerns.

The meeting was close enough he could walk home. Catching Patty's attention, he let her know he'd meet them at home and wandered out of the quaint two-story cottage—Grandma Katie's house. He passed a few houses before he focused on the address—it was the same. The time didn't conflict with the upcoming week's schedule. *Doc must have checked before setting the date.*

Grandma Katie met him at the side door near the concrete driveway and led him to a round table in a small dining room. She disappeared into the kitchen and emerged with a piece of pie. "Can you handle this, young man?"

Tom couldn't hide his smile. He'd heard about her pies. They were as good as Caleb had bragged—the light crust flaked into several layers, filling spiced with exactly the right hint of cinnamon and nutmeg, and sweet. "Who else is coming?" he asked between bites.

"Doc and Pastor." She stared at the clock on the wall. "At least someone's on time."

He would have stated the ED could be unpredictable, but the side doorbell chimed. Tom heard their voices floating up.

Pastor Hathaway opened in prayer after Grandma Katie served their pies. He and Doc exchanged glances and nodded at the elderly woman perched on a straight chair close to the kitchen.

"Did you ever hear our story?" She smiled with his head shake. "My father started this church when I was a child. Adam and I raised a family in this church." She sighed, "Times change, and our old building happened to be in the way of that fancy four lane traipsing down Main Street."

Pastor Hathaway picked up the story. "We settled into a storefront in a strip mall not far from here. Rent was cheap, but a few years before 756, they decided to gentrify the area and the rent quadrupled. We were in the middle of finding suitable land or a building when we realized the ramifications of the HCL laws." He leaned forward. "It's crazy. The politicians sold this like it would be the second coming—peace, harmony, diversity and love for all."

Tom laughed. "For the chosen few with the right beliefs. We've been sliding this way for a long time. It didn't happen overnight."

"You involved with the Hutton Bibles?" Pastor asked.

"My uncle kept me out of it to protect me, but the Task Force believes I've got some secret way of networking with the underground church." He described how they followed him to North Platte. "Eventually they'll follow me here."

"Ryan told us they didn't have anything on you. You'd proven you had submitted to the law."

Tom shook his finger. "Not complied—found the loophole. They outlawed hate crime literature, not speech. They know I'm resistant—why they blocked any good-time release. No, I'm still on their radar."

"Unless they've moved on to more promising targets." Dr. Wilcox sat back.

"I'm no expert on law enforcement tactics, but some of the agents took it very personally that I refused to go along with their attempts to drag us into the twenty-first century. I can't know anything, not a syllable, about Hutton Bibles in your region."

Pastor nodded. "We'd like you to lead the youth group."

Tom closed his mouth. The buzzing started in his head. "I worked youth groups while in college. We're way past fun and game time now. The church of America is not ready. It's asleep. Your teens are not ready for what I have to say."

"I believe they are, son," Dr. Wilcox said. "Do we look like a church still playing those games? Look at our numbers. The uncommitted have already walked out." He glanced at the small elderly woman sitting across the table. "Our members have counted the cost and are willing to take a stand for Christ. The light shines brightest in the darkness."

Tom nodded. He couldn't disagree with any point, but his heart struggled to say yes.

"What do you think of Caleb?" Doc asked.

"Having a hard time getting his life started, but that's not unusual for a 19-year old unless he or she has a passion to follow."

"He's 17 and a senior in high school. That's part of the problem—still in that in-between stage of acting out and growing up. He has his moments. Did he ever tell you he felt God called him to be a pastor?"

"Yeah, but he's not willing to put in the work. I told him he had to at least read his Bible through, cover to cover."

"He can help you find the teens and encourage them to show up."

Swallowing a groan, Tom said, "Can he keep our secrets?"

"We're working on that," Doc said, glancing at Pastor.

Hathaway paused. "Tell us about your journey."

Tom tried to give the short version, but they probed for the complete story. "Will you pray about it, young man?" Grandma Katie asked at the end.

Tom looked at the yellowed lace curtains obscuring the street-level windows. "Where do they meet?"

"Here," she said. Noting his look, she added, "Easier to explain they're visiting Grandma Katie." The elderly woman's laugh was as bright and mischievous as an eight-year-old.

He found himself saying, "Yes, for now." He'd see if they took to him, but more importantly if God gave him the vision to help the teens. He hadn't connected well with that age group before prison. Now he had even less patience for those not interested in walking the walk of faith with Christ or unwilling to pay the price.

Once the words left his lips, Grandma Katie rose, almost propelling herself from the armed chair. "Great. There's something you have to see." She winked at the other two. "More pie?" They declined the opportunity to overload on pastry, apples, and sugar.

Tom followed her through the kitchen. Katie pulled open a scuffed white door nestled between a pantry on the left and a wider door on the right. "Follow me." She ascended a narrow staircase that wound up to the second story, turning sharply near the top. Sliding a key in the only door in the short hall, she stepped back. "What do you think?"

Tom poked in his head. It partly resembled the attic room he had rented at Mt. Zion—the outer wall angled in where the dormer window cast beams of light through the dusty air. A twin bed along the opposite wall with a small stand and a mini-kitchen on the right with a small bathroom beside it felt cozy and warm. He could feel a gentle heat from the register.

"It's got AC and heat—same as downstairs. I lost my tenant last year. You interested?"

"You're sure?"

"Don't even go there, young man. My Adam's gone on to heaven years ago, and I aim to stay busy until my day. Are you going to grant me the opportunity to do my part?"

"Of course." Tom remembered similar conversations with Patty and Ryan. "Yes, and yes. Makes it easier, doesn't it?"

"Day by day, young man. My Adam was no preacher—a simple working man, but he lived God's Word every day."

His eyes teared at the evidences of a living faith in this group. "Thank you. You don't know…"

She stilled his speech with a warm hug. "Walk with Christ, young man, every day."

God's perfect timing touched his heart. Mrs. Ohr requested a residential address before the next payroll. Feeling a peace about renting from Grandma Katie, he followed her down the stairs where they finalized the arrangement.

He'd have to break it to Patty, or maybe let Ryan do it.

CHAPTER 83

Tom let Grandma Katie greet the teens at her side door. His heart pounded, and he rubbed his sweaty hands together, running through the message. The underground church did not meet every week, but at least three times a month. The services had more prayer with members often joining in with requests for spiritual growth over physical health issues. Pastor Hathaway's sermons spoke to the needs of Christians struggling to live their faith without compromise in a hostile culture. Tom knew where he wanted to be with the youth group in a month or two, but today, he had to see who was on board. He prayed again for grace to love them as Christ loved—truth with love. *Let me preach Your Word from a pure heart, Lord.*

Grandma Katie was the perfect hostess, serving home-baked cookies. She introduced Tom to each one who joined them at the large round table. Tom looked around with the time to start drawing near; Caleb had not yet arrived.

A pretty teen who looked like a senior laughed. "He's always late—that you can count on."

"Well, since he already knows your stories, let's share how Christ found you and why you consider this group important to you."

The blonde-haired senior began.

It was almost Tom's turn when Caleb pounded on the door.

Tom left his testimony for the last as it introduced his message—taking up the cross despite the cost, even if it led to family opposition. Tom had no notes; he worked from memory, cited passage after passage from Christ's own words. Everyone's face grew somber, and few had any prayer requests.

Some lingered, chatting with others or Grandma Katie. A few asked Tom how he was doing. Pleased at the show of concern, he still kept up his guard.

Caleb stayed after everyone left and asked to see Tom's room.

Tom nodded—it seemed the teen needed to say something.

"Yo, buster, you wanted to scare them off?" Caleb said before Tom could open the door to his room. "I mean, I thought you knew what you were doing. That's my group. I've been working it for a year, and it took a while to get some of them to keep coming even after we lost our digs. Now you…" he paced the room.

Tom sat on the edge of the bed, waiting for Caleb to settle down and fighting his own jumbled nerves. *What should I say? I'm not youth pastor material.* "I needed to see who was on board. We can't afford to have pretenders in the group."

That was the wrong thing to say. Caleb talked on for five minutes before sitting on a chair. "I've been looking for a reason to quit this church, and you just gave it to me."

Tom worked to keep his emotions out of it. "How long have you been wanting to change churches?"

"More than a year, I guess."

"You still live at home. Would your parents accept that decision?"

"Yeah, I think so—as long as I'm going to a good church."

"Have you prayed about it?"

"Every day."

"All right," Tom leaned forward and grabbed Caleb's hand, "Let's pray." He bowed his head and prayed for the teens, the church and Caleb's future.

"You'd be okay with me running out on you?"

"It's not our call, is it, Caleb?" Tom looked at the dark window and back, "Each one of us needs to know we are right where God wants us to be—wherever that is. It took me a while to accept He sent me to Hannibal and North Platte. We prayed your parents would be accepting this change if it is His will."

"And if they don't?"

"If you still feel strongly about this when you no longer live under their roof, you could make the change then." Tom sighed when Caleb nodded in understanding and agreement. "Who should I ask to let the group know about future meetings?"

"Cindy, the blonde who dominated your time tonight."

Tom laughed. "I'll connect with her at the next service."

CHAPTER 84

THE GROUP MET on his day off. Tom heard Caleb walk down the stairs and say his goodbyes. After he heard the side door close, he headed to the kitchen to help Grandma Katie clean up.

"What's on your mind?" she asked.

Tom shook his head and leaned against the counter with the drying towel in his hand. "Confession, I never connected well with youth groups."

"Sounded pretty good to me." She added, "They needed the challenge."

"Did I scare them away?"

Katie face Tom. "They need to know what's at stake."

Tom nodded and asked about the next meeting, and she set the next date. She brewed her nighttime herbal tea and headed to her bedroom with her Bible.

Tom felt for the keys in his pocket and headed out to the streets shortly after. The air was still and damp with the lingering warmth of a sunny fall day. Most homes were shuttered for the night, but a few blocks over, traffic passed by on the main city thoroughfares.

He walked to the sidewalk. A full moon hung over his left shoulder. Turning, he studied the moon while he walked. Bright areas with light spots and varying hues of brownish-gray almost resembled continents bounded by dark seas. Tom stepped under the shadow of a large nearby oak, misty tears clouding his eyes.

"Hi, Wallie, it's definitely a full moon tonight," he said quietly. *Look at the moon and remember me, buddy,* his best friend had said. Tom did that every night—even when he was scrubbing floors and he saw the moon in his mind. The ache returned.

He knew the neighborhood he would try next. Sticking to the larger streets, he crossed over and walked along side streets, listening for the sound of basketballs hitting pavement followed by shouts of encouragement or groans. Eventually, he heard dribbling down a narrow alley. Tom's heart tugged, but he measured his breaths and headed into the shadows, his senses alert.

Silhouettes of three playing two on one around a ragged basket perched on a sagging chain-link fence came into view. He didn't care who they were. He'd ask, just the same.

"Want to make it two on two?" Tom stepped into the light. An Asian, a Hispanic, and a black teen stared at him. He laughed, "Get some balance to your group?"

One frowned, the other looked puzzled, and the tall black shot the ball to him. Tom caught it dribbled past the two and let the tall one steal it. He took it back at his first opportunity and made a basket. "Name's Tom."

"Sean, Alec and Ron," responded the guy who was cradling the ball. "You live around here?"

"Next neighborhood over. Two on two?" He knew better than to ask questions; that would come later—if this group felt right.

"Ron and new guy." Sean gestured for Alec to join him. He smiled at Tom.

Tom shook Ron's hand. "You make baskets or know how to get the ball?"

"I can land 'em anywhere in the court."

"Good. Keep your eye on me." They nodded, took their stance and faced Sean and Alec. They exploded into action a few seconds later. Tom stole the ball; Ron made the baskets if he could get by Sean. They took the lead once they found their rhythm.

Sean whistled and cradled the ball, looking up the alleyway.

"Couldn't wait. That don't look like me," a large black man said, grasping Sean's hand and pulling him into a hug. "What's up with the new dude?"

"Name's Tom." He stepped forward, realizing just how large this man was.

"Wallace Moore."

Tom studied his face. At the same time, they both said, "Do I know you?"

Wallace shook his head and laughed. "Not likely. Out of Hannibal. That don't seem like your hood."

"Tom Hutton, transferred out a few years back; Bruce's block. You know a guy named Jordan?"

"Sure do, just left his pad in St. Louie."

"Glad to hear he made it out. Pulled eight years for his Bibles. I pulled five for mine. This your city?"

"Some folks left here. Finding my way." He dug a paper out of his back pocket, spread it open and handed it to Tom. "You that Tom?"

Tom wiped his eyes. He nodded. "Who'd you get this from?"

"The other Wallie."

He laughed. "My cellmate. He okay?"

"Nobody messes with Wallie."

Tom nodded, he read his short sheet on walking by faith, but it wasn't his handwriting. He tried to remember where he had seen this man before.

"L wing, Building Four." He crossed his arms.

Tom handed the paper back. "I wrote that, but Wallie copied it. You see me in the L?" The wing in the back end of the basement floor of Building Four—where the spitters lived 24/7 in dark despair.

Wallace nodded.

"I prayed, but Wallie preached. Said I didn't know how to say it, but he did. So, you made it out. Did Christ find you?"

"He did, and I came to hook up with Pastor Lincoln. You know him?"

"Seen him once. Don't know where he lives." He looked at Sean. "You know Pastor Lincoln?" The man nodded but didn't say anything.

"Connors watched ten of us leave the L. He's a friend of Wallie now." Wallace looked at the others. "This is the Hannibal preacher I been talking about. Can't believe we're in the same city. What you doing here?"

"Mop floors at a hospital. Work in the shadows, so to speak. They're never going to stop chasing me."

"Well, Lincoln'll want to meet you. We can shoot hoops any time. You want to come?" Wallace waited for Sean, Alec and Ron to answer. Only Ron walked with them.

Lincoln's house bordered a small playground. They cut across the park with sparse grass and ragged bushes lit by six streetlights. Wallace led them up the wooden steps of the front porch, pushed open the screen door and walked down the center hallway to a square kitchen in the back of the house. "Company," Wallace called out.

Betts welcomed them to the table. The group hanging out made room and placed cups of soda in their hands.

Tom nodded at the pastor. "Name's Tom. Saw you at the hospital night of the fire. How are Bibi and Ginger doing?"

"Bibi's in bed already, but Ginger's up front." Betts disappeared into the living room and she emerged with the shy girl.

"They staying with you?" he asked the pastor.

The pastor nodded and extended his hand. "Stafford Lincoln." He looked at Wallace, "You know him?"

"We met in Hannibal. Imagine that." He looked at Tom talking with Ginger. "You got to hear his story. He's the prison preacher I told you about."

Tom walked over to Ginger. "Been praying for you and Bibi. Doing okay?"

Ginger nodded, shrugged her shoulders.

Tom heard a quiet, "Fine." He looked at the cramped kitchen.

Betts nodded to Ginger who led Tom up the center hall and sat on the steps leading to the bedroom. Tom sat by her.

He asked various questions about their grades, school, and her friends. Then he asked, "How are you really doing, Ginger?"

She twisted the hem of her t-shirt around her fingers. "Our aunt didn't show up to take us in. I think she blames Mom for the fire. They think she was smoking, and they said it was accidental—cigarette or something." She looked at Tom, "But Momma was doing her drug thing. She doesn't smoke when she does that." Ginger shook her head.

"Ginger? Do you believe in Jesus?" He saw her head nod. "Do you think He cares for you?"

"Says so in the Bible." She spouted off two verses.

"Yes, that's right, and this is how you see God work." He longed to hug her, hold her hand, but he didn't want to frighten the slim girl. "Pastor and Betts will raise you in the Lord They'll help you. Can you and Bibi stay with them?"

Ginger looked into his eyes. "Yes. I know, but it feels…"

"Yeah, it feels bad when family don't do, but you are part of God's family now, and He will care for you. If you'd like, I could stop by when I'm not working and help with your homework, answer your questions. You like to play ball?" He saw her wrinkled nose and knitted brows. "Well, we don't have to play ball, but would it be okay?"

"Sure. You'd be like my Uncle Tom?" They both laughed.

"Or your big brother Tom. I'm not that old."

"Get out. Some your age be a daddy four times over by now. Pushing 30, right?"

Tom laughed. "Got my number." He glanced at his watch. "It's a school night, and I'd better let you get on with your evening."

Tom rejoined the group. Betts asked, "So, what's your story?" They listened without interruption and with no comment.

"Where's your church?" Wallace asked.

Tom laughed. "I'm an ex-con. No church's going to make me their pastor. I help out with a youth group. Will take it from there and see how it goes."

"Got to spread the faith, man. We not to put our light under a bushel. What you think I'm doing shooting hoops? Ron, here, he's seeing it in action, hearing the gospel."

"Glad to hear." Tom's eyes darted past the many eyes staring at him. "Thanks for the drink." He looked at the Lincolns. "Could I visit the girls? Help with their homework?"

"Of course. Drop by anytime." Stafford rose and led Tom out the back door. "The girls would love the attention. We give them what we can, but there's only so much to go around."

"Thanks for taking them in. They're special."

"They are."

Tom knew the city well enough to find his way back to Grandma Katie's. Wallace's words echoed in his mind. His chest pounded. What a disaster! At least he'd found the girls. It didn't seem they understood why he was reluctant to publicly lead a church—not with the Task Force on his heels.

CHAPTER 85

WHAT IS WRONG with me? The news from Wallace and Wallie's walk in Christ should have encouraged him, but the burden of the youth group persisted. Tom tried to cast down thoughts of feeling like a failure and a fraud. He also had to establish daily routines for his Bible study and memory work. He should be writing the next youth group message, even if no one showed up.

To keep his work schedule, he stayed up until late and slept into the day. His phone rang at noon. They needed him to come in early. It would count as overtime. Tom pocketed his summary of the next youth group lesson and latest verses to review when it was time to head to work. The long hours alone buffing halls or sanitizing rooms left him hours to think. He wanted to make sure he had enough distractions.

He didn't make it to the ED at once, but he did drop by to see if Dr. Wilcox was in. He found him in the ED staff breakroom.

"Dr. Wilcox, may I see you for a minute?" He sat down at the round table. "Quiet night?"

"You never can tell."

"Did Caleb say anything about the youth group?" Seeing the head shake, he said, "I needed to lay some groundwork—lay out the cost and commitment of discipleship. It's not always going to be like that, but they have to know." He sat back, wondering how to say it.

"Son, you don't have to explain yourself to me. Caleb's been conflicted for a while. If what you said shook him up, it's his issue. I would have been disappointed if you hadn't called them to a higher purpose, a more dedicated walk."

"That's good to hear." He laid out his plans for the coming studies. "Nice to know we agree. I'll keep praying for Caleb." He couldn't share anything they had talked about. "This helps."

"How you doing?"

Tom met his gaze. Tempted to say "fine" and walk away, he shook his head. "I don't know. I never thought I'd be longing to be back in Hannibal. Yeah, it's rough; most are your enemies—except for the ones God sends you. Get a chance to make a real difference. See God work. It's hard out here."

"I would suspect it's hard for anyone to adjust. Your friend Ryan seems to do fine, but then he has supports you don't have."

Tom nodded. "He's like my family now."

"We're praying for you, Tom. This is new territory for all of us." They jumped when a tech opened the door. "GSW, five minutes." The doctor rose and grasped Tom in a hug. "Don't give up. Keep on keeping on. Many are praying for you. Never forget that."

Tom headed back to his cart and his task list with a lighter heart.

He clocked out on time, grabbed the bus to Lincoln's neighborhood and headed for the park. *Maybe, just maybe.* He spied Bibi's pigtails bouncing with her run to make it first to the middle slide. "Miss Bibi," he called, "You share now."

She squealed and ran to him throwing her arms wide.

He knelt and hugged her. "Had to see how you've been. Praying for you every day. Glad to see you get to stay with Ms. Betts."

"My momma didn't make it. They checked around, but my aunties…" Bibi scrubbed the dusty dirt with her sneaker.

"I bet Ms. Betts and Pastor Lincoln will make sure you have a good home." He held her hand, and they walked to a bench. "The best is to know that Jesus will never leave you. Do you know Jesus?" He smiled, seeing her nod.

The other kids ran up. "Tell us a story, preacher man."

Tom laughed. He patted the side of the bench. "I'm your preacher man, huh? Glad to oblige. I'm going to tell you a story about a man named Jonah." He had no idea what he would do with the story. He told it as it came.

Pastor Stafford Lincoln approached from the side. "Fine storytelling, Tom. Join me for coffee?"

Tom sent the kids to play and studied the pastor. "All right. They good?"

"Fine. This neighborhood watches this spot. Dealers don't dare show their faces here." They turned to the house. "Betts and I once lived in the suburbs, but then this church lost their pastor and their building. God led and one thing after another." He stopped and looked at the house. "It's what they live. We're right with them every day. They can't say they hadn't heard."

Tom nodded. "How it worked in Hannibal. I suffered with them, but that didn't mean they'd listen. God gave me the privilege of sharing His Word in there. It's harder to do out here."

Stafford waited.

"Pastor," Tom shared his fears. "Full disclosure. I don't know what I'm supposed to do, just what I'm doing each day. Working at the hospital. Helping with a youth group. Sharing my faith when I get a chance."

"That's all it is—ministry is service, young man. Would love to fellowship with you a bit. Wallace is young in the faith and can be a little pushy at times."

"That happens. It would be an honor to sit with you."

CHAPTER 86

CINDY CONVINCED MORE than half of the group to return ten days later.

Tom settled into the next phase—the church of God and the Christian walk. "God gave pastors and teachers to train believers for the work of the ministry—equipping regular folk to live and share their faith. Even with these laws and going to a home church doesn't mean the ministry of the church is diminished. Far from it. The work of the ministry is the witness of each member, every one of us. That's what I want to share with you in the coming weeks. Come with your questions, and we'll look to God's Word for answers. Listen, hear, and put it to work in your lives. Bring your stories of how God is using you and your list of memory verses."

Grandma Katie smiled after the last one left. "Good work. Keep it up."

"Glad to see some came back."

"Young man, this isn't all on you. Our church is praying for these precious young ones. We prayed for a year for someone to come, and God sent you."

Tom helped her clean up.

"You find your way down to the DMV for your driver's license?"

"No, sorry."

"Well, when you get your license, I need you to take in Adam's car for an oil change. I can't drive at night and don't want to have to rely on Addie for rides."

"I remember."

It took a few weeks, but he found a time when Ryan could drive him for his road test. On their way that Saturday morning, Ryan said, "Doc Wilcox found out about me." He glanced at Tom.

"I didn't tell him. He asked me if I had assisted in emergencies before, and I said I had at North Platte but gave no names."

"He put it together." Ryan laughed. "Or maybe it's easy for one doc to spot another. He said there's a way I could get my medical license back." His voice softened. "A downtown clinic needs volunteer doctors."

"Do you want to go back?"

"It wouldn't be going back. I'd be a doctor for the right reason this time. Have to admit it's scary, but I'm different. The job would be different. Couldn't have my own practice."

"Think you'd ever sub at our ED?"

"He did ask if I had completed my emergency medicine rotation. I could, but..." He glanced over. "It's not cheap to work as a doctor. The liability insurance alone is more than what Patty and I make now. To volunteer, I'd have to work as a physician." They reached the DMV. "One day at a time."

Tom looked at Ryan. "Time."

"Go on. I'll wait for you." Ryan headed into the waiting area.

He forced himself to stay calm for the road test with Ryan's car. Of course, the results would come in the mail.

"You have something you have to do?" Tom asked, slipping out of the driver's seat for Ryan.

"Not really. Need to talk?"

"Yeah, not sure where."

"Patty's working today, so lunch at home."

"Sounds great." He tried to wait, but it poured out—his feeling outside of everything, as if he merely watched as he went through the motions. Ryan listened, adding comments in places, but never lecturing.

He was halfway through his sandwich when he set it down and stated, "I am afraid. I'm paralyzed, thinking what happened at North Platte will happen here." He shared Wallace's assessment that he wasn't out there for the Lord.

"Why am I feeling like I lost my way? Like the years in Hannibal were the best years of my life?"

"Part of this is natural—something we all go through. But you," Ryan paused, "lost your pastoral ministry. I saw it at North Platte. Even some of the officers respected your ministry of the Word. The residents let you be their pastor. Sounds like you had even more reach in Hannibal. It would take time if these were normal times for Christians, but they're not. Patty doesn't get it, but I saw what happened. I'm glad you're working under the radar for your sake as well as for ours."

"I'm not copping out, am I? I'm not holding back on the Lord?"

"Only you can answer that. An official position doesn't guarantee a person is walking with God. As you taught us, every believer is called to minister wherever he is. Give these doubts to the Lord. Take it day by day. I know you've made an impression on Dr. Wilcox."

"Thanks." He glanced at the clock. "Almost time to catch the bus."

"Patty will be home soon, and we'll all go to the meeting. It's at the Orh's lake cottage. Beautiful drive."

Tom nodded. "I'd heard. They say he's a real estate attorney."

He was surprised to see Caleb at the meeting with a beautiful brunette.

"Hey, Tom, meet Alice. She goes to White Steeple."

"Nice to meet you, Alice. I need him for a minute." Tom took Caleb aside. "Can you trust her to know about our meetings?"

"Dude, get a life. They haven't outlawed Christianity. This fellowship is careful about not having illegal items. You think they don't know every place we meet? It's not because we're hiding; it's because we're not going to send in lists of every member who gave a dollar to the church. No tax exemption means we can't afford a building. Relax. If she's not a real Christian, she's not going to put up with this. My little test."

"Fine." Tom added, "we're meeting at Katie's this Thursday. You're welcome to join us."

"We just might. Heard it was really good. Sorry I missed it."

CHAPTER 87

Two years to the day, Tom dressed in ED tech scrubs and headed for the front counter. More than a receptionist and managing patient paperwork, he was responsible to field in-coming calls and help those waiting to stay calm. He'd taken swing shifts, meaning he could be called to work anytime. Pastor Hathaway was more than supportive.

Tom fingered the car keys in his pocket. Grandma Katie had looked into moving closer to her son in Colorado and had signed the car over to him. Shortly after she had developed pneumonia on top of her issues with bronchitis. Tom moved out the day after she died. The funeral had been bittersweet. They all felt the loss, but Grandma had struggled her last year.

Pastor Hathaway's key verse ran repeatedly through his mind. Isaiah 57:1, *"The righteous man perishes, and no one lays it to heart; devout men are taken away, while no one understands. For the righteous man is taken away from calamity."* He knew she was rejoicing in heaven with her Adam, but they still grieved just the same.

Ryan and Patty had moved to St. Louis—he had accepted an emergency physician position at a city hospital. This allowed him to volunteer with a medical clinic he heard about through Jordan.

Tom looked up and smiled. Things were looking up in many ways. The youth group was growing and often held joint events with Pastor Lincoln's teens. He had a regular group of guys to shoot hoops, enjoyed helping the girls with their homework and bribing them with trips to the corner ice cream stand. He smiled; he no longer had the job of buffing endless miles of hospital hallways. Their church, while not always growing daily in numbers, grew closer spiritually.

It felt like the calm before the storm.

ACKNOWLEDGMENTS

Thanks to my husband who supported and encouraged, willingly allowing me the countless hours to work on this novel. Thank you to my patient editor, Linda Stubblefield, who continues to teach as she encourages.

I received the idea for this series when we left the mission field in 2000. We had been ministering to the Swampy Cree at Moose Lake, Manitoba, for eight years when the Lord told us our work was done. During that difficult time the question of how fellow believers and the church in America would deal with persecution was on my mind. However, the Lord in His wisdom knew I was not ready to write these books at that time; I had to endure more of my own trials, periods of testing, and learning better ways to cope with difficulties, obstacles and interpersonal struggles. Not that I have arrived, but that I am learning to see the signs when I need to repent, pray, and forgive with praise to the Lord and thankfulness for all things.

In humility, not pride, my first thanks is to God, Christ my Savior, and the Holy Spirit, who helped me write this. Unless we abide in Christ, we can do nothing (John 15:5).

Fiction allows us to save our favorite characters. There were many people at Gods Lake Narrows and Moose Lake for whom I prayed fervently for their salvation or courage to walk with Christ, but did not see it while I was with them. Fiction also allows us to create characters with abilities we long to have but do not possess. We are all to walk in our weaknesses so that the power of God will shine through.

END NOTES

UNLESS OTHERWISE INDICATED, all Scripture quotations are taken from the Holy Bible, the English Standard Version®, copyright © 2001 by Crossway, a publishing ministry of Good News Publishers. Used by permission. All rights reserved.

Scripture quotations noted NLT are taken from the Holy Bible, New Living Translation, copyright © 1996, 2004, 2007 by Tyndale House Foundation. Used by permission of Tyndale House Publishers, Inc. Carol Stream, Illinois 60188. All rights reserved.

[1] Luke 23:42 quote; Luke 23:39-43 paraphrase.

[2] Warren Henderson, *Managing Anger God's Way: Be Angry and Do Not Sin* (Dubuque, Iowa: Emmaus Correspondence School-A Division of ECS Ministries, 2016).

[3] Proverbs 16:7, paraphrase.

[4] Psalm 139:7-8.

[5] Matthew 10:28.

[6] Ephesians 6:10.

[7] Hebrews 12:2.

[8] Matthew 7:6.

[9] 2 Corinthians 12:7-10.

[10] John 16:33.

[11] Psalm 119:11, paraphrase.

[12] Philippians 4:11-12.

[13] Ephesians 2:8, NLT.

14 Titus 3:5, NLT.

15 Hebrews 4:16.

16 Ephesians 4:28, paraphrase.

17 John 17:17.

18 John 13:34-35.

19 1 Peter 5:8, paraphrase.

20 Ephesians 4:3.

21 Romans 6:23.

22 Ephesians 2:8.

23 Romans 1:16, paraphrase.

24 John 17:3.

25 Philippians 1:21, paraphrase.

26 James 1:20, paraphrase.

27 Philippians 4:13, paraphrase.

28 Psalm 139:13-15, paraphrase.

29 Hebrews 13:5, paraphrase.

30 Isaiah 53:6, paraphrase.

31 Jeremiah 29:11.

32 Psalm 139:12-13.

33 Romans 8:18.

34 Romans 8:1, paraphrase.

Made in the USA
Middletown, DE
30 June 2021